An Innocent in
New York

An Innocent in New York

Dolores J. Guthrie

Edited By: Katie King

Published by: Jim King

2014

ISBN: 978-0-9930329-1-2

Published by: Jim King

www.katiekingpublish.co.uk

Danielle (Dani) Sutton

The violent, passionate saga of a

fabulous beauty, who loved and lived

life so desperately

Preface

How fast the wind blows, swirling over the years. I lie in the stillness of the night and, within moments, my whole life rushes by.

I am a flower, growing in the wind. Why my beauty still grows only God knows, but the strength within my soul shouts, 'grow! Grow!'

What was once a tiny bud has become a full-flowering vine but each time a petal falls my tears water my roots and I keep on blooming.

Until the day my heart turns cold and my tears bleed dry I will continue to climb; reaching for my star in the sky.

Synopsis

Dolores Guthrie writes a frightening and cautionary tale, but manages to make her characters human as well as treacherous.

The tale is set in New York City, in 1965. Danielle Sutton (Dani) has recently learned that the man who has taken control of her wealth and her life, Anthony *'The Horse'* Mannelli, is a top lieutenant in the Carlo Gambiossi crime family. In the early 1960s, the 'Joe Banicci War' was in full swing for control over all the 'Families'. Dani, right in the middle of the chaos, had no idea that her dream of having a singing career would draw her inexorably downward into the subterranean sleaze that was the world of 'the Mob'.

Two years earlier, Dani had come to New York City, in a whirlwind of sultry energy, searching for a life of fame and fortune. Fascinated by the beautiful, the rich and the powerful, Dani soon realized she needed to have a plan in order to find her own eccentric, handsome tycoon. One such person, the owner and president of William H. Crawford & Associates, became Dani's first teacher, friend and confidant. However, Bill could not understand Dani's desperate drive to be in show business, referring to it as 'her paper and tinsel world'. So Dani kept on searching for the right man, the one who could make her dreams come true.

The rich metropolis of Manhattan was a target and vulnerable to the many organized crime-syndicates that spread like gangrene, poisoning and destroying all the lives they touched. Special Agent Ralph McMahon of the FBI, in a valiant, one-man effort to contain this gangrene, lurked in the City shadows searching for the vital evidence that would lock up *'The Horse'* forever. But the Mannellis were firmly entrenched within the powerful Gambiossi Family, which already controlled numerous enterprises throughout Manhattan.

One such enterprise was Anthony's Townhouse, on 49th and Broadway. It was known as a 'B-Bar', mainly featuring the untried talents of young women who had left their hometowns behind in search of stardom. For these girls it was glamorous and exciting to dress in evening gowns, to drink champagne with the customers and to sing and dance their hearts out. There was no turning back for these young starlets, who would sacrifice all in hope of success. They had yet to learn the unspeakable horror of a madman's ways. Fate was against them all from the moment these girls met Tony *'The Horse'* Mannelli.

Within Dani's circle of acquaintances, one girl would find her dream only to lose it again. Another would always live her life in fear and yet another would vanish completely, never to be heard from again.

Finding life in the big city lonely and drab whilst searching for success, Dani allows herself to be pursued by Howard S. Kline, known as 'HK' to his friends. He is Vice President of Xenon Corporation and twice Dani's age but he becomes enthralled by Dani's passionate beauty and intrigued by her innocent enthusiasm. HK makes Dani his 'queen' by placing gifts of jewels, furs, cars, boats, a mansion, stocks and money at her feet; nearly two million dollars' worth in one year!

Meanwhile, Nicky Mannelli, the sensual, handsome and dashing younger brother of *'The Horse'*, uses his Latin charm to entrap Dani, who falls in love with him. Nicky is the 'gofer' for 'The Horse' and so Dani becomes his moll...!

'An Innocent in New York' is an extraordinary first novel.

Etched in acid, the story's compelling characters are caught up in a maelstrom of danger, intrigue, passion and high drama that will leave the reader breathless.

Dolores J. Guthrie

Chapter 1

It was strange that she was able to recall that day so clearly but then, Dani had always been able to remember sunshine; it was in her soul. It must have been late afternoon for the sun was low but still shining brilliantly, despite the grubby window panes. Not brightly enough to hide the fear in Dani's eyes though.

Fast moving traffic provided background music outside that dingy room on 49th and Broadway. A room that reeked of stale cigars and the sweat of five nervous men, all menacingly gathered around one slender, terrified woman. Dani stumbled and sank down into a chair by the window. Tears flowed silently from her motionless eyes as Dani tried to comprehend what she had just recently learned about Anthony Mannelli; the man who had taken complete control of Dani's wealth, her freedom and her very life during the past two years.

In that year of 1965, the murky, criminal underworld of New York City was fighting for power amongst the various gangs, or 'Families' as they were known. Anthony Mannelli, or *'The Horse'* to give him his nickname, was a top lieutenant of the Carlo Gambiossi family and Dani, naively, found herself right in the middle of a battle for survival in their realm of violence and chaos.

Tipping the scales at over three-hundred pounds, Tony Mannelli stormed into that silent room and proceeded to pace around the floor, cracking his knuckles. He suddenly stopped in front of Dani and stared at her for a long time. Her mouth dried up, until it felt as if it were stuffed with cotton wool.

"Who the fuck do you think you are, bitch?"

Tony Mannelli paused for effect. Dead silence hung in the stale air of that stuffy room.

"I'll tell you who you are, you're some kind of nightmare sent to drive me nuts."

"Please, Tony, I haven't deliberately done anything to try to drive you nuts. You can have all of my money, if that's what you want, but just don't hurt me, please. All I want is to be left alone. I'll move far away from here and you'll never hear from me again, I promise."

Tony stood glaring at Dani, his steely, black eyes staring out from a well-creased face. He cracked his knuckles again.

"Such stories you told to your maid, Kay, too. I don't like stories, Dani, they upset me."

With a flare of her nostrils, Dani threw her head back in naive defiance at the injustice of Tony's accusations.

"I didn't tell Kay anything and anyway, my name is Danielle!"

"Whore!"

Tony roared as he backhanded Dani to the floor and then flashed a cold, icy smile in her direction.

"You think you're better off after going to the DA about me yesterday, huh? Naw, bitch, the FBI are my friends. They ain't gonna do nothin' to Tony Mannelli!"

Tony cracked his knuckles again and kicked Dani in the stomach as she tried to scuttle out of his reach.

"You're a fuckin scab, Dani, that's what you are! Look at you, now! You don't look so big now eh, crawling on your belly like a worm?"

Tony Mannelli raised his arm, menacingly and Dani screamed.

"Tony, please, don't hit me again! Things were happening around here that frightened me, that's all. I just got scared and thought I should get help from somebody on the outside."

"Well, I don't like my friends hearing bad kinds o' stories about me, OK?"

Tony motioned for a couple of his thugs to set Dani back up on her chair. Then he stomped back toward his private office, followed by the rest of his minders.

"Get my brother, Nicky, the fuck over here," Tony grunted, as the door to his inner sanctum closed behind them all.

Dani tried to slow her breathing as she leaned her head back against dirty, yellowed windowpanes. Time became a blur to her and it seemed only minutes before the door opened again, abruptly shattering the comforting silence. Tony bustled out of his office, ushering his younger brother, Nicky, out ahead of him. A cold, cynical smile still lingered around Tony's lips and he resumed his cross-examination of Dani as if there had been no interruption.

"Dani, you've been meaning to tell me all about Charlie now, haven't you?"

Dani didn't answer at first, just started trembling all over. But Tony's overbearing presence demanded an answer.

"Who?" she whispered, trying to buy time.

"Charlie Black, Dani? Or was it Charlie, *'The Blade,'* that you spent the night with, you know, over at his place?"

The big man smirked at Dani's obvious discomfort.

"Well now, Dani," what's ol' Charlie gonna do for you now then, eh? Gonna save you from big, bad ol' Tony is he?"

Dani's body was shaking so much that she could barely get her words out.

"Tony, it's true that I stayed over at Charlie's place that night." Dani deliberately avoided looking at her lover, Nicky as she answered.

"But Nicky had roughed me up pretty badly yesterday you know? And Joe DeCretis, well he saw me running down the street crying and he picked me up. Joe took me over to Charlie's penthouse, on Park Avenue and then Joe and Charlie told me all kinds of things about you and about all your friends too."

Tony roared. "They know nothing! It's all lies!"

"Nothing?" Dani screamed back at him "They knew a hell of a lot more than I did!"

For a second Dani thought Tony was going to hit her again, but she'd been raised on farm with brothers. Dani had learned at an early age how to stand up for herself and she was so angry by then that she simply forgot to be afraid.

"Call your secretary, Cele, in here then Tony. She can write it all down, in case you can't understand me!"

"Why, you fuckin bitch!"

Tony moved to hit Dani again but stopped short, smacking a huge, right fist into his other palm instead. He paced back and forth in front of his desk, in deep thought. Then, in a more restrained tone, *'The Horse'* spoke to Dani again.

"OK Dani, I'll hear you out, ma'am." Tony had obviously decided to humor her but his sarcasm was lost on Dani.

"So, what did those big scary men tell you then, eh?" Tony grinned broadly at Dani's serious tone as she began to speak again.

"Well for starters, how about John *'Sonny'* Crenziess. Charlie told me that he's an officer in the Faci organization but I thought he was just your friend... a nice guy, you know. But Charlie told me that Sonny was involved in killing Amie *'The Hawk'* Ruppilli, and that another friend of yours, Guiseppe Angelini was also a Faci lieutenant!" Dani's confidence was growing as she continued to speak her mind.

"And you remember that Joey Muck? Well, Charlie said that Joey is acting under-boss of the whole Caliminni Family and that Joseph Tarinelli, well, he's Joey Muck's bodyguard, isn't he? And all this time I thought you were all decent, tax-paying citizens, but you're not are you? You're *all* damn Mafia brutes!"

"Ya fuckin dumb broad, ya've been watchin' too many movies. There ain't no more Mafia."

"I think she is referring to the *'Cosa Nostra'*, Tony." Karl Hokowitz, Tony's personal attorney, cut in quietly. But Dani was determined to be heard.

"Well, I don't remember what damn name they called it, but it all means the same thing. You're all crooks and that's for damn sure!"

In an instant, Tony had reached across his desk and was talking on the phone to the aforementioned Charlie.

"Yes, I believe I *have* met the young lady you're referring to!" Charlie answered, hesitantly.

"Well now, see here, Blackie, you won't recognize the dame if you see her anymore." Tony snapped. "You got the picture?"

"Hey, whatever you say, Tony, this is your territory. I hope all this hasn't caused you any trouble."

"Naw, no need for trouble," Tony assured him. "I'm your friend, Charlie."

The conversation had only been brief but the blood vessels in Tony's forehead were throbbing as he put down the phone. He reached into his desk drawer for a bottle of Scotch and poured a large shot. Swirling it around in his mouth, Tony smiled with the coldness of all psychopaths. Then he walked over, knelt before Dani and started gently petting her face. Each stroke heightened her fear and tension but Dani could not block the man out of her mind.

His touch kept drawing her back to reality. Tony's huge hands were hot, sweaty and smelled of stale garlic, mixed with tobacco. Dani's mind was fighting both fear and nausea, so she simply allowed the hot tears to roll silently down her beautiful face.

"Such tears you have, Dani," Tony soothed as he wiped them with his rough thumb. "You look so very tired, my dear."

She turned her eyes toward her lover, Nicky and silently pleaded with him as Tony squeezed her cheeks together; so hard that Dani thought her teeth would break.

"Yes!" Dani mumbled through Tony's iron grip. "I *am* very tired."

"Well, so you should be." Tony approved of her reply. "You've been a very busy girl lately. What you need now is a nice, long rest." Looking around the room, Tony repeated himself. "Don't you guys think Dani here needs a nice, long rest?"

But the room stayed as quiet as a tomb.

Tony raised Dani up and walked her toward his younger brother. Nicky watched Dani's face anxiously, willing her to stay silent.

"Nicky, you know how much Dani likes Miami? I think you should take her home, so she can pack a small bag and then take her down south for a nice, long vacation."

Nicky's face was drawn and his eyes seemed as if they were bleeding inside. Silently, he took Dani's arm and led her out of the oppressive atmosphere of Tony Mannelli's office.

Still shaking, Dani made it down to the garage and started to get into Nicky's Cadillac. She had only recently bought the car for him, hoping it would make him stop hurting her, but it hadn't made any difference. Nicky had a temper just as bad as his older brother's. But to Dani's surprise, Nicky demanded *her* car keys instead.

"We'll take your car tonight."

Dani's heart felt so drained that it physically ached. Her crazy love for Nicky had left her spirit hurt and broken and she handed over her own car keys without a murmur.

Even after driving through heavy traffic they were soon pulling into the driveway of Dani's luxurious, New York mansion. The silence between them had been stressful during the journey. Now, as they entered into her beautiful home, named Hearthstone Manor, Dani felt a creepiness that made her even more uncomfortable.

"Nicky, where is my maid, Kay? I know they've questioned her already, but why isn't she here to meet me?"

Nicky didn't answer.

"What've they done to Kay?" Dani repeated. "Please, Nicky, don't let them hurt her."

"Danielle, would you just shut the hell up! Don't make this any harder than it is. Just go and pack your damn bag."

"Please, Nicky, help me," Dani begged, tugging at his arm. "I know you love me really, so how can you let Tony do this to me? Are you afraid to stand up to your brother?"

"My God, Dani, don't you think this is killing me inside? I've told you before, I can never marry you because of my family."

"Which family are we talking about, Nicky? Do you mean your wife, or Tony?"

"Shit, Dani, there you go again. Yes, it's Tony, OK. If I ever ran away with you, my brother would find me and kill me. He rules our family and those are just our laws; that's the way it is." Nicky lowered his head, miserably.

"Just go pack your bag, Dani. We have a plane to catch."

As Dani walked down the darkened hallways, she was somehow drawn toward the guest bedroom.

She carefully opened the door of that beautiful room, with its elegant furniture of black and gold, decorated with avocado-colored satin spreads and drapes. Dani could not shake the eeriness that had seized her from the moment they had walked through the front door. Then she saw a dark stain on the white carpet, in front of the closet door and reached down to feel it. She gasped and recoiled in horror. The stain was wet and it smelled like blood.

Shaking all over, Dani reached out and, little by little, she opened the closet door. Inside there was something large, tied up in a white, satin sheet. Dani's heart was pounding so hard that she could hear it inside her head. Then she saw her own, gold-monogrammed name, *'Danielle'*, on the edge of the sheet and blood, oozing out through what seemed to be bullet holes.

Dani tried to scream but no sound came out. She couldn't even move. She didn't know if seconds or minutes had rushed by before Nicky appeared beside her and quickly pulled Dani out of the room.

"Forget it, Dani!" he yelled. "Just pack!"

Dani staggered to her own bathroom, fell to her knees by the tub and started heaving. Then she leaned over and reached for the faucet, turning it on cold. As she was fumbling for a washcloth, Dani saw her darling poodle, Babette, lying motionless in the bottom of the tub.

'Oh my God, no! They've killed my poor Babette. Then that must be Kay, lying back there in the closet.'

It was all too much for Dani to take in. She collapsed over the tub in hysterical sobs. After a while, she picked poor Babette up, wrapped her pet in a towel and held her close.

"Babette couldn't have hurt anyone, she was just a little dog! Damn those bastards."

Gently, Nicky took Babette out of Dani's arms and spoke in a softer voice.

"Come on now, Dani. It was just a dumb dog." He hurried Dani along again.

"We've got to get outta here Dani, before they come back looking for us. Where's the shotgun I gave to you?"

"It was in my spare closet, where that…that dead body is."

"Well, it ain't there now so let's just get the fuck outta here. We've gotta be the next plane to Miami."

Nicky almost dragged Dani down the stairs.

"Wait, Nicky, I have to call Mr. Lopez to tell him about Kay. Someone has to take care of her funeral!"

"What the fuck, Dani, just forget it! We have to get the hell outta here!" Nicky yelled as he pushed her outside and towards the car. As they raced away from her beautiful home, Dani wondered if she would ever live there again.

Dazed and like a puppet on a string, Dani followed Nicky's orders all the way through the airport. She stumbled through the departure lounge, seeing nothing and then she climbed meekly aboard the plane, falling into her seat beside Nicky. Then they were airborne and the plane swooped out over New York harbor. As it began to turn southward, the pilot switched off the *'No Smoking'* signs and Dani and Nicky were finally on their way to Miami.

She looked over at Nicky who, thankfully, seemed to be already asleep. Although in shock, Dani was not completely stupid. She realized that she was going to have to keep her wits about her and try to figure out some kind of an escape plan, before they got to Miami. *'Well, it's obvious that Tony Mannelli wants me dead!'*

Lulled by the hum of the plane's powerful engines, Dani finally began to relax and her thoughts fluttered back over the previous 24 hours.

Charlie Black had given Dani a rude awakening the other night, when he told her that she was already well-and-truly under the control of the Cosa Nostra. Charlie had described Tony Mannelli as 'powerful and ruthless; a deadly enemy to make'. That was just before Charlie informed Dani that Tony Mannelli, also known as *'The Horse,'* was involved in nightclubs, protection rackets, shylocking, extortion and all kinds of illegal stuff.

'But, why involve me? Dani shuddered as she recalled that recent conversation with Charlie. *'I'm just a simple girl who loves people and life. Why was I foolish enough to go to the DA's office and spill my guts, when the only ones who got to hear about my valiant efforts at crime fighting*

were Tony and the 'Family'?' Then Dani thought about what had happened after she left the DA's office.

It was late afternoon and she had gone back to the Club where she worked, to pick up a hairpiece to have styled for her evening show. It had never occurred to Dani that she might have reason to be concerned about going back to the place where she worked.

Nicky had grabbed her as soon as she walked down the hallway, throwing Dani into a storage room and pushing her through a jungle of rubbish. Stacks of 45rpm records were sliding about under Dani's feet, causing her to fall. She landed on her back, in a pile of table cloths. As Nicky kicked her in the stomach, he slipped on one of the records too and fell on top of her.

"Stop it, Nicky, you're hurting me!" she pleaded. "Please, stop."

She had never seen Nicky so crazy mad before. Half-crawling and half-slipping on her knees, through the pile of broken records, Dani scrambled to get away but Nicky caught hold of her foot and twisted it hard.

"Why the hell did ya' have to go there, Dani," Nicky yelled?

Monty Salvadinni, the club's head waiter, ran into the room and started to pull Nicky away.

"What the fuck, Nicky? Have you gone crazy or what?"

"Naw Monty, let me at her. Dani went to the fuckin' DA today, to complain about 'the Family'."

Dani used Monty's interruption to pick herself up off the floor and make good her escape. Pulling her heavy woolen coat tight around her, the one that had softened the worst of Nicky's blows, Dani ran out of the club and down 49th Street, sobbing hysterically. A car pulled up out of nowhere but, to her relief, she recognized the friendly face of Joe Decretis, her 'Cadillac' dealer.

"What the hell's the matter, Dani? Get yourself in here."

Dani tumbled through the already opened door, onto the passenger seat. Joe drove several blocks before he parked. He lit a cigarette and handed it to Dani. She took a puff but then started coughing and choking. Catching her breath, she confessed.

"Sorry Joe, I haven't learned to smoke yet."

Shaking and crying, Dani told him what had happened back at the Club and about how afraid she was. She didn't know who to trust or where to turn. Joe put his arms around Dani in a fatherly way.

"Don't you have any family I can take you to?"

"No, not here in New York." Dani sobbed.

"All right, Dani. I have a friend who I think might be able to help you. Let's go!"

Joe drove off again, eventually turning onto Park Avenue and pulling up in front of an expensive, high-rise condominium. The front entrance was canopied and carpeted, right out to the curb and a matching, blue-uniformed doorman opened the front door for them.

While waiting for the elevator, Dani read the tenant register. *'Penthouse: Mr. Charles Black.'* Joe had already told her that if Charlie couldn't help her, no one could.

The penthouse they were invited into was so elegant that Dani absent-mindedly wished she had worn one of her furs that day, instead of the black-cloth coat she was wearing. Joe took her across to a bay window that overlooked Central Park and squeezed her arm reassuringly.

"Wait here a minute while I brief Charlie about your problems."

Dani smiled and nodded, helplessly. There were a number of men sitting around in the room, all talking on telephones and Dani wondered if they were bookies. She'd heard about 'bookie boiler rooms,' but this elegant apartment didn't quite fit the picture.

She watched as Joe walked over to a white, satin-covered couch and sat down next to a handsome, gray-haired man that Dani thought might be in his early 60's. He wore dark grey slacks, an open necked, mono-grammed, steel-grey silk shirt and the softest, grey-leather shoes she had ever seen. Dani even imagined him to be wearing grey-silk, opera hose underneath and felt her cheeks turn red at the thought of what he would look like *'au natural'.*

Dani turned away from the 'grey man' to look through the large, picture-window and watched the horse drawn carriages down in the park below. *'How peaceful they all look'.*

Joe talked quietly with Charlie, who kept glancing over at Dani. At one point he even stopped and stared at her, openly. Suddenly, Charlie snapped his fingers and called across to his men.

"That's all for today."

As each one finished his phone call, he unplugged his phone, put it in his briefcase and left without a word. Joe came over and took Dani's hand, leading her over to Charlie to make proper introductions.

"Dani, you're in good hands now."

Joe gave her another fatherly hug. Then he turned and walked out the door without a backward glance. Dani never saw him again.

In a soft voice Charlie invited Dani to sit next to him.

"Well, young lady," he began, "it seems you have some pretty big problems."

"I guess," Dani said, finding herself at a loss for words in this man's noble presence. Charlie pushed a button on the mirrored wall and a circular wet-bar appeared out of nowhere. He dropped two ice cubes, from a silver ice-bucket, into a crystal martini pitcher and then poured in an ample shot of gin. He looked over at Dani.

"Dry?"

She smiled as he swirled the glass rod twice then filled her stemware like a practiced bartender. Charlie handed her the glass, smiling into her eyes.

"This, my sweet, is a perfect martini to start a perfect evening with."

Picking up the house phone with a flourish, Charlie ordered a champagne dinner to be served in his private, sunken dining room next to the bar. Throughout the fabulous meal they exchanged life-stories, but what Charlie told Dani about the people she had known as friends for the past three years, scared the hell out of her.

'Keep calm, Dani, play it safe. Don't let him know you're afraid of him' she thought. Dani played with her last sip of champagne, coyly letting her eyes rest on Charlie's.

"But if these people are as bad as you say they are, how are you going to be able to help me, Charlie?"

Charlie, the gray man, moved smoothly as he carried the silver champagne bucket over to the couch. He came back to blow out the candles and then took Dani's hand. She seemed to float with him across the room to the couch. She could even hear the bubbles popping as he refilled their glasses.

"As I started to tell you earlier, I *can* help you, Dani. I'm known as 'The Blade' because of my expertise as an executioner."

Dani felt the blood drain from her face as she visualized what he had just told her. She ducked her head and took a sip of champagne to allow time to clear her thoughts.

Charlie gently put his arm around Dani and smiled again.

"There now, don't be afraid my dear. I've never actually killed anyone myself. I just set up contracts around the world for other people; people like Tony Mannelli."

Dani, shocked and speechless, followed meekly as Charlie took her hand and led her gently into his bedroom. The reflections of many scented candles danced all around its mirrored walls. Charlie carefully chose a silk nightshirt for Dani to use and then led her onward into his Grecian-style personal bathroom.

"I think you'll find everything you need here, my dear!" Charlie winked as he turned and left, closing the door quietly behind him.

Dani looked around and saw every kind of perfume and lotion that a girl could want but the French bidet was, for her, the crowning touch! The tensions of the day ebbed away from Dani's exhausted body as she relaxed in a hot, steamy bath, surrounded by the familiar scent of Revlon's 'Intimate' milk bath. Dani felt a warm desire come over her for this man of mystery and intrigue, as she thought of Charlie and all his kindnesses so far. She closed her eyes and became lost in her thoughts, losing all track of time until a soft voice interrupted the moment.

"What's keeping you, my dear?"

As she walked back into his magnificent bedroom, the silk nightshirt that Charlie had chosen for her clung to Dani's still-moist body, revealing hardened nipples. He pulled her down onto the bed beside his own, naked body. Then Charlie began brushing Dani's hair, tenderly, with an antique, silver-backed brush. He spoke softly as he brushed, telling her all about the new life they could have together, in Florida. If Dani would consent be his girl, she could live in his penthouse suite at the Doral Hotel.

As he continued whispering endearments to her, Charlie slipped the negligee from Dani's shoulders. He laid her back onto the black satin sheets, gently running his fingertips up and down her candle-lit body as he slowly peeled off the rest of the garment. Then he took warm, perfumed oil and rubbed it all over Dani's pulsating breasts and all the way down to her toes.

Any fears that Dani had were consumed by her burning desire for this mysterious man. Charlie's body was all she had fantasized about earlier and any lingering shyness flew away swiftly, as Dani crossed the threshold into a crescendo of passion.

Dolores J. Guthrie

Chapter 2

The pilot's voice, announcing their imminent landing over the inter-com, brought Dani back to stark reality. Looking down, she could see the coastline of Miami and the sparkling lights of all its hotels. Nicky, his head twitching more than she had ever seen before, still had not spoken a word to her. He only motioned to Dani with his hands; to guide her as they made their way out of the airport, then into a cab and on to the hotel. Only as they entered the hotel lobby did Nicky finally speak.

"Dani, go and register in your own name for two days and pay cash."

"Why just me, Nicky? Why aren't you going to stay with me?"

Dani was trying desperately to hold back the rising panic she felt, grabbing at Nicky's arm and digging her long nails into his sleeve.

"Please Nicky, I'm trying not to cry, but I'm so confused."

An uninvited tear crawled down one cheek as Nicky simply patted her hand and gently pulled her arm loose from his.

"Dani, I told you back in New York that I couldn't stay. Don't make a scene now, people are watching us. Just do like I've told you. I'm gonna go buy you a red rose now, so stop crying, okay?"

"I'm not crying!" Dani said, wiping her face with her fingers. "I just don't want you to leave me tonight, that's all. I can't stand what's happening to us, Nicky. Please, stay with me and take care of me. You do love me, don't you?"

Nicky took hold of her chin, turned her face upward and looked deep into Dani's eyes.

"You know I love you, Dani. I'll always love you. No one can *ever* take that away from us."

Nicky wiped away her tears with his handkerchief and Dani smiled faintly.

"I'll be okay now, baby!"

"That's more like my girl."

Dani turned and walked across the foyer to the front desk. As she waited for the clerk to attend to her she glanced back at Nicky and was surprised to see two men walk over to him. *'Nobody is supposed to know we're here!'*

Dani thought she recognized one of the men as Sonny Rialto. If it *was* him, she knew for sure that she'd be dead by morning. Dani turned away quickly, fearing that her face would mirror her thoughts. She knew that Nicky wouldn't be the one to do it because of his crazy, mixed up love for her. But Tony would love to make Nicky set up the scene for Dani's death, just to watch his little brother squirm.

'Yeah, Tony Mannelli would get a real kick out of that,' Dani thought, bitterly.

Nicky came back over to Dani and escorted her up to her room. With trembling hands, he unlocked the door and set Dani's bags inside. Standing out in the hallway, Nicky kissed Dani tenderly and handed her the rose, mumbling something about having to rush back to New York for an important meeting. He'd see Dani in a few days, he promised.

Dani noticed small beads of sweat on Nicky's forehead and that he was breathing heavily, but she didn't say anything; she didn't want Nicky to realize that she had already seen the men in the lobby. During their ride up in the elevator, Dani had ample time to figure out what 'The Family's' next move would be. Now they had got Dani out of their territory, they would have her killed quickly. They probably even planned to plant her body back in Charlie Black's penthouse.

'That would certainly even the score with Charlie for trying to interfere in Tony's business,' she reasoned.

Dani watched miserably as Nicky walked away toward the elevators. He looked back once. Dani smiled, waved and shut the door; trying to seem normal but all the time thinking, *'How the hell can I get out of here?'* She knew she couldn't take the elevator. Nicky's two friends would be watching the lobby. In fact, they could be coming up on the elevator even as Dani stood there. *'They won't waste time, that's for sure. They'll want to get this over with quickly.'*

Carefully, Dani opened the door a crack, just to be sure that Nicky had gone downstairs. Moving quickly, she picked up her bag and purse, not forgetting Nicky's red rose. Then Dani stepped out into the hallway, closing the door behind her. She had no idea where she was going, she just knew that she couldn't stay in that room.

***

"Fuck!" Nicky stumbled onto the elevator like a blind man without his white cane. *"What a shitty mess. Why the hell did Dani hafta go to the DA's office? And how the hell could I fall in love with such a dumb broad in the first place?"*

Nicky visualized how the two men down in the lobby would do the job. Probably chloroform Dani first, to make her look drunk and then take her back to Charlie Black's lavish penthouse and drown her in his bathtub.

'Hell, I can't help Dani now. It's too late to turn back. Besides, the bitch made her choice when she screwed 'The Blade' the other night!" Nicky was still deep in thought when the elevator doors opened. He stood in the corner, staring into space, until one of the waiting passengers began to get impatient.

"Sir, this is the lobby. Sir?"

Nicky came out of his daze and pushed through the group of tired travelers. Then he raced across the crowded lobby and jumped into a waiting cab. He snapped at its dozing driver.

"Get me to the airport and I mean fast!"

But the cab moved slowly, through hot, muggy night-air and congested traffic. Nicky's thoughts drifted back to their early days of love, when Danielle had given him every reason for feeling like a man. She'd driven him nuts, she was so damned exciting! Like that night when a spotlight had shimmered on her, wearing an Italian, emerald-green sequined gown. Dani's sapphire-blue eyes had fixed on Nicky whilst she sang, 'As Long As He Needs Me' - all the while holding an entire audience in the palm of her hands, as only Dani could.

'Hell, I can't let them kill her!'

"Turn this hack around," Nicky yelled. "Get me back to that hotel, quick as you can."

Nicky hardly waited for the cab to stop before he jumped out. Half-running through the lobby, he dove onto the first available elevator. The journey seemed to take an eternity and when Nicky reached Dani's door he began pounding on it like a madman. There was no answer. Nicky slumped to the floor in the shadows of the hallway, shivering with guilt and grief.

'They've already taken my Dani,' he sobbed.

***

Dani made it to the stairway door and as she pushed through into the fire escape, she could hear elevator doors opening behind her. She didn't look around, she daren't. Dani kept on running down several flights of stairs, until she found a waiting service elevator. She got in and pressed the button for the basement. When the elevator door opened to reveal total darkness, Dani groped for a light but couldn't find one. As her eyes slowly adjusted, she could see another stairway, outside of some glass doors on the far side of the room. Edging toward the lights, Dani banged her leg on something hard and sharp.

"Shit!"

It hurt like hell, but Dani knew she had to keep going. *'There has to be a way out of this place somewhere!'* On reaching the glass doors, Dani pushed through them and ran down some wide steps.

Swoooosh!

Down she went and, to Dani's surprise, she found herself lying flat on her back on the hotel's ice-skating rink. After what seemed a lifetime in some 'B' horror movie, of crawling across ice on her hands and knees, Dani finally found a fire door, opened it and ran out into fresh, night air.

The beach felt cold at night and sand was getting into Dani's shoes, cutting into her feet. *'These damn heels are not made for this,'* she thought, reaching down to pull her shoes off. Dani couldn't stop crying. She was drowning in a whirlpool of her own tears and her mind was spinning like a tornado.

'Maybe I'm going crazy, things like this don't really happen, only in movies. Maybe I should just go back to the hotel?' Then Dani remembered the two men she'd seen in the lobby with Nicky and the thought of going back sent a chill down her sweaty back. *'No, no, I'm not that crazy.'*

As she quickened her pace, Dani heard a noise behind, but as she turned around to look she stumbled over an embankment, hurting her knees. Dani was intent on inspecting her injuries when she felt a hand on her shoulder. *'Oh no, this is it.'* It was with immense relief that Dani realized it was only a beach boy. He stood quite tall though, towering over Dani as she lay there on the sand.

"My! My! What have we here?"

The youth bent down and held his lighter toward Dani's face so he could see her better. Then Dani realized that the youth was not alone!

"Shit! Hey, Larry! Come on down here and see this sweet gift from heaven."

Dani heard rocks rolling down the slope and then another lighter snapped its glow into her face.

"Yes siree, Jake, this is mighty nice. So, who gets her first, then?"

"Well hell, man, I found her! You just hold her down."

Dani was crying so hard by then that she didn't have any strength left to fight them off.

"That's it, you just take it nice and easy, baby. We won't hurt you if you're smart and cooperate."

But Jake yelled as he climbed on top of Dani for a second time.

"Ouch! You prick, Larry; you filled her full of sand! Now she's so swollen, I can't get it in."

"Hell, just jam it in, they all stretch, don't they?"

Dani screamed so loudly that Jake pulled out of her in panic.

"Jesus, Larry, let's just get the hell out of here before someone hears the crazy bitch."

Dani lay curled up in the sand, terrified, shaken and in agonizing pain. *'God, why is all this shit happening to me?'*

Then she heard someone else approaching and tried desperately not to breathe. Two figures passed within a few feet of Dani. Two young lovers, giggling, hugging and so involved with each other that Dani went completely unnoticed. She breathed a sigh of relief, then gathered her belongings and struggled to her feet. She could feel blood, grit and semen running down her legs and Dani felt so disgustingly dirty. God only knew what she might have caught from those bastards.

'I've got to get a bath and I mean soon!'

Dani ducked in through the back door of the first hotel she came to, no matter how run-down it looked. Using a false name, she tried not to faint during the time it took to check in. The room certainly didn't compare to her usual standard of accommodations but at least she could bathe and sleep. Dani was exhausted.

After carefully giving herself three good douches, she lay back into the hot water, aching in every muscle. Yet when she realized that she even had sand in her teeth, Dani almost laughed in spite of all she'd been through. She closed her eyes and sighed, deeply.

'Mmmmm, with my eyes closed even this old tub feels as good as the Ritz!'

***

Danielle's relaxed body had slipped down into the cooled bath water and she awakened with a start, sputtering as she sat up.

'Dammit! If Tony and those beach boys haven't managed to kill me yet, I don't want to drown myself in a dumpy hotel!'

Dani then asked herself a question she hadn't had time for until that moment. *'Now that I'm on the run, how am I ever going to fulfill that contract I was offered with A1 Sound Studios, to replace the star in their Broadway show, Funny Girl?'*

"Hell," she answered herself, aloud, "my singing career, at least in New York, is over. I'll never be safe there as long as *'The Horse'* holds power. I may not be dead yet, but 'The Family' has certainly taken a toll on my life."

Dani continued talking out loud, just for the comfort of hearing a human voice.

"God, I just hope they don't go after my son, JR, at his military academy. I really *do* hope they're too smart to make a dumb move like that."

What an injustice it would be if she had to take her only son out of school, for his own protection. JR already had an appointment to 'West Point' when he graduated, at the end of the next term.

'Damn!' Dani cursed herself. *'I've probably ruined my son's future too, just because I wasn't smart enough to see what was going on around me.'*

A shiver ran down Dani's back as she climbed out of the near-cold tub. She quickly dried herself, rubbing hard to get the blood flowing again and then she crawled into the welcoming bed. Tired as she was, Dani lay wide awake for quite a while thinking about food. She couldn't remember when she had eaten last! It could even have been back at Charlie's penthouse, the day before! *'Hell, no point in thinking about that now! There probably won't be any room service in this crummy hotel anyway.'*

Finally, Dani closed her eyes but just before drifting off she made plans for the next day. *'I'll call Papa in the morning. He'll know what to do and I'll be in better condition then.* And as quickly as the thoughts left her pretty head, Dani was asleep.

***

When she woke next morning, Dani realized how much she had needed last night's sleep. Her body was still sore and bruised, but her mind was much clearer and she felt ready to take on the problems of getting herself to a place of safety.

Her mother answered Dani's phone call.

"Hello? Mama?"

"Dani? Dani, is that you?"

"Yes, Mama! But can I talk to Papa, please?" Dani asked, fighting to hold back the tears that were welling up again in her still-swollen eyes.

"Are you okay, Dani?"

"Yes, I'm all right, Mom, but can you just get Papa for me please."

"Harold, come quick, it's Dani. Something's wrong, I'm sure of it."

Only a brief moment passed before her father spoke and Dani felt such relief at hearing his voice.

"Oh, Papa, I'm in trouble. You tried to tell me about my friends, back in New York. Well...oh Papa, you were right! I just can't stop crying. I'm so afraid and it's so hard to talk."

"Now, Dani, just calm down and answer my questions. Where are you now?" Harold spoke in his familiar, soothing manner.

"I'm in Miami, Papa but they're trying to kill me."

"Who is?"

"Tony Mannelli has two guys out looking for me, but I think I'm okay for now. I got away from them last night. Should I go to the police down here?"

"Hell, no! Mannelli probably has men all over the place down there. Do you have any money with you, Dani?"

"Yes, Papa, I have enough cash to get home. But can I come home?"

"Dani, of course you can come home but you must do it right. Just do exactly as I say, OK? Now, I want you to rent a car first and drive up to Tampa. When you get there, get on a bus to New Orleans and then fly from New Orleans to Seattle. Do you think you can do all that?"

"Yes, Papa, I can do it."

"Okay. Now Dani, don't you go getting' all dressed up either. Try to look plain, if that's possible!" Harold Gunther knew his daughter well!

"And don't call here to the house again either, Dani. When you get to Seattle airport we'll be there to meet you, don't worry. Go to the *Lost and Found* desk to pick up a message that I will leave there for you. Now, have you got all that, Dani?"

"Yes, Papa, thank you. I love you, but I'd better get going now." Dani hung up and began looking in the nearest yellow pages for a car rental agency. She needed to find one close by. *'Don't want to be spotted, walking all around town!'*

Later, driving along Highway 75 toward Tampa, Dani reminded herself how lucky she was to have such a family to go home to.

Chapter 3

Unable to sleep, Lindsay, Nicky Mannelli's wife, stumbled from their marital bed and into the en-suite bathroom. *'Damn, I forgot to buy aspirin.'*

In desperation Lindsay plunked two seltzers into a glass of water. She walked back through the bedroom and over to the French-doors that opened onto a pool area. It was cold outside, but the fresh air made Lindsay feel better. She smiled broadly as she drew a deep breath and lifted her seltzer toward the sky, in a mocking toast.

"Goodbye forever, Danielle! Thanks for the million dollars; for the new home and furniture; for the Cadillac; the yacht, oh and let's not forget the N&D Corporation! It's been worth sharing my husband with you for all of that but, after tonight, my handsome Nicky will be all mine again."

The seltzers had already helped ease Lindsay's physical discomfort. "Yes!" she continued, rubbing her large, pregnant belly. "Your father will be back from Miami soon and then we won't have to share him with 'Miss high & mighty, Dani' anymore."

Lindsay started to move back inside, but doubled over with a cramp in her leg.

'God, I should feel great, but I feel like crap. If I go to bed, maybe the morning will come around sooner.'

***

Struggling to get a cab out of Kennedy Airport, in the early morning traffic, was almost too much for Nicky after such a miserable, long night. As he entered his home, in New Jersey, Nicky was still sick to his stomach about what he'd allowed to happen the previous day.

'Shit!' he berated himself. *'Not only am I an accessory to murder, but it was to help kill the one woman I really love. OK, I've got Danielle's money but I've still got two children and a new one on the way. And, yes, I've still got Lindsay; oh sweet, nagging Lindsay, who's even worse when she's pregnant!'*

Lighting a cigarette, Nicky went over to the bar and poured himself a double shot of scotch. He leaned back and drained the glass in one, then shook his head as if trying to clear it of the troublesome thoughts that were roiling around inside it. He poured another drink and took a deep drag of his cigarette but the smoke burned his eyes and left him coughing. Impatiently, Nicky flicked the butt into the sink on the bar and dragged himself upstairs, into the bedroom. Complete exhaustion numbed his body. All Nicky wanted was a shower and then some sleep, plenty of it.

But Lindsay awoke with a start as Nicky lowered himself onto the edge of the bed. She looked at the clock, then stretched and yawned.

"Gee, hon, you're back fast. Did everything go okay?"

"I don't want to talk about it."

"But, did it?" Lindsay insisted.

"Yeah, yeah," Nicky growled, jumping up. "Just leave me alone, will ya'? I said I don't want to talk about it."

Nicky stomped outside to the poolside in his stocking feet, kicking at some moldy leaves that were laying in a large pile and getting his socks covered with smelly gunk for his trouble. In disgust, he picked up a chair and hurled it across the patio.

"Jesus Christ, just look at this place, Lindsay. It looks like we're living back in Brooklyn again. You've already got a damn maid and in future I want a gardener here, once a week! Lindsay, do you fuckin' hear me?"

But Lindsay knew when not to reply and this was definitely one of those times. Then the bedside phone began ringing and Lindsay rolled over to pick it up. It was Tony, his gruff voice harsh and demanding. She muffled the phone into the pillow as she called to her husband.

"Nicky, it's your brother."

"Who?" Nicky stomped back into the bedroom.

"It's Tony."

"Shit, how the hell did he know I was back," Nicky hissed, grabbing the phone out of his wife's hands.

"Yeah, Tony, what's up?"

"You fuckin' punk kid! Where is she?"

"Who?"

"I knew you couldn't do it? Where the fuck is she?"

"Hell, Tony, I don't know what you're talking about. The boys took Dani, I know they took her, Tony. You *are* talking about Dani, aren't you?"

"You sorry motherfucker, get your ass down here, now!"

"What are you talking about, Tony? What's wrong?"

"I'm talking about that goddam broad, Danielle, that's who. Get your ass down here, goddam it; to the office, that's where!"

Tony had slammed the phone down hard and the violent sound still echoed in Nicky's ear. He stood in silence, his face as white as a sheet and wondered where the hell Dani had gone. *'This means she's still alive.'* A sudden feeling of relief ran through his gut, or was it the fear of his brother's wrath. Either way Nicky was feeling sick again.

Lindsay jumped out of bed, demanding to know what was wrong but her husband didn't answer.

"Nicky! What's going on?" she demanded again.

"I don't know, but I gotta get to the office!" Nicky snapped as he headed for the bedroom door.

"But, hon, you need a shower and some rest first."

"I'll shave in the car. Just find me some clean socks, will ya'?"

As he drove back into the city, Nicky knew all too well the full wrath of *'The Horse'* that awaited him.

When Nicky walked into the office, his big brother was pacing back and forth, chewing on a dead cigar. Vinnie *'Cueball'*, Tony's bald-headed, right-hand man, sat idly thumping a pencil on a tabletop. Karl Hokowitz, attorney for 'The Family', sat at another desk drinking coffee, calm as all hell. But then Karl was always calm and quiet and that made him very dangerous. Nicky had never really thought about it before; about Karl being Jewish and not Italian, like the rest of 'The Family'. Nicky wondered, idly, where Tony had first met Karl.

As Nicky hesitated in the doorway, Tony grabbed at his brother's arm and tried to twist it behind his back, but slipped on one of his own discarded cigar butts and landed flat on his back. The breath was knocked hard out of him. Everyone ran to help lift Tony's heavy frame back onto his feet, but he shook them all loose. His face was purple with rage.

"Just get this wimp brother of mine the fuck outta my sight!"

"I just got here. Ya want I should leave already, Tony?"

Nicky was anxious to place the blame at someone else's door.

"I've just been flying all over the fuckin' East Coast doing your damn dirty work. Then ya' drag me the fuck' back in here from Jersey, fighting the fuckin' traffic all the way, when it's your fuckin' torpedoes who fucked up down in Florida!"

Nicky swung around and began to head out of the still open door, just as Tony's phone rang.

"Hold it kid. Get your ass back in here. We got Florida on the squawk box, right now!"

"Tony? It's Benny Kurtzin here. I got all my boys out looking for that bitch. Arnie Silversmith's men too; they're all over the airport and bus station. Does the broad have any friends down here she would go to?"

"Naw! I don't think so. You never can tell about that Dani though, she could always pick someone up in a flash with those 'goo-goo' eyes of hers."

"Yeah, don't you and I know it? Okay, Tony, I'll get back to you as soon as there's anything new."

"Yeah Benny, you do that. Hey and tell Sonny Rialto that I gotta talk to him 'fore he finds her. My man at the DA's office says the story leaked out already that Dani was there the other day."

"No shit, Tony?"

"Yeah, so we better put a hold on the hit for now, eh? Things could get hot on this one and reflect badly on us all. Ya' get my drift, Benny?"

"Yeah, yeah; I get it!"

"One more thing. Her ol' man's a sheriff or something big, back up there in Yakima."

"Hell, Tony, that's not good. I'll get back to you soon as I hear anythin', okay?"

"Yeah, okay!"

Tony clicked off the speaker, picking at his tooth with a pencil. He sucked in air through his gums while he thought things over.

"Karl, you got any ideas where the bitch might have gone?"

"Hell, Tony, I figure if she was smart enough to ditch the boys down in Miami, she won't be talking to anyone, or showing up around here, anytime soon. Maybe you should put some bugs out, amongst her friends and family out West."

Tony glared long and hard at his younger brother, before speaking in as calm a voice as he could manage.

"You knew her best, Nicky boy; what do you think?"

"Well, I reckon' she musta' guessed what we had planned for her. I think maybe she saw Sonny Rialto come up to me in that hotel lobby. Maybe our young Dani *can* add two and two, after all!"

"Shit! How in the fuck did that happen?"

"Hell, Tony, I left Dani at the desk, signing in, but Sonny came up to me as I waited in the lobby."

Tony cracked his knuckles in a gesture of disgust. He wiped his brow with the end of his already sweat-stained tie and cleared his throat. He loosened his collar too. It felt like it was strangling him.

"Shit, Nicky! Sonny Rialto told me on the phone that when you came down and left to get a cab, they went straight up to Dani's room. But the bitch was already gone, bag-and-baggage and, for sure, she didn't go out through the lobby."

"Well, she didn't just vanish, Tony, she's gotta be there someplace."

"No shit! I'll call the bank, anyhow. Frank'll let me know the minute she gets money from any place in the country, any place at all."

"But that'll take time, Tony. Ya' know Dani always carries a wad of money with her and a purse full of credit cards, too."

"Yeah, you're right there, Nicky."

"Well, I reckon Dani's bound to show up there in Yakima, where her family lives," Nicky ventured.

"Yeah, ya' gotta point there. Get Celie in here will ya', before you leave," was Tony's less than subtle dismissal of his younger sibling.

Celie Temarko was a matronly, gray-haired woman whose husband, Frank, had been a lieutenant in the Faci Family. Rumor had it that his death in 1959 was what started the whole Ballo-Faci war. Anyhow, after Frank's death *'The Horse'* had taken Celie under his protection and she had been loyal to him and his kind ever since.

"Celie, call Tucson and get Joe Banicci on the line for me will ya'."

"Tony, that might be a problem," Celie replied quietly. "You know very well that the only way Joe will *ever* take a call is if his attorney can set up a specific time, for a pay phone connection."

"I don't care how you do it, Celie, just do it and fast! Tell him *'The Horse'* wants an audience!"

"Okay, Tony. I'm on it."

As Celie set up the proper connections, she started thinking back to 1957, when her husband had gone over to Joe Barbara's house, to that fateful Mafia meeting. Frank had been sitting next to Joe Banicci when the FBI had made their hit on the house. Somehow the Feds had gotten the names of every single one of the sixty three Mafia members attending. The 'godfather' of the whole of California was arrested at that meeting, but most of the others had escaped by running through the woods. Heads had rolled after that affair, Celie remembered.

But Joe Banicci, the Godfather of all the godfathers, had escaped. When he finally did return to his Tucson paradise, his empire had been blown out from under him. Only he, and his faithful Doberman, *'Easy,'* had survived and the news media quoted Joe as saying,

'They kill me, I die but then I come back.'

But Joe Banicci, knowing that he didn't really have nine lives, retired to live in the desert. He hadn't expected his doting 'family' to follow him to his hideout but they all did. Celie reflected that Joe Banicci would remain the 'Don of Dons' until he was laid to rest.

'Oh, my! And Tony wants a favor from him?'

Celie didn't actually manage to make contact with Banicci himself, but with one of his main lieutenants, Santo Perrone.

"Sure," Santo said, when Celie explained what was up.

"Whatever Tony needs, we can do. We have a real ladies' man for that sweet young broad, if she ever shows up in Yakima. His name's Digger Rosselli - doesn't look at all Italian, his mother was a Swede - and trust me, the man is one real, smooth operator."

"Ok, Santo, Tony is waiting, so I'll connect you now!"

"Santo? Tony, here. Ya been able to set up a meet with Joe yet?"

"Naw, Tony, it's a no show on Banicci. He's out of the country right now, but I gotta good man for the job you need. The Feds are looking for him on some land swindle and he needs a quiet life for a while. What's the plan?"

"Hell, Santo, if he's that good he'll figure a plan out for himself. I just want to know that dame's every move, even if this fella has to marry her. That'd tie up the rest of her money and keep her from making any waves about 'The Family' back here."

"Sounds perfect, but what makes you think she'll marry Digger?"

"She's running scared, an' that makes her vulnerable."

"Is she a two-bagger?"

"Naw, she's a real beauty, but she's stupid so just give her the right kinda' bait and she'll bite.

"OK, Tony. Anything else we need to look out for?"

"Yeah, just a minor thing; her ole man's a sheriff or some such back there in Yakima!"

"No shit," Santo laughed. "But that shouldn't give our man Digger any trouble. I told Celie, the guy's a real charmer. So long, Tony, I'll get back to ya' later."

Tony smiled, leaned back in his big, swivel chair and pushed down on the intercom button.

"Celie?"

"Yes, Tony!"

"Get Nicky on the phone. I wanna' be the first to tell him there's going to be a wedding soon."

Tony was glorying in the fact that his younger brother would really be hurt when he learned of the plan that had been worked out for Dani's future. Yet another reason for Nicky to curse his older brother and proof that Tony wasn't known as *'Crazy Horse'* for nothing.

From under his desk Tony pulled out his old-faithful, Thompson sub-machine gun, opened the breach and inserted a magazine. As he caressed the weapon lovingly, Tony suddenly thought way back to his sixteenth birthday, when older brother, Louie, had given him the prized possession, telling Tony that he had personally taken it off of a dead 'G-Man', many years before.

On that same birthday, Louie had also taken Tony for his first 'lay' at some fancy, downtown whorehouse. Getting more excited at his memories, Tony began to polish the old Thompson vigorously. He always kept the safety catch on because he was afraid it would blow up in his face, but he sure scared the shit out of his own boys when he waved it around in the air, screaming at them.

'They all know Tony Mannelli ain't no street hood,' he smiled at the notion. *'My guys know I'm Mr. Big alright!'*

Tony looked around then at his fancy new offices, covering both the 26th and 27th floors of the Time & Life Building. Celie sat outside, at her huge horseshoe-shaped reception desk, surrounded by three large enclosures made from bullet proof glass. The glass had been installed so that Tony could safely survey all the elevators, but his personal office also had windows that overlooked the Rockefeller Center.

Tony held the keys to his own little Mafia kingdom in a little black book, with all the names written in code. As long as he had that book, Tony would always be the boss and his boys, and their guns, would always stand by him. Tony even believed that someday his power would spread his own Family's influence all around the world, just like back in the old days.

"Yes," Tony whispered aloud, still caressing the Thomson cradled in his lap.

"You will all kiss Tony Mannelli, before I sleep the 'Big Sleep'."

Chapter 4

Digger Rosselli checked into 'The Chinook Hotel', in Yakima, only a matter of hours after getting his mission orders from Santo Perrone. Dressed as if he had just walked out of a Sears & Roebuck catalog's western-clothing section, Digger even spoke with a phony, western drawl.

"Ya'll send my bags up to my room, now? And tell me, do ya'll have a good bar here in this little ole town?"

"Yes sir, we have a lovely lounge right here in the hotel, just down the hall to your left.

"Well' thank ya, ma'am. This western atmosphere is just makin' me feel right at home."

After ordering a Beefeater-on-the- rocks, with a twist, from the bosomy blonde behind the bar, Digger was quick to acquaint himself with the fellow seated on the next barstool. Ray Darby, as the man introduced himself, quickly let it be known that he owned a car dealership, right there in town. It didn't take Digger long to also find out that Darby considered himself to be a good friend of Sheriff Gunther and family. Darby was obviously the chatty kind, which suited Digger just fine and the man went on to say how the Gunthers' daughter had flown home to Yakima, from New York, the previous year. It seemed that the lady had gone into Darby's showroom and paid cash for a fully equipped *Grand Prix,* as a gift for her teenaged son, JR.

"Not only that," Darby carried on, enthusiastically, "but she paid for a top-of-the-line *Oldsmobile Starfire* for her eighteen-year-old sister too, all on the same damn day!"

"Boy," Darby grinned broadly at Digger, "that dame was sure some looker, too. I remember her from way back, when she was nothing but a skinny, pony-tailed kid and now they say she's in show business!"

Digger ordered another round before seeking more information.

"Is the lady in these here parts right now, Ray? She sure sounds like someone I'd like to meet."

"Naw, Digger. I heard she just got a contract for some new Broadway show, back in New York. Guess that's why she had to sell her ranch, out in Selah."

"And what ranch would that be?" Digger inquired subtly.

"Why, the 'Suzy Q' o' course, just about the largest cutting ranch here in the Northwest!"

Darby was enjoying his role as an informer.

"Story has it she lost about $200,000 on the sale, too."

"How the hell did that happen?"

Digger kept on with his skillful probing.

"Well, from what I heard, her attorneys back East tricked her somehow."

Ray Darby looked at his watch.

"Say, Digger, the sheriff's department is only a few blocks from here. If you want, I'll call to see if Gunther's there and then we'll go over and I'll introduce you to the man."

"Thanks, Darby, but I want to shower and clean up afore I get to moving around. I've been on the road awhile."

Getting up from his stool, Digger winked at the bosomy, blonde bartender.

"Say honey, could ya'll bring a li'l ol' bottle of gin up to my room when you get off work?"

"Sorry, sir, but you'll just have to trot your li'l ol' buns down the hall, where you can buy all the bottles of booze ya' want."

She winked, exaggeratedly, back at Digger as she stalked off.

"My, my, quite a frisky little filly, wouldn't you say, Ray?"

"Shit, Digger, don't you worry about her, she's married anyway. Most of the other gals in this town are pushovers."

Digger stood up and stretched.

"Well, maybe I'll catch ya'll a little later then, Darby."

"Sure, Digger, see ya 'round. You got my card, anyhow."

Up in his room, Digger thumbed through the well-used phone book. *'Well, lookee here,"* he muttered, *"isn't that something. H. R. Gunther, on*

Euclid Avenue. I think I'll hire me a private eye for a few days. He can do a little diggin' while I enjoy a few of the spicier things in this hick town.'

***

Harold Gunther packed the last suitcase into the car and also several bags of groceries that his wife, Laura, handed to him.

"I don't think there'll be supermarkets up in the mountains, Harold and the resort store will be far too expensive for coffee and such, so I stocked up."

Smiling up at her husband as he stood so tall and handsome in his sheriff's uniform, Laura thought how proudly he carried himself. Harold bent down, pulled Laura's small frame to him and gently kissed her soft, velvety lips.

"Umm, what's for dinner?"

He was surprised at how well his wife was holding up. Only ten days ago she had been released from hospital after major surgery and now she was concerned for Dani's welfare. He smiled down at his wife's upturned face.

"I thought we'd eat on the way to Seattle," she smiled back. "We'll have plenty of time before Dani's plane gets in."

As Harold backed out of the driveway he noticed Yakima's only private investigator's car, staked out a little way up the street. Laura noticed it too and the slight frown that crossed her husband's face.

"Is something wrong honey? I thought I saw that private investigators car parked around back?"

"Don't worry about it, hon, it's probably just someone getting caught playing house where they shouldn't be!"

That seemed to satisfy his wife but Harold couldn't understand why the car was now following them. Not wanting to alarm Laura further, he told her he would stop by the Sheriff's office to change cars before they left town, just in case. Then Harold drove out down all the back alleys, hoping the maneuver would lose their tail before they were finally on their way to meet Dani.

***

Dani had boarded the Greyhound bus to New Orleans and looked carefully at all the people already on board before deciding she was in the clear. Taking a deep breath, she adjusted her seat, settled back and closed her eyes. The sway of the bus as it rounded corners and the humming of its motor, soon lulled Dani into a half-sleep, full of thoughts and memories of exactly how and when her nightmare had started.

New York City in 1964 meant much more than just the Statue of Liberty, or the Empire State Building to Dani. It represented everything she had ever longed for in life: fame, fortune, glamour and, most importantly, her freedom and independence.

As a bride of sixteen, Dani had married Peter, a tall, dark, handsome Gregory Peck-type and all that a romantic youngster could have hoped for in a lover. But what had seemed important at sixteen was not so important fifteen years later. Peter had simply wanted a 'wife' and had never been able to accept Dani's burning desire to be a professional singer. He had allowed her to do benefit shows for the VA hospital, and concerts at the town's Civic Club and the like, but that had turned Dani's singing into some kind of harmless hobby, like needlepoint or stamp collecting. Whether her husband had felt threatened by Dani's talent, or whether he simply thought she couldn't cut it professionally, Dani didn't know. Whatever his reasons, Peter would not give in and so Dani had been forced to leave him, to find out for herself if she could make it on her own.

Dani had been in New York for only a few short weeks when, one hot, muggy night, she sat alone in her drab room in the 'Barbizon-Hotel-for-Women', on Lexington Avenue. Noise from the street below was punctuated by excited laughter and music coming from an apartment building, across the rooftops. Its terrace doors were wide open and sheer curtains were billowing gently, seemingly in time to the music.

Dani saw a tall, slender girl in the doorway, champagne glass in hand and dressed in a white-satin gown that showed off her golden hair and smooth, tanned skin. The girl moved out onto the terrace to stand next to her gentleman friend. She brushed her tongue across the rim of her glass as she looked up into his eyes. She licked her lips and then kissed him as he held her in a long, passionate embrace.

The man was handsome, dressed in a tuxedo and with greying hair and bronzed skin. Dani guessed him to be an outdoor kind of person; a well preserved 60year-old, or thereabouts.

Dani was an illicit observer to this fantasy scene; envious of what she saw, but reassured by remembering the many gifts she already had.

Dani had been blessed with a rare beauty. At five-feet seven- inches tall and with long, black hair, sapphire-blue eyes and a 44-22-37 figure, she had just won the New York *'Miss Cleopatra'* contest for an Elizabeth Taylor look-alike. As Dani slid down into her own, cheap, hotel bed, she imagined that her sheets were made of satin. *'Someday, I too, will have beautiful things, just like that girl across the rooftops.'* Dani took a deep breath, closed her eyes and drifted off to sleep to the sounds of partying, drifting across the New York rooftops.

***

Dani awoke, happy and determined the next morning. She quickly slipped into her favorite sun dress, the one she had worn the night she won the contest. Out on the street, Dani hailed a cab to take her to the Time & Life Building, where she had no trouble finding the offices of William H. Crawford and Associates. Dani approached the reception desk with bravado.

"Is Mr. William Crawford in, please?" Dani sounded confident, even though she was nervous.

"And you are?" The receptionist eyed Dani up and down as she asked the question.

"Miss Danielle Sutton."

The receptionist buzzed the intercom to speak to her boss and Dani heard Bill Crawford reply without hesitation.

"Send her right in."

It seemed such a long time ago now, but Dani had met Bill the year before, in Rochester, NY. Since then she had spoken to him only briefly, when he had called her at work, but from their first meeting Dani had been attracted to this man. In his mid-forties and impeccably dressed in a double-breasted suit, Bill had worn a hat and carried a leather briefcase and umbrella whenever Dani had seen him.

He had seemed a quiet man, whose ideals, Dani suspected, were as impeccable as his attire and his tastes.

"My loves in life,' he had once told Dani, "are the opera, the theater and Chinese Bronzes."

And now Bill was greeting her with open arms.

"My God, Dani! What are you doing here?"

"Well, it's a long story, Bill, but I'm here in New York to stay and if you have time for lunch, I'll tell you all about it."

"I'll make time, Dani, for you! After a couple of phone calls, I'll be free for the whole afternoon. Would you like to have lunch at 'The New York Athletic Club'?"

"That sounds fine," Dani murmured, "but I don't really feel like swimming."

Bill laughed gently at her innocent mistake.

"You really are such an innocent, Dani. It's an exclusive country club, with one of the finest dining rooms in the whole city, or the whole country for that matter!"

That lunch was Dani's first encounter with *'escargots'*, *'salad varie'* and *'mint juleps'* and it was the moment she understood, without doubt, that New York was the right place for her.

"Bill, do you remember when I first met you in Rochester? It was last spring, while I was still studying at the beauty school."

He nodded, smiling. "How could I forget?"

"Well, the night after you returned to New York, several of us girls from the beauty school went over to the Sheraton Hotel. This older, but very drunk, gentleman kept asking me to dance with him but I kept refusing. He was really persistent and finally he laid out two hundred-dollar bills, just for a dance. But I was so embarrassed that I threw his money back at him and ran upstairs to my room. Well, I guess it impressed him that I couldn't be bought, because the man found out where I worked, at the beauty shop in Syracuse. Oh, Bill; he sent me flowers, he called me at work and in general the man drove me crazy. I really felt guilty at the way I treated him but I knew I had done nothing wrong. To make things worse, he sent a brand new TR-4, registered in my name, to our house and even sent several thousand dollars to me, in the mail!"

Bill listened, aghast.

"What on earth did that do to your relationship with Peter?"

"He knew I wasn't seeing anyone, but our friends didn't and they made some pretty nasty comments. Finally, I just couldn't stand the gossip any longer so when the chance to model for Eastern Travelers was offered to me, I took it. On my first job, in Boston, the president of the company I was working for would come into the showroom, which was where I had to sleep and make advances to me. I fought him off for two whole weeks and quit as soon as the show was over. That's when I came here, to New York. But now that I'm away from my old life, Bill, I really don't want to go back home."

"Well, what about your son, JR? Are you going to leave him behind, too?"

"No, no, Bill!" Dani insisted. "I just need some time to get on my feet and then I'll bring him here, to be with me."

"I see." Bill looked doubtful. "Dani, you didn't say who gave you all those presents?"

"No, I guess I didn't, did I? His name is Howard S. Kline, but his friends all called him 'HK'."

"And what does he do for a living?"

"He was hired by the man who was with him that night we first met. That man's father is J C Williams, Sr., the founder and president of the Aloid-Xenon Company."

"HK told me that after he had finished at Harvard Business School, the Xenon Company hired him as 'controller', whatever that is! Then, in 1954, he got promoted to 'treasurer' of the company and now HK is the company's Vice President! Even when he retires, later this year, he told me he'll still stay on as a member of their Board of Directors. He seems a nice enough guy, Bill, I've talked to him on the phone many times, but he's fifty eight! I really think that's too old for me."

"Aren't you going to call him though, to tell him you're here in New York?" Bill asked, quietly.

"I don't know," Dani admitted. "If only he were closer to my age, I wouldn't hesitate, Bill. I'm not sure I'd like being with a much older man."

Bill looked at Dani for a long time and then shook his head, gently.

"Dani, I think you should head straight back to Peter, in Syracuse. This city is too big for a girl as naive as you are."

"No," Dani told him, firmly. "I won't go back, Bill. I want to become a singer and this is my chance."

Bill was obviously skeptical about her plans, but that didn't matter to Dani.

"I know it's going to be tough and that I'll have mountains to climb but, Bill, I have to try."

Bill was quiet for a long while but Dani believed she could read his thoughts. She continued to toy with her drink and look deeply into Bill's eyes and when he finally spoke again, it was in the voice of a man who knew he was doomed.

"My God, Dani, what you can do to a man's willpower is unbelievable. I've never met anyone like you. I know damn well that if I give in to the overpowering drive that I feel building within me, you would draw me into the very depths of those blue eyes and I'd never know reality again!"

Dani leaned across the table and ran her fingers lightly up and down his. Then she picked up his hand gently and slowly kissed his fingertips, one at a time. In a childlike voice, she asked him, "your place, or mine?"

Bill's hand started to sweat and tremble. "Well, I do keep a room here at the club, Dani, if you really want to? I mean..."

Dani suddenly felt something new, bubbling up within her and the recognition of a power that had lain dormant until that very moment. A woman's power over a man. Dani smiled, inside herself. *'It's a shame I can't bottle this to sell.'*

The cold, sparsely furnished room felt pretty unwelcoming until Bill turned on the steam heat. They climbed into bed, all the while Bill telling Dani, again and again, what a quiet, uncomplicated life he had led up until then and how he didn't want it all upset. Dani ignored his protests and disappeared beneath the covers.

"Dammit, Dani! What are you doing?"

As Dani came up for air, she kissed every inch of Bill's lean, muscular body along the way. She breathed in his manly scent, before whispering into his ear.

"I want to bring out the animal that's hiding beneath your Wall Street image, Bill!"

Dani emphasized her statement by kissing him hard on the lips and Bill gave up without a fight.

***

The next morning, even more determined than ever, Dani asked to be taken to every theatrical agency that her cab driver knew. Stopping before a building on Broadway, the man waved his hand, airily.

"This whole place is *full* of agents."

And the man apparently knew what he was talking about. The reader-board on the wall was covered with agent's names. After a great deal of study, Dani picked out the 'Phil Taylor Agency' and made her way up to the office. A small man, as disheveled as his desktop, smiled broadly as Dani entered his door. He lit up a Tiparillo and leaned back in his chair, looking at Dani over the top of his half-moon glasses. His inspection took a while and by the time he finally spoke Dani felt like a fine, but rare, steak.

"So, what can I do for you, young lady?"

When Dani had finished telling him what she wanted, the man nod-ded, sagely.

"Well, I've got the contacts, honey and with your looks, you can go far in this town. Can you carry a tune too?"

Dani nodded, confidently.

"Well, that's a plus, then!" The strange little man snorted at his own joke. Dani expected that next he would be telling her how he could, 'make her a star for certain exchanges' but to her surprise, Phil Taylor did nothing of the sort. His only interest seemed to be in his own 15% cut from the one-year contract that Dani signed with him. After taking her to several different lounges, Phil and Dani finally stepped into 'Anthony's Town House', on 49th and Broadway.

When she walked through the door, Dani's first impression was that the place looked like a set from some TV crime series about Elliot Ness and Al Capone. Phil took her over to the bar but didn't offer her anything to drink. He just told the barman to let the manager know they were here.

Dani twisted around on her barstool and took it all in, like a child in Wonderland.

The main room was only dimly lit but Dani could see that the decor theme was red and black. Tables were all decorated with artificial flowers and blood-red, teardrop candles. The whole room was filled with hand-some men and beautiful young girls, all listening to a jazz combo. The band was playing 'Yellowbird' and their singer, an older lady with a good figure, was quite good. Dani leaned toward Phil and whispered, quietly.

"What's the singer's name?"

"Mata," he responded, curtly. "One thing you gotta learn fast around here, Dani, is not to ask for last names, or to ask too many questions. Just do what you're hired to do; you sing and you go home. Oh, yeah, one more thing. Do you drink?"

Dani knew she couldn't drink very much, but said 'yes' anyway.

"Good, because when you're not singing you're supposed to drink champagne with the customers. You get a commission on every bottle that you drink each night."

Dani was horrified.

"But, Phil, won't I become an alcoholic?"

Phil looked at her in exasperation. "Don't you know what a 'B' girl is, Dani?"

"Do you mean I have to go to bed with all the men?" she gasped.

Phil stifled a smile. "No, it means that when the bartender sets a glass of champagne in front of you he will also put up a tall, frosted glass of water. You'll drink half the water first and then, as you talk to the customer, you simply take a sip of champagne and spit it back into the water glass, without him knowing. Don't worry, the other girls will teach you how."

"And another thing," he added, "they'd better not catch any prostitute working out of here because it wouldn't be healthy, believe me. There are other bars for the 'pros'."

Phil stood up then and made introductions as the manager of the Club came over to them.

"Nicky Mannelli, this is Dani Sutton and she wants to become a star."

Nicky smiled at her. "We'd better see what she can do then. You wait here, Phil," he said, leading Dani over to a quieter table. Nicky was a good looking young man somewhere in his thirties and around five-feet, ten-inches tall, with black hair and deep brown eyes. If he'd had a lighter complexion, she could have mistaken Nicky for Marlon Brando. The only thing Dani could find unattractive about him was a constant nervous twitching of his head. Nicky never seemed to take his eyes away from the front door, either, even as he questioned Dani.

"I'm not altogether sure you're old enough to work here, you know. Can I see your driver's license, Dani?"

Nicky examined it closely and when he seemed to be satisfied, he motioned Dani forward.

"Get up on that stage then, girl and let's hear how you sound!"

Dani went over and introduced herself to George Taylor, who was the black leader and to the rest of the band. After she had finished her audition, the audience roared approval and Dani saw that both Phil and Nicky were smiling.

Dani had her first real job - from seven pm to four am, six days a week, with Sundays off – and all for the grand total of $85 a week!

Dolores J. Guthrie

Chapter 5

After a few months of working at 'Anthony's Townhouse', Dani's funds were beginning to run low. No longer able to afford cab fare to and from her lodgings, Dani decided to move to the Plymouth Hotel', on 49th and Broadway. It was only one block from the Club, which meant Dani that could walk to work, but that was its only advantage. 'The Plymouth' was exactly what you would expect from a cheap hotel. The smell of stale grease rose up from a ground floor coffee shop, the odor of rank liquor filled all the hallways and a general, damp mustiness permeated the air inside Dani's 'one-room-and-bath'. And for entertainment, there was always the spectacle of nightly cockroach races around her room! *'Some of 'em are so damn big, you could put a saddle on 'em!'*

But Dani still figured that she was lucky. Her room faced the street and the hotel's neon sign flashed a nocturnal glow across her bed, adding an awesome night-life feel to Dani's room. With the added touches of a matching bedspread, drapes and towels; lots of green plants, fresh flowers and a daily burning of incense, Dani could escape stark reality, at least temporarily. It was only a matter of weeks though, before the dinginess began to overwhelm and depress her. This was not the kind of life that Dani had been dreaming about. From time to time she thought about calling Bill Crawford again, but kept telling herself that she was too busy. In reality, Dani just couldn't face Bill's stubborn opposition to her staying in New York.

Dani's thoughts gradually turned back toward HK and she wondered if the older man would still want to hear from her. After days of hesitation, Dani finally called information for his office number, in Rochester. She dialed and waited anxiously. His secretary answered and said that Mr. Kline was on a European holiday, but she would have him return Dani's call as soon as he returned.

Disappointed, Dani hung up. She lay back on the bed, letting her mind wander aimlessly. She watched two flies in the act of mating and idly wondered if she would be able to hear the rats in the walls of her room, 'getting it on' at night, if she listened carefully enough.

Suddenly, the phone rang, bringing Dani abruptly out of her reverie. It was HK on the line and his voice was shaking.

"Oh, my dearest, darling, Dani, I'm so excited! You don't know how happy I am that you've finally called, Dani. I had always hoped you would, you know, if I gave you enough time."

"HK," Dani purred, "it's so good to hear your voice again. But I only called your office a short while ago. How did you get the message so quickly? And where are you, anyway?"

"Hell, I'm somewhere in Germany, near the Black Forest, I think. I'm trying to renew my vitality and health, Dani! I've been to all the great spas of Europe trying to ferret out their secrets, but until now none of them has helped much. I'm in someplace called Baden, for their famous 'de-tensing' therapy, known as *'Entschlachungskur.'* It's a technique of self-hypnosis that makes me feel just as refreshed as a full eight hours of sleep."

"Oh, but Dani, just your phone call has given me a warm surge running through my whole body; the kind of thrill that nothing else could possibly give me. I knew in time you would call, my darling."

"Oh, Howard!" Dani breathed his name, huskily.

"Hell, have you forgotten already, Dani? Call me HK, please."

"Okay, HK! Listen, I've called to tell you that I'm living in New York City now. I've left Syracuse *and* Peter, for good!"

HK began yelling excitedly down the phone line. "I'll get the next flight back to New York, Dani! We'll have the whole weekend together!"

"But HK!" Dani tried to explain her situation. "I'm singing at nights, in a place called 'Anthony's Townhouse'. And I work Monday through Saturday nights."

"Oh, my little darling, don't you worry your pretty head about all that. I promise you, my dearest, you'll never have to work again. We'll talk about everything after I get there tomorrow. You'll be my 'queen', Dani! Won't that make you happy?"

"I'm not sure I know what you mean, HK"

"But you will, Dani, you will! Give me your address now, so I can make my flight arrangements."

Dani blew kisses down the phone. "I'm staying at the 'Plymouth Hotel', on 49th and Broadway. Until tomorrow then, HK. I'll be waiting for you."

"Until then, Dani." HK replied.

After Dani had hung up the phone, she spent a long time wondering what on earth HK had meant, about making her his 'queen'. But she came to the conclusion that there was no sense dwelling on the puzzle.

'After all, a man as impulsive as HK might just as easily change his mind and not show up at all,' she decided.

***

HK leaned back in his massage chair, smiled and then frowned. *'Damn, if I don't finish this spa treatment I won't get my money's worth.'* Yet even as HK pondered financial issues, a warm surge of delight ran through his body. *'Hell, I'm getting an erection just thinking about that girl, Dani.'*

HK absentmindedly stroked his growing cock. He knew that one night with Dani would eliminate any need to go to spas for 'rejuvenation'. HK's heart began to race. Just the very thought of Dani quickened his breathing. He reached for his nitroglycerin tablets, but his hands shook so badly that HK had difficulty getting the pill placed under his tongue. He sat as still and quietly as possible, to let the angina attack subside and regain his composure. Looking around the hotel suite that he had booked for an evening away from the rigors of the health spa, HK considered his lifestyle.

'I would have been better off tonight if I had stayed at the spa.'

He surveyed the empty champagne bottles and dirty ashtrays that were littered all around the room. HK could feel his pulse-beat slowing down at last. Swaying a bit, but carefully pulling a satin robe over his nude body, HK made his unsteady way back into his bedroom.

There were two young women inside, sprawled across his king-size bed. The blonde one seemed to be asleep but her long legs were spread wide open, allowing the redhead to feast upon her displayed womanhood. Throwing a wad of money onto the bed, HK yelled.

"Enough is enough. Leave now!"

"Listen prick, I'm not through here," the redhead mumbled!

The blond moaned as she grabbed the redhead by the hair and went into an intense orgasm.

"Oh! Please, please don't stop now. Oh shit, don't stop now!"

HK picked up his money again and walked back to the main lounge, shaking his head in bewilderment.

"Whores!" he grumbled. "They're all alike: 'cold as ice with a man who pays, and hotter than hell with a woman who plays'!"

HK picked up the phone and barked at the receptionist.

"Get me 1st class reservations on the next available plane to New York."

***

At 'Anthony's Roadhouse', nothing went right that night for Dani.

First of all, amid roars of laughter from the customers, 'Papa', the cook, had chased a customer out of his kitchen, yelling in Italian and waving a pan in the air.

Tony, the owner, had been in and out of the Club all night and on manager, Nicky's, tail. In turn, Nicky bitched at all the girls but at one point he pulled Dani into a back room, where he shook her angrily.

"Are you stupid or what, Dani? Use your spit glass and stop drinking the damn champagne! Those assholes out front don't give a damn whether you drink it or throw it on the floor."

He shook Dani even harder.

"Can't you understand? Are you really that dumb? Most of those guys are so lonely that they'll cough up for drinks just so's a girl will sit with them for a while!"

Nicky grabbed the back of Dani's neck, flashed a smile that showed beautiful white teeth and then relaxed his grip and gave her a long, lingering kiss. He released Dani just as quickly and spoke in a more friendly tone.

"Now, go sing me a pretty song, eh?"

With tears in her eyes Dani went out onto the stage and sang her heart out. Twisted emotions, for both Nicky and HK, pulled her in all directions, but Dani managed to make it through the rest of that night without any more trouble.

Leaving work as early as she could, Dani arrived at her hotel's greasy spoon café at around four am and ordered the 'breakfast special'. She needed some comfort food. Dani wearily stepped around the drunks in the hallway on the way up to her room until, with a tired sigh, she finally locked the door securely behind her. Once her food was eaten, Dani soaked away the day with a hot, perfumed bath before falling into her bed, exhausted.

Desperately needing to believe that HK would arrive like a knight in shining armor, Dani fell asleep dreaming of what he would be like.

When she awoke, early the next afternoon, Dani slowly dressed in clothes that she imagined HK would approve of. A navy blue, Italian-knit jacket, trimmed in bone tones and with a matching bone-colored dress, shoes and bag.

'Yes!' Looking into the ornate, full-length mirror that she had rescued from a garage sale, Dani decided that her selection would definitely meet with HK's approval.

***

Isabella Goldstein, owner of *'Le Parisian'* beauty salon, had the rare talent of being a good listener. It made time spent in her boutique a real pleasure, especially for those entertainers who were her regular customers. They all told Isabella their stories; some happy, some sordid or sad, but all told with many tears.

That afternoon, Dani told Isabella her own story. About her fear of Tony, the boss; about the sexual desire she had for Nicky, his younger brother and about her need for voice and acting training. Dani wanted to get into Broadway musicals, but because she was working so many hours it left her little time for school, or for rehearsals. And Dani also told Isabella that on that very day, a man was coming to New York to make Dani his 'queen'. Isabella already knew that most girls were attracted to Nicky, but she agreed that maybe HK would be the better prospect, at least for Dani's future ambitions in the theater.

Dani then asked Isabella about the man that people called *'The Horse'*. When she had heard people use that nickname, Dani always assumed they were speaking about her boss, Tony Mannelli, but she wasn't sure. Dani only knew that Tony seemed a very powerful man and that she didn't want to get the way of his temper.

But Isabella flatly refused to answer any of Dani's questions about *'The Horse'*.

After a few hours in the beauty salon, Dani was on her way back to her hotel to meet HK. She felt a bit anxious, but ready. And there he was, sitting amidst the grime of Dani's hotel lobby! She had almost forgotten how handsome HK was. About five-feet, nine-inches tall and on the thin side, with brown hair and a pencil thin mustache, HK resembled David Niven, but older, with warm, brown eyes twinkling out from behind his glasses.

Jumping up as he caught sight of Dani, HK hugged and kissed her as if they were old lovers. Arm-in-arm, Dani took him up to see her room, but she was not prepared for his reaction.

"I can't believe this hovel!" HK said in a shocked voice. "My poor, poor Dani! Come on, we're going apartment hunting, right now!"

Hailing a cab, HK gave the driver directions to take them to 'The Envoy Towers', on Second Avenue and 47th Street. The building manager, a Mr. Fellman and HK seemed well acquainted, Dani noticed, as she listened to the way they spoke to each other. Mr. Fellman took them up to the most beautiful penthouse Dani had ever seen. Everything impressed her, from the French, antique furniture and the oil paintings in heavy gold frames, to the terrace view of the whole bay and of the United Nations Building.

Just when Dani thought there was nothing else she could be impressed by, she looked across to an adjoining terrace, where a gentleman sat sipping tea. The gentleman looked up from his book and smiled at Dani. She was stunned.

"Mr. Fellman, is that man, on the terrace there, who I think he is?"

Smilingly, the building manager answered Dani's question.

"Yes, ma'am, Peter Ustinov will be your neighbor, but you probably won't see very much of him. He is a very quiet and private person."

Mr. Fellman also told them that a number of other people involved in the arts were tenants of the 'Envoy Towers' and that there was even a TV studio within the building. Dani's eyes widened as HK turned to her.

"With your permission, Dani, I'll write a check right now to cover your rent for six months."

Dani nodded, hugging his arm like a little girl in a candy store as HK handed over the check to the building manager.

"Will you watch over Dani," HK asked Mr. Fellman, quietly. "She's all alone here in New York and for the time being I have to remain in Rochester. It will comfort me to know that she has you close by if she needs help."

Shaking HK's outstretched hand, Mr. Fellman promised to take good care of Dani.

HK seemed like a little boy again, happy and proud as he and Dani walked the short distance to the Chemical Bank, on Second Street. There, HK opened both a savings and a checking account in Dani's name and deposited $10,000 in each.

Dani called in sick for work that night!

Everything was happening so quickly that Dani was having trouble keeping up. HK wanted to celebrate by taking her to a very elegant restaurant, 'Barbara Hutton's Town House', over on the East Side. She and HK were served *'escargot in burgundy'*, *'Rouen duck'*, 'Veuve Cliquot' and 'Ponsardin Champagne-1772', whilst classical guitars filled the air with wonderful music. Dani's eyes could see only one, wonderful man, through all the flickering candles. For her, no other diners existed.

Dani completely forgot their age difference during that evening, too, except for the moment when they had first entered the restaurant. She was sure then that everyone had noticed the 'younger' woman and the 'older" man'. But HK was a man in love and he was ecstatic.

After their magnificent meal, Dani reached over and took HK's glasses off, looking deep into his eyes.

"You, my darling, are so wonderfully unpredictable. You're an ego-centric, romantic but I love your style. You know what you want and you go after it."

Dani brushed her fingers across HK's lips and then leaned closer. She picked up her glass, licked the rim and whispered.

"I think you need some sugar."

HK patted his sweat-beaded brow with a Hermes, silk handkerchief.

"You know, my darling, for over a year I've been waiting, thinking of you every day. I began to despair that we would ever be together. But we *are* together now, aren't we Dani?"

"Yes," she assured him, "we're together, HK."

Dani realized that she wanted desperately to be with HK forever but when she told him what she was thinking, he suddenly seemed upset.

"*Damn!*"

HK almost knocked over the table as he jumped up. "I have an important phone call to make."

"HK, a phone call? Right now?"

Dani was alarmed by his urgency.

"Don't worry, my darling. I'll be right back. It's a surprise, that's all."

"I don't know if I can handle any more surprises today," Dani groaned, "but I'll try!"

When HK returned there was no sign of his earlier distress and he called for their bill. The couple were ushered into a waiting taxi outside the restaurant and Dani overheard the doorman tell the driver, *'Waldorf Astoria.'*

The 'Waldorf Astoria' hotel represents a whole different world, from a long-ago era. The carved ceilings; the wood-paneling; the staircases, crystal chandeliers and artworks of the masters were all so elegant that Dani was afraid to breathe. Like Cinderella, she feared she would awake and find herself back in her own dingy bed at the Plymouth Hotel. But instead, Dani and HK were escorted up to a beautiful hotel suite.

'So, this was HK's important phone call!'

On the table were three dozen, red roses to greet Dani. Then HK led her into the luxurious bathroom, where Dani could see a full case of opened bottles of champagne, sitting next to the bathtub. HK was beaming with pride as he drew Dani into his arms.

"A queen should have the whole world Dani. I'm sorry I can't give you that yet, for I am still a married man. But my darling, one day I will build you a castle on a hill overlooking the ocean and I will cast the key into the sea, so that no one else will ever feast his eyes on your beauty.

That, my darling, will save you only for me."

"You are so poetic!"

Dani giggled, as she tweaked HK's nose and then kissed him lightly. She could not believe how sincerely the man loved her, after knowing him for such a short time. It gave Dani a warm, safe feeling inside and the difference in their ages seemed to matter less and less.

Dani asked HK to unzip her dress. Then she turned around, stepped out of it and stood before him, wearing just her hose and shoes. The look on HK's face told Dani he wasn't disappointed. He knelt before her, removed both her shoes and kissed one of her legs all the way down to the toes. Then, with a flourish HK filled one of Dani's shoes with champagne and drank a toast.

"To Dani; my 'queen'."

Taking her by the hand, HK asked Dani to climb into the bathtub and while she lay there, giggling, he poured the full case of champagne all over her naked body. Cold bubbles tickled her as they fizzed and popped all over her skin. Yet, even as Dani begged him to stop, the coldness suddenly began to raise her body temperature within, making her feel hot in a way that she never had before.

In that moment, Dani realized that *she* now had even more than that 'girl on the terrace'; the one that Dani had envied during her first few, lonely months in New York.

Dani was indeed HK's 'queen'.

Dolores J. Guthrie

Chapter 6

The morning air was crisp and cold as HK opened the bedroom window. Dani, drawing in a deep breath of fresh air, realized that last night had not been a dream after all. She was still in the 'Waldorf Astoria Hotel' and in the distance Dani could hear the resonating chimes of St. Patrick's Cathedral. *'This is going to be a very special day.'*

Outside on the sidewalk, HK tried to keep Dani from falling as they both slipped and slithered their way down an ice-glazed Fifth Avenue while trying to hail a cab. HK had to catch a plane back to Rochester but, later today, Dani was going to move into her new apartment. The excited churning of her stomach made her feel like a child on Christmas morning. HK turned and hugged Dani tightly as his taxi pulled up by the curb.

"Honey, you've made me the happiest man in the world. Hell, I wish I didn't have to leave so soon, but just you wait for your next surprise!"

He kissed Dani again. "I love you, I love you Dani. Don't work too hard my darling and I'll call you tomorrow, sometime."

But Dani could hardly hear HK's final words as his cab pulled noisily away. Crunching through the frozen snow, it left a blast of cold, exhaust fog to surround her.

After hailing her own cab, Dani felt as if she was being paroled from jail as she returned to the run-down Plymouth Hotel. *She was checking out of that rat hole for good.* Within an hour, Dani had packed everything she owned, called another cab and driven away without a backward glance.

The doorman of the Envoy Towers opened the cab door for Dani, with a flourish.

"Good afternoon, Miss Sutton. We've been expecting you."

Smilingly, he handed Dani a florist's box.

"These just arrived for you. You go on up and I'll bring the rest of your things up right away."

As she put HK's roses into water, Dani thought how easily she could settle into this new kind of life. Only when Dani had put everything away that she brought with her, did she suddenly realize how weary she was.

The move to a new home, the champagne from the night before and all the excitement of the past twenty-four hours were beginning to take their toll. Dani took a quick shower and slipped into bed, intending to take a nap before work, but her mind kept on reviewing recent events. It would not let Dani sleep, as tired as she was.

Dani was still filled with awe, but it was slowly getting easier to accept all that had happened to her over the last few days. Dani may never have seen $20,000 before, but now it was in her very own bank accounts and that was a wonderful feeling. Dani had to share her good news, she decided; it was too good to keep all to herself.

Bill Crawford was out of town for a week, his secretary told her. Then, wishing that she didn't have to go to work that night made Dani think about Samantha Carrol, known as 'Sam', the friendly, daytime bartender at the Club. *'Maybe Sam and some other employees from the Club would like to come over after work, to see my new apartment?'*

After the club closed at 4:30 am, Sam, Nicky, Luigi, the headwaiter, Frankie and Mike, the night bartenders and a few others that Dani had invited all headed toward her new apartment. From an all-night diner, just across the street from the Envoy Towers, Dani bought enough hamburgers, fries and shakes to feed them all. *'What a joke! My first party in the plush 'Envoy Towers' gets catered for by a lowdown diner!'* But everyone was happy; relaxing, talking and listening to the stereo. Dani walked out onto the terrace with Sam to find Nicky already there, looking out over the lights of the city. He turned and gave Dani a look that caught her off guard.

She was glad that Sam had her back to them both and couldn't see it. Without saying a word, Nicky loosened his tie and fixed his piercing eyes on Dani. She stared back, not hearing a word that Sam was saying to her. *Was Nicky really making a play for her?* Dani just couldn't figure the man out and decide she didn't really want to know either, her life was complicated enough with HK in it. Impatiently, she went back inside.

Sam and Nicky came in from the terrace later, just as everyone else was getting ready to leave. As she put on her coat, Sam gave Dani a big hug and suggested that they all get together for lunch, someday soon.

"Sounds good to me," Dani answered.

Nicky lagged behind as the group left. He had opened his shirt collar by then and his tie was hanging loose over his shoulders. Dani wasn't sure if she should close the door or not as Nicky just stood there, staring at her. After several moments he walked toward Dani, never taking his eyes away from her. He grabbed her by the hair.

"It's late, baby, get some sleep."

Releasing Dani without otherwise touching or kissing her, Nicky was gone in an instant. She locked the door behind him and leaned against it, puzzling over his strange behavior. A cold shiver ran through her whole body. She decided to go to bed and not think about Nicky anymore. But the whole scenario had left Dani feeling very unsettled.

***

The next few days went by so smoothly at work that Dani began to wonder what was happening. The atmosphere was all different, somehow, and everyone seemed especially nice to her. Nicky played 'peek-a-boo' each time they ran across each other, sending hot vibrations all through Dani's body without even touching her.

As hard as she tried to keep Nicky Mannelli out of her thoughts, he just kept popping right back in.

Dani's excitement over Nicky kept steadily growing. She found herself fantasizing about him, night after night. In one of her dreams, they were both in an all-white room filled with fluffy pillows. A breeze was blowing white feathers all around the room and Dani, in a white, filmy gown, was lazily bouncing on the pillows. Nicky was trying to touch Dani as she floated back and forth. She took his hand and together they floated up to a cloud where she lay back, breathing rapidly and with her thighs spread, invitingly. Nicky floated toward her and Dani was waiting for his hot thrust when HK suddenly appeared.

Dani awoke with a start. But her life spun by like a fairground carousel over the next few weeks, keeping her bewildered and off balance.

One night, between songs, Dani was sitting at the bar with some guy buying her drinks, as usual. He was telling Dani how lonely he was and what an animal he was in bed. Dani told him to just drink up and be good, otherwise she'd say goodnight and leave. Then the guy said something to Nicky, who happened to be working behind the bar that night. It must have been something about Dani, because Nicky suddenly lunged over the bar, landing on top of the guy. He began beating on the customer with his fists. It took a few minutes for the bouncers to wade in and pull Nicky off and then the guy was taken out into the back alley and stuffed into a garbage bin. He was never seen at the Club again.

Another night, Dani was finishing her last set on stage when Tony and 'Moose', his body guard, came in. They took Nicky over to a back table to join with Vinnie *'Blackie'* Balianti, for one of Tony's regular meetings.

Anita was Vinnie's mistress of eight years and she and Dani had become close friends, over time. On slow nights, Anita had told Dani many stories about her own earlier career in the Ziegfeld Follies and about her life with Vinnie. When Dani asked about puzzling things at the Club, Anita always seemed to give straight answers to her questions and Dani liked that.

That night, Anita was telling Dani that Vinnie was a four-time loser and that the next time he was caught, it would be a life sentence for him. But Dani found it hard to believe that Vinnie was a real 'gangster'. In fact, when she had first met him she thought Vinnie was a cop! Always friendly and pleasant, he often complimented Dani on her appearance and on her singing voice. Vinnie liked to go to the 'Village' to hear Vicky Karr sing and then he would come into the Club to listen to Dani. He once told her that he wished he could manage them both; he thought they were both 'star material'.

Then, one night after the Club had closed, Vinnie and Anita, Nicky and Dani went for some Chinese food, down by the waterfront. Afterward, Vinnie drove their car, without lights on, around an eight block area, stopping at each corner to wait for a man to step out from the shadows. Each man would wave and then step back, before Vinnie would drive on to the next comer. Dani was uncomfortable with all of this, but tried to convince herself, naively, that they were all part of some FBI undercover team. She soon found that this was definitely not the case.

Vinnie got out of the car and disappeared. Nicky moved over behind the steering wheel and when Vinnie returned, only a few minutes later, he threw what he was carrying into the back seat, with the girls.

Dani heard gunshots as Nicky floored the gas pedal and their tires burned rubber as they made a fast getaway.

"Fuck! The fuckin' bastards got me in the leg," screamed Vinnie.

"Where in the hell did they come from?" Nicky yelled, as he headed out of the city.

Dani had slid off the back seat onto the floor and under what she soon realized were fur coats that Vinnie had slung into the back. She was shaking so hard that her teeth were chattering. Above Vinnie's moans and Nicky's cursing, Dani suddenly heard Anita yelling,

"Stop the car! Stop this goddam car and let us out!"

"Shit! I forgot about you fuckin' broads!"

Nicky slammed the car to a halt and yelled.

"Out, out, out, an' take the fuckin' furs with you. Grab a cab an' go home, will ya'."

The two girls jumped out with coats in their arms and ran into a dark alley. They startled some cats rummaging in garbage cans, which frightened the girls even more. They both leaned against the nearest building, holding onto the furs and to each other, trying to stop shaking and catch their breath.

"What the hell happened, Anita?"

"Hell, I don't know!"

"So what do we do with these furs then, stick them in the trash?" Dani demanded to know.

"Ya gotta be kiddin' Dani. We'll put 'em on and we'll walk 'til we find a cab. We should be alright. Who's to know these coats aren't ours?"

So Dani lived ever after with a dark secret and with what she found out later to be one very expensive, black, Russian sable coat! Meanwhile, HK called every day to give Dani his love and to tell her that they would soon be together.

***

As time went by, Dani and Sam, the daytime bartender, became inseparable friends and went everywhere together.

One night at 'Jilly's', a famous nightclub in the city, Sam suddenly grabbed at Dani's arm and hissed in her ear.

"Oh, my God! Dani. See that guy sitting over to the left of the Exit sign?"

Dani looked over.

"Yeah, what about him?"

"Don't stare at him, Dani, but I think that's Carlo Gambiossi. But Tony told me the guy was in hiding, somewhere in the Caribbean on a yacht."

"I don't know much about those people, but I *do* remember reading somethin' about that name. What did Tony tell you, Sam?"

Sam explained that the guy had been Anastasia's right-hand man, until Gambiossi had taken over the Brooklyn 'Family', back in 1957 Anastasia was once considered the most brutal killer in Mafia history, but had got himself murdered in the Park Sheraton hotel barber's shop, while his face was covered with steaming towels.

"Two gunmen just went in and shot him all to pieces! They were never caught, although the big guys always reckoned they knew who the hit men were," Sam said. "The whole thing had started because of petty squabbles among the lieutenants of the Brooklyn 'Family'. Carlo Gambiossi was Anastasia's ambitious under-boss. So, a contract for Anastasias' execution was put out, Joey Ballo accepted and, that was that!"

"What a great memory you've got, Sam! You sound like you're reading from a Mickey Spillane novel! I've heard Nicky talk about Joey Ballo before, but he said Joey was in prison. How many years did he get?"

"Only about ten," Sam said, "even though Robert Kennedy described him as 'public enemy number one'! It took the government until 1961 to finally nail Joey and then they only got him for extortion, not for murder."

"Sam, let's get out of here," Dani said. "I'm getting nervous just looking at that bunch over there."

"Yeah, you're right, Dani. Just forget what you saw and heard here tonight, for your own good."

Dani nodded, but she couldn't stop thinking about how the pieces were falling together like a jigsaw puzzle and she didn't like the picture she was seeing. The next day, Dani decided to take the weekend off, to go up to Syracuse and see her husband and young son. *'Maybe this city is too big and scary for me to handle after all?'*

But it was a wasted trip. Dani cried most of the weekend, as old friends constantly called up to tell Dani how horrible she was, to have left Peter the way she did. Their nasty phone calls only confirmed what Dani had long felt, that she was no longer accepted as Peter's wife. She was hurt to see him looking so thin and drawn too and to leave her young son, JR, in his care. Through bitter tears, Dani finally realized that she could never go back to her old life.

Her future now lay in a different direction and she must follow her heart.

Dolores J. Guthrie

Chapter 7

"Damn it, Danielle, you did what?"

"Now, don't get all excited, HK," Dani said, trying to calm his unexpected wrath.

"I went up to Syracuse last weekend, just to see my young son, JR. I have to figure out some way to get him here to New York, with me. And, while I was there, I picked up that TR4 that you bought for me last year."

"Oh that," HK said, matter-of-factly.

"Well, there I was walking along Broadway after I got back and there *it* was, right in the showroom window; a customized, blue-metallic, Cadillac 'De Ville' convertible. I just couldn't help myself, HK, I fell in love with it. So, I hope you don't mind but I used the TR4 as a down payment on it. I figured I could easily handle the rest of the repayments out of my earnings."

HK just sighed, looking at Dani with a wounded expression.

"My little darling," he said in a low voice, "don't you realize that you're my 'queen'. I don't want you worrying about anything."

HK stood up.

"Let's go see that dealer right now! Hell, I'll write him a damn check out in full payment."

Dani jumped up and gave HK a long hug and a lingering kiss.

"Just give me a moment to freshen up?" she said.

Dani went into the bathroom, all the time telling HK about how Shelley Winters had paid to have the car customized but had never picked it up. She came back and stood before her lover, twirling around for his inspection.

"Do I look okay?"

"Good enough to eat," HK announced, pulling her toward the bedroom, but Dani managed to avoid his advances long enough to convince him that food would be their best option right then.

Never one for a simple hamburger and fries, HK took Dani to 'The-

Tavern-on-the-Green', in Central Park. As they were sitting on the terrace, a warm breeze wafted Dani's yellow, spring dress upward to reveal her layered, eyelet petticoat.

"Damn, Danielle, you're so soft and feminine. Just looking at you makes me want to put my arms around you and never let go."

"You're missing out on some good lox and bagels here, HK," Dani countered, trying to divert the man's attention back to the subject of food. After a moment of silence, she asked him a question that had been on her mind for a while.

"HK would you like to come to the Club sometime, to hear me sing?"

You'd have thought Dani had asked a six year-old if they wanted to go to Disneyland.

"Oh, my; I thought you'd never ask me, my darling! I've so much wanted to hear you sing, even though I don't really like the idea of you working anywhere!"

HK's voice became more somber as he continued.

"As soon as we are both divorced, I can't allow you to continue working, Dani, not a man in my position. God, what would my Board of Directors say?"

They both knew how important Dani's singing was to her, but it was a touchy issue and HK realized that now wasn't the time to address it.

"But, HK, what will the Board think when they find out about your pending divorce?"

"Don't you worry about that, my dear. The Board knows that my wife and I have been estranged for several years, now. They even know that Grace makes me sleep in the garage and that I started drinking because of it. Hell, the only thing that's kept the two of us together all these years has been our son, Don."

HK mentioned his son, Don, often and each time with the same pride in his voice. He told Dani that Don was studying to be a doctor of radiology and would be qualified to practice very soon.

"But when will I meet Don?"

"That boy is too much like me Dani! One look at you and I wouldn't stand a chance, especially since Don's your own age and handsome with it!"

Dani understood HK's concerns, so she tactfully let the subject drop. After a few moments of companionable silence, HK spoke again.

"Dani, I have another surprise for you. I've been thinking about how you were trying to get JR here with you. I don't really think it would be a very good life for a young boy, especially with you working at the Club all night, almost every night, in fact."

"I know that HK, but what else can I do?"

"Dani, I took the liberty of calling a friend of mine at the Valley Forge Military Academy, in Pennsylvania. I've already written a letter of recommendation so JR could be enrolled in time for the fall term."

HK pulled a letter from his briefcase and handed it to Dani, along with all the necessary enrollment forms and a check for full tuition fees.

"This should take care of his schooling, Dani and I've also set up trust funds; one for you and one for JR, which you'll receive ten years after my death. I'm afraid there will be many unscrupulous people who will try to take your money from you if something should happen to me, although by then, JR should be old enough to help take care of you."

Dani's emotions overflowed at HK's generosity and she reached for a handkerchief to wipe her eyes.

"People will wonder what I'm doing to you, Dani; please stop crying, my dear."

"It's just that you're so generous to me, HK."

"Well, hold onto those tears my 'queen', because there's more," he said, reaching for Dani's hand.

"I'd like you to go to Mexico for a 'quickie' divorce, so there won't be anything holding us up when my own divorce is finalized."

"But I'll need a lawyer for that, won't I? Do *you* know a good attorney, HK, here in New York?"

"No," he replied, "but I can ask around for one. Perhaps the manager of your Club, that nice young fellow you mentioned, what's his name, would he know of one?"

"You mean Nicky Mannelli?"

"Yes! I'm sure the Club must have an attorney of their own.

"I suppose so," Dani hesitated. "I'll ask Nicky the next time I see him.

"No, I don't want you to ask him," HK insisted. "I'll ask him myself."

"That means you'll have to come to the Club though."

"Well, you did ask me to come and hear you sing." HK reminded Dani.

Dani wavered. The Club had a strict policy, forbidding boyfriends to visit when the girls were working.

"OK, but you'll have to buy a bottle of champagne and ask for me to sit with you. Ask for a back table, where we'll have more privacy."

"But, honey, you can't drink for all of the time that I'll be there."

"Then you'll have to come later in the evening. Why don't you go see Chubby Checker, at the 'Peppermint Lounge,' first? That way you'll arrive after midnight and then it'll be only a few hours until I'm off duty."

HK smiled and reached into his pocket.

"Before you go, we'll have to stop and deposit this check into your bank account. You'll need extra money for your Mexican divorce, as well as for airplane tickets, lawyers and such."

HK handed a check to Dani. She looked at it, then stared at it and then looked back at him.

"HK, I think you've made a mistake. Aren't there too many 'zeros' on here?"

"No, my 'queen'; the check is supposed to read 'one-hundred-thou-sand-dollars'!" he grinned.

***

That evening seemed to last forever for Dani. She couldn't keep her mind on the songs or concentrate on what was said to her by the customers. Pretty soon Nicky realized she wasn't her usual self.

"Dani, is anything wrong? D'ya wanna go home.

But Dani just smiled, mysteriously.

"Of course not Nicky'. Things couldn't be better."

Nicky walked away confused, twitching his head and thinking how he'd never understand 'prima donnas' and their temperaments.

But Dani had her own thoughts. *'It's just so hard to keep your senses, and your life, in balance when you've been handed a check for one hundred thousand dollars!'*

One o'clock finally came and Dani had just begun a new set when HK walked in. Her first crazy thought as she saw him was, *'How can I drink for three more hours?'* She watched as HK asked for a back table and specified, 'but with a good view of the stage please, and the company later of Miss Danielle Sutton.'

There was quite a stir as the waiter told Nicky what the man had requested. Nicky, always the good manager, pulled Dani off stage after only a couple of songs.

"We've got a live one here, Dani. He's already paid out a wad and with your help, he'll probably drop a lot more."

Dani looked at Nicky in disgust as she walked over to HK's table, thinking, *'the joke is on you, Nicky Mannelli.'*

HK had already ordered $500 worth of 'Mumm's' champagne but refused to drink very much. He told Dani he didn't want to waste precious time with her by getting drunk. She was becoming disgusted by the whole Club setup and instead of spitting the champagne back into the water glass, Dani started drinking it. Nicky could see that she was becoming tipsy and sent a waiter over to ask her to meet him, in the back room.

She excused herself from HK and went towards the office but on the way she stopped in the ladies' room. Nicky, angry and impatient, began banging on the door.

"Get out here, now Dani. I want to talk to you."

Then he flung open the door and barged in. "What the fuck's wrong with you, Dani? I keep telling you broads to spit the champagne back in the fuckin' water glass, but not you! No, you have to play all 'high society' and drink the fuckin' stuff. You know you could die with disease of the liver, Dani?"

Dani tried to act sober.

"The word you're looking for is 'cirrhosis' and that gentleman that you want me to hustle is my fiancé."

"Fiancé, hell, that old fart is just putting you on! All he wants is to buy you a few bottles of wine and play big shot so you can make his old prick hard again. I've been in this business so long I can smell them the minute they walk in the front door."

"Well, I quit! Do you hear me, Nicky?" Dani screamed at him. "I quit! You can take this damn job and shove it, Nicky Mannelli."

"You couldn't be more wrong about that man. Today he paid off my Cadillac *and* deposited a hundred thousand dollars in my bank account as well! So you can get off my ass, or I'll buy this place and become *your* boss!"

Nicky stared at Dani but before he could think of a reply, HK had forced his way into the restroom.

"What's going on here? Hell, I've got three fast broads out there who all want me to buy champagne for them. What kind of a place *is* this you're running? What the hell is going on?"

Nicky walked over and put his arm around HK's shoulders.

"Calm down, sir. Dani here was just telling me that you two are going to get married. Is that true?"

"That's right, young man, just as soon as I get my finances settled."

"Well, that's a whole different story. Come on out to the bar, sir and I'll buy *you* a drink."

HK looked over at Dani and winked.

"You see, honey, he's not at all upset that I'm your boyfriend."

HK gave Dani a big hug, then turned and walked out to accept Nicky's invitation of a drink.

***

All a cold shower could do for Dani that night was to make her feel clean and cold: it certainly didn't make her head feel any better. Yet HK was already opening another bottle of 'VO' cognac! The thought of more liquor made Dani turn back toward the bathroom. HK came to the door and crooned to her, solicitously.

"Honey, oh ho-ney, where's my little 'queen' hiding? Daddy has another surprise for you. Hurry here to big daddy, Dani."

As if she wasn't sick enough, that kind of sweet talk could keep Dani in the bathroom all night. She sincerely hoped that HK wouldn't be in the mood for sex; she wouldn't be able to muster the strength to argue. She took another shower then dragged herself over to the bed, not even bothering to put on a gown. She pretended to pass out.

But HK began humming, 'Diamonds Are a Girl's Best Friend' and laying pieces of paper all over Dani's nude body, making her laugh in spite of herself.

"Stop it, HK; that tickles! What on earth are you doing?"

"Hold very still, my darling," he told her. "We don't want to wrinkle or tear these precious pieces of paper!"

Dani opened one eye, to see official looking documents lying all over her and the bedcovers.

"Hell, Dani, where is my camera? I've just wrapped you up in one million dollars' worth of Xenon stocks!"

"You've done what?" Dani exclaimed. She couldn't believe what she had just heard and her headache wasn't helping things.

HK carried on, ignoring her.

"I've already transferred all the certificates into your name. See, your sweet little name is right there?"

HK emphasized his point by holding up one of the certificates in front of Dani's face.

"With these, my 'queen', I've made you independently wealthy. You, Danielle Sutton, are now worth over a million dollars!"

Tears streamed down Dani's face.

"I love you, HK," was all she could mumble.

HK hugged Dani to him for a long while as she repeated over and over again, through a waterfall of tears, that she loved him.

Dolores J. Guthrie

Chapter 8

Yet Dani still felt guilty about Peter. In order to 'put things right', as she explained it to HK, Dani sent ten thousand dollars to her soon-to-be ex-husband, telling him it was to cover any bills she'd left behind. Dani also signed over her portion of their Seneca River waterfront home, including all the household furnishings.

Her friend, Sam accompanied Dani down to Mexico to get the 'quickie' divorce, together with an attorney, Karl Hokowitz, whom Nicky had recommended. There were no problems in getting Dani's divorce and as soon as it was all settled, she and Sam flew to Las Vegas and checked-in to 'The Dunes' Hotel. They had no sooner entered their two-bedroomed suite than the phone rang. Sam answered it.

"We'll be there." she squealed and hung up, turning to Dani in excitement.

"Nicky's here, in the same hotel. He wants us to meet him for dinner later. Isn't that a coincidence, Dani, Nicky being here at the same time?"

Dani didn't make any comment, but seriously doubted that Nicky was in Las Vegas by coincidence.

Sam was excited, though.

"Let's do it right tonight, Dani. Can I wear your powder-pink, satin gown and carry the long, black Russian sable?"

Dani agreed. "It does accent your lovely hair and olive complexion." She had often thought that Sam's dark, auburn hair was like the color of a rich, burgundy wine. *'She could easily model for Vogue Magazine'.*

Dani decided to wear a black strapless gown, slit all the way up one side and bordered with black-fox fur. She carried a matching, black-fox muff and, of course, she wore the engagement ring that HK had given to her before the Mexico trip. The ring was magnificent; a seven-carat, marquise diamond, with one-carat, baguette diamonds set on either side. All heads in the room were turning to look as the 'maître d' escorted the two beautiful women over to Nicky's table.

Nicky was absolutely loving it.

The Ford Motor Company was filming a commercial in the dining room that night. The producer had asked if he could get a shot of Dani's ring as it glittered in the reflection of her wine glass. To complete the scene, Dani was asked to look into Nicky's eyes. It was so much fun, being part of a film production that it never occurred to Dani what any consequences might be. She became a mere spectator as her own life spiraled even further out of control.

As the cameras shot the scene of Dani looking into Nicky's eyes, she could sense the unspoken message he was sending. The whole, romantic spell of *'Romaro and his Violins'* playing love songs, with sparkling fountains dancing in time to their music, completely overwhelmed Dani. She could fight her suppressed desire for Nicky no longer and her eyes silently returned her acceptance of his mute invitation.

After the filming and dinner, they all moved into the casino to see what kind of action they could find there. Before long, Sam was onto a winning streak at one of the blackjack tables and so the involved pair left her there.

***

The bedroom door burst open.

"Ok, you two, I caught you!" Sam cried playfully. Dani sat up, startled and embarrassed and trying to cover her nakedness with sheets. She felt herself blushing all over and looked across at Nicky, who seemed just as embarrassed.

"Dani, I thought you locked the door," he hissed.

Ignoring the pair's obvious discomfort, Sam continued her dramatic entrance by dragging a fully loaded breakfast cart into the room behind her.

"Try these cheese blintzes," she announced, licking her fingers, "they're better than sex!"

Dani and Nicky half-smiled at each other in spite of their circumstances. She didn't know what to say or do, so Dani reached out a hand for one of the delicacies that Sam was offering. As she savored the flavor, she turned to Nicky and offered him a bite.

"Um m, this *is* good, but I can't agree with Sam about it being better than 'you-know-what'!"

Nicky seemed in a great mood, too. Dani had never seen him so happy. The three of them later had lunch by the pool and made plans to catch the 'Jerry Lewis' show that night.

"Sam," commanded Nicky, "make the reservations through Hokowitz. Tell him to say that 'Anthony Mannelli' sent us and then we'll get the best seats in the house!"

Lying by the pool, soaking up the sun and Nicky's attention, Dani pondered. *'Why does all of this good stuff have to happen at once?'*

Dani's trip was supposed to be to get a divorce, so that she could marry HK. Her future home was only one payment away from being completely hers. All of her new furniture was being built by the Vassiminni Brothers of Italy, last of the great craftsmen. With HK, Dani knew that she would never have a financial worry again. She would be his 'queen' and the world would always be in her palm.

But Dani also knew that she couldn't marry HK anymore; not now that her love and desire for Nicky had finally been realized. *'I've cheated on HK and I can't possibly marry him now'.*

Succumbing to Nicky's allure had tangled Dani's life far more than she could have ever imagined. Immediately upon her return to New York, Dani called HK to tell him that she was no good for him; she couldn't marry him and he was to forget all about her. There was nothing but silence on the other end of the phone. Dani's words ran on and on, telling HK that she was so confused and needed time to sort things out.

"I know this will hurt you, HK, but I don't want to hurt you any more by marrying you and causing you more pain in the future."

"Hurt me, hell!" HK said, crying like a bereaved man. The pain and grief in his voice cut right through Dani's heart.

"I'll give you back all the money and stocks I have left, HK. I don't know what to do about the house, though?"

Dani also began to cry, unable to control her sobbing.

"Hell, Dani, I'm not worried about the goddam' money. If it were just my money you were after, then you're pretty short-sighted. I am twenty years older than you and women always live longer than their husbands. When I die it will all go to you, Dani, if we are married, that is. You have no idea how wealthy I am, do you child?"

"I'm sorry, HK, but I think it would just hurt us both too much. I need time to think, please."

***

Dani stayed away from work for several weeks after that phone call, afraid that HK would show up there. She was too ashamed to face him. But, finally, Dani forced herself to return to work, fearing that if she didn't her own career goals would start to fade. Many changes had been made during Dani's absence. For a start, Anthony's Townhouse had been re-named Anthony's A-Go-Go. Tony Mannelli had also hired some new, young talent.

One was named Adrienne Baluchi; a sweet girl with dark hair, a nice body and a cute dimpled face. Another girl, with the temperament of a bobcat, was Sheri DeVito, ex-wife of lounge singer Joey DeVito. Steve Condos was to be the 'star' show dancer and there was to be an MC in future, the renowned 'B.S. Bully'. *'So many changes!'*

The most startling change of all though was no more drinking with the customers; the Club was 'legit' now, according to Nicky.

Adrienne, Sheri, Sue Shetland and Dani became the first 'go-go girls' to ever dance in New York and maybe even in the entire country!

With the grand re-opening of 'Anthony's A-Go-Go', the newest craze in entertainment, called 'Disco', spread like wildfire across the nation. Walter Winchell even wrote an article about Dani in his news column. *'Danielle Sutton's dancing is enough to drive men crazy, but her real talent is her voice.'* Everything was going great in the new Club, with no more crises until just before Christmas.

That night the Club was packed, as it had been every night since it re-opened. Then Tony came in, brushing snow off his huge shoulders. He was followed inside by Pinto, Cueball and someone else that Dani had never seen before. The whole room came to a standstill. Even the customers sensed that someone powerful had just arrived. The whole mood of the Club was changed in an instant.

Tony yelled up toward the stage, "You'se dumb broads, nobody dates a customer from this place in future. If ya' wanna hustle, go work the streets. There's lotsa' room for y'all out there."

With that, Tony turned on his heels and, to underline his point, hurled the Club's fully-decorated Christmas tree clear across the room. Then, Tony slammed his way out the main door, with his entourage right behind him.

Adrienne, Sheri, Sue and Dani stood on stage looking at each other; rooted in shock and completely baffled by the whole episode. But, like the show people they were, they began dancing again as if nothing had happened. The band launched into their version of 'Shout' and the fringes on the girls' dresses began flying. That number gave them quite a workout and was always a big hit with the customers. Hot and perspiring though she was when she came off stage, Dani went straight over to Nicky.

"What the hell got into Tony tonight? He has some nerve, embarrassing us all like that!"

Nicky sipped his scotch and water and stared at Dani. Finally he broke the silence.

"Did you see that guy with Tony? He's Phil Simms, manager of the Bank of Florida, one of our interests."

"You mean that bank that Tony wants me to buy?" Dani queried.

"Yeah, that's the one," Nicky replied. He seldom talked about his older brother's interests to Dani and she wondered what it meant now that he had. But, as she stood there pondering, there was another intrusion.

A huge black man burst through the doors of the Club and began throwing aside people in his path, left and right. Reacting quickly, Nicky and Mike, the bartender, grabbed two bats kept behind the bar for just such an occasion. Mike came up close behind the crazed man and swung the baseball bat with all his strength. It connected with a crack that would have knocked anyone else out cold, but the wild-eyed man seemed completely unaffected by the blow. He spun around, grabbed hold of Mike and threw him into some tables, as if he had just tossed a ball for a pet dog.

Nicky got close enough to hit the guy, but only managed to break the bat. It took three more large men, working together, before the intruder was finally brought down. Then, Nicky and the boys kicked him repeatedly until he was bleeding badly.

During the entire melee, the man's only sounds had been animal grunts. When they finally finished with him, Nicky and the boys dragged him out into the street. About an hour later word began to circulate that the wild man was a junkie dealer, probably high on his own stuff. Dani was completely shaken by it all.

"You didn't have to keep on kicking him after he was down!"

Annoyance crossed Nicky's face as he looked at Dani. His shirt was soaked with sweat and blood and his own hand was bleeding through a towel he'd wrapped around it.

"It's nothing!" Nicky snarled. "Get our coats, Dani. I'll take you home."

Nicky was cool and detached all the way back to Dani's home, off the Belt Parkway, in Brooklyn. She invited him in, even though Nicky had never visited since Dani had begun to live there.

"I really don't want to be alone tonight," Dani whined, trying to appease Nicky and pulling him gently toward the staircase.

"You're a big girl now, Dani. I've had a long hard night an' I gotta get some sleep," Nicky mumbled, as he kissed her goodnight and left.

Dani could hear the snow crunching as Nicky's car ploughed its way out of her driveway and onto the road. She watched him disappear into the night and sadly closed the door. Dani's mind flashed back to the day that HK had driven away, after their first, wonderful weekend together in New York. Grief washed over her as she thought of how HK had bought all of this, just for her and yet he didn't even know she had moved into the house!

Dani stood there for the longest time, looking at all the beauty around her. She had always felt so fortunate to have found that beautiful Carrera-marble statue - 'Madonna and Child' - to stand life-sized in the foyer. Gold-veined mirrors covered all the walls, reflecting Dani's image dressed in sable and diamonds.

'Fifty thousand dollars' worth of clothing and jewelry on my body, and yet there's no-one here with me to appreciate it!'

Dani's wildest fantasies had all been fulfilled by HK. Now, without him, she felt more empty and alone with each passing day. Why had she felt she had to leave him? Yes, he was older than Dani, but he sure knew how to treat a woman. Dani slowly climbed up the marble staircase toward her empty bedroom, hating herself for having hurt HK so badly. *'And all for what?'* Nicky certainly wasn't living up to Dani's expectations.

She removed her make-up and dressed for bed, feeling depressed and needing sleep. She closed her eyes, praying that a new day might bring her new hope. Dani even thought about going to church. She hadn't been in a Catholic church for years, but thought she might go the very next morning. She lay there for what seemed like hours, with tears falling from her sleepless eyes and trying not to let dark thoughts drag her down.

But there was no escape for Dani until she had cried herself to sleep.

***

She awoke early, to the sound of trucks and cars bringing workers to labor on the other houses being built in her area. Half asleep, she became aware of sobbing sounds coming from the hallway outside her bedroom door. Dani got out of bed and reached for her robe. Yes, she definitely heard someone crying.

"Who's there?"

Dani called out in her most commanding voice as she stood behind the closed door. When she eventually plucked up the courage to open it, Sam was lying in a heap in the hallway, beside the guestroom door. Her face was all bloody and streaked with tears. Sam looked up as Dani approached her and allowed Dani to help her to the guestroom, but when she saw her friend in the daylight, Dani gasped, involuntarily.

"Whatever happened to you, Sam?"

"It was that fat slob Tony. I'll kill him one day, I swear!"

"You mean Tony Mannelli did this to you?" Dani asked, disbelievingly.

"That fat son of a bitch, I'll kill him," Sam repeated. Through tangled hair, blood and tears, Dani could see that one of Sam's front teeth barely clung to her top gum and her right eye was swollen shut.

"Sam, you need to see a doctor, right away."

"No. I can't go to a doctor, Dani" Sam cried, getting upset again. "He'd have to report it and then the police would ask questions that I can't answer."

"You don't have a choice, Sam. You need attention right away!"

Sam slumped down onto the bed. "Dani, please, I only want to sleep. I'm so tired."

Dani didn't know what to do for the best. Her friend was just lying there silently, with both eyes closed.

"Sam, I can't make you go, but there's no way that I can do what a doctor can do for you."

There was no answer but Sam was still breathing strongly so Dani decided to let her friend sleep, for the moment. She made Sam as comfortable as she could and then closed the door quietly and went back to her own room. Dani's black maid and surrogate mother, Kay, came in as usual at 11:30 am, with Dani's breakfast.

"My goodness, Miz Dani," she said, clicking her tongue. "It ain't right and proper. Comers-and-stayers, comers-and-goers, so much blood on them sheets in the guest room too."

"Ah declare, if the Lord be willin,' y'all get to live through 'nother day."

"What's happened Kay? Isn't Sam in the guest room?" Dani scrambled out of bed.

"No, ma'am, but this here note was on the bed. It says Sam went to see the doctor."

Dani's maid knew all about Sam and Tony.

"For the life o' me, I jus' don't figure why a pretty young thing like Samantha keeps on agoin' back to such an animal."

"I don't know either, Kay." Dani admitted. "He's twice her age, he's mean and he gives Sam nothing but trouble. It's stupid, but what can I say or do to make her stop seeing the fat slob. And he's not even satisfied with having both a wife *and* a mistress; he screws every new girl that Nicky hires at the Club."

"He didn' get to y'all, did he?" Kay asked, horrified.

"God no, but only 'cause Nicky told him to lay off. Lord knows, Tony tried," Dani remembered with disgust.

While they were still talking, Sam walked into the room, looking like death. She had been to see a dentist, who had put a temporary cap on her tooth, hoping to be able to save it. Also, she *had* gone to see a doctor who advised her to report the incident, but promised that he wouldn't report it himself.

"Did you tell the doctor who did this to you, Sam?"

"My God, Dani, d'you think I'm nuts? Tony'd kill me if I turned him in." Later, as they sat in the kitchen talking over cups of coffee, Dani decided they had both earned a trip to Atlantic City. Quickly, the two girls threw some clothes into a bag and drove away for a few relaxing days of playing tourist on the Boardwalk.

***

Life seemed much better when they returned to New York and both girls decided to be more sensible. Sam was going to date other men, apart from Tony Mannelli and Dani was going to call HK again and agree to marry him, if he still wanted her.

It had sounded like such a wonderful plan, back when the two girls were enjoying their holiday break but Dani couldn't shake the feeling that a dream was all it could ever be.

Dolores J. Guthrie

Chapter 9

Dani's professional dreams were beginning to take shape, at last! Thanks to Walter Winchell's column and many other good reviews of her Club act, Dani's name was becoming known in the entertainment world. To continue to promote her career, Dani scheduled a recording session at the A1 Sound Studios. Steve Lawrence, the recording star, was also there that day. Impressed by Dani's voice, he sent a copy of her recordings to the producer of the Broadway musical, 'Funny Girl.' Not long after that the producer called, asking Dani to try out for the lead role because their current star was leaving in order to make the movie version.

And if that wasn't enough, Dani also got a call from Tex Beneke, leader of the Glen Miller Tribute Band. He wanted Dani to join them on their up-coming European tour, right after they finished their current season at the 'Americana Hotel'. For the first time in Dani's life, she truly felt that she could have a successful, singing career and her confidence was riding high. Dani's personal life, though, was still not happy. Although living in a beautiful home, built for her by a man who loved her more than she had ever imagined possible, Dani knew that if she went ahead and married HK she would be compelled to give up her promising professional career!

But this was not the only dilemma Dani was facing.

Lately, Nicky had done a complete about-turn in their relationship. He took Dani aside one night and told her that he thought HK was a great guy and that Dani was making a mistake; she should call him again and tell him she'd marry him. Dani was thoroughly confused. *Nicky, who had flirted and pursued her until she had given up HK for him, was now telling Dani that she should marry the older man!*

Dani couldn't handle the pressure any longer and she finally challenged Nicky.

"Is this your way of telling me that we'll never be together Nicky, because you're already married? What kind of marriage do you have anyway? You're never with your wife!"

"Shit, Dani! I couldn't marry you even if I wasn't already married," Nicky replied sadly. "Not only are you divorced, you're not Italian either.

The 'Family' would never accept you, Dani. And even if I was to leave my wife and kids for you, my brother, Tony, would find me and..."

"Yes?" Dani prodded.

"Never mind, Dani, I just can't marry you and that's that."

"But Nicky, I love you," she pleaded.

"Dammit Dani, I'm with you more hours in one day than I am with Lindsay in a whole week!"

Nicky continued to emphasize to Dani the wonders of marriage to HK, until she really couldn't decide whether it was the fact that she and Nicky could *never* marry, or the fact that Nicky kept promoting HK, that hurt her the most.

A lot of time had gone by since Dani and HK last met. He had not called her on the phone, stopped by at the Club, or called by to visit at Dani's new house. One quality she'd always loved about HK was his persistence and it really puzzled Dani that months had gone by with no word from him at all. About a week later, on a cold, wintry morning, Dani was carefully picking her way along the icy sidewalks of Fifth Avenue along with dozens of other busy shoppers when, suddenly, there HK was. They both stopped dead in their tracks, facing each other. HK beamed broadly, even as the tears streamed down his face.

"Oh Dani, Dani; do you know where I just came from?"

Dani struggled to speak, afraid of spoiling the moment. "No, where were you?"

"I was inside St. Patrick's Cathedral, praying that I'd see you again and I'm not even a Catholic! And now, here you are! Dani, you're truly an answer to my prayers."

Dani struggled as the tears welled up in her own eyes and began to spill over onto her cold cheeks.

"I've thought about you too, HK, so very much," she whispered.

"And?" he prompted her to answer.

"I guess it's time we had a talk about things, HK." Dani stepped closer and gave him a hug.

"Great!" he shouted. "I know the perfect place; somewhere we won't be interrupted."

"Where, HK?"

"Florida, Dani! Florida!"

***

Dani smiled as she watched from across the room. HK was definitely her kind of man. The day before, they had checked into the 'Fontainebleau', HK's favorite resort hotel. Dani was sure that was because the hotel had a special room, filled with ticker tape machines that were connected to the New York Stock Exchange. HK liked to sit there for hours, watching his money working for him!

They were having a wonderful time in Florida. HK was happy, buying out all the boutiques for Dani and she was happy to let him. On their second night there, while having a private dinner in their suite, Dani decided it was time for their 'talk'.

"HK, I didn't leave you because of anything that *you* had done. It was because of something that *I* did."

"Let's just forget about it all, Dani. It's not important now, anyway. I'm just glad we're back together again."

"No, it *is* important to me HK and I can't just forget it. I was unfaithful to you, HK" Dani confessed.

"Oh, my darling child! You are so charmingly innocent and naive. I never expected you to give up your youth for me, Dani!"

HK didn't seem at all surprised or angry by her confession. Instead, he gently caressed her trembling hands.

"Believe me, Dani, I understand. I do! You are a beautiful young woman, with needs that I cannot always be there to fulfill. I simply want you to love me, Dani, that's all and I feel that you do. You do love me, don't you?" He desperately searched her face for reassurance.

"I *do* love you, HK!" Dani answered in a soft voice and looked deep into his eyes."

"Then that's all I can expect for now," HK smiled back at her. "After we're married though, it'll be a different story, you know," he said, trying to sound stern.

"HK, I'm so very lucky to have you take me back!" Dani whispered in her lover's ear and they embraced for a very, long time.

The rest of the week passed far too quickly and, at the end of it, neither of them wanted to return to their respective responsibilities. But they did. When they arrived in New York, she and HK said fond farewells at the airport and went their separate ways, HK promising to come back to Dani just as soon as he could.

Dani had already called her friend, Sam to come to the airport to help carry the mountain of luggage that Dani had brought back with her; six new suitcases, all full of new clothes! Dani's maid, Kay, squealed with delight as they were unpacking it all.

"Ah do swear, Miz Dani, ah ain't nevah seen so many beautiful new things at one time in mah whole life. That there Mr. HK sure is somethin' else! If I was you honey, I'd stake my claim real fast, 'fore some other young'n gets her hooks into him."

Dani hugged her maid. "Don't you worry Kay, I'm working on it."

At the Club that evening, during one of her regular breaks, Nicky came over to welcome Dani back. She gave him the news that she and HK were back together again. He seemed genuinely happy for them both, which made Dani totally unprepared for his next statement.

"Dani, I've been thinking 'bout how you and I can see more of each other. If we were to become business partners, well that would give us a good reason to travel around and be together for most of the time, wouldn't it?"

Dani was stunned and tried desperately to figure out what he was really saying. She never knew what was coming next with Nicky; it was like being on a roller coaster. *'If only I could just walk away from him,"* she wished, silently. *'If only I wasn't so damned attracted to the guy.'*

As he went on to explain his proposition, Nicky seemed nervous, which was most unlike him.

"You know, babe, we should set up a proper corporation, to invest your money in. Wha'd' yah say, Dani? It'd be great for both of us and Tony'll help. He's already said so."

Dani couldn't hold back her emotions. This man, who had once said he loved her, now seemed to think of Dani only as a business partner!

"What do you mean, 'business partners', Nicky?" Trying to get her thoughts in order, Dani gestured around at the Club.

"*You* don't have any money, Nicky; this is all Tony's."

Nicky just smiled at her.

"We'll set it up with *your* money, honey. Three-hundred-thousand dollars should do it. Investing it here, in the Club, would double your money in six months. After that, we'd become full, equal partners. Come on, babe, wha'd'yah say?"

Nicky fumbled with his tie as he waited for her answer, but Dani was so stunned she couldn't find one. Then Nicky's next idea came from way out in left field.

"And, if you're a good girl in bed tonight, I'll make you a little more Italian. You'd like that, huh, wouldn't you Dani?"

She went weak in the knees, just thinking about Nicky's passionate lovemaking. Dani wanted him so much and the man damn well knew it. '*Is it fear that makes him so attractive to me or just the excitement of the unknown?* But those were questions that Dani just couldn't answer.

***

Later that night, in bed, Nicky teased Dani; nibbling the skin up and down her back, sucking on the lobes of her ears, her neck and her nipples until she was ready to climb the walls. As good as it was, though, Dani sensed that Nicky was holding back; that he wanted to do more but wasn't able to rise to the occasion, so they eventually just fell asleep in each other's arms. Early next morning, Nicky shook Dani awake.

"C'mon Babe, we have to get going and set up that business corporation at the bank!"

Groggy and hung-over, Dani crawled obediently out of the warm bed and headed for the bathroom. '*Hell, what am I, a damn puppet?*' Dani complained as she showered. '*I should never have gone to bed with Nicky again. Damn him, will he always use me like this?*'

On their way out the door, Nicky turned back toward her. "You've got your checkbook in your purse, don't you, Dani? You'll have to write out a check today, hon'."

'Karl Hokowitz, Attorney at Law' was the name on the brass sign outside a small office door. Dani realized, with horror, that it was the same attorney that Nicky had found for her Mexican divorce, the previous year. From behind the battered desk of his bleak, two-room offices on Broadway, the lawyer swiveled around in his chair as they entered. With his squat build and the prolific chest hair that poked out from beneath his shirt collar, the dried-up lawyer reminded Dani of a gorilla and she shuddered, involuntarily. *'The man is barely kindred to mankind!*

The only time that Karl Hokowitz acknowledged Dani's presence in the room was when he threw some typed pages across his desk, toward her. Quickly skimming through the contract, Dani could see that the wording was exactly the way Nicky had suggested things to her the night before, *'three hundred thousand dollars, six months, partners, etc. etc.'*

Dani fleetingly thought that it was an interesting coincidence, but the fact that the contract had already been typed out hardly crossed her mind. Without further thought, Dani signed on the dotted line. Karl insisted that she write two checks, each being for one-hundred-and-fifty-thousand dollars. Greedily snatching them from Dani's hand, the gnarled lawyer promptly declared the meeting over and ushered them, hastily, out of his office.

As Dani and Nicky waited for the elevator, Tony appeared out of nowhere and waited with them. He and Nicky said nothing to each other and Dani could figure out neither Tony's presence there, nor the expression on his face. On anyone else, Dani might have thought it to be sympathy, but that was not an emotion Tony Mannelli possessed. No one spoke at all in the elevator, but Dani's mind was reeling. *Had she been hypnotized, somehow? Was she part of some odd dream? Was she even really there at all?*

How Dani wished she could just wake up and find that it was all a mistake. As they stepped from the elevator and walked towards the street, Dani became aware of the stains on the drab, grey walls of that hallway. Its ancient steam heaters, the dimness of its dirty, fluorescent lights, the background street noise and the smell of hotdogs that wafted inside was suddenly overpowering to Dani and she was glad to get outside. It was Tony who broke the silence between them all.

"Dani, you catch yourself a cab and go on home." He waved his ever present cigar toward her, dismissively, "Nicky and I are gonna have a meetin'."

With that he put his arm around younger brother, Nicky's shoulder, patting it in congratulation as they walked off together.

"Yeah, I'll see you at work tonight, babe" Nicky called back over his shoulder as they walked away from Dani.

Dazed by the whole morning's proceedings, Dani slowly began to feel the full impact of what she had done.

"Hell, the least you could do is to take me to lunch."

'My God," Dani thought, as reality finally took hold of her emotions. *"What the hell have I done? And, what the hell am I going to tell HK?"*

She began to walk back down the street, toward the bank that Nicky had long ago insisted she switch her accounts to. *'It will yield higher interest,'* Nicky had told her.

Dani found Frank Dunicci, the bank manager, standing in the lobby and demanded to know how she could stop payment on two checks that she had just written! Dunicci excused himself politely and disappeared into his office. Returning after only a few minutes, he explained to Dani that the checks had already been notarized and therefore could not be cancelled.

"Well, how in the hell did they get notarized so fast," Dani demanded to know. "I only wrote them a few minutes ago?"

A very nervous Mr. Dunicci cleared his throat several times before replying.

"Er, I can assure you that Mr. Hokowitz took care of everything while you were in his office, Miss Sutton."

In her upset condition, it never occurred to Dani to wonder how the bank manager already knew to whom she had written the checks!

***

When Dani eventually arrived home, miserable and exhausted, Sam was already there. Over a cup of coffee, Dani tried to tell Sam what had happened that morning.

"You fool!" Sam cried. "You damn fool. Sometimes I can't believe your stupid head, Dani Sutton!"

Dani was startled by her friend's outburst, but Sam hadn't finished.

"Frank Dunicci is Tony's inside man at the bank, so I wouldn't mention stopping any payments again if I were you, Dani. You haven't seen how really crazy Tony can get. He isn't called *'Crazy Horse'* for nothin' you know. You *do* know, don't you, Dani?"

"Well, no, not really, I've heard so many different stories about Tony, but what do you know, Sam?"

Dani's friend hesitated for a moment before answering.

"Well, I've been told that a young singer from 'The Family' wanted a contract with a big producer in California, but he wasn't gettin' anywhere. Tony approached the producer on the singer's behalf but he was told that 'the likes of Tony Mannelli couldn't tell the producer how to run his own business'. Not long afterward, that same producer awoke to find the bloody head of his priceless race horse lying on the pillow beside him. Need I say more?"

Coffee no longer satisfied Dani's thirst and she asked Sam to make them both a Bloody Mary. Mixing their drinks whilst looking at Dani in bewilderment, Sam asked the question that Dani had already asked herself a hundred times.

"What are you going to tell HK about this?"

Dani hung her head, like a child caught dipping into the cookie jar.

"I know HK loves me deeply and will do anything for me, but Sam, I'm terrified that these three-hundred-thousand dollars I've just signed away might push him over the edge."

Knowing that she had to call HK sooner or later, Dani reluctantly reached for the phone and HK's secretary put her through right away.

"HK here." he said, in a playful voice. "Is this my little honey? Is it my little 'queen'?"

Dani wondered how long HK's mood would last after he heard her whole story.

"HK, I have to talk to you, about something very important."

"Yes, my honey lamb; what is it?"

"No, not on the phone HK. Could you come into the city later, so that we can talk about it face-to-face?"

"Oh my darling honey, you make me so happy when you need me. Alright, we'll talk about it when I get over to our new home tonight. Have your maid leave early, Dani. I want my horny 'queen' all to myself."

"HK, not on the phone!" Dani reprimanded him again, gently. "But I love you, too!" she whispered.

Sam sipped at her drink, shook her head and smiled at her scatter-brained friend.

"Damn it. Dani, you either have no sense at all or a lot of guts. I suppose you want me to tell Nicky you won't be working tonight?"

"Yes, if you will, Sam. And tell Kay that I'll be using the main dining room, tonight. Tell her that Mr. Kline will be there for dinner and I think that leg of lamb is in order."

HK was pleased as he surveyed their new house. Crystal chandeliers sparkled in candlelight from all around the dining room. To HK's right was a Vassiminni Brothers, hand-carved, seventeen foot long, cream-and-gold Venetian breakfront that covered one entire wall!

The rest of that lavish room complimented such a large decorative piece, though. From the huge gold, Florentine-style mirror hanging over the bar to the French, velvet drapes over cream-colored Venetian sheers that hung softly at the marble bay windows; to the thick, cream colored carpet that covered the whole floor. Dani glided into the ornate dining room in a low cut, white, beaded-gown and stopped by HK's chair to kiss him. Then she walked down to her own seat at the other end of the large table, set for two.

"Damn it, Dani, you're not going to sit that far away from me are you?"

Kay magically appeared in the doorway.

"I can move Miz Dani closer to you. Mr. Kline, sir.

Dani nodded her agreement and Kay hummed merrily as she rearranged the table settings.

"And especially for you, Mr. Kline sir, ah's made one of my banana-cream pies to fatten you up."

Kay giggled and then left the room as quickly as she had arrived.

Dani and HK were sipping their after dinner liqueurs of Chabot X.O. Armagnac, before Dani finally plucked up the courage to tell her fiancé what she had done.

"Goddam, it Dani! Goddam it, girl, three-hundred-thousand dollars?"

HK face was turning scarlet so he stood up, took off his jacket and loosened his collar and tie. He paced around the room several times, taking deep breaths, before he was able to continue in a calmer voice.

"Why in the hell do you do these things, Dani? Why on earth didn't you ask me before you did this? I didn't become Vice President of Xenon by being stupid, you know. I could be a great help to you with your investments, if only you'd let me. How could you possibly do such a foolish thing without asking me?"

"I honestly don't know, HK." Dani spoke meekly, hanging her head. "So many things have happened to me lately that I'm really confused. I just can't explain why I did it. I suppose I thought that since Tony was in the investment business, I might be better investing through him than risking my money in the stock market."

Dani couldn't possibly tell HK how Nicky had suggested the idea only last night, just before taking her to bed; nor could she tell him how completely used and stupid she felt! Meanwhile, HK continued to pace, back and forth, the full length of that huge room. He stopped for a moment, fighting to regain some of his normal composure.

"My dearest darling, Dani. I realize that you don't have the education to understand high finance and so I'm not going to blame you. But, you really don't know those people very well at all, do you?"

"Well, I know that Tony owns a brokerage firm *and* a bank in Florida. So I figured he must know *something* about how to handle money. And he loans money to small business people who get into trouble, too."

HK smiled, wanly.

"This 'Tony' sounds like a loan shark to me."

"What's that?" Dani's eyes opened wide in alarm.

"Never mind, my darling." HK took Dani's hands in his and kissed her forehead, gently.

"I don't want this money thing to upset you any more or to spoil the rest of our evening together. I'll attend to business tomorrow. All I want you to worry about tonight, my darling Dani is slipping your voluptuous body into your prettiest, most revealing, negligee. It's been far too long since I've caressed my very own 'queen'."

Dani was so relieved that HK didn't go on any more about the money that she hugged him fiercely. *'He forgives me so easily.'* It was such a relief to see HK getting back to his old self.

"You're crazy, but I love you!" she teased him. "Just give me a few minutes and then join me upstairs."

Dani dabbed 'Shalimar' perfume here-there-and-everywhere, before slipping into a baby-blue peignoir, an outfit that she knew made her blue eyes look deep violet. When she came out of the bathroom, HK was already there, sitting on the bed in the nude with pen and pad in hand, checking his finances. His briefcase was open next to him, revealing his constant companion, a bottle of V.O. He smiled as he looked up.

"Dani, you may not believe this, but you make Christine Keeler, that high-class escort from England, look like a frump. Hell, the way I figure it, if you charged me for every time we had sex, I'd have happily given you seventy-five-thousand dollars a trick!"

It took a moment for the thought to get through to Dani's brain but then they both began laughing; so hard that HK slipped off the bed and fell onto the floor.

"Dammit, these satin sheets are slippery," he grumbled as he tried to cover his modesty, which only made Dani laugh even harder.

"Oh, my dearest, please marry me soon so that we can be together forever."

Dani's mood swiftly changed to a more serious one at HK's sudden reference to marriage.

"HK, do you remember that month, early in our relationship, when we were apart?"

"Yes?"

"I had such mixed emotions back then, HK. I thought that as long as we kept seeing each other I would just keep on hurting you more and more. There's such an age difference between us, you see, and I..."

"I've told you already, honey," HK interrupted Dani's flow of thought. "I understand that a young woman like you needs a young stud to service you while I'm out of town. That's the reason you ran away from me, I know Dani. You were afraid to tell me about Nicky, weren't you?"

HK calmly reached into his briefcase, bringing out the bottle of V.O. along with a couple of silver shot-cups.

"It happened in Las Vegas," Dani admitted as her eyes looked everywhere in the room but at HK.

"It was when I was on my way back from Mexico after the divorce. We stopped over in Vegas and Nicky was there too and...well, things just..."

"Hell. Dani! I *paid* Nicky to watch out for you, to see you home safely and to take care of all your needs while I was out of town!"

Dani looked at HK in utter disbelief, shocked by such matter-of-fact statements.

"You mean you *paid* Nicky to make love to me? When did you do that?" Dani demanded to know.

"Hell no, Dani, not love; it was only sex, my darling. A long time ago, in fact the very first night I came to the Club, I made a pact with young Nicky."

The room spun crazily around Dani and everything seemed to be caving in on her.

"I can't believe you would *pay* Nicky to do that," she snapped.

On seeing how upset she was, HK wiggled closer to wrap his arms around Dani and he kissed her tenderly.

"I'm so sorry, my sweet. I just thought you'd be better off having sex with someone I controlled, that's all. I didn't want you going with just any young guy off the street while I was away in Rochester."

Dani stared at him.

"Well, if you're so damn clever, Mr. HK, what the hell do I do now that I've fallen in love with Nicky?"

"Love, hell! Lust Dani, it's only lust."

"Well, I don't know whether I love him or lust him," Dani sobbed like a child. "All I know is that I'm afraid of him now, HK. So, maybe I should just run away and forget the both of you?"

Crying hysterically by then, Dani couldn't speak so HK rocked her gently in his arms and stroked her hair until she could breathe again.

"Now you listen to me, my darling Dani," he said, firmly but gently. "You always told me that your aim in life was to become a millionaire one day. Well, I've given you that, Dani and now you expect me to give you up? Think of all that you could have in the future! As my wife, after my death, you'll be entitled to half of my entire estate, plus an income from my corporation for as long as you live!"

"You stand to make at least another five million dollars, Dani. And remember, you'll most likely live at least thirty years longer than I do."

HK's eyes were becoming inflamed from shedding his own tears.

"I love you so much, Dani. I could never live on if you left me again. I'm so sorry that I hired Nicky. It was a crass idea and very thoughtless of me."

"There you go again," Dani pouted. "I know how much you love me HK, but you don't seem to understand that, deep down inside, this showgirl has some very old-fashioned ideas about life. I want us to grow old *together*, HK and that's the only reason I wish you were younger. I need more time to think about everything."

HK nodded and forced a smile while Dani tried to lighten the mood with her best coy expression.

"Well, I sure don't feel like making my seventy-five-grand tonight, now!"

"What?"

HK looked at Dani with dismay, not getting her joke at first and his expression turned to disappointment.

"Oh, all right, then." Dani relented. "Give me a jigger of that horrible V.O. stuff you carry with you everywhere. Maybe that will settle me down and make me worth your money!"

The cognac felt like molten lava as it drizzled down Dani's throat.

"So, is my 'queen' ready now?" HK asked, hopefully.

"Ready!" Dani replied, wiping her lips.

"The lady is hot and ready!"

Chapter 10

When Dani invited her friend on a two week vacation to Yakima, Dani's hometown, Sam thought it was a brilliant idea. For some reason though, the notion upset both Nicky and Tony Mannelli but neither could persuade the girls to change their minds. After exchanging a few odd glances, the boys dropped the subject.

Kay buzzed around happily, helping the girls to pack and she even baked a chocolate cake for Dani to take home for her father.

***

Once airborne to Seattle, it seemed that neither girl had a care in the world. Sam chattered like a teenager on her first trip away from home, as they found their first-class seats and settled down for the long trip. With the initial excitement over, Sam became her usual curious self and began asking Dani what married life with Peter had been like.

"For the fourteen years that we were married, we lived right on the Seneca River, in Baldwinsville, New York. Pretty much like back in New York City, the weather there was usually hot and sticky in the summers, beautiful in the fall and freezing cold from Halloween to Easter!"

Dani smiled wistfully at the memories.

"One winter, our water pipes were frozen for a whole six months and we carted water all the way up from the well, in milk cans. If we wanted hot water, it was heated on the stove."

'How different my life was back then.'

"Peter was a good husband really, but most of all he was a wonderful father to my son, JR. Our married life was quiet, though. We spent time with friends, neighbors and the church but our local social life was always pretty busy and, oh, there was the 'Moose Club' too!"

Sam interrupted Dani's flow of thought.

"What do you mean, *your* son, Dani? Are you saying that Peter isn't J.R's father?"

"I didn't even know Peter back then," Dani confessed. "JR was conceived after I played 'doctor', in a haystack, with one of the neighborhood boys. I was only fourteen then."

"You've gotta be kiddin' me, Dani!" Sam studied her friend closely. "But you're not, are you?"

"No." Dani admitted. "JR's father and I got married, but being hardly more than children ourselves it was real hard for us. *He* left town before JR was even born. And I had to resist my parents too; they didn't want me to keep the baby."

"Gee, Dani, that musta' been awful."

"It was, but five years later I met Peter, when he was in the Air-Cat Division stationed at Yakima Firing Center. Peter and JR got along so well that when Pete asked me to marry him, I said yes."

"So when did the three of you move over to New York?"

"It was after Peter's discharge. He wanted to go back to where his family was based, so the three of us packed up and headed across country. Peter got himself a good job with an optical company; you know spectacles, microscopes and such? He made a comfortable income and I worked too, for a department store in charge of their 'Revlon' beauty products."

"I've often wondered why you have so much of that stuff in your bathroom." Sam smiled.

"I guess I just never changed brands! I really enjoyed my job, too Sam, except for the damn cosmetics manager, who chased me around the back stockroom whenever he got a chance! You may not believe me, but I was *always* faithful to Peter, even though men flirted with me all the time, telling me how pretty I was and asking me why I wasted myself behind a cosmetics counter. That kind of flattery was hard to take sometimes, too. I'd missed out on a lot of growing up stuff, you know; dates, proms and things like that."

"Yeah, I know what you mean," Sam agreed. "I didn't get to do many of those, either."

Dani went on with her musings.

"I'd *always* wanted to sing. I took voice lessons for quite a while and from a good teacher too. I knew I was good and wanted to prove that I could sing professionally, but Peter wouldn't ever let me do more than sing around our little ol' town. He would never let me accept any money for my singing, either. It always had to be 'just for the fun of it'."

Dani went quiet. Sam carried on at sipping her drink until curiosity got the better of her again.

"Who hired you at the Club; Dani, was it Tony or Nicky?"

"Nicky."

"Didn't Tony ever try to take you to bed, then? He regards it as his personal job to break in *all* new girls, usually by taking them to room 1906 at The Towers Hotel on 49th Street!"

"Well, he might have been working up to it, but the other girls had already told me to watch out for *'The Horse'*. That's the reason I let Nicky start driving me home at night. I thought if Tony knew his own brother had designs on me, he'd leave me alone."

"That's never stopped Tony before, not that I know of anyway," Sam made a sour face.

"Maybe you're right!" Dani voiced a sudden recollection.

"One night Tony, full of smiles, asked me to join him at his table after work. He poured some good wine and told me he 'liked what he saw and heard'. Then he said he could do a lot for me, like piano lessons and such, so that I could do solo work at some of his better clubs."

Sam spluttered into her drink. "I can just see that awful smirk on his face. Although a 'leer' is more like it."

"Sam, I'll always remember that night, because he never did stop smiling. I was getting real nervous, especially when he loosened his tie, making himself comfortable. I'd always thought that Tony was different, you know, kinda strange and I really didn't want any part of him. So I told him, - *'no, sorry but I don't have the time for piano lessons, Tony. All I want is to sing but hey, thanks anyway'.* Nicky passed by our table right then, so I asked him to drive me home."

"Damn, I hate that pig, Tony!"

"Sam, if you know all these things about him and they upset you, why do you still put up with the man?"

"Dani, you really don't know?" Sam turned to her friend in genuine surprise. "The guy's a real animal in bed and I just can't let him go."

***

There is something about a long journey that lets a person loosen up, lets them confide feelings that they wouldn't normally like to talk about, so Sam carried on chatting.

"Dani, why haven't you and HK got married yet?

Dani smiled, mistily.

"You know, Sam, HK isn't a young man any more. He tells me it takes him all night to finish what he used to do all night!"

"Well, maybe you're not doing the right things for him, then."

"He says it's because of all the pills he takes, for his high blood pressure and heart problems.

"Anyway, I really think I'd have difficulty being true to HK and I *do* believe that's an important part of any marriage. I don't know, Sam, maybe I build my life too much around sex."

"You're just a nympho, Dani."

"Oh no, not me," Dani denied the idea strongly. "But believe me, by the time the night is over, HK does manage to take very good care of me, Sam."

"You know that look you get in your eyes, Dani? Men call that 'bedroom-eyes'. It's a shame you're not working as a high-priced call girl; you'd make a fortune."

"As much as I enjoy sex, I could never sell myself. Doing it for money would destroy my sexual desires completely, Sam. So far there have only been four men in my whole life and that's three too many, already!"

Just then, their flight attendant announced 'The Hustler', starring Paul Newman as their in-flight movie.

"Wasn't that filmed inside Amy's pool hall, back on Broadway?"

"Yeah, I wonder if they kept the scene that I was in." Sam's eyes sparkled at the recollection. "They needed crowd extras and I just happened to be there that day. It was really exciting. Did you get in on the filming too?"

"No, I missed that day. But Amy, the owner, has always been a good friend to me. Every time I see him he tells me I should leave New York. I guess Amy thinks he knows what's good for me."

***

The two girls walked down the ramp of Seattle Airport into a brisk, April evening. Dani's parents greeted them with hugs and kisses and Laura handed her daughter a beautiful rose, picked from her own garden.

Sam was rendered speechless during their drive over the mountains, away from Seattle. She just couldn't believe the wild beauty all around her in the majestic pine trees and snowcapped mountains. Sam had never experienced such peace and stillness. Her world had always been filled with continual noise, within a city of dirty concrete.

Dani, too, had almost forgotten the wonderful serenity of the landscape and the freshness of the mountain air. But it was wonderful to return to the ranch-style house that Dani had bought the previous Christmas, with the first money that HK had ever given her. It had been a surprise gift to her parents.

Sam and Dani relaxed for the first few days, enjoying the company of Dani's extended family. As well as Dani's parents, there were two brothers, each with their wives and children and also Dani's seventeen-year-old sister, Brandy. During one particular, quite lengthy conversation with Sam, Harold questioned her about life back in the 'Big Apple.' Sam's usual forthrightness gave Dani's father a much greater insight into his own daughter's lifestyle, but what he learned didn't please him. Later, he took Dani aside and advised her to put some of her money into a bank in Yakima. At least that way there'd be something left of Dani's wealth if Harold's suspicions about the Mannelli's proved correct in the future.

Dani acknowledged her father's wisdom and the very next morning went to a local bank to transfer two-hundred-thousand-dollars into her new account. That same afternoon, Dani and her sister, Brandy, were driving Sam around, showing her the delights of the area. As they rounded a bend in the road, Brandy suddenly let out a squeal of delight.

"Oh, Dani look! There's that 'Suzy-Q' ranch I've been telling you about. Oh, it's so beautiful. Don't you think so, Sam?"

The enormous, white-fenced property that Brandy was excitedly pointing at contained a large, but empty house slumbering atop a gentle slope and overlooking extensive acreage.

Dani was already aware that the ranch was famous for having the largest, indoor horse-show arena in the whole North-western U.S., plus it had indoor stalls for almost two hundred horses. One horse in particular, 'Pacos Man', was a five-time, grand champion in 'cutting' events and had come from this ranch's own stables.

But the most important feature for Dani was the large 'For Sale' sign that hung on the ranch's five-barred gate. *'Maybe this is my way out of New York City!'* Thoughts tumbled around in Dani's mind as she hurriedly scribbled down the telephone number. When they got back home, she immediately called to make an appointment to discuss buying the ranch. Then she called HK, to tell him how great a place it would be for them to live after they were married and HK was retired; a place where the two of them could relax when they weren't traveling the world together. HK reluctantly agreed, on condition that he wouldn't have to care for any horses, admitting he was terrified of the damn creatures.

"Ah, what the hell!" HK declared, finally. "I'll just hire a manager and then we'll be in business."

Dani truly believed that she would be able to straighten out her life at last, but her happiness was short lived. Early next morning, the Yakima bank manager called to say that her New York bank had put a hold on her money transfer. She immediately called Karl Hokowitz, hoping he would tell her that it was all a mistake. Instead, he informed Dani that she couldn't invest that kind of money in Yakima, it was needed to pay 'gift taxes' back in New York.

"Karl, what the hell are you trying to pull? My taxes are all paid. Is your memory that short?"

But the lawyer insisted that there was no mistake. Frustrated and unable to control her temper, Dani slammed down the receiver. She was trying to calm herself before calling HK, when the phone rang again so Sam answered it.

But, after saying a startled 'hello', Sam stood there holding the phone for a long time; mostly listening and occasionally muttering.

"But, Tony!...okay, yeah...okay, okay!"

She slowly replaced the receiver and turned to Dani.

"That was Tony and he's mad as all hell. He says I have to get you on a plane and back to New York as fast as I can."

"Oh, Sam, what's happening to me? Everything is such a mess. Why has Tony got my money so tied up that I can't do what I want with it? I'm going to call HK, right now!"

But Dani was sobbing so hard that she could hardly speak when she finally got through to him.

"Dani, Dani, stop crying my darling and tell me what the matter is? I can't help you if I don't know what's wrong."

She took a deep breath and tried to calm down.

"Oh, HK! The New York bank won't transfer the money for the ranch. I called Hokowitz and he says 'it's needed to pay gift taxes' or some such rubbish. And now Tony just called and told Sam to take me back to New York!"

"Dani, of course there's a mistake. All the taxes have been paid on my gifts to you. It's all right, honey, you come on back to New York. I've been doing some checking on Hokowitz and those Mannelli's anyhow. It seems I'm not the only one who's interested in their activities, either. An FBI agent came to see me the other day and scared the shit out of me, until I realized that they thought the Mannelli's were using *you* to siphon money from me. I told them flat out that wasn't the way it was; that you and I are getting married, my darling."

"The FBI?" Dani wailed, unable to take it all in.

But HK wasn't finished with his news yet.

"By the way, Dani, I've set August 1st as the date for our wedding! Tell your Mom and Dad that I will be over there to make all the arrangements as soon as I return from Greenbrier Health Spa, in Pennsylvania. I'm going there first to get myself all rejuvenated for you, my darling 'queen'."

"Okay, HK, I'll tell them."

Dani's head was spinning, but HK still wasn't done yet.

"Shall we cruise around the world, my love, or shall we just fly from country to country? It's your choice my darling, whatever makes you happiest."

HK had done it again! He always made everything seem right, at least as far as Dani was concerned.

"Let's go on a cruise ship and then we won't have to pack and unpack all the time."

Dani seemed to have completely forgotten all about what had upset her only moments before; Tony, Nicky, money, even the ranch. But there was one thing that Dani hadn't forgotten and all this talk of weddings suddenly brought memories flooding back.

"HK, do you remember your estranged wife's heart attack, on the day she signed your own divorce papers? Your son, Tom, asked you to go home until your wife had pulled out of her illness, do you remember? You didn't want to leave but I'd never have forgiven myself if anything happened to your wife because of me."

"Yes, yes, I remember," HK said, patiently, "but don't worry my dear, her health is fine now. And she's accepted the way things are, especially since we made the property settlement!"

HK chuckled at his own joke. "Don't concern yourself with all that stuff anymore, my love. Our wedding date is set for August 1st and that's all you have to remember."

"But what about Tom?" Dani persisted. "Will he accept me as your wife?"

"I've told you before Dani, the only reason I haven't introduced the two of you yet, is because I'm afraid my son will steal you away for himself! He's a lot like his ol' man, you know."

HK was doing his best to calm Dani's fears.

"Seriously, my sweet, the last time I saw Tom he told me, 'Hell Pop, you've had so little happiness in your life, only lots of hard work. I've never seen you as happy as you've been since you met Dani, so go for it!'

"What's the real problem, honey? HK inquired, gently, "Are your feet getting cold, again?"

"I think they're frostbitten, HK!"

Dani tried hard to lighten up the mood. She didn't want to seem un-grateful for all that HK had done.

"Okay, HK, we'll plan for the first of August then," Dani declared, with far more confidence than she actually felt.

"Sam and I will fly back to New York tomorrow. I love you, HK" she whispered, "and I'll call you as soon as I get back there.

Dolores J. Guthrie

Chapter 11

Without knocking, Nicky came bursting through the front doors of Dani's New York home.

"Fuck!" he yelled. "Dani, what the hell's going on in that pea-sized brain of yours? First you take Sam to Yakima for no good reason and then you go buying some dumb ranch! Tony just about broke my head over that one, until I got it stopped!"

"You mean *you're* the one to blame?" Dani yelled, defiantly. "Nicky Mannelli, you had no right to interfere with my buying a ranch. And what's more, I don't like the way things have been going with my money at all. Remember when Hokowitz, Tony and you talked me into selling most of my Xenon stock? That was back when I wasn't seeing HK, remember?" she reminded him.

"Yeah and that was the best investment ya' ever made. You just wait and see," Nicky grinned back at her but Dani threw all her anger back at him.

"Well, HK told me later that it had to be the most stupid move he'd ever seen. *'Anyone with any financial sense knows that you don't sell a million dollars in stocks in the same fiscal year that they're bought!'* - that's what HK said."

"Aw, this HK don't know everything."

"Oh yes he does!" Dani screamed. "He's made millions on the stock market during his career. Damn you, Nicky Mannelli, I'm a fool to ever have listened to you and your crooked buddies."

Nicky spluttered in amazement. "Who the fuck d'ya think you're talking to, bitch?"

His face grew scarlet with anger, but Dani blindly carried on with her tirade.

"You listen to me, Nicky Mannelli. This trip you guys are on, working over 'good-ol' Dani Sutton', is ending; right here and right now! I won't live like this any longer. I'm marrying HK on the first of August and then *he* will be taking charge of all my finances, so that'll be an end of it."

Dani's eyes were flashing and she stood defiant as she raved on.

"HK's not at all happy with your great attorney, Karl Hokowitz, either you know."

"Hokowitz is a damn good attorney. He's worked for our 'Family' for years," Nicky countered.

"Your 'Family', that's a joke! They were the only clients Karl had until I came along. Get out of my house and out of my life Nicky; you and your so-called 'Family'. I've had it up to *here* with them all!"

Dani hit her own chest with her fist as she demonstrated the meaning of 'up-to-here', not noticing that, by then, she had pushed Nicky over the edge. He swore loudly in Italian and rammed his fist clear through the nearest wall, without flinching. Reaching for Dani's long, black hair he twisted it tightly and pulled her toward him until she cried out in pain.

"Nicky, stop it! You're hurting me!"

'Damn, he's going to pull it out by the roots!'

"Yes, you hurt, don't you Dani?" Nicky sneered.

"Yes, I hurt! Let me go Nicky, please!"

But Dani's begging fell on deaf, Italian ears.

"I *mean* to hurt you, you bitch! And I'm going to drive the fear of our 'Family' right into your head, once and for all. Ya' got that, Dani?"

Nicky's black eyes were wild with excitement as he dragged Dani into the bedroom, throwing her onto the bed by her hair. Then he ripped off all her clothes.

"I'll show you *who* you love," he roared, rocking his powerful body above hers.

And Dani's body reacted of its own volition. Spontaneously, she surrendered totally and rose to meet Nicky's dominant passion. The new idea of unconditional surrender sent chills of excitement rippling through her body, even as her naked flesh was torn with every thrust of his huge cock.

When he had finished with her, Nicky stomped over to the bathroom to clean up. After the wild heat of passion, sanity kicked in and Dani lay on the bed feeling like tossed away garbage. Tears stained her satin pillows as she stared at the ceiling, thinking of all her vows to HK. *'When will this nightmare ever end?'* Dani beat her fists upon the wet sheets, knowing that she'd just been raped by the man she once thought she loved.

Refreshed by his shower, Nicky came out of the bathroom as if nothing were wrong. His head twitched only slightly as he put on his most charming manner.

"Dani, ya know ya gotta put this marriage thing outta your head, if you wanna stay healthy. We reckon this HK is good for another million at least and baby, you're the one that's going to get it for us. OK?"

Then he turned and walked toward the bedroom door, glancing casually back over his left shoulder.

"Don't get up, babe. I know my way out."

Dani watched, mesmerized, as Nicky admired himself in the mirror by the door; patting his black, silky hair and straightening his ice-blue tie and matching handkerchief.

'Even though I hate him right now, the damn man is as handsome as ever and in perfect physical condition.'

Catching sight of Dani's reflection, watching him, Nicky flashed pearly-white teeth at her in one of his trademark, barracuda smiles. Then he cocked a thumb and two forefingers in imitation of a gun and pointed at Dani's image.

'Click!' he mimicked. "Remember, Dani. No weddings babes, or else…!"

The sound of her own front door closing hit Dani like a cold slap in the face. She stayed where she was, crying and curled up on her tousled bed, for what seemed like hours until her ribs felt as if they were crushing her chest. She had screamed into her pillows until she couldn't scream anymore. Dani's life was a total mess and completely out of her control.

Eventually, she struggled out of bed to get a glass of water from the bathroom. Standing before her open medicine cabinet, Dani casually read the label on a vial of pills. *'Tranquilizer: for the relief of anxiety, tension, fatigue and agitation'.*

After only one, tiny hesitation, Dani stuffed as many pills as she could swallow into her mouth and washed them down with water. She did that again and again until the pill bottle was empty and then she leaned against the sink, breathing heavily. Minutes passed. Slowly, Dani crumbled onto the cold, marble floor as her exhausted mind-body-and-spirit succumbed to the powerful drug. In an unexpected moment of clarity, bright images of her beloved family flashed before Dani's eyes and she struggled to get up again. *'No; this is wrong. How can I do this do them all?'*

Mustering just enough strength to crawl across to the telephone table, beside her bed, Dani pulled on the cord until it fell onto the floor.

But she didn't even have the strength to pick up the receiver and dial 911. Curling up into the fetal position around a soggy, satin pillow that had fallen off her bed, she drifted away.

***

A familiar voice began to invade Dani's new, warm and peaceful world.

"Dani, Dani! Oh, my God, Dani, what the hell have you done?"

Sam's voice kept fading in and out and then Dani recognized another voice too. It was her maid, Kay and she was muttering a funny little phrase, over and over again.

"Oh my; oh my!"

Dani couldn't feel her own body at all, but she could clearly hear the sounds of Sam and Kay all around her. Their voices grew louder and louder, until Dani was conscious enough to realize that they were holding her up between them and dragging her around her own bedroom.

"Walk, Dani; walk. You've got to walk!"

Dani didn't want to walk. She just wanted to sleep. Even working together, Sam and Kay couldn't keep Dani moving around enough to get her circulation going. In desperation, Kay recalled an old-fashioned anti-poison remedy that her mother and grandmother had used. Finding and mixing together in a blender as many ingredients as she could, Kay then helped Sam to pour the powerful brew into Dani's mouth and make her swallow. Then they waited. And they prayed.

Dani finally came around, retching and heaving, under the stinging jets of a cold shower. And Sam, fully clothed, was standing right there beside her friend, holding her up.

***

Next morning, Dani's head felt as if it was alternately shrinking and expanding. She couldn't imagine that even a binge on 'sloe-gin' could feel any worse than the way she felt right then. A lecture from Sam, on how stupid she'd been, only made Dani feel even worse. Even a more 'motherly' talk from Kay didn't help, either.

'Sleep will be the only cure', Dani decided as she drifted off in her own bed again, under the watchful eye of her faithful maid.

***

Several days later, realizing how much she really *did* want to live, Dani expressed her gratefulness to her saviors by writing Sam and Kay a check for $3,000 each.

"I thought of calling an ambulance, honest I did, but I called Tony first, instead," Sam confessed.

"And Tony said it was best if I didn't call an ambulance. He wasn't going to be dragged into no police investigation, he said, just 'cause some dumb broad tries to commit suicide. I *was* going to call 911 anyway, Dani, but then I remembered that OD's are always taken to *'Bellevue'*, instead of to a normal hospital! Hell, Dani; you aren't crazy, you're just stupid, so Kay and I decided to take care of you ourselves."

Dani squeezed Sam's hand as Kay came back to check on her mistress.

"Nothing is going to deter me from my marriage plans now, guys. I'm going to sell this house and move out of New York City for good. And HK will get me the rest of my money back, from out of the Mannellis' hands."

Kay tearfully told her mistress that she was doing the right thing. A knot of emotion tightened in Dani's throat as she realized just how dearly she loved her black housekeeper; the simple, down-to-earth woman who had always been there when Dani needed a friend.

Soon afterward Dani began shopping for her 'big day'. But she was quickly reminded that her troubles weren't *all* over yet. The first surprise came when Saks, on Fifth Avenue, called to say that Dani's $4,000 check had been returned, marked 'insufficient funds'. Dani immediately spoke to the manager, Mr. Dunicci, at her own bank and he delivered the second surprise.

"Mr. Anthony Mannelli has power of attorney over *all* of your money now, Dani and the account is set up for his signature only. Of course, we'll be happy to give you a loan for the amount you need!"

Dani immediately phoned HK at his health spa, who told her that he already had people looking into her financial problems. He would mail her a check to cover her bill at the store and she was not to worry; he just had 'a few more loose-ends to tie up', including going to Allentown to visit his elderly mother.

"Just think, my darling," HK told her, "in only three more weeks, you'll be Mrs. Howard Kline and you'll never have to worry that pretty little head of yours ever again, about anything. You'll be all mine, to love and to care for, forever. God knows, they'll be the longest three weeks of my life but I'll call you every day, I promise."

"They'll be long days for me too," Dani cut in. "I need you now more than ever, HK."

Once again Dani was comforted by his promises to take all her worries away, but not for long. After confiding to Kay what HK had said about having people looking into Dani's money problems, her maid asked a question that set Dani thinking.

"Has that crooked attorney fella' returned your car, yet, Miz Dani?"

"No," Dani answered, getting angry again. "No, he hasn't, dammit and to quote *'The Horse'*, himself, I'm about ready to 'bust some heads' about that!"

She reached for the phone again but Hokowitz' answering service said he was gone for the day.

So Dani called HK again, but was informed that he'd already left his room and gone down to dinner. She began to pace the floor nervously and Kay was worried that her mistress might do something silly again during the night. But Dani assured Kay that she would take a long, hot bath and go straight to bed with a good book.

"Well, alright, Miz Dani, as long as you're sure. I'll draw you a bath right now then, before I leave."

***

Next morning, when HK called with his usual morning love and pleasantries, Dani brought him up-to-date straightaway.

"You won't believe this, HK. It's been four lousy weeks now since Hokowitz borrowed my Cadillac for his wife to use, he said, while I was away in Yakima. Now he has the nerve to ask me to sign over the registration to him, saying I still owe him at least the car's value in legal fees! Hell, HK; only the other day I gave Nicky $50,000 to pay Hokowitz with. I'm not sure what it was for though," she conceded, meekly.

"Now, honey!" HK soothed her in his customary, calm manner. "Don't get so upset, my love. Legal fees *can* add up and I should know; I've paid enough of them in my time. But I'll give him a call right now. Don't you worry, he won't be keeping your car."

"But Nicky got mad at me for loaning Hokowitz the car in the first place and then, when we went to see Hokowitz together, Nicky denied that I ever gave him any such amount!"

"But surely Dani, you have a cancelled check to prove payment, don't you?" HK asked her, incredulously.

"No, I gave Nicky cash," she confessed, meekly, "but I challenged Hokowitz right there, in front of Nicky, about the whole transaction."

"And then Nicky told Hokowitz to bring my car back the very next day. Well, the car still hasn't arrived yet, HK."

But there was more bad news to give him and Dani braced herself before continuing.

"While I was in Hokowitz' office, I also asked him why *'Nathans',* of Miami, has gone into bankruptcy. You remember, HK; that restaurant they had me buy, down in Florida. Well, Hokowitz said it was because salaries were too high; the 'officers' alone were making $50,000 a month, he told me!"

"Who are the officers, Dani?"

"I don't know, HK; he didn't tell me!" Dani was beginning to get very frustrated at her inability to understand finance.

"I really think you should bring someone down to check out all this mess *before* we get married, HK. It's beginning to look like I'm losing everything!"

Dani began to cry.

"There, there my darling. Come on now, pull yourself together. You're going to spoil your looks with all these tears!"

HK put on his most mollifying, boardroom voice.

"I admit it does all sound very fishy, but this Agent McMahon I told you about, from the FBI, is already looking into it for us and he wants us to leave it all in their hands."

"The only things I want my darling fiancée to worry about are buying herself a whole new wardrobe and having the house all ready to close up when I get over there."

"But when will you move your things out of Rochester, HK?"

Dani was still not completely calmed.

"The only possessions I have to show for all those years of marriage are my books, my briefcase and me! I haven't told you this before, Dani, but for several years now I've been living in the garage of our marital home, with only my stereo for company. And I had to fight Gladys to keep even that!"

Dani was astounded. "I can't believe that with all your millions you ever had to live like that?"

"Well, it was my own choice, my darling, but I won't be doing it anymore!"

They talked on happily for a while longer about their wedding arrangements; HK insisting that Dani take everything in her stride and not worry. He told her that his last meeting before leaving Allentown, would be with his Board-of-Directors. That would be the first the Company would know of HK's forthcoming marriage!

When he was assured that Dani understood everything, HK told her again that he loved her and finally hung up. She had been aware of clicking on the line all during their conversation and, after hanging up, Dani called out.

"Sam, were you listening in, on the extension?"

"Well, I did cut in a few times" Sam confessed. "You were on the phone for well over an hour and I needed to call the Club. I haven't seen Tony in so long I feel like a virgin again!"

"Have you told Tony about my wedding plans, Sam?"

"Well, yeah, last night. He just asked a few questions about your honeymoon plans and where did HK's mother live; how long would he be up there visiting her. You know, dumb stuff like that. He didn't seem at all upset though."

"And did you tell him about my car, too?"

"Yes, he said you should get it back this afternoon. Or maybe he meant tomorrow afternoon?" Sam finished, lamely."

"Sam, what did Tony *really* tell you?" Dani demanded to know.

"Oh, all right then! He said, *'tell the fuckin' broad she'll get the car back by Monday'*."

Dolores J. Guthrie

Chapter 12

Dani was awakened by movement inside her room. It was Kay, opening the drapes. As the maid returned with a breakfast tray and slid it onto her lap, Dani stretched lazily

"Miss Dani, you sure were sleepin' awful fitful last night; a tossin' and a turnin' the whole night you were. Why, ah never seen the likes of it. Ah knows it's a bit early still, but I thought you'd be better off awake."

"You're right, Kay, I did have some horrible dreams. In one, I dreamed that my father was reaching out to me but our fingers never quite touched. It was awful. I wonder why I'd dream something like that. Maybe it's because of having so much on my mind, lately."

Sam came into the room, rubbing at her own eyes and complaining about the ungodly hour.

"You sure are awake early, Dani girl."

She sat on the side of the bed and poked around at the tasty-looking bacon on Dani's plate.

"Sam, do you want Kay to bring you some breakfast in here, with me? I'd like to talk to you."

"Sure, why not? But its coffee I need first, please," Sam said, smiling beseechingly at Dani's agreeable housekeeper.

After Kay left the room, Dani confided in her friend.

"Sam, I had some terrible dreams last night and since then I've been thinking back to our trip to Atlantic City."

"What about it?"

"Well, you remember that palm reader on the Boardwalk, the one that read both our palms?"

"Sure, it's not easy to forget someone who tells me that my first-born will be handicapped and that I'll commit suicide before I'm forty!"

"Well, my reading was just as crazy, Sam. He said that if I stayed on my present path, it would lead to my death within six months but that if I moved to a new environment, I would live. My numbers were in threes, do you remember? Like, two-times three makes six and so on."

"Sam, there are seven 'threes' in the upcoming year of 1966! The clairvoyant said I'd meet a fair haired man in the New Year and that three months later I'd marry him. In the sixth year, 1972, he told me that I'd be alone again but still alive, having lost a great wealth and that then I would be poor for a short time. Three years after that, I would marry a red-skinned man; my true and last love. The fortune-teller also said that *'my moccasins would walk in many lands and that there would be many tears and an abundance of wealth'.*"

Dani looked solemnly into her friend's eyes.

"Yes, I remember all that," Sam assured her. "But, didn't he also see a man crying and say that someone you loved would be dead within three months?"

"Oh; I'd forgotten all about that!" Dani gasped in horror.

"My god Sam; it's been three months now! I don't know who he could have meant, though. Everyone we know is in good health?"

Dani shook her head, deep in thought. Then she laughed out loud at her own superstitions.

"Oh, what the hell Sam! Besides, HK and I are getting married on August the first, so that blows the fair-haired, Greek-god theory out the window as well, doesn't it?"

***

Kay was busy baking pies. Sam was getting the liquor and beer stocks ready and Dani was elbow-deep in making her Mom's famous 'potato-salad-and-baked beans' recipes. The weather was perfect for a July 4th cel-ebration aboard the 'Danielle One'; Dani's 28-foot luxury cruiser. JR, was home from Valley Forge Military Academy for the holidays and he had already left for Sheepshead Bay to get the boat ready to sail. He usually brought home a buddy or two at weekends anyway and Kay always kept them all well fed.

Dani was proud of her freckle-faced, red-haired, handsome cadet, who towered over his mother at a straight-backed, well-proportioned six-foot, five-inches. Her 'baby' was definitely all grown up now and had the girls swarming around him. JR would often look down at Dani, grin and say, "Mom, the girls just love me!"

Amidst all these festive preparations, the phone rang. It was HK, calling, to wish Dani a happy Fourth-of-July from his country club, up in Allentown.

"Hi, honey! Boy, it's a hot one today! I just came off the 9th hole but I decided not to play the back nine today. I want to save all my energy for my 'queen' when I get there. Guess where I'm calling you from, my darling."

"I couldn't begin to guess."

"From the men's locker room and I'm stark naked!" HK giggled down the phone line. "I wanted to get a rub down, but I can't seem to find the attendant anywhere around."

"Oh, my darling, Dani," he continued, "I'm so excited and I feel just great. Now, I want you to tell Nicky that this is to be your last weekend working at the Club. I've already spoken to him, but you should remind him anyway, Dani"

"Just think, my love; in three days' time I'll be leaving Rochester for good to begin our beautiful, new life together."

"Oh, HK; I can't believe it's finally going to happen, either. I'm excited, too, but I wish you could be here with us all today. JR's home, with some of his friends and we're taking the boat out later. We're having fried chicken, potato salad and all the works!"

There was no response but Dani could hear rustling noises down the phone line.

"HK, are you there? Hello?"

There were more noises at the other end and then Dani heard HK yell out.

"What the fuck! God dammit! No...! Somebody, help me!"

Frantically, Dani screamed into the phone.

"HK, where are you? What club are you at?"

There was simply silence; more terrifying to Dani than strange noises. Then someone hung up the phone at HK's end and Dani shrieked in panic.

"Sam! Kay! Something's happened to HK! He was struggling with someone and calling for help and then the line went dead. What can I do? I don't even know where he is," Dani howled, helplessly.

HK's office was closed for the holiday weekend and she couldn't even remember where his son lived. She knew that HK had planned to be in the offices on Monday morning because he wasn't leaving to meet Dani until the Tuesday. All she could do was wait. And weep.

***

It was a long weekend of not knowing but at precisely nine o' clock the following Monday morning, Dani called HK's office.

"Hello, this is Dani Sutton. I've been trying to locate Mr. Kline all weekend. Have you heard from him this morning?"

HK's secretary burst into tears at the sound of Dani's voice.

"Dani, you mean you haven't heard?"

"Heard what?"

"Poor Mr. Kline is dead," the secretary whispered."

Dani's throat went dry and her body felt frozen. She could barely understand what the girl was saying through the tears they were both shedding.

"Poor Mr. Kline," his secretary wailed, "but he knew better! The doctor told him that he wasn't supposed to take saunas; not with his high blood pressure and bad heart."

"What are you talking about?" Dani gasped. "HK never took saunas."

"Well, that's where they found him Dani, in the sauna in the men's locker room. Lord knows how long he'd been there, but he died later that afternoon of a cerebral hemorrhage!"

Dani couldn't believe what she was hearing. Sobbing and unable to speak any more, she silently hung up the phone. Her beloved HK was gone. Another of Dani's petals had fallen.

***

By early afternoon the news had spread and people began calling Dani to offer help. Even Karl Hokowitz and his family showed up to return

Dani's car, saying she'd probably need it for the funeral. They were acting very strangely too; going through Dani's home as if it were their own and opening drawers, touching her things. Dani was completely taken aback by Mrs. Hokowitz' announcement that she would accompany her to Allentown, for HK's funeral. To Dani, they were behaving like vultures, ready to pick at her bones. She felt so helpless without HK.

Dani retreated into the safety of her bedroom and Sam followed.

"Can I do anything, Dani?"

"Oh Sam; HK was so close to happiness after all those years of hard work. It's so unfair. I just *know* that someone was there, in the locker room at that club, to keep HK and me from getting married. But I don't know how I can prove it and who the hell would listen to me, anyway?"

"Dani, stop right there. Those kinds of thoughts will only cause you more trouble than you can handle. I agree that something's definitely wrong and I don't like it any more than you do, but you and I could end up just like HK if we start getting too smart."

Dani half nodded, whilst blowing her nose. She knew Sam was right but didn't want to admit it.

"But I'll be damned if Mrs. Hokowitz is going with me to HK's funeral!" Dani stated, indignantly. "That woman has got some damn nerve. She didn't even know HK! You'll go with me, won't you, Sam? Just you, JR, and me. I don't want to tell Nicky where we're going, either. Please don't say anything to *anyone* at the Club about all this, *please* Sam."

***

They had deliberately set off early, but the Pennsylvania turnpike was already burning hot with summer heat, intensified by slow moving traffic. Dani was driving, but was so distraught that she missed their Allentown exit and her mistake took them twenty miles out of their way. Realizing that she was becoming a danger to herself and all those around her, Dani handed the driving over to JR. When they reached Allentown city limits, he pulled into a gas station to get directions to the funeral home.

"Oh, you folks must be here for Mr. Kline's funeral. Lotsa people have been asking me for them same directions today. Well thought of in this here town, Mr. HK was."

As he slowly cleaned their windshield, the elderly man droned on.

"HK's financial knowledge helped a lot o' folk 'round here make some good and fair investments. Made millionaires out of lotsa folk in Allentown, HK did, and my uncle was one of them. Yes siree; ol' HK talked my uncle into buying a hundred shares of 'Aloid', back in '42. Now, he's my boss. My uncle, that is, not HK!"

The old man chuckled at his own humor but Dani's mind was screaming.

'Will the old fella never shut up?'

JR thanked the old man and drove on to a hotel near the funeral home so they could all freshen up. Dani decided to call HK's son.

"Hello, Tom? This is Dani Sutton, your father's fiancé. You *do* know who I am, don't you Tom?"

"Yes Dani, my father spoke of you many times and I'm looking forward to meeting you. Are you in town now?"

"Yes, I'm here with a friend and my son."

"Well," Tom spoke with a slight quiver in his voice, "the service starts at 10:30 am tomorrow. I expect you'll be able to get here by then?"

"I'll be there Tom, don't you worry, but won't it be awkward with your mother being there too?"

"No, it shouldn't be a problem. She won't be told who you are."

"Tom, HK's name and his honor are very important to me. I know that the people of this town loved and respected your father very much and I wouldn't want to do anything that might affect his reputation. I think it's best if I wait until after the service and then pay my own respects privately, when everyone else has gone. HK will know that I'm there with him," Dani added, quietly.

"Thank you very much for your thoughtfulness, Dani. Will you come to Rochester later, for the reading of the will?"

"I understand my father set aside a trust fund or something, for you and your son" Tom paused and took a deep breath, before continuing. "Dani, I want to thank you, just between ourselves, for making Pop's last days so happy. I hadn't seen him so happy for a very long time."

Dani thanked him, but she was suddenly reminded of the way in which HK had died. She couldn't help but think of the Mannelli's and of how her previously vague fears of that Family were coming more and more into focus.

***

Dani, JR and Sam found the large cemetery easily enough, but it was very cold and forbidding. They had all been looking for a huge funeral canopy, something worthy of HK. Dani couldn't understand why the site was only a fresh pile of naked dirt, with no name, no great wreaths of flowers to show respect for such a wonderful man. There was only one spray of flowers there – hers - with a simple card that read, *'I love you, from your 'queen'.'*

Dani fell to her knees and looked up toward the sky, unaware that her fingers were absently playing with the spray of flowers. She pulled off all the petals, one-by-one and let them float away in the breeze.

They tumbled across her lap and spread out over HK's lonely grave like snow-white tears, as Dani wept for what could have been.

Dolores J. Guthrie

Chapter 13

Dani stared through falling mist at the darkening sky. The whine of the northwest-wind pained her tortured heart like a saw blade. JR gently reached down to touch his mother's arm.

"Come on, Mom, we should go. It's starting to rain now."

Dani stood motionless by HK's sparse grave, watching the remaining rose petals fluttering away in the wind. She imagined them soaring up to him in some faraway galaxy. At last, smiling up at the handsome young man beside her, Dani straightened her shoulders and took a long, deep breath.

"Yes, we'd better go. There's nothing left for me here."

She took one last glance at the barren grave, knowing that HK would always be with her, wherever she went.

JR drove. It was just as well, because the turnpike was a complete blur to Dani as the three of them headed back to New York City. All was silence, except for the *crump, crump* of the car's windshield wipers as they skimmed back and forth. Dani's mind was on fire as her vision of the world slowly went in and out of focus through the windscreen. She wished it were all just a bad dream, but knew that it wasn't. It was her nightmare.

Dani looked out of the side window, searching the dark sky for comfort but she couldn't find any. She rubbed at her forehead and cleared her raw throat, in an effort to control the tears before she spoke.

"Dammit, this has been one helluva day and tomorrow isn't going to be any better. I feel as though Tony, Nicky and Hokowitz are all trying to trap me. I need to get myself a good lawyer; someone who can help me to plan a proper plan of attack on *all* of them."

"Oh, hell, Dani," Sam cut in, impatiently, "why don't you just shut up! No one is out to get you *or* your money. That's all you think about lately and now HK isn't around anymore to pick up the pieces. Just give Nicky a bit more consideration, will ya'. The two of you own a corporation together, so you'd better just..."

JR interrupted and tried to cool things down.

"All right you girls, just put a lid on it! It's been a long day and we're all tired. We should stop somewhere for the night and finish this journey tomorrow. Is this place OK, Mom?" he asked, stopping the car in front of *'Howard Johnson's'* diner.

"Sure, why not!" Dani agreed. The idea of a drink, some dinner and some sleep seemed far better than fighting each other, the rain and the traffic.

A drink at the bar revived their spirits a little but later, as they waited for the waiter to serve their meal, Dani and Sam were well settled into their own, private reveries. The whole meal passed in silence until after dessert when JR, not liking the tense atmosphere, leaned forward.

"To change the topic of the day, it's been rumored around College that the last phone call that Marilyn Monroe made, the night she died, was to President Kennedy supposedly crying over his baby brother, Bobby."

"That's strange!" Sam spoke without moving her body at all. "I heard that Marilyn was the President's girl."

"Well, the FBI has been keeping it all hushed up, naturally." JR commented.

"Well, it doesn't surprise me, JR," Dani joined in. "At the Club one night, a while ago, some guy was boasting about being with the FBI and he told me that same story, just before hustling me for a date!"

JR realized that it felt good to be in the company of two beautiful women, even if one of them *was* his mother!

"Don't get me wrong, Mom, I'm not knocking JFK. I think history will prove that he was one of this country's best Presidents and I'm damn proud to be an American!"

JR was emphatic.

"But it sure seems to me that the people of this country had better wake up, before it's too late. There's a struggle comin' soon, between Capitalism and Socialism. Our own Government will eventually have total control over all production, all distribution of goods and services, all banks, credit cards, hospitals! In other words, they'll control everything and everybody. It could even have us under the rule of another Caesar-type leader, if we're not careful."

"JR," Dani began, "I love you, son, but isn't this all a bit heavy? You know I don't understand about politics, or about things like socialism. And even if I did, I'd be just like Scarlet O'Hara in 'Gone with the Wind' - I'd worry about it another day!"

"OK, Mom, but just answer me this. Why are all the *really* wealthy people, folk like the Hunts, the Rockefellers, etc., why are *they* all for Capitalism?"

"You mark my words," JR went on, confidently. "Someday, instead of sharing the wealth, the wealthy will just be getting' richer and paying lower taxes while the poor will be getting poorer and paying *more* taxes."

"My god, JR, you sound like a real politician," Sam commented. "But tell me, isn't young David Eisenhower going to school at Valley Forge right now. Is he in your class?"

"He's a senior, Sam, so he's not in my classes. But I see him around campus, pulling duties just like every other cadet."

JR turned back to his mother.

"Mom, you remember that picture you gave me? The one of you wearing that long, black dress.

Dani nodded, sipping her after-dinner drink.

"Well, I hung it on my wall in the dorm, but they made me take it down. No one would believe that it was my mother! And when I complained, I got put on garbage detail. Every time a senior cadet came by, I had to sound off, saying, *'Bong, Bong, my name is Lurch.'* I wonder what detail they'd have given me if I'd told them what I *really* thought."

They had all finally relaxed after the traumatic day and were having a good time when their hostess announced that the dining room would soon be closing.

'Time to hit the road back to reality again', Dani thought, wearily, as they each made their way up to their rooms.

$$***$$

As they got closer to New York City and drove through the Brooklyn-Battery tunnel, a faint smell of the sea, mixed with the sulfurous smell of fuel, began to seep into their car. Dani felt nauseous. The fatigue of the last few days was weighing heavily upon her. She took a deep breath, to settle her stomach, but it came out as an audible sigh causing JR to briefly glance at his mother in the rearview mirror. Dani never noticed; she was too busy wondering if she would be able to retain her prized home, 'Hearthstone Manor'.

HK had asked that Dani name their mansion 'Hearthstone Manor', because of all its marble fireplaces, staircases and the natural stone structure of the whole building. It seemed that the property also had a haunted history though; part of which was that it had once been home to a 550-pound gorilla of incalculable strength!

Dani managed a smile as she recalled the old story.

'Not even the animal's keeper, who every day for years had fed and cared for it, dared to get close to that animal, especially after the poor man was viciously attacked by it.'

The story of Dani's New York home had begun back in 1937.

'John and Henry Ringling-North, who jointly owned 'Barnum and Bailey's Circus', were staying at the Ritz Hotel, in New York, when a lady telephoned. She claimed to be the owner of a fully grown gorilla, named Buddy and offered to sell him for $10,000.

Naturally, the Ringling Brothers smelled a bargain and immediately took a taxi to Brooklyn, to her elegant, water-front, brownstone mansion. Mrs. Lintz, a small, middle-aged lady, led them through her dimly lit house and out to the back yard. Behind empty horse stables, they entered a shed, permeated with the heavy odor of wet fur. The gorilla's keeper, Richard Kroener, sat reading a book by the light of a dim lamp hanging from a nail. At the far end of the shed, a huge coffin-like box had been constructed, braced by heavy timbers from both the ceiling and the side walls.

Mrs. Lintz informed the Ringling brothers that she had been an ocean-liner passenger many years earlier and had heard about an infant gorilla being shipped from Africa. She had taken an interest in 'Buddy', and learned that he had been badly burned and disfigured from acid being thrown into his face by a sadistic crew member. Mrs. Lintz purchased the baby gorilla and brought him home. Her husband was a plastic surgeon and had attempted to repair Buddy's face, but without great success. The fearsome go-rilla's face peered out at the two men after the iron bar door of its steel box was raised.

As the animal grew older and stronger, Mrs. Lintz told them that she had become increasingly afraid of Buddy. Once, he had got out of his cage and come into her bedroom. Mrs. Lintz awak-ened to find him touching her hair and that was when the gorilla's cage was strengthened!

When Buddy roared and beat upon his chest with his im-mense hands, it sounded like a cannon firing. On hearing such a terrifying noise, her neighbors had become concerned about what went on behind the mass of overgrown ivy that hugged Mrs. Lintz's massive walls and gates. Buddy had never left the grounds at any time, but they were fearful that the animal would one day get loose and terrorize the neighborhood in the dark of night. So the neigh-bors were not at all unhappy to hear that Buddy was to be sold to the circus.

Buddy was renamed as 'Gargantua, the Great,' and billed as 'The world's most terrifying living creature; the largest and fierc-est gorilla ever to be brought before the eyes of civilized man'.

Gargantua made his first appearance in a 1938 pageant and was a prominent feature of the circus world until his death. He died in Miami at the age of twenty-one years and by then the ani-mal had a majestic, silver coat of thick hair. Dr. Yerkes, of Yale University, performed an autopsy and prepared the animal's skel-eton to be displayed in the University's own museum.

Gargantua, in death, had become a 'Yale man!'

***

Aside from worrying about keeping Hearthstone Manor, Dani was also thinking about her other money problems. Now that she didn't have HK to take care of things for her, she would have to play the Mannellis' devious games by herself. But her reveries ended abruptly when JR stopped their car at the white-stone, pillared entrance to her New York home. They had expected to arrive to an empty house but dozens of people were going in and out, unloading two, huge catering trucks. Dani scrambled out of the car and stalked up to one of the men.

"What the hell is going on here? What is all this?" she demanded, sweeping the scene with a wave of one hand.

The man turned to Dani with a grin that showed yellow-stained teeth. A half-chewed cigar was stuck to his lip like a permanent growth. The man chuckled and scratched at his head.

"I hear the rich broad who lives here is having a big celebration. A 'wake', or something, I think."

Furiously, Dani turned to JR and Sam.

"Can you believe this? Am I dreaming?"

Dani strode into the house and found Kay in the basement party room, hands on hips and shaking her head in dismay. When she saw Dani, Kay ran over, her voice shrill with emotion.

"Miss Dani! Ah sure is glad you done come home! Ah's jus' 'bout gone crazy with all this going on."

Kay wiped sweat from her forehead with the back of one hand and rubbed it down her apron.

"That Mr. Nicky, he said you knowed all 'bout this here party. But, ah tol' him I didn't know anythin' 'bout it, not with your mournin' for poor Mr. Kline an' all!"

"Calm down, Kay; I'll find out what's going on here. Where's Nicky now?"

"Out by the pool, telling those cooks how to roast a whole pig the last ah saw, Miz Dani."

Nicky seemed in complete control as Dani strode toward him with fire in her eyes. He arrogantly flashed her a beautiful smile and playfully pulled her toward him.

"Welcome home, baby! I've missed you."

Their eyes met as he held Dani tightly and, for a second, the world suddenly rushed by her at top speed. She tried to fight off the frightening panic that was overwhelming her and pushed Nicky away.

"What the hell's going on here, Nicky? I'm not in the mood for any damn party! How could you do this to me?"

She picked up a dish of antipasto and threw it in his direction, but Nicky ducked and it splattered all over the pig that was turning on the spit. Stepping backwards, Dani tripped over the pool-man and overbalanced, pulling him into the pool, along with her and the bottle of chemical he had been pouring. Sputtering and trying not to scream, Dani began to cry. Through her blurred eyes the whole scene looked like a volcano erupting. Chemicals were bubbling violently; spewing noxious fumes and covering the surface of the water with a green, oily film.

Nicky reached down to pull Dani out, but as he gripped her hand she gave a jerk that brought him into the water too. Surfacing and gasping for air, Nicky sputtered.

"What the fuck d'ya do that for? Here I am, trying to be a nice guy an' throwing you a surprise party to make you feel better, an' this is the way you thank me? Just like a dumb broad!"

JR and Sam rolled with laughter as they stood on the sidelines, surveying the chaos.

"Come on Mom, don't be a spoil sport, let's have a party. There's no need to let all this good food go to waste and some guests have already arrived, anyhow."

"Oh my God, where are they?"

"They're in the bar, getting drinks." Nicky held his hand out to Dani and smiled. "Truce?"

Kay was still shaking her head as she helped organize a bunch of men to begin cleaning the oil slick from the pool. In water-logged clothes and shoes, Dani and Nicky squeaked their way to the master wing to shower and change.

'Keep cool and play the game', Dani kept telling herself as she showered. She shampooed her hair and was just beginning to settle down when Nicky stepped into the shower behind her. He began rubbing shampoo over her nipples, which soon became as hard as marbles. Then he pulled her down onto the floor of the shower. Dani grabbed at his hair, pulling his lips close to hers.

"Damn you, Nicky Mannelli, when this party is over we need to talk?"

"Dani, just shut the fuck up, will ya'! Ah shit! See what you fuckin' did with your fuckin' mouth flappin'?"

Nicky looked downward in distress. "I lost my goddam hard-on."

"Great!" Dani grinned, sadistically. "Now maybe we can get dressed, or have you forgotten about your party guests?"

"Naw, I ain't forgotten the fuckin' party guests!"

Nicky muttered angrily as he dried and dressed. Then, at the bedroom door, he turned and flashed his famous smile again, giving Dani the finger.

"Gotcha!"

Angrily, she hurled an expensive perfume bottle across the room. It missed its intended target and shattered against the bedroom wall and Dani watched in horror as the precious liquid ran in sparkling, fragrant rivers down her silk-damask wallpaper.

"You bastard!"

Chapter 14

HK was gone for good, she knew that now. Alone and beyond pain, Dani wandered in a world of faceless people, reaching out to them only to find more, dark numbness. *'If this is my life, I don't want to know it.'* In her mournful stupor, she let the sunny, summer days, with all their happy outside activities, pass her by. Things she had once enjoyed with child-like gusto no longer brought a smile to Dani's beautiful face.

One morning, she looked outside to find that the Ming trees in her garden were already leafless. Wondering, in shock, where time had gone to, Dani's thoughts turned to the approaching fall season. Reality began to slowly pull her back and created in Dani the maternal desire to see her son, JR. So she called him, at Valley Forge Academy, to let him know that she had packed her valise and was already on her way!

Dani deliberately chose the winding back roads for her drive so that she could relax and enjoy the sights, especially the trees. The stunning colors of the foliage, the weathered-stone walls that lined the roads and the rustic bridges that crossed over natural brooks all gave Dani the feeling of driving through a 'greeting-card' landscape. Amid such spectacular surroundings, the numbness of grief was slowly leaving her soul. For the first time in months, she felt that her life might actually become worthwhile again.

When Dani arrived at the Academy, JR greeted his mother with a big hug.

"Gee, Mom, you sure surprised me when you called to say you were coming. I thought you wouldn't feel up to the journey just yet. But we'll show these guys around here now, won't we?"

A few seconds passed before Dani realized what JR was talking about. Then she remembered their conversation on the day of HK's funeral, when JR told her that no-one believed it was his mother in the picture she'd sent him!

Dani really enjoyed watching the cadets 'full dress' parades and all the other ceremonies over the weekend, especially when JR received a medal for his marksmanship. And, at the traditional 'Mother-and-Son Ball' on the final evening, they proved to any non-believers that JR's mother was indeed the 'lady-in-the-picture'. Made them both feel on top of the world!

As Dani prepared to leave after the long weekend, JR begged to be allowed to leave school so that he could take care of her. But, for once, Dani was determined to do things right.

"JR, you know how much it meant to HK for you to get an education. No matter what happens, we can't let him down. You *must* finish your education, honey."

Reluctantly, JR agreed. Standing tall and straight, he gave his mother a smile and a smart salute as she drove away. Watching him in her rearview mirror as she passed through the Academy gates, tears of pride trickled down Dani's cheeks. *'I will cherish this moment forever.'*

***

November found Dani taking solitary drives out to Long Island, in the wee morning hours. She took lonely walks along the seashore, watching the seagulls diving for their breakfast. Then that would make Dani think of food and she would head over to Sheepshead Bay, for steamed, little-neck clams. On one of those walks, Dani's mind flew out over the tide too, like the seagulls swooping low in search of their morning feast. She pondered on how strange were the twists-of-life that had haunted her so far. As a child, Dani had loved her older brother, Hal, so deeply that she would have climbed mountains to get his approval and recognition. She knew that Hal loved her anyway, but Dani constantly tried to prove to him that she wasn't just some dumb girl. That she could do anything her brother could do, if only he would let her tag along with him and the other boys!

She leaned down to pick up a handful of clean, cool pebbles. Brushing the sand away absent-mindedly, she put the pebbles into her jacket pocket and then climbed to the top of a huge, flat rock. Dani lay down and adjusted her body for comfort; on the sunny side and out of the gentle, but chill, morning breeze. She lay there for hours, skimming her gathered pebbles into the surf, one at a time.

With the rhythmic calling of the seabirds and the gentle *swooshing* of the waves, Dani's mind drifted back to her years in McKinley Grade school, where so many boys had tried to make advances to her. Big brother, Hal was always there to put them in their place; always there to protect Dani from the world, in much the same way that HK had always been there for her. Until she lost him, last summer!

Dani closed her eyes and drew in several deep breaths of salty, air. She carried on remembering and a smile crossed her face as her mind drifted even farther back; back to when she would run through ripening cornfields with big brother Hal, playing cowboy and Indians. Dani was always the one who got caught and burned at the stake; or hung by the townspeople; or tortured in some evil, homemade laboratory.

'And, come to think of it, wasn't I always the first to try out any new invention that my big brother could dream up?'

Dani recalled when she had been too afraid to go to their outhouse by herself; how brother Hal had bundled her up so she'd keep warm and then waited outside for her, so the 'boogie-man' wouldn't get her. Yet, if Dani didn't obey his every command, she would have to do all Hal's chores for a week or he would tell the boogie man to get her!

Dani never did figure out how to get the best of her adored big brother. Over the years, she'd mowed lawns, ironed clothes and babysat; anything to make extra money. She would save up to buy Christmas presents for everyone in the family and every year she'd sign their cards 'from Dani and Hal', even though her brother never contributed a cent of his own money!

As long as she did things for him, Hal let his little sister hang around with him and noticed that she existed. But to him and his friends, Dani was always just a dumb girl and a dreamer at that.

So, Dani played with her dolls, fantasizing that one day she'd be a famous ballerina, dancing in Europe. She loved to sing so much that she joined every church in town. Hal teased her, saying that every time he turned around, he had to save Dani from another baptism! He called his sister, little 'Miss Hollywood'. Dani even dreamed that when she eventually met her own 'Prince Charming', he would look just like her big brother.

But she truly believed that she had broken her brother's heart. Right about the time that fourteen-year-old Dani got herself pregnant and was forced to marry Hal's best friend, Johnny Kingston, Hal had enlisted in the Navy and gone away to war. Dani's life was never the same after that. Daily, she prayed for Hal's safe return but knew in her heart that she had lost her hero. As she lay there reminiscing, it struck Dani that she had always felt a desperate need to please her menfolk or risk losing them, just as she had lost Hal.

Her mind wandered forward to the men in her recent life, Nicky, in particular. She hadn't seen *him* since the day of that awful, surprise party and wondered if HK's death and the manner of his dying, had left Nicky feeling too remorseful and ashamed to come visit her. Dani also pondered whether Tony had learned of her suspicions, about how and why HK had died. Just the thought of Tony Mannelli knowing her thoughts sent a cold chill through Dani's body.

"Shit, I hope not!" she said aloud.

✳✳✳

December came all too suddenly for Dani. The snow was piled high out in the pool area before she even noticed. Then Kay began fussing over Dani's summer clothes, saying she was sending them all to the cleaners.

"Jes' in case, Miz Dani! You sure do need to take a trip to find some sunshine; get some color back into yo' face and some happiness in yo' life."

"You're right Kay," Dani agreed, looking down at her pale skin. "As soon as Christmas is over I'll go down to Bermuda. I'm as white as a ghost."

Kay paused in her activities and expressed some old fashioned, moral concerns.

"Do y'all think it be proper, Miz Dani, ah mean a' comin' an' a' goin' to all them ritzy hotels', all by yo' lonesome?"

Dani gazed at the warm, loving woman that she had grown to care for so dearly. Yet she realized that she knew very little about either Kay, *or* her family back in the Bronx.

'Have I really been so self-absorbed that I've let the best things in my life pass by unnoticed?'

But before Dani could answer her own question, Sam staggered into the bedroom. Her face was completely drained of its natural color. Dani watched as her friend laid a towel on the emerald-green satin, Louis XIV loveseat, before carefully lowering her shaking frame down into a half-sitting, half-lying position.

"Don't say a word, Dani. I know I'm crazy to even think that Tony Mannelli would ever leave his wife for me, even though she has never conceived, nor even *tried* to give him a son."

"My God, Sam, you look like death warmed over. What on earth's happened to you?"

Sam eased herself back against the antique upholstery.

"I've just aborted my third fetus, that's what; this time for that bastard Tony. But if he wants to be a 'Don-without-sons', then I guess that's his problem."

"You know what that slob has had the nerve to do, Dani?"

Dani shook her head, mystified.

"Well, the other night we were out to dinner and Tony introduced me to some guy called Ralph Martini. Very handsome he was, with lots of charisma and he reminded me of a young Dean Martin."

Sam winked at Dani before carrying on with her tale.

"Anyway, those two men calmly sat there and told me that the next morning this Ralph was going to take me to some doctor for an abortion. Tony then said I should take a two-week vacation and then never look back on my relationship with him, or speak of him, to anyone. Ever again! As soon as I feel better, I'm s'posed to start dating this 'Ralph' and then - get this - once we're *married*, Tony will give the two of us our own club to manage, in Queens!"

Dani was horrified.

"Sam, you're being a fool! Tony's not giving you anything, he's just using you. It's like putting yourself in a glass jar on a shelf and having Ralph keep the lid on!"

"Hey, you're not telling me anything I don't already know, Dani. This is Tony's way of getting me off his back and yet still having control over me, forever, I know that. But I don't have much of a choice do I? I know too much about his business. Tony can't just toss me to the dogs, not unless he's backed into a real bad corner."

"So are you *really* going to marry this stranger then, Sam?"

"Hell yes, Dani, you should see the man. He's big *and* beautiful. And besides, you know what we think they did to HK? I've been around Tony for too long. I know what he's capable of when something, or someone, gets in his way."

Sam hesitated.

"I've known for a while that I was on my way out, Dani. I guess getting pregnant was just the last straw for Tony."

"Sam, you're a complete nut, but I must say that anyone is an improvement over Tony Mannelli," Dani offered. "Do you think maybe Tony has a new girlfriend and that's the real reason he wants you gone?"

"I don't know about that, girl but I *do* know why you haven't seen Nicky since HK died."

Right then, Kay strolled into the bedroom pushing a trolley, filled with food for brunch. She had obviously overheard quite a lot of the girls' conversation because she kept shaking her head, back-and-forth and clicking her tongue.

"Buzzards and chickens always come home t' roost and yo' bad deeds is gonna haunt you, Miz Sam."

"What do you mean?" Sam snapped.

"I mean, gittin rid of yo' baby," Kay replied, with another click of her tongue.

"Well, everythin' that goes around in the dark ain't no Santa Claus, either," Sam threw back.

"What on earth does that have to do with giving up a baby, Sam?" Dani was bewildered.

"It means, don't hit a hornet's nest with a short stick," Sam countered and then they all started laughing at their own nonsense. Dani was happy for any change in the mood of the room as Kay left them both to enjoy their lunch.

"Sam, what was it you were going to tell me earlier, about Nicky not seeing me since the day of the funeral 'party'?"

"Oh, right! Well, *he's* the one with a new girlfriend, not Tony! He's got himself an Oriental dancer and her name's 'Hot Kimchee'. It's rumored that she gives a fantastic rub down and great 'head,' if you know what I mean. You know how much Nicky loves his massages, Dani."

"Tell me about it," Dani said, ruefully. "You have no idea how this news makes me feel, Sam. I went into the Club the other day, to let them know that I was ready to go back to work and Frankie told me that I didn't have a job to go back to! He said I'd been replaced by a Korean girl, would you believe it. Is *she* the one, Sam?"

"Dani, whad'ya' mean, *'how it makes you feel'*; you haven't worked in over five months! They couldn't wait forever, you know." Sam had carefully ignored Dani's final question.

"Well, I don't care! With all the money the Mannellis have taken from me in the past, I probably own the goddam joint by now, anyway," Dani snapped. Then she remembered something.

"Oh, while I was in the City the other day, I went into my bank."

"Which bank?" Sam queried.

"You know, *Tony's* bank. I asked to speak to anyone except that Mr. Dunicci, 'cos I know he works for the 'Family' and not for *my* best interests, at least not as far as I can see. And who d'ya think came out to talk to me? None other than Mr. Dunicci himself, that's who. Another man was with him, but he didn't say anything, he just stood there."

"Dunicci explained again that my funds are tied up in a special account under Mr. Tony Mannelli's control and that if I need money, the bank will make me a loan. I just happened to have these with me so I showed them to him." Dani pulled a bunch of papers from her purse.

"Where did you get these?"

"They came last week, in the mail."

"But who sent them?"

"I've no idea! The only one who could have known about this was HK, but he sure as hell didn't send them, did he? Anyway, I didn't question where they came from, I just accepted them as a gift from heaven!"

Sam took the papers from Dani's outstretched hand and began to read.

"To whom this may concern:

"Howard S. Kline has bequeathed Danielle Sutton, the following 'Xenon stock'. Total shares 7,500

RC7U 2768*	in trust 1,000
RC/U 2770*	in trust 1,000
RC/U 2807	Sold 1,000
RC/U 2868/69/70	Sold 2,500
RC/U (numbers withheld)	2,000"

Dani passed over another piece of official looking paper.

"Sam, here's a letter from HK, saying that he received the shares I'd returned to him, the ones with his own name certified and transferring them to me. Now it seems that the estate of Howard Kline has misplaced these two certificates at the National Rochester Trust Company!"

Sam was a fast reader and she began to bombard Dani with questions.

"Dani, look at this other stock certificate copy. Do you have any idea who the hell 'Baggett & Co.' are? And who's 'a nominee' of the Prince National Bank of New York'?"

"I've no idea, Sam. That's definitely not my signature, but it's been guaranteed by Tony's bank manager, Dunicci!

"It looks to me like the 'Family' has either stolen my 2,000 shares or kept the money, if they've sold the stocks. I sure as hell don't have either the stocks or the cash! How can a bank do something like this? Don't they have to protect their depositors?"

"Dani, I don't know, but it sure looks like the Mannellis have got you good. What are you going to do about it?"

"Hell, I don't know. I'll worry about it all tomorrow, as usual," Dani sighed.

"Have you gone to Tony about any of this, Dani?"

"No, I'm too afraid to. Why?"

"I think you're right to be afraid, Dani. I'm not 100% sure, but I think

Tony owns 'Baggett & Co.' and he maybe even owns the 'Prince National Bank' too."

"Shit, Sam, I've got a lot to worry about tomorrow, don't I?"

Dani smiled on the outside but she felt as cold as ice inside her heart.

***

Next morning, when Dani awoke, her satin sheets were cold and soaked from a fever that had developed during the night. She felt terrible. She let out a long sigh as tears came streaming, unbidden, down her face. Dani was full of anger, bitterness and sorrow at losing both her self-respect and all control over her own affairs.

She sat up in bed, the damp sheets a wrinkled, sodden wad between her legs. She looked up to the white-painted ceiling as if she could see right through it to the heavens and to HK.

"If only I could run away and hide, leaving all this mess behind me," she wished, aloud.

"HK please hear me. I'm not a 'queen' anymore, I'm just a lost soul. Please take my hand and help me to get through another day."

She remembered how good it had been with HK around to fix everything so that she could just laugh and play like the child that was still within her.

Sam stuck her head around Dani's bedroom door.

"Who are you talking to? Anyone I know?"

"What are you doing up so early?" Dani smiled.

"Oh, I have a 10 o'clock appointment with my doctor today, to see if everything's okay after the 'you-know-what'. What're your plans for this afternoon, Dani? Maybe we could meet up for lunch?"

"I'm really not feeling very good, Sam, but I'll try to meet you. How about at the 'La Bella' Restaurant, on Queens Boulevard; say about one o'clock?"

"No, we're not going near that place anymore. How about 'The Playboy Club' and then you can meet my Dean Martin look-alike?"

"Great, Sam. But what's wrong with 'La Bella' all of a sudden?"

"Oh, it's got fantastic food, as long as you don't mind sitting around with all the *'Appalachian Dons'*; those gangster types that hang out there these days."

"Okay, Sam. I understand."

"Wear something warm, too. It's really a bitch outside," Sam cautioned, stepping over to touch Dani's forehead.

"God, you feel like you have a fever, Dani! I hope it's not contagious. In my run down condition I sure don't need any more health problems!"

"I'll be okay, Sam, as soon as I shower and get myself going," Dani reassured her.

Sam blew her a kiss and headed for the door.

"See you at *'The Playboy Club'* then and let's make our meeting at noon!"

"OK!"

Wearily, Dani dragged herself out of bed and headed for the bathroom.

***

Dani dropped her car off for its routine checkup at the garage, intending to take taxis for the rest of her day.

'Sam's right, it is cold today.'

She pulled her coat tighter around her. In New York, there is never a cab in sight when you need one. It seemed ages before one appeared and Dani instructed the driver to take her to Tony Mannelli's new offices, in the Time & Life Building. Until Dani entered the building she hadn't given any thought to the fact that Tony was now in the same building as her old friend, Bill Crawford. *'Even stranger that Tony Mannelli can now afford such a high-rent district.'*

Sitting behind her huge, horseshoe-shaped desk sat the familiar face of Celie, Tony's girl-of-all-trades. She seemed surprised to see Dani but hid it well and was all smiles, as usual.

"Tony's out just now, Dani. Can I be any help?"

Dani just gave her a cool smile.

"Well, why don't you just show me around this fabulous new place, while I wait for him?"

"Are you sure you want to wait, Dani? Tony may be quite late getting in!"

Celie tried her best to dissuade Dani from hanging around, afraid of what she might see and hear.

"Oh, yes, I definitely want to wait."

In her feverish state, Dani had already lost all track of time and thought she had plenty of time before meeting Sam for lunch. The bank of elevators was still visible from Tony's new office, Dani noticed and she paused to tap on its thick glass.

"Bullet proof, is it?"

"Most likely!" Celia smiled as she ushered Dani ahead of her, continuing to guide her on a tour down the hall. She pointed out Tony's two, fully-equipped kitchens and the wine cellar that was hidden behind a secret wall. There was also a large conference room with its own refrigerated bar. Several, smaller offices were clustered at one end of the hall. *'For all Tony's underlings, I'll bet!'* After the tour, Dani sat herself in Tony's office, where Celie served her coffee in a black mug, decorated with the crest of a golden, horse-head.

'How original,' Dani thought, sipping her coffee as her eyes wandered over the rest of Tony's office decor. A paperweight of a black onyx hand particularly caught Dani's eye but, as she leaned over to read the inscription, Tony suddenly entered the room.

"Looking for something?"

He quickly, but smoothly, covered up some papers on his desk as he sat down behind it.

"No, not really, but that black-hand paperweight is very interesting, Tony. Isn't that the call sign of the 'Mafia'?"

Jumping up, Tony hammered his fist on the desktop, raging like a madman.

"Ya got some goddam nerve, coming in here like 'Miss Innocence'. You're nothin' but a worm, Dani Sutton. I'll beat the shit outta you in front of Nicky's eyes if he can't keep you down where you belong."

Dani's eyes widened and she reeled backward at Tony's unexpected outburst. Wiping sweat out of his eyes, Tony pushed the intercom buzzer and bellowed at his secretary.

"Celie, get Blackie in here, on the double and then find Nicky. Tell them to get the fuck over here, right now!"

'Why the hell does Celie keep on working for such a terrible man?'

Dani, quiet all through Tony's tirade, decided that it was time to put him on the defensive and she began yelling back.

"Tony, you and your thugs are nothing but toy soldiers that suck air every time they fart!"

Tony knocked over a big leather chair as he came around the desk. Dani threw her hands up in defense, but she carried on yelling.

"You might scare your boys, 'cause you have your hand on their crotches, but not me, Tony Mannelli. Not anymore!"

"You fuckin bitch! D'ya think you can just waltz in here telling *me*, Tony Mannelli, what to do?"

"Tony, you don't have any cause to come after me, but you *do* have something I want. I want you to return my money and my stocks and then I'll stay away from you all and stay quiet for good. Agreed?"

Tony's fleshy, bottom lip dropped open, showing the huge gap between his front teeth. The remains of a dead cigar hung there on his lip, a sight that would either scare the hell out of you or make you plain nauseated. Disbelief at what Dani had said left Tony muttering to himself. Slamming his fists together, he straightened his shoulders, took a deep breath and roared at her.

"You got no fuckin' edge over me, you dumb bitch. You ain't got no fuckin' brains either, barging in here past my asshole secretary. Next, I suppose you'll be tellin' me you wanna be the big boss?"

Grabbing her long black hair, Tony twisted Dani's head back sharply and looked down at her.

"How can anyone so beautiful be born with no fuckin' brains?"

With a savage twist, Tony threw her to the floor. His eyes bulged, wide and wild, as he shook his outstretched hands, palms up, at his two henchmen, Santo and Blackie. They had just walked into the room.

"What the fuck. You guys ever see me with any of this broad's money?"

"Naw," Blackie replied, "not me, Boss."

No one moved or spoke as Tony reached under his desk for his faithful, old, Thompson submachine gun. Inserting a magazine into the open breach, he grinned menacingly at Dani, who was still crouching on the floor. Tony kicked her in the head and then stepped back.

"See this?"

He pointed the gun in her direction, with a mocking, *'Ah-ah-ah-ah-ah-ah' noise,* imitating the terrifying sound of a functioning machine-gun. Dani prayed that the old piece of junk would blow up in Tony's face. *'It'd serve him right!'*

But he continued to rage at Dani, who was still face-down on the office floor.

"You know nothin, bitch,' ***nothin***'!"

Then he turned his back on her. No-one moved. No-one spoke. No-one dare. After several minutes of pacing the floor, Tony had composed himself and he turned back to Dani again. He waved an arm around his fancy, new suite of glass-walled offices and then grinned down at her.

"Ain't it grand, bitch? And it's all mine!"

Tony half-heartedly kicked at Dani once more before walking back to his desk and laying down the gun. He reached into his back trouser pocket and pulled out his 'little black book'.

"Ya wanna know why they call me *'Crazy Horse'*, Dani? I'll tell ya my secret; it's 'cause everyone's afraid of me, see? I'm the big boss 'cause this here little book holds coded keys to everything in my world and, as long as I have this little book, I have the power. Everyone will kiss my ass before I die."

Tony seemed calmer now. But even when he was calm and cool, he could be more dangerous than anyone Dani had ever known. He lit another cigar as he paced the room again, back and forth. The only sound in the room came from Santo as he thumped a pencil, rhythmically, on a tabletop. Dani, in trying to get away from Tony's wrath, had backed herself right into a corner of the huge office. She was shaking all over, but managing to keep silent. Not only was she shaking from the coldness of the marble floor and her fear of Tony, but a burning fever had begun to rage up from within Dani's shuddering body.

"While we're waiting for my no-good brother, Nicky, to show up, why don't you tell me and the boys all about what you *think* you know, Dani Sutton? Tell us about this fuckin' 'edge' you think you have over us; the one that's makin' you so cocky all of a sudden!"

Dani's throat was so dry that when she opened her mouth to speak, there was no sound. Tony, feigning consideration, poured her a glass of water from the silver decanter on his desk. Beads of sweat trickled down Tony's face and neck as he waited for Dani's answer. Grateful for some time to think, she slowly sipped at the cool water.

'Make this good, Dani; it may be your only chance to come out of this office alive.'

She took another sip before she finally answered.

"I... I gave a notarized letter to a New York Times journalist, who is going to expose you and the rest of your 'Family' if anything happens to me, or to my son, JR."

Through pursed lips, Tony blew out a long, hard sigh. "You fuckin bitch, you got more balls than Eva Braun to try something like this on with me."

Then Nicky arrived and rushed through the outer glass doors into Tony's office.

"Hell, but it's fuckin cold out there!" Nicky's eyes made a fast sweep of the room, taking in the scene. Without being told, he could see that Tony had been having one of his frenzied outbursts.

Big brother, Tony, spat his cigar butt out onto the carpeted floor. Lunging like a wild animal, he grabbed Nicky by his tie and lifted him clear off the floor.

"Whad'ya gonna do about that bitch of yours, over there?"

Nicky started to take a swing at his brother but Santo and Blackie were on top of him in a flash, pinning his arms back. Then Tony doubled Nicky over with a punch to the stomach. Santo caught him and led him over to a chair. Nicky sat there in silence, rubbing his stomach until he could speak again.

"Ya didn't have to do that, Tony. I don't even know what's going on here, yet. Dammit! You hurt me, you bastard. I gotta go to the john now."

Tony nodded to Santo to let Nicky pass.

"On second thoughts, Nicky, just get your brain-child there the fuck outta my sight and teach her some respect. Or, maybe you wanna leave her here with us and we'll put the wrath of 'diablo' into her."

Nicky, still holding his stomach, reached down and helped Dani up off the floor.

"Just forget it, Tony. She looks like a walking corpse, anyway. I'll see that she don't bother you again."

"Yeah, you do that, little brother."

Dani could barely keep her legs from folding as Nicky helped her toward the bank of elevators. Once inside, she was counting the floors down to her freedom. *Sixteen, twelve, eight!* Dani looked at her watch, but her eyes couldn't focus on it. *Four, three!* Their elevator stopped and another person joined them. The elevator started to move again and then stopped with a jerk. Dani looked up and could see that the indicator light was stuck, between the third and second floors. Then all the lights went out.

Dani could hear pounding, yelling and someone screaming from somewhere above her. In the darkness, she found Nicky's arm and tugged on it in terror.

"Oh, my god!' *'The Horse'* wouldn't go this far would he, Nicky?"

Dolores J. Guthrie

Chapter 15

The sweaty, odor of seven frantic people hung heavily on the still air inside the elevator. Dani's fever made her feel as though she would suffocate long before anyone came to rescue them. From within the darkness, somebody said that if the elevator fell, they would be less likely to have broken bones if they were all sitting down. So here they all were, legs entangled, sitting on the floor of a dark, stuffy, stinking tin box.

'If only I had met Sam at the 'Playboy Club', instead of playing tough-mama with Tony.' Dani berated herself. *'Or better yet, I should have just stayed in bed this morning.'*

Several times Nicky put his arm around her but so far he hadn't said anything. *'Is he just trying to show friendly concern, or is it real love he's showing me?'* But for the moment, Dani decided to put aside her own feelings.

"Did Tony hurt you much, Nicky?"

His reply was a sharp jab to Dani's ribs. Stifling a cry, she moved as far away from him as she could. After what seemed hours, voices could be heard nearby. Then there was total silence, as they all strained to hear the first signs of rescue. A few moments more and there was movement on top of the elevator. *'Thank god, someone is working to open up the ceiling trap door.'*

Everyone remained calm as a battery-operated light was lowered down to them, along with a jug of water and some paper cups.

"Guys, hang on down there! We'll have you down at lobby level within the hour," their rescuers promised. They all began asking questions at once, but one husky voice resounded above the others.

"What the hell is going on outside? Why all the screaming?"

"All we know for sure is that the whole city is blacked out. No lights anywhere, but don't worry; we'll get you all out soon. There are others worse off than you, believe me. I hear they're delivering a baby in one of these other elevators!"

When their elevator finally creaked its way downward and its doors were forced open, nothing but a sea of flickering candles could be seen. It took a few minutes for any of the passengers to actually move. Dani had terrible pains in her legs, after being cramped up like a sardine for several hours.

The brisk evening air and the freshness of newly fallen snow were a welcome relief as they made their way the three blocks to Nicky's Club. There they found wall-to-wall people, all drinking the night away. Commuters who couldn't get out of the City back to the suburbs or across town to their fancy, high-rise apartments. A massive power blackout had stopped 'The Big Apple' dead in its tracks!

Dani didn't want to stay around Nicky all night, but she didn't know what to do. She hadn't been able to pick up her car that afternoon and getting a cab was going to be impossible now. Then she remembered that JR's Pontiac *'Grand Prix'* was stored in the parking garage, next door to the Club. While Nicky was busy in the back room, getting more liquor for the bar, Dani made good her getaway.

Looking back later, she couldn't explain how she had ever found her way back home. Just creeping through the darkened garage to find JR's car was a nightmare all on its own. And even when Dani had the car out onto the street, the going was slow. The darkened streets were eerie, with only each car's headlights to see by. Yet Dani was amazed at how the people of New York worked so well together that night; they were actually taking turns at the intersections! Pedestrians with powerful flashlights were even standing out in the streets, directing traffic. The camaraderie of that shadowy night in the 'Big Apple' was nothing short of a miracle.

Unused to a manual gearshift, Dani jerked and ground her way through the gears as she struggled homeward. Traffic was re-routed over the Brooklyn Bridge because there was no power available to suck exhaust fumes out of the tunnel. On the car radio, Governor Rockefeller was saying it was the worst blackout in New York's history but, so far, no tragic results had been reported. Dani sat talking to herself as the car started to smoke in protest from the ill-used clutch. *'Shit, Rocky, I'll probably sit here and burn up the Brooklyn Bridge. Then you'll have your disaster.'*

Dani finally made it home, only to find Sam sound asleep and completely unaware of the riotous events outside. She decided not to wake her friend and softly closed the door. Details of her nightmare day could wait until morning.

Under the shower, Dani's thoughts grew fuzzy and tangled from the rising fever. Slumping heavily against the shower wall and taking a deep breath, she watched as the soapy water ran down her legs. Hallucinating by then, Dani imagined that her strength was going down the drain too, with every soapy bubble. She shook her head several times and turned the shower over to the cold setting to clear her head. At last, she fell into bed, completely exhausted.

When Kay tried to wake her mistress next morning, she realized that her temperature was way too high. Kay was busy applying cold alcohol packs to Dani's feverish body when Sam wandered into the room.

"Please, Miss Sam, call for a doctor. Ah's scared that Miss Dani is in a mighty bad way. Her fever is 106 and that's way too high, even for a young'n like her."

But Sam, as ever, called Nicky first and she told Kay that he said *not* to call the doctor.

"He says that fevers usually burn out in their own time."

"But, what if it doesn't, Miz Sam? Miz Dani'll just lie there and burn to death?"

In the middle of this conversation, the burglar alarm went off as someone tried to break in downstairs. Kay stood rooted in shock, dripping the cold, wet cloth into Dani's face and eyes. Her mistress was awakened by the screaming of the alarm bells and the shock of the cold water and she tried to push herself up onto one elbow.

"Sam, get the shotgun from my closet. It's loaded, so don't aim it unless you intend to shoot it."

Dani's alarm system was hooked into the local area police department and so it wasn't long before the house had officers swarming through every room. One of them took one look at Dani and grabbed for his radio.

"Call an ambulance to my current location. Urgent! This young woman here is almost comatose."

***

Dani kept repeating herself, over and over again, like a little girl

"I want my Momma. Please don't let them kill me, Momma."

The hospital staff, working over her, looked all fuzzy to Dani under the huge, white lights. Still hallucinating from the high fever, she had to be restrained so that she wouldn't hurt herself as she thrashed around. She had no idea where she was. As they wheeled her bed through the cold, basement corridors toward the X-ray section, Dani was convinced that she was in an institution for the mentally ill.

It was a full week before she began to respond to treatment and feel something like herself again. Every time they wheeled her downstairs for tests and X-rays, Dani shuddered, for even in her right mind she found the vast, maze-like hospital unnerving.

Sam visited her every day, bringing stuffed animals, flowers, cards and letters from home. Once, she even tried to slip in a plate of *spaghetti* and a bottle of 'Chianti'! The senior nurse, 'Jaws' as everyone called her, caught sight of Sam just as she was about to enter Dani's private room carrying a large, wicker basket filled with food and drink.

"Miss, I don't want to seem mean, but young Dani here has acute *'Pyelonephritis'* and can be only fed intravenously. She could spend the rest of her life on dialysis if she isn't careful. We wouldn't want that to happen, now would we?"

'Jaws' picked up the picnic basket and turned toward the door,

"You can pick this up at the main desk as you leave, miss!"

Dani laughed, weakly, after the nurse had gone.

"Damn it, Sam, I've been lying here for over two weeks with stuff dripping into my veins. I feel like a damn porcupine. How can I ever get out of this torture chamber?"

"Hold on now, Dani. Have you given any thought as to what Nicky and Tony might have in store as your homecoming present?"

"Well, I haven't conjured up any ideas yet, but I'll have plenty of time to think of something. The doctor says, I'll be here for at least thirty days. It's not the Ritz Hotel, but I'm really too weak to care, or to do anything stupid, or brilliant, for that matter," Dani added, jokingly.

"I talked to your Mom the other day," Sam told her.

"She's worried about you, Dani and naturally, she's upset that she can't be here to watch over you herself. But she's been in contact with the doctor and is well aware of your progress here."

"I'm surprised she hasn't been here already Sam, she's never let me down before."

Sam looked Dani in exasperation.

"Don't you remember? Your sister, Brandy gets married in two weeks' time and it's going to be a big posh affair."

"No kidding? I don't remember hearing anything about that. She must be marrying her high school sweetheart, ol' Bill Unger."

"Dani, I thought you knew all about it. She's not marrying Bill." Sam shook her head in frustration.

"Guess Mom and Dad were waiting for me to get better before they told me. Who is Brandy marrying, then? Do I know him?"

"Well, maybe not. Remember when you bought her that 1965 'Starfire'?"

"Sure, that was a big thrill for me, just seeing my little 'Sissy-Poo' have a dream come true."

"Well, not just a car it seems but also her dream of a young, handsome guy, named Steve Fowler. He saw Brandy pull up to Eisenhower High School in that flashy sports job and it was all over for poor ol' Bob Unger."

"That's too bad," said Dani, sadly. "Brandy and Bob had been sweethearts for years. You know, first love innocence and all that stuff!"

"Hell, Dani, I wouldn't know *anything* about that. Tony was the first guy I ever dated and I wouldn't call the things *he* taught me at seventeen 'innocent'. They were shocking, even to me."

"I've always wondered what made you pick up with a savage like Tony and at such an early age too."

"I've wondered that myself Dani, many, many times. I came alone to the big city, just like you did, to find excitement and glamour. I got my first job as a bartender in one of Tony's clubs and that was the end of the line for me. You must admit that Tony is always exciting, though?"

"Exciting! Hell, don't you mean frightening?"

"Well, maybe a little but he's kept me interested, even after all these years. Still, I can't cry over spilled milk, Dani. That's just life!"

"Funny you should say that, Sam. I wrote a poem while I've been lying here and it sounds exactly like the feelings you've just expressed. You wanna hear it?"

"Sure, why not!"

Dani cleared her throat. "I call it, Life."

I am your shining star.

I have come to you from afar.

I have sprinkled the moon beams and made you a street.

It leads you to heaven with every heartbeat.

Your tears have been heavy and weighed you down.

You have managed to walk tall and not carry a frown.

I've seen you when you're up, I've seen you when you're down.

I've seen you roll with laughter, like a silly little clown.

I've seen you take those punches, without falling down.

I have this degree, befitting to thee.

A sprinkle of star dust I'll blow through your hair.

You'll stay healthy and young and not have a care.

I'll take a pinch of the rainbow and color your street.

I'll get pennies from heaven, to drop at your feet.

I'll catch all your tear drops and water God's soil.

Your life will bring love, in your first bundle of joy.

You'll forget your old love, with your dreams of the past.

I will strengthen your new love with dreams that will last.

Your life will be happy and life you will give

To some special 'somebody', for as long as you live.

Dani paused, waiting for Sam to speak.

"Well, what do you think?"

"Hell, Dani; you must be getting some of your strength back. Maybe you'll make it to Brandy's wedding after all."

She gave Dani a quick kiss on the forehead.

"I gotta go now, hon. Catch you tomorrow."

***

In the quiet of that dark night, when most patients were sound asleep, Dani tossed and turned. She opened her eyes and could see a hallway light through the half closed door of her room. She lay quietly, slowly absorbing the feeling that someone was inside the shadowy room with her. Dani fumbled for her call buzzer but it seemed to take forever for someone to respond. Dani smiled in the darkness, thinking that when Nurse 'Jaws' came in, she'd be enough to scare any intruder away but it wasn't Nurse Jaws who came in.

"Where's Miss Carter?" Dani asked.

"Oh, she got off at midnight, she can't work all the time you know, dear. Do you need a bedpan?"

"No, I just feel uneasy. Is there someone out there in the hallway?"

"Now, now Dani, there are no boogie men wandering these halls." The nurse reassured her nervous patient.

"We are very secure in this hospital so there's nothing to worry about. Would you like me to get you something to help you relax?"

"Well; maybe that would help."

Dani was angry at herself for giving in to such silly fears, but she couldn't help it. She lay tense and fearful until she heard the comforting sound of the nurse's rubber soles squeaking on the linoleum as she strode back down the hall.

"There, that should get you to sleep."

The nurse stayed to make sure Dani had swallowed the pill and then out the door she went.

'Damn, she's closed the door!' was Dani's last recollection before drifting away into a warm cocoon.

***

She was brought back to unwelcome consciousness by the overpowering sensation of danger. All her senses were telling Dani that someone was inside the room with her. She tried to open her eyelids, but the sleeping pill had done its work well. She could only mumble, drowsily.

"Nurse, is that you?"

But the voice that answered her didn't come from any nurse.

"Be quiet, Dani! It's me, Vinnie."

"Who?"

"It's me, 'Cue Ball'!"

The man Dani knew as Tony Mannelli's number one 'hit man' was standing right next to her bed. She whimpered in fear.

"What on earth are you doing here in the middle of the night, Vinnie? Don't you know I'm sick?"

Vinnie turned his flashlight on Dani and then gave the rest of the room quick sweep with its wide beam. He took away the handset for her call-buzzer and light-switch and dropped it out of reach. She was struggling to raise herself up but Dani was dopey from the medication and all the intravenous tubes were pulling on her arms, keeping her down. She fell back against her pillows, weak and terrified.

'Has Tony finally sent Vinnie to kill me?'

She tried to call out but no screams would come. Then she felt Vinnie's hands, moving all over her helpless body.

"Dani, just relax," he said, pulling her bedcovers down to the foot of the bed.

"Is this a joke, Vinnie 'cos I'm not laughing? Turn on the damn light and let's talk."

"I'm not here to talk, Dani but don't be afraid."

Vinnie's breathing was becoming short and shallow as he taped up Dani's mouth and tied her hands to the bed rails. Then he slipped his rough hands under her nightgown. She squirmed, trying desperately to get away from his revolting touch. Silent tears streamed down Dani's face.

"Easy baby, I'm not going to hurt you." Vinnie crooned into her ear. "I've waited for this moment for a very, *very* long time, Dani. It's just you and me now, babe."

Vinnie's voice quivered as he mounted her, whispering to her constantly in the darkness.

"So nice, baby! Oh, you feel so good."

Dani turned her tear stained face away from him as Vinnie thrust away at her until he reached orgasm. Her only thought was whether he would leave her unhurt once he was finished, or was this going to be the end. After he was sated, Vinnie lay on top of her for a quite a while before rolling off the bed. She heard the zipper of his pants and then his footsteps as he walked across to the door. Only then did she turn her head to look. Vinnie peered out into the hall but then, to Dani's horror, he turned and walked back toward her bed!

"I'm going to untie you now, Dani and take off all this tape. But not a sound before I get clear of here. And don't you go mouthin' off about this night to anyone, d'ya hear me?"

"You know there ain't no-one, or nothin', that can stop me if you cause me any problems with the law. I'm a five-time loser Dani and it ain't from rapin' little girls. Get my drift, doll?"

Like a cat Vinnie had entered Dani's room and like a cat he left. Carefully, Dani took the needles from her arm before drunkenly making her way to the bathroom. As she was busy throwing up, the nurse appeared again, seemingly out of nowhere.

"What are you doing out of bed, Dani? And, why did you take out your IV's, young lady?"

Dani daren't tell the night nurse what had just happened. Not only because of the threats Vinnie had made, but also because the nurse hadn't believed her when she thought there was someone in her room.

'So why bother?'

"I woke up tossing and turning and I guess they must have just pulled out."

Dani meekly let the nurse lead her back to bed.

"You were the one who was worried about the boogieman earlier, weren't you?" asked the nurse curiously, as she tucked Dani up in bed and reaffixed her IV tubes.

Chapter 16

The rest of Dani's stay in that hospital was filled with terror as, every night, she lay wondering if Vinnie would reappear. And when she wasn't worrying about Vinnie, then she was worrying about *'The Horse'*. Over and over, Dani kept telling herself that if she just let Tony Mannelli keep her money and stayed out of his way then, maybe, she would be safe.

Her weeks in hospital had seemed like months but, slowly, Dani's strength began to return. Three days before her sister's wedding, Dani announced her decision to be there and told the doctor, in no uncertain terms, that she was leaving that very day.

"I don't care what you say, Doctor! I feel quite strong enough to go home to my own family and, if I need to, I can always check into the local hospital there. You can speak to Dr. Brundage, our family doctor in Yakima and tell him what care I need."

"You certainly are one stubborn young lady, Miss Sutton."

Dani smiled sweetly and squeezed his hand.

"My Great-Grandfather Gunther always said I was born 'as stubborn as a government mule'!"

"Well, it's against my better judgment, Dani, but I'll have your discharge papers ready for noon today, OK? But please take very good care of yourself, young lady."

Dani was over-the-moon not to have to endure one more night in hospital. The episode with Vinnie had really unnerved her. She called her maid with the good news and asked her to come over with Sam, later that morning, bringing a bag packed for Dani's trip home. She didn't want to go anywhere near her New York mansion before catching a plane to Seattle.

"And Kay, have Sam make me a reservation on the very next plane, please. She knows which travel agent I always use."

***

"Has Nicky been to see you?" Sam asked as she helped Dani to dress.

Dolores J. Guthrie

"No, I haven't seen him in over a week. We don't seem to communicate very well, lately."

"Did you tell him that you were leaving hospital today and going over to the West Coast?"

"No!" Dani was horrified at the very idea of Nicky Mannelli knowing where she was going.

"Sam, please don't tell Nicky, or anyone else for that matter. When people ask where I am, just tell them you don't know!"

"My, my, Miz Dani!"

Kay shook her head and frowned.

"That Mr. Mannelli sure has you up against it and that's a fact. Y'all better get yo' daddy down here to help you, or y'all won't have a pot to piss in an' nary a window to throw it out of neither, not if you're away from New York for too long."

"Now, Kay, don't you worry, everything will be fine. Just close up the house and go home until you hear from me, OK? Will you take Babette with you too? Take all her food dishes and her doggy bed. If you put one of my old nighties into her bed, then she'll know I'll be coming back."

Then Dani quick-fired questions at the two women.

"Did you pack plenty of clothes for me, Kay?"

"And Sam, were you able to get me a seat on the very next plane out of here?"

"Yes, yes, Miz Dani, everything you need is already in your car, downstairs."

"We'll get you to the airport in plenty of time to pick up the ticket for your flight, Dani."

Sam sighed, wistfully.

"I sure wish I was going with you, girl."

"Well, why don't you?"

"Oh, I'd love to, but I kinda' like what's going on in my life right now with this new guy, Ralph Martini. If I go away with you, he might just forget all about me while I'm gone."

***

Dani's long flight was far more demanding than she had anticipated. She arrived at Seattle Airport feeling very weak, but still able to walk off the plane on her own. As she struggled up the long walkway, toward the waiting room, she could already see her folks and waved to them excitedly as the distance between them slowly closed. Laura and her daughter sat in the waiting room, chatting, while Harold rounded up his Dani's luggage and brought the car around front.

The three-hour journey home passed quickly enough with all the chatter and excitement between her and her mother, but Dani's strength was almost gone by the time the car pulled into their driveway. She was barely able to greet her younger brother, Ted, and all his family who had gathered in welcome. Dani quickly whispered her 'goodnights' and 'I love you's' to them all and struggled upstairs to her waiting bed.

As Laura bent to kiss her daughter goodnight, Dani mentioned something that was bothering her.

"Momma, why wasn't Brandy here when we arrived? Didn't they have a bridal shower for her tonight?"

"Your dad and I are a bit worried ourselves," Laura confessed.

"Brandy was supposed to pick up her gown from the seamstress this morning and then have lunch with her bridesmaids at the Elks Club. She told me this morning that she planned to be here when we got back."

Dani squeezed her mother's hand and smiled reassuringly.

"She probably just got involved somewhere, Mom, you know how Brandy can be. It's been a long day, today. But I'll feel stronger tomorrow, I promise."

Laura's brow wrinkled with concern but she put on a brave smile.

"You know, Dani, you were a little foolish to make such a long trip in your weakened condition. You and I are going to check in with Dr. Brundage, first thing tomorrow morning! But right now it's time to rest, honey."

Laura switched off the light and blew her daughter a kiss. "I love you, sweetheart. You'll call me if you need anything?"

***

Voices from somewhere inside the house awakened Dani later. Turning on the light, she saw that it was three-o'clock in the morning!

'Is that Brandy, only just now coming home?'

Dani slowly made her way downstairs toward the sounds of excited voices.

"Oh!" Dani hesitated. "Excuse me, but I thought Brandy had just come in."

"No, Brandy's not here, honey" her mother replied. "Dani, I'd like you to meet her fiancé, Steve Fowler. He was about to tell us all *why* Brandy isn't here."

Steve was pacing back and forth, wringing his hands. He looked as though he could cry at any moment, but nodded an acknowledgment in Dani's direction and then turned back to her father.

"I just don't know how to tell you everything, sir" Steve's voice was shaky. "But, first of all, Sandy is all right now!"

Laura frantically grabbed at Steve's arm. "What do you mean, she's all right *now*?"

Harold leaned forward urgently.

"Dammit' Steve, just tell us! Has Brandy been in an accident?"

Steve rubbed at his forehead as he tried to control his roiling emotions.

"Yes, she has, but she'll be okay!"

Laura put a motherly arm around her future son-in-law's shoulders.

"What hospital is she in, Steve?"

"She's at St. Josephs, but....! She lost...well...*we* lost our baby."

Harold Gunther's face turned red and Dani could see the whites of her father's knuckles as he spoke.

"You mean to say that our Brandy was pregnant? Why, you bastard, I'll beat the living crap out of you!"

"Harold! Steve! Both of you stop it right now," Laura cried, as she stepped in between the two men. "Can't you see what this is doing to the young lad, Harold?"

"Well, this wedding will be called off, right now," Harold declared as he stalked around the room. "No daughter of mine is going to be forced onto any man, never again!"

Her father's meaning was not lost on Dani.

"But you don't understand, Mr. Gunther. I *love* Brandy, very much and I still want to marry her. This accident may have taken our first child but I'll be damned if I'll lose Sandy too. We're getting married and I don't care what you say or do!"

Harold towered over the young man and his manner softened.

"Well, I'll be damned! Young Steve here might just have the kind of grit that it takes to handle our Brandy," Harold conceded. "I think we all could use a drink about now."

But the policeman in Harold continued to quiz Steve whilst he made the drinks.

"So, exactly how did this accident happen, then Steve? Were you in the car with her?"

"No, it was after her lunch with the girls. Brandy was on her way home when a car went through a red light and hit her on the driver's side. The other car left the accident scene, with the police in hot pursuit."

"So, it wasn't our Brandy's fault, then?"

"No, sir, Brandy had the green light. She's just very bruised and shocked but the doctors say they'll release her in the morning, so long as they don't find anything else wrong before then."

After further discussion, it was decided not to mention the loss of the baby and for the couple to continue with their wedding plans, as arranged. It was too late, though, to change the wedding theme that Brandy had chosen. She had picked a theme of three, intertwined, golden-hearts in all the flowers and decorations, to represent Steve's heart, the baby's and her own. It would make the ceremony even more poignant.

***

At St. Timothy's Episcopal Church there was pandemonium, as before any big event. Before they departed for the church, Dani had made sure that tradition was followed. She placed a penny in one of her sister's shoes and also gave her 'something-old-and-something-new'!

Then she had presented both her mother and sister with blue velvet, jewelry boxes. Each held a heart-shaped, diamond pendant, matching the one that Dani was already wearing.

"This will represent *our* three hearts now, together forever." Dani spoke with tears in her eyes. "I'm sorry Brandy, but I hadn't realized when I ordered them that they would coincide with your own theme."

Dani had been asked to sing her own rendition of 'Tonight,' from the musical, 'West Side Story' before the wedding ceremony proper began. She didn't want to disappoint her sister, but in her weakened state, Dani barely made it through to the end of the song, leaning heavily on the arm of some young man in a white tuxedo as he ushered her back to her seat. Then, to the rich sounds of St. Timothy's church organ, Brandy floated down the aisle on her father's arm, looking like a pure white cloud in her beautiful, French-lace wedding gown.

As Dani watched, she remembered her baby sister; first as a toddler showing Dani an '*owie*' on her chubby, pink chin and then as a young girl, riding her favorite horse bareback. Brandy had always been a happy child, always laughing and that was how Dani would always remember her.

After the church ceremony, the couple's many friends and relatives attended the 'Chinook Hotel' for the official cake-cutting and photographs. Then, the immediate family returned to their home for a private buffet. One of the young ushers, Scott, volunteered to take the wedding presents over to the family house and offered to give Dani a ride.

He said he needed to stop by his own house first and steered their car up into the hills. Then he turned into an orchard that overlooked the entire Yakima Valley.

"Scott, what the hell are you doing?"

Dani struggled to pull away as the young man drew her toward him in an embrace.

"We're expected back at the house and I really don't feel up to this kind of messing about. Please, Scott, just take me home," Dani demanded.

"All Brandy ever talks about is her beautiful 'big sister', back in New York. And Dani, you *are* beautiful," Scott breathed.

"I've never known a woman as exciting as you. I just want to touch you and kiss you and then I'll take you home, Dani."

Scott was trembling as he kissed Dani's neck and then her ears, before climbing all over her weak, quaking body.

"Damn it, Scott, my eyelash just came off and you've torn the strap of my dress. Enough is enough!"

But the flood gates of youthful passion were opened wide.

"Oh, goddam it, Dani, I've got to have you, please!" Scott begged.

"Okay, okay!" sighed Dani, pushing him away, "but not like this. I like things to be right. I want a hot bath, a bed with clean sheets and exotic oils to rub over your body; not this kid's stuff in the backseat of a car!"

Scott sat up and straightened his bow tie. He took a few deep breaths and cleared his throat before he started the car.

"I'm sorry Dani! I really wanted take you to a motel, but I don't have enough money on me. I just couldn't miss this chance to be alone with you."

On the drive back to the family home, Dani's breathing became calmer but her mind was working overtime, trying to out-think the handsome, young stud. *'My god, even Yakima has night crawlers!'*

"Scott, why don't we make an appearance at the party and then slip out later, when no one will miss us. I need to get some things from my room first, and some money too."

Dani felt as though a spotlight had been trained on them as they walked into the wedding party room. Everyone was staring at Scott, who had make-up all over his spotless, white, tuxedo jacket. Amidst all the whispers and giggles, Dani took her opportunity and disappeared upstairs, never to see young Scott again.

Several days later, Dani asked her favorite Aunt, Marjorie, to accompany her to Las Vegas for a short vacation. She needed more time to recuperate, she decided, before returning to the perils of New York and the Mannelli's.

***

Their suite at *'The Dunes'* hotel had two separate bedrooms, two bathrooms, a living room with its own bar and a magnificent view out over the Las Vegas 'Strip'. As they gazed out of the panoramic windows, Marjorie turned to Dani, excitedly.

"All these years of being a wife and a mother to five kids, as well as working weekends too! I've never had the chance, or the time, to see what the rest of the world was like, Dani."

"Well, don't get too carried away, Marjorie. You are far better off with *your* life than I am with mine, believe me. I envy you."

"Dani, how can you possibly say that?"

But Dani didn't want to get into specific details.

"Just trust me, Marjorie! Let's just enjoy today, shall we?"

Dani outlined her plans for their first day.

"First on our agenda will be a 'face-and-full-body' massage, then a sauna, then a body-wrap and we'll finish with a Jacuzzi. After that lot, we'll visit the beauty salon. And when we're finished there, we'll go shopping for a 'Las Vegas' wardrobe for you to take home with you."

Walking hand-in-hand down the hallway to the hotel gym, Marjorie squeezed Dani's hand.

"Oh, Dani, I think I'm dreaming."

It had been several weeks since Dani last had a massage. Her hospital stay hadn't included that kind of treatment and she was looking forward to this. Just the thought of someone massaging and touching her body was enough to put Dani into a tranquil, almost drowsy state. Marjorie thought she had died and gone to heaven and said as much when they got eventually back to their hotel suite.

"My God, that was a marvelous day, Dani. I feel like a new woman. I could sure get used to your way of life if I didn't have a family. I don't know if Yakima is going to be ready for me and all these fancy clothes when I get back."

"Well, everything you picked out looks great on you. And you can wear them anywhere, so don't worry," Dani said, truthfully, as Marjorie twirled around, showing off her chosen outfit for the evening.

"You look just beautiful, Marjorie. C'mon, let's paint the town!"

After cocktails and dinner they wandered around the gaming tables until Marjorie couldn't stand the excitement anymore. She sat down to play blackjack, having decided that was her game. She didn't win much, but kept ahead for most of the time. Dani wasn't much of a gambler and as she waited for Marjorie, she marveled at how the ever watchful pit-bosses kept track of all the fast-paced action.

Looking around at all the other gamblers, Dani made a game out of guessing what part of the country each person was from, just by the way they were dressed. Several men spoke to Dani briefly, but she ignored them and continued to sit alone with her thoughts.

'Why do I feel so alone here? I could have my pick of any of these men?'

Then a tall, lean fellow sat down beside Dani and began complaining to a buxom waitress, close by.

"Give me a triple Manhattan, ma'am, a very dry one, to help me forget that I just lost $30,000!"

"Come on, Chester, there's more where that came from, surely?" His friend had overheard his complaints.

"Hell, I'll be playing catch-up for the rest of my life, George, trying to overcome tonight's losses."

The man called 'Chester' turned and gave Dani a half smile.

"Could I buy you a drink, ma'am, with the small amount of pocket change I have left?"

"Sure, why not," Dani laughed.

The mood of her evening began to slowly change as the two of them continued exchanging small talk and banter.

"For someone depressed, you sure are a comedian," Dani said, but Chester's mood became more serious as he explained to her that he was a doctor, a kidney specialist, from Boston. It was a stressful occupation and he sometimes needed to let his hair down.

"Well, that's a real coincidence! I'm here in Vegas to recuperate from a serious kidney illness," Dani confided.

"Well, my dear, you come on over to Boston and I'll take good care of you, should you have any more problems."

They talked on, ignoring everyone else in the room. Later, Chester suggested they go somewhere for a quiet nightcap. Marjorie was intent upon her own games and Dani reckoned that she would remain at the tables for quite some time.

"Sure, let's go up to my suite, Chester. Marjorie looks well occupied for a while."

"Losing tonight would almost be worthwhile Dani, even with only a kiss and your good company."

Dani beckoned Chester to follow by a simple flick of her shoulder. Neither of them spoke more than a word or two more until the door to her suite had closed behind them. Without turning on the light, or going any further into the room, Dani whispered to Chester; her own excitement growing.

"You'll feel better when you take my dress off!"

"Oh, damn, yes!" Chester gasped in anticipation, his surgeon's fingers turning into thumbs as he worked to unzip Dani's skin-tight, gold satin gown. The dress slid to the floor and his hands frantically hunted for Dani's sensuous spheres, the ones he'd been eyeing for several hours. Neither of them heard the key turn in the lock, nor the door open. But they heard Marjorie's voice!

"Come on in, why don't you!"

Before they could move, all the lights came on and Dani and Chester were facing Marjorie and several other people she had invited back with her.

Dani shrieked as she tried to pull up her gown and whispered to Chester.

"Oh, dear, this just doesn't seem to be your night at all, does it?"

Chester didn't even try to hide the bulge in his pants as he headed out of the door.

"I wonder, can a person drown themselves in a shower?"

Everyone laughed and began making themselves at home as Marjorie headed for the bar to mix drinks for everyone.

***

The next morning told its own story.

"We must have had a great time last night, Marjorie. I feel as though I fell into a vat of booze and then drank my way out!"

"Don't fret, Dani, I'll make you my famous 'Bloody Mary', with clam juice; guaranteed to cure even the worst hangover."

The phone rang as she passed and Marjorie answered it.

"Is this Dani Sutton?"

"No, but I can take a message for her? She's not able to come to the phone at the moment."

"Just tell her that a friend called to give her a message. Tell Dani that she should leave Las Vegas. They're going to hurt her."

"Who is this? Hello? Hello? Dammit, Dani, they hung up."

"What did they say?"

"They asked for you. They said they were a friend and for you to get out of Las Vegas; that someone was going hurt you."

"Oh, it's just some prank call. Who around here would want to hurt me?"

"Well, I'm calling the house detective. He can stay with us until we get packed and get outta here," Marjorie said, dialing down to the main desk.

"Oh, come on, Marjorie, it was just a prank," Dani insisted.

"Dani, just look at all that damn jewelry and furs you walk around wearing. Any two-bit hood can see that you're dripping in money."

"So what? Look, I'll put everything into the hotel safe for the rest of our stay, if that'll make you feel better."

"Sorry, Dani, but that's not good enough for me. I'm packing up and going home. My five kids aren't going to grow up without their mother so I plan to be on the next flight to Yakima. Are you coming with me?

Before Dani could answer there was a knock at the door. Dani jumped and Marjorie hurried over to answer it.

"Who's there?" she called through the door.

"Hotel Security. You called, ma'am?"

"Who?"

"Ma'am, I'm the house detective. You just called down to the front desk and asked for me?"

Still unsure, Marjorie cautiously opened the door to see a man in a brown suit. He looked safe enough, peering at her through horn rimmed glasses.

"May I come in?"

He extended his identification card for Marjorie to read and she stepped back, allowing him to pass into the room. After he heard the story of the phone call, he agreed with Dani's aunt.

"Yes, ma'am, I think it would be best if you were to leave. The hotel and I prefer not to have problems with our guests' safety. When you are ready to go, I'll personally drive you to the airport."

"Marjorie, I don't want to go back to Yakima." Dani was being obstinate, although she had to admit that she was a little spooked. She looked from Marjorie to the security guy and back again.

"Oh, OK. I guess I'll just go back to New York and try to finally settle things back there. I'll sell the house and everything and then move back out to the West Coast. What do you think about me living the quiet life and marrying a farmer, Marjorie? Or maybe a rancher?"

"You? Marry a farmer? You've got to be kidding me?"

"Well, the idea sounds damn good to me right now, I can tell you," Dani sighed

Chapter 17

In the huge games room of Hearthstone Manor, a cigarette smoldered in one of several dirty ashtrays on the coffee table. Sam was sleeping soundly on the black leather couch, oblivious to the fact that someone was staring down at her. Dani shook her head in disgust, both at the state of her beautiful home and of her friend. *'I wonder how long Sam's been in this condition.'*

Dani picked up an empty vodka bottle and a couple of dirty glasses and walked over to the bar. She found its usually pristine sink chock-full of dirty cocktail glasses and stinking ashtrays. Angrily, she dropped the empty bottle and glasses among the rest of the debris. Sam stirred on hearing the clatter of broken glass.

"Who's there?" Sam demanded to know, trying to clear her liquor-soaked brain of its confusion. She rose up on one elbow, rubbing at her eyes.

"It's me, Sam. I'm home."

"Dani! What are you doing back already? She paused, woozily. "Er, I think Tony's upstairs somewhere, asleep."

"What?" Dani was fuming "Why in the hell would Tony be upstairs in my house? I told you the house was to be closed up while I was away. Dammit', Sam! You know better than to let that bastard into my home! Looks like one helluva party went on here too, behind my back!"

"I'm sorry, Dani," Sam whined, "but I had no choice – I had to let him in."

Dani couldn't believe her eyes and ears. *'Will I never be free of these damned Mannelli brothers?'*

"You'd better have a damn good reason, Sam."

"When Tony arrived yesterday he was raging drunk, Dani. If I'd tried to keep him out, he would've just broken down the door anyway!"

"I honestly don't understand you, Sam. Aren't you supposed to be going out with, what's his name, Martini? That guy Tony gave his blessing to months ago?"

"I am, Dani, but Tony was so drunk yesterday that he forgot all about breaking up with me."

With a heavy heart, Dani trudged upstairs but couldn't find Tony Mannelli anywhere.

"So, where do you think he's gone, Sam?"

"God, I've no idea, but I'm glad he's not still here." Sam sighed with relief but looked at Dani in despair.

"Dani, Tony says he wants your house and I am so afraid he's going to get it."

"Damn Tony Mannelli; he'll never get my mansion if I can help it!" Dani vowed.

"Sam, do you think you could go and stay at a friend's apartment for a little while? Maybe Dawn wouldn't mind, would she?"

"No, I guess not," Sam hesitated, "but you know that Robbie has moved in with her now."

"Robbie? You mean, Tony and Nicky's *youngest* brother?"

Sam nodded and Dani groaned.

"Well, just tell them that you're afraid to stay here without Kay, or me, around."

"Well, that's no lie for damn sure," Sam declared. "It really is spooky at night in this great big house."

She tried to stand up but fell back onto the couch.

Dani looked at her friend with real concern.

"Sam, you really oughta ease up on your drinking, you know. Lines are beginning to show in your lovely face and that's a damn shame for someone as young as you."

Sam eventually managed to stand up but swayed as she leaned over and tried to pick up more dirty glasses.

"Never mind about all that, Sam!"

Dani shooed her away.

"I'll have Kay come in early tomorrow and give this whole place a good cleaning. It smells like a brewery!"

"Dani, I don't think it's safe for you to stay here alone tonight. What if Tony finds out that you're back?"

"Hell, Sam, he doesn't have a door key, does he?"

"Nooo, I don't think so." But the elusive look on Sam's face made Dani think her friend wasn't telling the whole truth.

"Well, I won't be around here much, not if I can help it, so I'll just have to take a chance on that."

"I'll get my things and be out of here as soon as I can, Dani. You know how to reach me if you need me, don't you?"

"Sure, I know Sam. But *please*, don't tell *anyone* that I'm back in town."

After Sam left, Dani went into the back part of the house, trying not to turn on any obvious lights. The big, empty house even gave Dani an eerie feeling now that she was alone and she spent a restless night. Until the sounds of music and of men talking and laughing awoke her at around five o'clock in the morning! Dani threw on a robe and in total darkness she cautiously moved downstairs, toward the games room. *'Dammit, Sam did lie to me. Tony Mannelli does have a key!'*

Dani peeked through a crack in the doorframe. Through a haze of cigar smoke she could make out the silhouettes of several men huddled around the bridge table, playing cards. She recognized most of them; Nicky, Moose, Tony and Joe-Faci. Someone else spoke too, but Dani didn't recognize the voice. Then she noticed an empty chair and realized with a shock that someone must be visiting the bathroom, behind her.

A chill shuddered through Dani as she turned to make a quick exit, but it was too late. A hand covered her mouth and another hand grabbed her arm, pulling her away from the door. Dani's body was pressed close against the man's but she didn't struggle, somehow she didn't believe that the man meant to harm her. Then a familiar voice whispered in her ear. It was Vinnie!

"I've had a meeting with Tony since I last saw you, Dani. He reckons he's going to lay-off your case, just so long as you don't make no more waves around him, if you know what I mean. And remember now, not a word about that night in the hospital, Dani. That's our little secret, forever," Vinnie whispered, kissing her cheek tenderly.

He took his hand away from Dani's mouth, touching her hair in a soft gesture and then he spun her around, kissing her lips hard.

"C'mon with me now, Dani, you'll be all right, I promise."

Dani tried to pull back, but Vinnie insisted.

"Trust me," he whispered and so she followed him like a lamb.

"Well, lookee-here, who's come home," Vinnie announced, pulling Dani into the room behind him.

"Hi there, Doll!" Nicky flashed a perfect white smile in her direction. He motioned for Dani to come closer and hugged her, but she never took her eyes away from Tony's massive presence. She well remembered the beating he'd given her the last time they met.

Tony stared hard at Dani before tossing his cards into the center of the table.

"Deal me out, guys."

He reached over and scooped up his money, then jerked his head at Vinnie to follow him.

"Let's tie it up for tonight, guys."

Nicky looked at Dani.

"I'll be right up, Doll," he said, winking and patting her on the rear as he passed by. Dani didn't like the sound of that but didn't question him. She was just relieved that there hadn't been a big scene and that she was still alive. Meekly, Dani went back up to her bedroom to wait for Nicky Mannelli.

∗∗∗

As she lay wrapped in the strong arms of her controlling lover, Dani felt safe, at least for the moment. Her fingers absent mindedly stroked Nicky's satiny, olive-toned skin as it stretched over the ripples of his well-honed muscles. His breathing was relaxed and even. Nicky wrapped his arms around Dani's waist, pulling her closer to him.

"I've missed you, baby. You know I love to have you touch me. I've missed those soft lips of yours and the way you nibble on me. You're like no other woman I've ever known, Dani Sutton."

"I hear that you and Lindsay are going to have another child soon," Dani asked, as unemotionally as she could.

"Who told you that stupid rumor?"

"I don't remember now," Dani lied, "but *are* you?"

"Naw, don't listen to stories like that, Dani. Do you really think I need another kid?"

"I also heard that the reason you didn't want me to come back to work at the Club was..."

"Was what?" Nicky demanded, raising himself up on one arm and opening one eye.

"Well... I don't really believe it, anyway." Dani purred, toying with the dark, curly hairs on Nicky's chest.

"You don't believe what, dammit'?"

"Well, that you replaced *me* with that Korean girl," she coaxed.

"You mean replaced you at work, or what?"

"At work *and* at 'you-know-what'," Dani said, crossly.

Nicky laughed, closed his eyes and flopped back onto the bed.

"Are you talking about 'Hot Kimchee'?" he chuckled.

"Yes," pouted Dani, "but I don't think it's very funny."

"Well, it *is* damn funny Dani, because Kimchee's a goddam dike!"

"You've gotta be kidding me!" Dani couldn't believe her ears. "Why would anyone tell me that you took her to bed, then?"

"Who told you?" Nicky's curiosity finally got the better of him.

"*She* told me," pouted Dani, "and she also said she felt damn good doing it, too!"

"Well, now, that's mighty interesting." Nicky gave Dani a crooked, half-smile.

"One night after work, Mikey, I and Sheri went over to Kimchee's apartment. We guys watched the girls get their jollies off together and then we beat them both up!"

"My god, Nicky, what an awful thing to do!" Dani was genuinely upset. "Did you hurt them?"

"Naw, they both loved it. You know how it is, when folk are into S&M."

"What's S&M?" Dani felt stupid at how many things in life she didn't know.

"You know, like when folk *enjoy* being hurt." Nicky kissed Dani and then whopped her hard on the rump, just before rolling out of bed.

"I heard someone come in."

"It's probably only Kay. I called her last night to come in early, to clean up.

Nicky stared deep into Dani's violet-blue eyes.

"If you think you're strong enough, maybe you could come back to work tonight, huh? I've really missed having you around, babe and, you know, maybe we could get back to the good-old days again?"

Dani sat on the bed with her legs crossed, studying the strange, but fascinating man looking down at her. She was worried about all the changes she'd noticed in everyone, especially in Tony Mannelli.

'Oh, what the hell?'

Dani drew in a deep breath.

"Sure, why not? I do feel a lot stronger now and I've missed the entertaining a lot."

"You mean you haven't missed *me*?"

"Of course I have, silly!" Dani smacked him, playfully. "What time should I show up tonight?"

"Same as ever, seven o'clock. See you tonight then, babe."

Nicky blew her an exaggerated kiss as he departed and she smiled to mask her swirling thoughts.

'Yes, I'll see you, Nicky Mannelli. I'll play your games. I just hope I have enough time to get some outside help before you all strike at once!'

As Nicky went out, she heard him apologizing to Kay in the hallway before the maid came bustling into Dani's bedroom.

"Why, Miz Dani, it's so good to see ya'll lookin' so much stronger, but ah'd best start getting some fat on them there bones. Ah swear, child, didn't yo' momma feed you while you was away?"

***

It felt strange, walking back into familiar scenery at the Club that night but everyone seemed happy to see Dani after her long illness. Well, almost everyone! After all the welcomes, Dani went back into the girls' dressing rooms to find herself a clean costume. She was dressing when Sheri came in and stood in the doorway, looking defiantly at Dani and with her hands on her hips.

"You fucking bitch, whad'ya mean by gettin' my Kimchee fired?

Dani stared in amazement.

"I don't know what you're talking about."

"Kimchee told me that Nicky called, telling her not to come in tonight because *you* were replacing her. What would *you* call that, Dani, 'cept getting someone fired?"

"I wouldn't call it anything," Dani answered calmly. "I was told to come back to work, so I did."

"You fucking bitch! Just because you're screwing the boss's baby brother don't give you the right to be gone for weeks and then come back here any time you please."

Sheri gave Dani's costume a yank.

"And you've put on the wrong damn costume," she added for good measure.

Dani threw Sheri's hands aside.

"I'm very sorry about the costume mistake, Sheri but don't you use that foul language with me. I'm a lady and I expect to be treated like one."

Sheri hooted at the top of her voice.

"Why, Miss *'Lady'* Sutton, d'you think your cunt smells any better than mine?"

That remark cut right through Dani. "I've had just about enough of your filthy mouth. Get out of my sight or I'll have *you* fired as well."

Sheri brought up her middle finger and thrust it in front of Dani's face.

"Up yours, bitch."

Dani went crazy. She doubled her fist and swung her arm up hard, right under Sheri's chin, knocking her backwards. Sheri looked totally shocked, just for a second, but she came back slugging.

Papa, the cook, heard the racket and came running out from the kitchen. As he opened their dressing-room door, both girls fell out into the hallway. Dani grabbed at Sheri's hair but it came off in her hand. Looking at the wig in horror, they both paused momentarily before resuming battle. At that point, Dani was on top.

"Hit her again, Dani! Hit her again!" Papa was yelling!"

Nicky and Mikey ran over and pulled the girls apart.

"What the fuck's goin' on here?" Nicky yelled. "I got a house full of thirsty customers waiting for a show and back here I got me two prima donnas tearing the shit out of each other."

He silenced their indignant protests about who-hit-whom first.

"I don't wanna hear another word outta' either of ya'. Ya' got just ten minutes to get cleaned up and get your asses out there on that stage!"

Dani picked up her things and took herself off into the bathroom of Nicky's private office. But after taking a look in the mirror, she started to laugh. *'What a sad sight!'* Her eyelashes were hanging loose and mascara was running in dark rivers down both cheeks. *'Well, at least I finished on top!*

Sheri opened the door a crack and lobbed in another costume, hitting Dani on the head with it.

"Wear this, bitch!"

Several people congratulated Dani on her moral victory and, when the show finally got going, she was on a real high. Dani hated liquor and she didn't take dope either, so she guessed it was just an excess of adrenaline left over from the fight.

Just before closing time, Nicky Mannelli's wife, Lindsay, came into the Club. She stood in front of the stage looking straight at Dani, until

Nicky rushed over and took her over to where Vinnie and Anita were already seated. Lindsay's appearance upset Dani, but she carried on and remained in control, even whilst cursing Nicky.

'That lying bastard, Lindsay is very pregnant!'

When Dani came off stage, she angrily followed Nicky into his office.

"So, how come I've never seen Lindsay in the Club before, eh? And why'd she come in tonight, of all nights, Nicky?"

"Guess she's heard all about you, babe!" Nicky grinned. "She was sure looking you over good, wasn't she? But don't go back on stage tonight, Dani. I'll take her home soon."

"I'm too upset to go back on stage, dammit. I hadn't realized that your wife would be so pretty."

"Aw, she's nothing compared to you, babe," Nicky wheedled.

Lindsay Mannelli stood five-feet, ten-inches tall, with long blond hair and a willowy figure even though she was obviously pregnant. Nicky had already told Dani that his wife used to be a long-legged show girl, in Vegas. That was where he had met and married her, but Dani hadn't expected her rival to look quite so good.

'Damn all men!' Dani swore under her breath, as she watched Nicky lock up the safe. He was just about to leave when Dani yelled at him and began to cry.

"Nicky Mannelli, you flat out lied to me!"

He turned, stunned. "I lied?"

"Well, Lindsay *is* pregnant, isn't she?"

"So! I lied," Nicky confessed, nonchalantly, kicking at the office door as he left. "I'll catch you tomorrow, Dani, on the boat."

'Oh, shit! I can't tell him it's in the boat yard, for sale!'

"Nicky, wait! We can't meet at the boat."

He stuck his head back around the office door

"Why the hell not?"

"Er, well, it's in the yard, having some work done."

"Okay, then; I'll drop by at the house."

***

Sam had been on 'hat-check girl' duty that evening and after the doors were locked she flopped down next to Dani at the bar.

"Boy, you were great tonight, Dani. I could have sold tickets for that fight if only I'd known..."

"Leave it out, Sam! This has been one helluva night and I don't want to be reminded of any of it, thank you very much. I wish all the bars weren't closed already. I'd like to get very drunk tonight."

Mikey overheard and offered a suggestion.

"I know where there's an after-hours joint, down on the waterfront!"

Frankie, the other bartender, cut in.

"But can we get booze there or is it only pop?"

"Booze, I swear it," said Mikey. "I've been there, already."

"Then let's go!" Dani shouted.

"Oh, oh! This sounds like trouble to me," Sam said, to nobody in particular.

"Okay, we all go then but for god's sake, no one tells Nicky, or Tony, that we took you girls to that place, right?"

Mikey made them all promise.

***

Dani and Sam followed behind Frankie and Mikey and they all parked their cars on a wharf, across the street from, *'The Hideaway'*. The bar was choc-a-block with people having a great time but Dani wondered how on earth they had all gotten there. She hadn't seen any cars parked outside. The place was real dark inside and cigarette smoke hung in the air, thicker than fog in 'old London Town'.

When the rough-looking bartender gave Frankie his change, he jokingly said that he'd paid with a twenty dollar bill and that the bartender had shortchanged him. In a flash, the bartender reached over and yanked

Frankie over the bar by his tie. Frankie's eyes were bulging but he tried to laugh it off.

"Hey, man, I was just joking. Hell, I'm a bartender, just like you."

"Joking, huh?" The barman released Frankie's tie and reached under the counter.

"Oh, my God!" Dani gasped as the bartender pointed a snub-nosed revolver, right at Frankie.

"You gotta be kidding me, pal, it's only a fuckin' toy gun, right?" Frankie snickered.

"Oh, yeah? Well the joke's on you, pal."

The bartender fired a single shot into Frankie's stomach. His mouth opened in shocked disbelief and he looked down at the blood, oozing through his clenched fingers.

"Son of a bitch, the bastard shot me."

Shot or not, Frankie charged after the bartender and folk began screaming and running for cover. Dani slipped to her knees and crawled towards the door. She heard four more rapid shots and then Frankie, yelling.

"Jesus, I'm shot to shit."

She ran outside to her car, fumbling for the keys as Sam came running up behind her.

"Come on, Dani, open the damn doors!"

They tore away from there, burning rubber as they left. Dani stopped at the first phone to report the incident and request an ambulance but when they asked who was calling, she hung up. Dani was shaking so hard that she could hardly drive. Her knees stung like hell from crawling over broken glass and her hose were shredded. Her eyes were filled with tears.

"Poor Frankie, he must be dead by now."

"Yeah," Sam agreed. "I wonder if Mikey is still with him."

"Well, we're not going back to find out!"

Both girls agreed to never, *ever*, let Nicky or Tony know how they had gone with Frankie and Mikey to that god-awful place!

The next afternoon Mikey reported, discreetly, that Frankie was still alive and in hospital.

"That kid's got real guts, I tell ya'. He was torn all to hell but he's so damn stubborn that the doctors say he's actually going to make it. None of the slugs hit his heart or anything, but if they'd been .38's instead of .32's, the chief doc' says Frankie woulda been dead on-the-spot."

When Nicky and Tony were out of the way, Dani and Sam went with Mikey to visit Frankie in hospital. As they entered the private room and saw him, lying so still and with so many tubes in him, Dani had to fight back her tears. She touched his arm, gently and Frankie's eyes opened. He looked at Dani, then over to Sam and then to Mikey. He tried to raise himself up but the pain wouldn't let him. It took his breath away.

"I think I got a map of New York City carved on my chest and stomach." Frankie coughed and then winced, trying to laugh at his own joke.

"Don't talk, Frankie," Dani whispered. "Save it 'til you're stronger."

"I'll kill that bastard," Frankie spat. "When I get outta here, I'm gonna find him and then I'll hang him by his cock and watch him bleed to death. If you guys wanna watch, you're more than welcome!"

"Oh, Frankie, you can't even think that way," Dani pleaded. "He's probably some kind of nutcase. You know, completely 'off-his-rocker' and anyway, he's probably goin' to be in jail for a long time."

"I don't think they caught him yet." Mikey cut in. "He ran out back, into the alley but I didn't go after him. I was more concerned 'bout Frankie and, besides, I thought he might still have had one bullet left for me!"

Mikey's honesty made them all smile. Then a nurse came in.

"I'm sorry, but you need to leave now. This young man needs all his strength; he's going to have a long road back to full recovery."

Several weeks later, Frankie was released from hospital for the weekend and he came into the Club. After closing, Nicky invited everyone down to the annual Italian Festival, on Mott Street, for 'hot-sausage-and-peppers' to celebrate Frankie's recovery.

"But won't the tents have closed by now, Nicky, it's after four." Dani revealed her inexperience once again.

"Dani, you just don't know Italians." Nicky shrugged his shoulders. "Some tents'll be open all damn night!"

Nicky didn't like the look of the sausages in the first tent they came to. As they turned to leave, a group of kids came bursting in, breaking the necks off of beer bottles as they came in. At first, Dani thought they were after them, but the gang zeroed in on a kid of about sixteen.

"We warned you, you fuckin' faggot, we don't like queers like you on our turf."

A horrifying sight exploded before Dani's eyes as the gang gouged at the kid's face with their broken bottles. Women leaned out of windows and doors, yelling for their own youngsters to come back home. Police appeared from all directions with sirens screaming, only to find they were too late. The poor kid was a bloody mess and very dead.

Dani came out cautiously from behind garbage cans where she had been hiding and ran like hell. She and Sam reached their car at the same time and dived inside, locking all the doors. Dani drove like crazy for about twenty blocks before stopping the car; she was weeping, breathless and shaking from head to toe.

"Hell, Sam, we forgot about the guys but I had to get us both out of there," she wailed.

"I don't think I'll ever be able to forget that kid's screams. It was awful!"

"Forget it, Dani, if you can. As for the guys, they can find their own way home. This is *their* neighborhood and they know it like the backs of their hands."

"Sam, this City is crazy. What the hell are we doing here? I just want to go where it's peaceful and quiet, where people pretty much keep their blood to themselves."

"Let me know when you're ready, Dani and I'll go with you."

***

Dani had not made any definite plans, but had begun to realize that any time she had left, to get safely out of New York City, was getting shorter. Over the next few days, she put on her thinking-cap and started planning her escape to sanity. The days passed quickly.

Her precious 'Hearthstone Manor' was listed on the market with a private agent for $300,000. She had sold the boat easily, but at a loss. Dani's *'General-Bronze'* stock also went for less than she'd paid for it. Her furniture was worth well over $200,000, plus all her clothes, jewels and furs but Dani figured that maybe she could get all them back to Yakima without the Mannellis' knowledge. Tony seemed to be aware of Dani's every move though and she suspected that Sam might be the one who was telling him, so she began keeping *all* of her plans to herself.

During this period, Dani often felt that somehow HK was guiding and protecting her. She also remembered the guy who had helped her when she first came to 'The Big Apple'. Maybe Bill Crawford might be willing to advise her one more time.

She called and arranged to meet for dinner, at *'Michelle of Paris'*. To her surprise, Bill brought his best friend with him, a priest named Father Queen. Strangely enough, Dani felt comfortable and at ease with them both, telling them everything that had happened in her life since first arriving in New York.

Father Queen believed that Nicky Mannelli had some hypnotic power over Dani; that he was a man skilled in psychology who could weed out, and prey upon, a person's weaknesses. He advised Dani that she should forget about monetary things and make saving her own life her main priority. She should return, without delay, to the safety of her family out on the West Coast.

Bill strongly urged Dani to heed his friend's warnings and to let him know when she had arrived home safely. They had her best interests at heart, she knew that, but before Dani left, she decided to ask one more person's advice.

'There's just so much money to leave behind!'

She called HK's friend; the owner of her first New York penthouse, Mr. Feldman. Surely he must know how to either walk away from his possessions or, if possible, how to fight for them. She knew that he had lost several Cuban properties when Castro overthrew the government during the revolution.

Mr. Feldman agreed to meet Dani later that morning for a light breakfast. Yes, he knew from personal experience what it was like to lose millions of dollars but told Dani 'that was the gamble any person takes when they invest in a foreign country'.

"But Dani, here in America we have laws to protect citizens like you from corrupt folk like the 'Mannellis'."

Mr. Feldman kindly escorted Dani to the District Attorney's office to visit a personal friend, someone he was sure could help Dani. They really were in the DA's office – Dani read the sign on the wall as they entered the building - but she wasn't sure if she was speaking to the actual DA himself. One thing she did feel sure of, was that the people around her were finding it very hard to believe in her incredible story. It was a nerve-racking day for Dani Sutton.

A male stenographer recorded the entire interview, whilst three other men came and went at various times. Mr. Feldman's friend questioned her at great length and in great depth, about the Mannelli's and their connections with her money. After sitting for such a long time, Dani had to excuse herself and stand up. Her leg muscles were cramping. She limped slowly around the room to ease the stiffness and pain. As she passed the office window, a clock on the courthouse steeple opposite struck five o' clock and it startled her.

'My god, we've been stuck in this tiny room for more than four hours!'

Dani leaned back against the window sill and watched as her interviewer swiveled his chair around and talked to someone on the phone for a long time. Then he turned back to the room, clasping strong hands across his chest but keeping a blank expression on his face. He looked at his watch and then pushed back his chair.

"What say we all meet back here tomorrow morning to continue this discussion?"

Dani and Mr. Feldman waited together for a cab. He apologetically told her that she would have to visit the DA without him the next day, as he had other commitments. But he told her not to be afraid. She was finally in the right hands and his friend would advise her in a right and legal way. But even his sincere apologies left Dani feeling naked and alone and it must have shown in her face.

"Were you thinking of leaving town tonight, Dani?"

Mr. Feldman's razor-sharp question surprised her. It was as though he had read her mind. Sensing her discomfort, Mr. Feldman put a fatherly arm around her shoulders.

"I won't leave town, *just* yet," Dani promised. "I'll work at the Club tonight so no one will get suspicious and I *will* finish what I've started.

"But I need to be all packed and ready so that I can leave town to-morrow afternoon."

"Please don't let me down, Dani! Be there at the DA's office, first thing tomorrow morning."

As he climbed into his waiting cab, Mr. Feldman smiled.

"You know, Dani, I'll miss you, even though it's been a roller-coaster ride trying to keep up with you, young lady!"

He hugged her warmly and kissed her on the cheek. Mr. Feldman called out one last time as his cab began to pull away.

"Write to me after you've settled in, Dani."

She smiled and waved until he was out of sight.

Because of her friendship with this charming man he would soon vanish, never to be heard of again. But Dani couldn't know that.

Nor did Dani foresee that she would never keep her next day's appointment with the DA.

Chapter 18

The pilot announced their approach to landing at Seattle's *'SeaTac'* Airport, putting an end to Dani's contemplations. She stretched her stiff limbs and walked to the rear restroom, where she attempted to use her cosmetic skills to cover up deep, dark circles beneath her sunken eyes.

'Damn! I look every bit as bad as I feel.'

Her right cheekbone was bruised and extremely tender to the touch as she applied rouge. She tried to freshen up her mouth too, using a scrunched up napkin since she didn't have her toothbrush handy. Finally, with a squirt of mouth spray that she found in the bottom of her purse, Dani hoped she'd pass inspection. In truth, she knew it wouldn't fool her mother for very long.

Back at her seat, Dani winced as she reached up to the overhead storage locker to collect her meager belongings. Her whole body was racked with pain after her vicious beating in Tony Mannelli's office. She even had bruises in places she hadn't known it was possible to get them! The horrors of her last few days, plus the long hours on the plane, had taken a severe toll on Dani's body, mind and spirit.

As she stepped out onto the tarmac, she took a deep breath of fresh air and looked around in hesitation. Then she remembered that her father was going to leave a message for her somewhere. *'But where?'* A moment's panic followed until she remembered about the 'Lost and Found' office. Dani asked for directions and then stood in line impatiently, until the clerk had finished helping others.

"Do you have a message here for me, please? My name is Miss Dani Sutton?"

"This is the 'Lost and Found' desk lady, we don't take messages."

Spoken without even looking up at Dani!

"Oh, please, you must have one. I was told to collect a message from here when I arrived. I'm sure Papa left it here. Is there someone else you can ask? Please!"

At that the clerk grudgingly looked up and instantly melted under Dani's desperate gaze. He agreed to ask his superiors and when he returned from the backroom he was mumbling under his breath.

"Well, I'm told there's a message here some place. Sure ain't a regular thing, though." He carried on muttering as he searched; poking around under the counter for what seemed like ages. Finally, he found a white envelope with Dani's name on it and handed it to her with a flourish. Her father's note simply told her to call the airport's *'Holiday Inn'* hotel, but gave her no room number. Dani timidly asked for Mr. & Mrs. Gunther's room and when she heard her father's voice, she almost collapsed with relief.

"Papa, I'll be right outside. I don't have any bags with me so there's no need for you to park; just pick me up!

She had just settled onto a bench, hoping not to have to wait too long, when the familiar car pulled up. Before Harold had even come to a stop, Dani's mother was out and running, like a mama bear to her cub! They were clinging to each other and sobbing by the time Harold finally caught up with them.

"My poor baby! Laura reached out to caress her daughter's bruised face. "What have they done to you?"

Dani winced in pain. "Please don't touch, Mama, but I'm okay, really I am. The bruises will go away in time. I'm just grateful I'm alive."

"I'll get those bastards!" Dani's father cursed all Italians as his wife tried to calm him.

"Oh, Harold! Don't' talk that way, honey; you'll only get yourself all steamed up. Dani's home now."

Harold steered them toward the car. "Come on you two. We can all talk on the way home."

"Honey, why on earth didn't you call us before things got so bad?"

"Oh, Mama, I just didn't know where to turn! I was trying to salvage what HK had given to me but I couldn't seem to do anything without the Mannelli brothers finding out. And I was trying to protect you and Papa...and JR too."

'Who am I kidding? '

Dani hadn't been able to protect anyone had she, especially Kay.

'Her poor body is probably still wrapped in a satin sheet in my guest room closet, back in New York.' She thought of how bad the smell must be by then or if someone had found Kay yet. Dani couldn't imagine telling her parents about such a grizzly episode! She shook herself, trying to lose the distressing images from her past, but her mind was so focused on New York that it took several seconds before Dani responded to her father's voice.

"Dani? Can you hear me, honey?"

She nodded agreement, through the rearview mirror, so Harold carried on.

"I couldn't tell from our phone conversation just how much trouble you are in, Dani, so I've borrowed a friend's cabin, way up in the mountains. We can hide you there until we know exactly what to expect from these Mannellis. We haven't told anyone that you're here, not even our closest family."

"But won't they wonder what's going on Papa, if you and Mom aren't at home?"

"The plan is to leave you *both* up at the cabin for the moment. Your Mama could use some vacation time anyhow, after her surgery."

"I'll head straight back down the mountain tonight and I'll be at the Sherriff's office for work first thing in the morning, as normal and on schedule."

Dani smiled at her father's habitual, military correctness.

"I've arranged for a neighbor to answer the house phone. She'll tell folk that your mother is resting and can't be disturbed. Messages will be passed to me at the Sherriff's office and then I'll pass them on to y'all up at the cabin. Laura can call folk back later, if necessary.

"It might work," Dani replied, although a bit dubiously. She knew from experience how hard it was to fool the Mannellis.

"Aren't all these measures a bit extreme, Harold?" Laura asked, but Dani answered before her father could.

"Mom, please listen to Papa. There's probably someone already checking out our home in Yakima, looking for me!"

"She's right, Laura!" Harold Gunther patted his wife's knee encouragingly and turned slightly in his seat, to speak to Dani. "Honey, do you feel like bringing me up-to-speed with everything, as we drive?"

She nodded, taking a few deep breaths first to steady her nerves.

"The other day… oh, I can't remember exactly what day it was, Papa. It all seems like a dream now that I'm back here with you and Mama."

"Take your time, honey, you're safe now!"

Dani paused to compose herself before resuming her tale.

"You remember Mr. Feldman, Papa? He was my apartment building manager, when HK was still alive. Well, I asked his advice and he took me straight over to the DA's office, to speak to a friend of his. I was supposed to go back again the following morning – hell; that was only *yesterday* morning Papa, wasn't it."

Dani was shocked at how much she had lost track of time.

"Anyhow, Tony Mannelli found out about it all, somehow. It was him that roughed me up in his office and then he made Nicky take me down to Florida. Tony told his brother, *'Dani needs a long rest'*!"

"Well, I was pretty sure I knew what Tony meant by that so I had no choice, Papa; I had to play along and go to Miami with Nicky! I'd already made my plans for leaving New York and didn't want Tony Mannelli to get wind of them!"

Dani searched for the reflection of her father's eyes in the rearview mirror and they smiled encouragement back at her.

"Go on, honey!"

"Well, when we got to the hotel in Miami, Nicky wouldn't stay with me. He said he had to get back to New York for a business meeting or some-such and that he would see me in a few days. But as I was checking in at the desk, I saw two guys I recognized. They were a couple of Tony's hatchet-men, standing over by the lounge entrance."

Dani was adamant about what she had seen.

"I'm *sure* it was them. Then they were talking with Nicky and then Nicky came over to the reception desk and escorted me up to my room. But he wasn't like himself, you know? He seemed subdued, Papa, and he wouldn't look at me. He gave me a single, blood-red rose, just before he said goodbye outside my room and that was when I knew for sure that something was definitely wrong."

She shuddered at the recollection.

"I had to think *real* fast, Papa! I peeked out the door to make sure Nicky had gone and then grabbed my purse and coat and ran down the emergency stairway. I ended up in the basement before I found a service door and got out onto the beach and then I called you first thing the next morning."

Dani deliberately left out the part about being raped on the beach! There was only so much she felt able to reveal about her ordeals, even to her closest family.

"Well, you made the right move in coming home, Dani," her father reassured her, "but I sure wish you had done it sooner, hon! You're a very lucky girl!" Harold shook his head in amazement. "Mighty lucky, indeed!"

"I know Papa. "Dani sighed and leaned back against her mother's shoulder.

***

When they reached their destination, Harold Gunther drew up right in front of the rented condo. But Dani still had one more question.

"Papa, before he died, HK told me he had spoken to you about an FBI man; Paul McMahon, I think he called him. Did you ever talk to him, Papa? Do you think he'll be able to help us?"

"Yes, yes, honey! Now, don't you fret anymore, OK? I'll take care of all that stuff first thing in the morning, I promise." Harold soothed his troubled daughter.

Their cabin was delightful, with exposed structural beams and a wide overhang of the roof at the building's front and sides. A glimmering, white, snow-blanket weighed heavily on all the surrounding trees. The whole complex reminded Dani of a *'Hansel-and-Gretel'* storybook village. She loved the crunching of the crisp snow under her feet as she helped to carry in supplies. She loved the clean, fresh air, too and the fragrance of pine logs, burning in the open fireplace. But, most of all, she loved feeling safe again.

Dani shivered, not from being cold but from relief at being away from New York City, with its tall apartment blocks that put her in mind of concrete coffins.

It was getting late when Harold finally set off back toward Yakima. Laura and Dani waved until he was out of sight and then headed back inside to the warmth, arm in arm.

"I love you, Mama. Thanks for being here for me. I'm so sorry to cause you and Papa so much trouble, but things will get better soon."

"I hope so, Dani." Laura Gunther kissed her daughter's bruised face tenderly. "I really hope so, hon!"

By the time they had finished unpacking, they were both done in and turned in for the night. Dani drifted off into a deep, comfortable sleep, feeling safe for the first time in many months.

***

"Dani! Dani!"

"Mmmm?"

Dani grunted, trying to rouse herself from her deep sleep.

"Honey, I hate to wake you, but you've been snoring for fourteen hours straight and I'm afraid you'll harm those precious vocal chords of yours!"

Laura giggled as she pulled back Dani's covers. Dani squealed and pulled the covers back around her.

"You've gotta be crazy, Mama; it's cold in here. Look, I can see my breath and I'm still under the covers!"

"Well, it's not going to get any warmer and the afternoon's wasting away so get dressed and come on down. How do you want your eggs, honey?"

"Over-easy, please, Mama. *Mmmm!* I'd almost forgotten how good coffee smelled up in the mountains."

In complete ecstasy, Dani passed her nose over the delicious aroma that was wafting up from downstairs.

"Well, after you eat, honey, we'll go over to the Main Lodge, and buy you some warm clothes. We may be staying here for quite a spell."

Later, Dani and Laura walked out of the resort store, resplendent in new outfits and ready for the ski slopes. They asked directions to the bar, only to be told that there wasn't one. Dani whispered into her mother's ear.

"I might go into shock, Mama! What kind of place is this, without a bar?"

But the indignant desk clerk had overheard Dani's remark.

"This is a family-oriented resort, ma'am and so there hasn't been any interest in having a lounge, or even a restaurant, in the past. However, we hope to make some changes in the future.

"You mean, we can't even eat unless we cook in our own cottages?"

Dani was horrified, after being used to all the twenty-four-hour eating choices back in New York!

"We *do* have a cafeteria, ladies. You can get chili, hamburgers, hot chocolate and that kind of thing there, but only during the daytime. And, of course, there is always the grocery store in the village, up the road a'ways."

The clerk spoke this final sentence with a slight toss of the head.

Time passed quickly for Dani and Laura as they chattered away, catching up on all the family happenings. The last time they had seen each other was at Brandy's wedding. With the sun's rays bouncing off of blinding, white snow, Dani's cheeks gradually regained their natural, rosy-hue.

And, at nights, she found herself sleeping so well that she actually accused Laura of putting 'knock-out-drops' in her night-time cocoa!

Dani was definitely starting to feel more like her old self again and tried hard not to think of the old memories and fears that still lurked in the shadowy corners of her mind.

'I'll worry about all that tomorrow,' she told herself, in characteristic, ostrich-like fashion.

Laura, in spite of still recuperating from her recent hysterectomy, was amazingly full of vigor. She was, after all, a mother hen looking after an ailing chick. But, from time to time, Dani noticed her mother wince painfully and realized that she was putting on a brave face for her daughter's sake.

'Time to start making my own entertainment and give Mama a break.'

So Dani signed herself up for ski lessons. With the benefit of having long, strong legs and natural dancing agility, she had often been told that she would take to the ski slopes with ease. And she did!

Her instructor was Herr Marcel Schuster; a German, ex-Olympic skier from several years before. He and his wife, Olga, managed the whole resort between them. Olga was a typical Bavarian woman; short and heavyset and with long, brown braids wound tightly around her chubby, rosy face. Sadly, Olga spoke only German but she always had a big smile and a cheery, *'Guten Morgen,'* for everyone she met.

Late one evening, Dani was stoking up the fireplace in their cabin when she heard footsteps on the porch. Then the door opened and Dani squealed in childish delight.

"Papa!"

Harold Gunther carried in a fresh stock of groceries for his women-folk and they both tried to hug him at the same time.

"Hang on a minute you two or I'll drop all these damn bags!"

Harold grumbled on the surface, but he was very happy to see them both looking so well.

"But what brings you here tonight, honey? Don't you have work to-morrow?" Laura asked.

"I need to talk with Dani, honey and I can't do it over the phone," he explained. "Could you fix me some coffee for my thermos, to take back with me later?"

"Oh honey, I really hate for you to drive back down that mountain at night; it's so dangerous." Laura pleaded with him as she started a fresh pot of coffee. "Couldn't it have waited 'til tomorrow morning?"

But her husband just shook his head, sadly. Dani sensed the serious-ness in her father's tired voice as she sat down beside him.

"Dani, you are in a far bigger mess than I could have ever believed," he began. "By rights I shouldn't even be anywhere near this case, you being my daughter and all, but I managed to convince the FBI that you just wouldn't talk to anyone else. They've agreed to allow me this one interview but then I'll have to take a back seat, for while at least."

Harold rubbed at his brow. Laura bent over and laid a gentle hand on her husband's reddening forehead.

"Why, Harold; I swear you have a fever!"

"I think I *do* have a touch of the flu," he admitted, pushing his wife's hand away gently, but firmly. "Honey, go sit down over there and let me do my job. I'm here because I need to find out some things from Dani. Then I'll go home, take some aspirin and go right to bed, I promise."

"Papa, what is it you want to ask me?"

"Kay called my office today, Dani, looking for you."

"What!

She jumped up, but the blood rushed to her head so fast that she saw stars. Dani sat down again, hard.

"Are you *sure* it was Kay who called you, Papa?"

"Yes, I'm sure," he said, looking at Dani in an odd way. "Are you all right, darlin'?"

"Kay is alive!" Dani repeated those three little words, over and over again, whilst crying hysterically.

"Yes, of course she's alive, Dani. Whatever made you think she wasn't?"

She stammered through a cascade of tears.

"I... I thought it was Kay's body, back there in the guestroom closet. Especially after finding my poor li'l dog, Babette, dead too!"

"If you thought all of that, Dani exactly when were you going to tell *me* about it?"

Her father's voice had become stern and she wilted under his gaze.

"I was just too tired to tell you everything on that first night after I arrived, Papa," Dani whispered. "I meant to tell you the next time you came back up the mountain, honest I did!"

Feeling about ten-years old again, Dani blew her nose and dabbed at her rapidly swelling eyes.

"I guess I just didn't want to talk about the nightmare I'd escaped from!"

"No one's dead, Harold, so don't be too hard on the poor girl? She's only just getting back on her feet again."

Laura, ever the diplomat, tried to ease the tension between father and daughter but to no avail. Harold pointed a stern finger in Dani's direction.

"*No-one's dead?* Dammit' all to hell, Dani; I want to hear the *real* story - and I mean the *whole* story - right now, goddam it! There is an all-points bulletin out for your arrest; for murder!"

"But *I* didn't murder anybody, Papa! Yes, I saw a sheet full of shotgun holes and a whole lot of blood, but I didn't ever actually see a body!"

Harold Gunther couldn't believe what he was hearing. "You mean you didn't check to see if there was somebody still alive in that closet, before you left for Florida?"

"No, Papa!" Dani wailed in desperation. "Nicky wouldn't let me do *anything* except pack a bag and get the hell out of there.

"And besides," she added, defiantly, "just because a body was found in *my* closet, that doesn't prove I killed anybody, even if I *was* in town at the time."

"Well, trust me my girl, the FBI has more than enough proof for an arrest warrant."

Harold shook his head, miserably.

"But Papa, they couldn't possibly have any proof! How could they, when I didn't do anything?"

"Honey, they found *your* shotgun in the trunk of *your* car, parked up at the airport in New York. *Your* fingerprints, along with Kay's, are all over that weapon!"

"Well, I don't know how, or when, that shotgun got into the trunk of my car, Papa."

Dani's tears had all dried up and she was getting angrier by the minute at all the lies she was hearing.

"Sure, I left my car at the airport that night. That's when Nicky and I flew down to Florida."

"So, why weren't you in Nicky's car if he was the one driving?"

Harold had toned his anger down a notch as he listened to his daughter's breathless explanations.

"I really don't remember, Papa."

She was getting frustrated with her feeble memory as she tried, once more, to recall the details of that awful night.

"OK, we picked up *my* car at the garage next to the Club and left Nicky's car there. I don't know why he wanted to take my car, but that's what we did, Papa. Then Nicky drove me home to pack for my supposed 'vacation' in Miami."

"OK! Let me get all this straight." Harold was getting into full Sherriff-mode.

"You *both* went to Hearthstone Manor, in *your* car and that's when you saw this 'body' in your closet?"

"Yes, Papa."

"Did you see, or touch that shotgun, Dani?" Harold's voice was serious, but he sounded tired.

"No! I definitely remember telling Nicky to look around for it, but he said it wasn't there. And of course my prints are on it, Papa, it was *my* gun and I often took it out of that closet."

"Whatever for?" Laura was horrified at the very idea of her daughter with a gun.

"Sometimes, if I heard strange noises at night, I would bring it out of the closet and keep it next to my bed, just for comfort. That big ol' mansion is beautiful, Papa, but it could be pretty scary at night when there was just me and Kay there."

Dani was getting emotional again, but she carried on.

"Oh, and the last time I saw that gun Papa, was the night when I went down with my bad fever. Our alarm system had gone off and I remember telling Kay to go get the shotgun. That must be how *her* prints got on it, too. Oh, Papa, you do believe me, don't you?"

Dani searched her father's face for reassurance. "Hell, I don't even know who got killed," she finished with a whimper.

Harold Gunther took a small tape-recorder out of his shirt pocket, laid it down onto the table between them and snapped it to the 'off' position. Then he leaned over and took Dani's small, trembling hand in his own giant paw.

"Dani, I knew you hadn't murdered anyone all along, honey, but I needed to record your testimony for the benefit of the FBI."

"You recorded all of that, Papa?" Dani asked in disbelief. Laura sank back into her chair, in shocked silence.

"I had to, Dani, unless you prefer that I simply turned you over to the Feds to interrogate you! They know we have you safely in hiding and they also know how dangerous the Mannellis are. They believe that you were set up, Dani, but what they don't know is, *why*?"

"So who got killed then, Papa if it wasn't Kay?" Dani whispered.

Harold spoke gently. "It was Mr. Feldman, honey. I'm so sorry, because I know he was a good friend to you and HK."

Dani beat a white-knuckled fist against her leg. "Those bastards! I'll bet the whole thing was some kind of vendetta."

"What are you talking about? Wait a minute."

Harold switched the tape recorder on again. "Repeat what you just said, Dani, for the benefit of the tape."

"I said, I'll bet it was some kind of vendetta against poor Mr. Feldman, because he was..." Dani struggled to find the right words.

"Go on, honey!"

"Well, I think Mr. Feldman was *gay*, Papa and the Mannelli's don't like *'queers'*, if that means the same thing."

"Honey, that's not a good enough reason to take someone's life."

"Well, maybe it was because Mr. Feldman took me to see his friend at the DA's office, then, on my very last day in New York. That's when I told the DA everything I know about the Mannellis and the whole 'Family' thing! That was why Tony Mannelli beat me up so bad."

"Dani, I think you just said the magic words!"

Harold Gunther winked at her as he turned off the tape recorder once more and placed its precious recording safely back into his uniform pocket.

"I think this will be enough to satisfy the boys back at the FBI."

"You mean I can stay up here with Mama?" Dani asked, relieved.

"Yes, honey. The FBI knows the importance of keeping you well out of sight, so you and your Mama should just relax now and enjoy yourselves. I'd better head on back down the mountain and get myself to bed. I hope I haven't given ya'll this damn flu."

"Don't worry, Papa; I've lived through tougher things!"

Harold Gunther hugged his two favorite ladies and strode out into the cold night air.

Dolores J. Guthrie

Chapter 19

Dani had taken to the ski-slopes every bit as easily as Herr Schuster promised. Before long, she was gliding over the entire mountain, feeling every ripple of its packed, crusted snow beneath her highly polished skis. Her lithe young body moved across the sparkling slopes like a ballerina performing Swan Lake, just as Dani had often dreamed of doing during her childhood dancing lessons.

Dani's health was healing fast. In the fading afternoon sun, she and Laura would often sit out on the open-deck area, enjoying the camaraderie of their fellow skiers. Her natural, sparkling personality was almost back up to its usual tempo as she quickly made friends with the resort regulars.

Dani and her mother were sipping hot chocolate one afternoon when a tall, handsome man with curly, salt-and-pepper hair sat down next to Laura. With a smile, he extended a hand and introduced both himself and his younger companion.

"Hi, ladies! I'm Ira Moore. Would you mind if my friend and I joined you?"

The ladies nodded their agreement and the younger man sat down beside Dani. When he spoke, it was with a heavy, foreign accent.

"Good afternoon, *'Mademoiselles'*. My name is Andre Ramos."

The young man's voice was rich and had a wonderfully poetic lilt to it but he constantly looked toward Ira, as if to be reassured of the correctness of his words. Dani smiled at the two fascinating strangers as she made her own, official introductions.

"How do you do, Andre and Ira. I'm Dani and this lady is my mother, Laura."

"It is indeed a pleasure to meet you both," Andre replied.

"Almost daily, my companion and I have been watching your excellent progress on the slopes, Dani. Perhaps, one day, you would like to ski the expert run with us?"

"I'd love to, just as soon as Herr Schuster permits me to," Dani answered, cheerily. "Your accent intrigues me sir. Are you French?"

"Oui, *Mademoiselle*! Fifteen years ago I came to visit your country, but I fell in love with it and decided to make it my permanent home."

"Do you ever go back to see your family?"

"Oh, many times in the past but my father died five years ago and then my mother came to live over here. I haven't been back to France since."

Andre briefly glanced at Ira before speaking again.

"Now that we know each other ladies, would you care to join us for dinner this evening, in our cabin? Ira is cooking tonight."

Dani looked to her mother, who politely replied for them both.

"Thank you very much for asking but I don't think so gentlemen. I don't believe that my husband would approve of our going to another man's home for dinner, not without him there."

With a secretive little smile, Ira took Laura's hand and patted it gently.

"You need not worry about a thing, my dear ladies. Andre and I have been happily married - to each other - for the past fifteen years!"

"You mean that you're...? Oh, dear! Oh, my!" Laura put a hand up to her mouth to hide her embarrassment.

"Mother, it's quite all right," Dani cut in discreetly. "Ira, we would love to join you both this evening."

She extended a hand to each man in turn as she and her mother stood up to leave.

"We need to change before dinner, though, so where shall we meet you gentlemen?"

"Just come over to chalet number fourteen, at seven o'clock," said Ira, bowing slightly.

"Until later, ladies."

***

Dinner preparations were well in progress when Dani and Laura arrived. Ira was bossing Andre around the kitchen, just like any wife would, but the meal they eventually produced was superb. Laura quickly forgot her initial reservations about the couple's unconventional domestic situation. After dinner they all sipped coffee in the warmth and glow of an open fireplace.

When both the fire and the conversation had begun to fade, the ladies agreed to join Ira and Andre in their nightly sauna routine. There, they swapped many more stories together, before each retired to their own beds.

As the days passed, it became clear that everyone in the resort knew and loved Ira and Andre. Dani and Laura came to accept their friendship, without question, as the mountain community began to prepare for the coming high-season. On one especially clear, sunny morning, Dani made her way to the *'Mile High'* chair-lift, where Andre was already waiting for her.

"Good morning, Danielle."

Andre greeted Dani with a big hug and steadied the ski lift for her as she climbed on board.

"Good morning to you too, Andre, but where's Ira? I thought he was going to make the first run with us."

"He was, my dear, but an old friend of his arrived very unexpectedly, late last night. He hadn't realized that it was not possible to just walk in and rent a room at this time of year, so Ira invited him to sleep on our couch until he can find himself suitable accommodations. Ira is at home now, awaiting a phone call from another friend of ours who owns a small hut here."

"That's very considerate of you Andre, to take a stranger under your wing like that."

"Oh, that is just our natural, European hospitality."

Dani smiled at Andre as she gazed out over the landscape. Then she looked down to watch their own shadows swinging across the ground, far below them. The surface of the snow was glistening like diamonds under the bright sunlight.

"The top is getting near now," Dani suddenly shrieked, "and look; I can see Ira!"

They jumped off the chairlift together and giggled as they almost fell at the feet of Ira and another man. Dani looked up and was surprised to see such a handsome stranger at the top of a freezing mountain.

'Things are certainly looking up!' They silently appraised each other and then the stranger smiled, extending a hand to help Dani to her feet.

"Hi there, ma-am! I'm Digger Rosselli, from Texas. Ira here tells me that you've been trying to work up the courage to ski down the *'Mile-High'* with them."

"Yes, I come to the top here every day," Dani said, motioning toward the lookout-point benches.

"I love this mountain and this is a great spot to just sit and dream. I meditate for a while and then I ride the chair-lift down to a lower station and ski down from there."

The men offered Dani a cigarette as they lit up their own but she politely refused.

"Sorry boys, but I won't contribute to contaminating this wonderful champagne air."

"Don't you smoke then, Dani?"

"No, it's not good for a singer to smoke."

Her eyes were riveted on Digger and on the emerald green, one-piece ski-suit that was stretched over his muscle-toned body. A matching, stocking cap was perched jauntily on the back of his thick, golden hair, accentuating his tanned handsome face. Deep-blue eyes winked back at Dani as Digger adjusted his aviator-style sun glasses and extended a gloved hand.

"Come on then, Kitten, I'll get you down this little ol' hill, real slow and easy. You just follow in my tracks."

"Oh, I *really* don't think I'm ready." Dani was hesitant, even though her blood was stirring at the nearness of this handsome man from Texas. Digger whispered into her ear in that seductive drawl

"I won't let anything happen to you, I promise. No ma'am, not one thing."

Before Dani realized it, she had floated out into space. To her amazement, she found herself hugging the mountainside and following Digger's manly silhouette with surprising ease. He waited at every open area to allow her to catch up and he coached her gently, as if he were her own personal instructor. Digger reminded Dani so very much of *Star Trek's* 'Captain Kirk'. He even talked and moved like the famous actor.

'Perhaps it really is him using an alias. After all, famous stars have to get away from their fans once in a while, don't they?'

Dani was totally exuberant as she reached the bottom of what was one of the toughest runs in the skiing world, but hoped she'd never have to do it again. Once was enough for Dani, in spite of the massive thrill. Herr Schuster suddenly appeared at her side and voiced his unhappiness at Dani for doing such a foolish thing without an instructor present.

"But, since you have successfully made the run, I am obliged to present you with your *'Mile High'* pin!"

He chided Dani gently as he clipped the prize to her lapel.

"I insist, though, that you wait for *me* the next time you take a run down that route. Do you promise, Dani?"

Chagrined, Dani stammered her promise in front of the gathering crowd.

"Yes, Herr Schuster, I will wait for you. But I doubt very much that I'll ever try *that* again!"

***

A full week passed with Dani only getting brief glimpses of Digger Rosselli, even though he would ski the mountain daily. Then, early one morning, her father called with some welcome news. The 'all-points bulletin', issued against Dani by the FBI, had been withdrawn and the murder charges had also been dropped. The Mannelli's would be the prime suspects if anything were to happen to Dani in future. Paul McMahon, HK's original contact with the FBI, was now in charge of a full-scale investigation into the Mannellis' activities.

Harold told his daughter to relax; the pressures were over for the time being.

"Thanks for the good news, Papa, but I guess I've been feeling more relaxed ever since I found out that it wasn't Kay who got killed."

"I'm bringing Steve and Brandy up to the mountain later tonight," he told her.

"I'll bring *wieners* too and we'll have a *'wiener-roast'* for anyone who's brave enough to try it. Invite all your new friends, too."

And her father also suggested that maybe Dani should invite the young Texan he had heard so much about already!

"Bring Kosher, though Papa. I don't like *'tits and lips'*."

"What on earth do you mean, Dani?"

"I learned all about the kinds of crap they put in regular *wieners* from my restaurant days down in Florida." Dani shuddered at the memory.

"Well, I'll see what I can do, honey. I don't know if the 'deli' in Ya-kima knows the difference, though. See y'all later."

***

On his way to the chair-lift, Digger spotted Dani clamping her skis on and called out to her.

"Hey there! Seeing your face is like gettin' a vitamin shot-in-the-arm after the evenin' I had last night."

Dani grinned.

"You do look as though you tied-on-a-good-one, Digger. But where on earth did you find a bar around here?"

"It was at a private party, over at one of the instructor's cabins. I thought I might see you there, but no such luck."

Digger adjusted his aviator glasses and put on his thermal gloves as Dani spoke again.

"You remind me so much of *'Captain Kirk'* that I have to ask you; is Digger Rosselli your real name?"

A quizzical look flickered across the Texan's face, just for a brief moment, but he answered without hesitation.

"It sure is, ma'am. Now, I have a question for you. Where did *you* find such an unusual ski outfit?"

Digger pointed to the colorful, striped suspenders that curved around Dani's large bosom. She climbed onto the chair beside him, not realizing she was getting on the *'Mile High'* lift again.

"I bought this here when I first arrived."

Dani took a deep breath and opened her jacket a little, she was getting warm. "I hope these suspenders don't make me look like a boy."

Digger laughed at the idea.

"You'll never have to worry about that, ma'am. You're more woman than I've ever had the pleasure to meet."

Sexual electricity flashed through the air between them as Digger moved his ski poles over to his left hand and put his other arm around Dani.

"I've been working up the courage to ask you to do something with me one evening, but there aren't any restaurants or bars around here. I don't have a kitchen in the place where I bunk, either. I only have a pot-belly stove for warmth and so I have to cook whatever fits into one pot! That's hardly the kinda' place to take a lady out to dinner, now is it?"

Dani could feel his strong arm around her shoulders and her inner temperature began to climb. Her heart was beating too fast already and she needed to slow down the mood a little.

"Well, you're in luck tonight, Digger. My father is coming up later and bringing everything we need for a *'wiener-roast'*. I was going to ask you if you'd like to come, anyway."

"Sounds great to me. When we get down off the mountain, I'll drive down to the village and buy us a case of *Mogen David* wine.

"*Mogen David*? Isn't that the wine the local Indians drink and get 'loco' on?"

"I don't know about any Indians, Dani, but I *do* know that a *'wiener-roast'* ain't much of a roast without *Mogen David*!" Digger laughed as their chair-lift reached the drop-off ramp.

"Come on, Dani, we get off here."

Realizing at the very last minute that she was at the top of the *'Mile High'* again, Dani hesitated for a fraction too long. The chair had already left the platform by the time she jumped. The front zipper on her open jacket caught in the chair and she dangled below it as it went over the summit.

"Drop your ski poles, Dani!" Digger yelled out. "Now wiggle out of your jacket sleeves!"

Dani hung on until the ground got closer and then dropped, landing hard on her skis. But the fall was further than she anticipated. Her knees buckled and she slid for a quite a distance, finally stopping in a bank of snow. She was unhurt, but her skis were still strapped on. Alone in the quietness and without gloves, jacket, or ski poles, Dani realized she had to move quickly. Removing her suspenders, she made a sling out of them, to tie her skis onto her back with. Tearing large chunks from her undershirt, she then wrapped two pieces around her hands, like gloves.

Dani decided that climbing up to the top would be closer than going down. But with each step, she sank into soft snow up to her knees and her legs were soon covered with ice. It was slow going and frightening. Then Dani heard voices, calling her name.

Digger and others were out searching for her. *'Oh, thank the Lord!'*

When they reached her, Digger gave Dani his coat and one of his ski poles. Another skier gave her one of his poles too. Then down the hill they all went. She was triumphant to have conquered that majestic mountain one more time, but vowed it would *definitely* be her last.

Dani Sutton had had enough of life threatening escapades!

Laura and Ira had been the first to see Dani's red jacket, dangling from the empty chair as the ski-lift returned to the Lodge. It took some time before the Ski Patrol was ready to head out but they had just convened at the bottom of the hill when Dani herself came into view. Seeing her alive and well, the whole patrol gave an enormous cheer. Laura was right there too, with a warm jacket for her daughter.

Dani hugged her.

"Mom, I think I'll just stay a 'lodge bunny' from now on!"

***

Laura had invited everyone in sight to their *'wiener-roast'*, in cele-bration of Dani's safe return. Brandy looked as if marriage agreed with her, as she hugged her elder sister and promised they would get together the next day and have a good, long talk.

Digger came armed with a case of *Mogen David*, as he had promised and had been busy building little igloo-type wine cellars all over the area, to keep the bottles cool. Later, as they were all relaxing around the camp-fire, he took a long-stemmed, corncob pipe, filled it and then lit it using a smoldering twig from the fire. He puffed on it until the pipe was smoking real well and the party gradually settled into silence. People were wondering what the handsome man was doing.

Digger then handed the pipe to each guest in turn, asking, "You smoke'm peace pipe?"

Good naturedly, they each took a puff from the pipe and then handed it back to Digger. When it came to Dani's turn, Digger took a long drag himself before handing it to her.

"You smoke'm peace pipe too, before big feast?"

Dani struggled to take a deep puff but she choked on the smoke and Digger began laughing uproariously. She never did find out what was in the pipe, but everyone ate, drank and had a good time until they could eat and drink no more!

Between the fire, the wine and Digger's arms, Dani began to feel warm for the first time since earlier that afternoon. As they stared into the embers, Digger pulled Dani closer to him and kissed her lustily. The crowd around them ceased to exist anymore, until someone began to yell.

"OK; everyone get ready for the Swedish Dip!"

Digger released his embrace and whispered to Dani.

"What the hell is a Swedish Dip?"

"You either have to be a natural-born Swede, or just completely nuts to do it," she giggled. "A sauna is hot and moist, right? Well, you stay in there until you sweat and then you jump into the cold pool. Then, you go outside and roll around in a snow bank. Then, it's back into the sauna again. You do it over and over."

"Do you feel nuts tonight?" Digger asked, as he helped Dani to her feet. She began running towards her condo.

"I'll meet you in the sauna in ten minutes! I have to get my suit and some towels."

"Suits? That'll take all the fun out of it," Digger shouted after her.

"Yes, suits!" Dani shouted back.

At the cabin, she slipped into a pink, lace-bikini and tied her long, black hair up into a ponytail.

'How am I supposed to look feminine wearing snow boots and a ski jacket?' Dani shrugged, grabbed some towels and headed back to the party. *'Oh, what the hell.'*

Brandy, Steve, Harold, Laura, Ira, Andre, Marcel, Digger, Dani and two ski-instructors were all crowded into the same sauna. The warmth felt good but Dani had never seen so many people in one sauna before. When they all jumped into the cold pool, the water was so cold that Dani didn't feel her bikini top float away!

No one else noticed either, until she climbed out of the water and everyone laughed hysterically! Digger handed her a towel to hide her modesty while her father retrieved her bikini top. Heading back to the sauna for another round of *'Swedish Dip'*, Digger pulled Dani away, towards the small condo he was staying in.

In the back room, there were bunk beds at one end, plus a rough, wicker rug; a small oval reading table; a lamp and a smoldering pot-belly stove. Digger opened the stove door, threw in another log and left the door wide open for extra heat and some ambient light. He took a blanket and laid it on the rough floor, then pulled Dani down beside him. She was shaking from the cold as much as from her unexpected abduction. Digger reached out for the towel that was still wrapped around her but Dani hugged it tightly, until he kissed away any resistance by nuzzling at her neck and arms. Then the towel slipped away unnoticed.

Digger took a fresh towel and began drying Dani, rubbing her skin hard to warm her. He stared at her voluptuous breasts as they glistened in the firelight. Then he slowly caressed them; first one side and then the other, back and forth with his lips.

"Like two large, ice-cream cones that are too cold to melt," he whispered.

Dani's inner temperature rose rapidly. She had never felt as alive as at that very moment. Her body had become a roaring oven and Digger was the one who fanned the flames. She relaxed completely and gave herself over to the moment.

***

After hours of sexual bliss, they stood by Digger's cabin door, kissing goodnight. Dani had only a blanket wrapped around her as she had left everything else back in the sauna dressing rooms. *'I'll have to try and retrieve my stuff discreetly, tomorrow!'*

Digger looked deep into her eyes.

"I don't want you to go, baby. Maybe we could do it all over again?"

As they were trying to decide whether or not to go for round two, a rough voice came booming out from somewhere deep within the cabin.

"Either get it on again, or say goodnight so that I can get some goddam' sleep!"

Dani slipped off through the snow, giggling and moving quickly to keep herself from freezing. She sneaked inside their own condo and closed the door softly behind her.

"Is that you, Dani?" her mother's voice queried from somewhere within the darkness.

Dolores J. Guthrie

Chapter 20

Laura, long overdue for her six-week, post-operative checkup, was packing for her return home. She had missed Harold, although he said he was happy enough with *'Gigo'*, the dog, for company!

All kidding aside, Harold was lonesome too and he felt that Dani was safe enough now, with Digger and her other new friends up on the mountain. He had secretly feared that Nicky Mannelli might show up there, to try to win Dani back. Getting involved with Digger would help heal Dani's broken heart so Harold had been all in favor of the idea of the tall, Texan going along on her proposed, cross-country expedition. Harold made Dani promise to call home though, as soon as they returned safely to the ski lodge.

For her part, Dani decided that the week-long trip would accomplish two things. Firstly, she'd receive her cross-country skiing badge, which was no mean feat in itself.

Secondly, if she could handle being alone with Digger, away from everyone and everything for a whole week, she'd agree to travel the State Fair circuit with him as he had already asked her to do. Dani couldn't imagine the Mannellis looking for her there and so it would be a great place to hide; keeping those New York goons well away from Yakima and Dani's precious family.

The morning was bright and beautiful as the three intrepid skiers began their trip, braving the icy foothills of that big mountain. Marcello, the professional, led them and his expert pace made it difficult for Dani and Digger to keep up. It wasn't long before Dani could feel the weight of her backpack pulling at her shoulder muscles, probably caused by all the little 'extras' she had squeezed in. She daren't complain as they moved deeper into Mt. Rainier National Forest and the shadow of the mountain slowly engulfed them. It was a challenge, avoiding all the huge pine trees, the tricky ravines and wash-outs along the way.

At one point Dani was lagging way behind and she saw something running off through the trees. She couldn't tell if it was a wild dog or a wolf.

"Damn!" she yelled. "Wait for me!"

Temporarily losing control, Dani went end-over-end and landed in a gully. After the two men had assured themselves she wasn't hurt, they had a good laugh. Then Marcello spoke to her seriously.

"So, Dani; now you learn lesson number one. When you fall, you must make your own recovery!"

"But I can't get my skis untangled!"

She waited in vain for the men to help.

"All part of the course," Marcello told her, matter-of-factly, as he pushed off again. "Come on Digger, she'll catch us up in a few minutes."

"Hey, wait a minute, there was a wolf or something back there!" Dani yelled after the retreating pair.

"Dani, I've never known of *any* authenticated case of violence on *any* human, from a wolf or a wild dog!" Marcello yelled back, over his shoulder.

Dani muttered as she struggled to take off her own skis, but finally she hauled herself out of the gully she had landed in. She heard another noise but kept her composure as she put her skis back on and followed in the men's' tracks. The laughing duo was waiting for her, not very far up the path, but Dani was not at all pleased.

"You rats! I'll probably be frozen stiff by morning and you won't be laughing then."

"Sure we will," Digger replied. "We'll sit you by the fire and watch you defrost!"

As the air temperature slowly fell, the snow became crusted and very slippery and the going was getting harder. Just as Dani began to wonder if they'd ever be allowed to rest, Marcello, standing atop a small knoll, began gesturing. A short distance down the hill, she could see a quaint log cabin, nestled among some trees. A river raged nearby, the past winter's thaw making the rapids run, foaming white. Several cords of wood were stacked by the cabin door, neatly protected from the weather with a tightly tied-down oilcloth. Smoke was coming out of the chimney.

"Look!" Dani shouted, with a sinking feeling in her stomach. "Has someone else rented our cabin?"

'Damn! I'll never be able to make the return journey back to base tonight.'

A woman came out of the cabin door and emptied a pan of dirty water over the end of the deck. As she turned to go back inside, Marcello called out to her and then pushed off down the hill towards his wife!

"Digger, how do you suppose Olga got here ahead of us?"

Ignoring her question, Digger blew her a kiss.

"Come on, I'll race you down."

As they got nearer to the cabin, even over the noise of the pounding river Dani could hear highway traffic in the distance. Then, at the corner of the cabin, she saw the resort's jeep, parked up.

"You rats!" she yelled. "We could have *all* driven here."

"Of course Dani, but then you'd never have made your cross country badge, would you?" Marcel smiled, wickedly.

She hesitated and thought for a moment.

"Does this mean that we can go back next weekend by jeep then?"

"Yes, I'll pick you up on Sunday around noon!"

Marcello gave her a smile and a wink. After explaining about the cabin, the food supplies and all about the surrounding area, he and Olga bade them both a fond farewell. With chains on the tires, their jeep slowly made its way through the trees and down a snowy, winding track toward the main highway.

Digger waxed their skis, ready for the morning, whilst Dani changed into her after-ski clothes; a powder-pink, silk jump suit and white fur, Indian moccasins. She ran a brush through her thick hair and licked her lipstick-free mouth. *'I don't need makeup in the middle of the mountains, do I?'*

She was hungry after their long day in the snow and savored the aroma of Olga's beef stew wafting up from the cast-iron pot over the fire. On the other side of the fireplace hung a cast iron teapot, steaming through the spout.

"Dani, go look in the side pocket of my backpack. You'll find some small bottles of booze in there."

"How come you still have these?" she asked, returning with several individual-sized, bottles of spirits. "I always drink mine on the plane."

"The stewardess was extra nice to me. But you can buy these little bottles in most liquor stores, too."

"I don't believe I ever went into a liquor store, not even while I lived in New York."

"But didn't you say you had a bar in your Brooklyn home?"

"Yes, but my maid stocked the house with everything for me. I never did any of that stuff, Digger."

"I need to talk to you, Dani."

Digger's voice had suddenly became serious.

"You know, if we travel together, on the State Fair circuit I mean, you're going to have to learn to live in cheap motels and eat in diners. Adjust to *my* way of living is what I mean. I'm only a poor *'Carnie'* worker and I can't afford luxuries like the kind you're obviously used to."

"We won't have to live in *total* poverty, Digger. I'll pay my own way and between us we should at least be able to live in a 'Travelodge'! But it has to be clean!"

Dani was suddenly horrified at her own tone of voice.

"Oh my; here we are, together for only a few hours and already we're into a heavy discussion. Let's save it for another day, Digger. It's a shame to let all this lovely hot water go to waste. And I've made some hot, buttered-rum 'toddies' for us both."

Dani handed him his brew and raised her own glass in a toast.

"To tomorrow being the first day of the rest of our lives!"

Digger added his own comment. "And I hope we'll be together 'til the very end."

They savored the warmth and flavor of their drinks for several minutes of silence until Dani spoke again.

"You know, Digger, the cupboards here are very well stocked for just a rental place. If you're so poor, how can you afford all this just for a week?"

"Come on, Dani; save it for another day, remember?"

***

Darkness separated their small hideaway from the rest of the world. Digger lit kerosene lamps for illumination and Dani closed all the heavy curtains to keep in the warmth. She dished up the stew and it really hit the spot, for both of them, after such a long, physical day.

Straightening up the kitchen ready for the morning, Dani peeked out through the window.

"Wow, it's really snowing out there. I'm glad the owners have installed indoor plumbing here. I hate outhouses with a passion and I won't ever use one."

"What, *never*?"

"Never," Dani repeated, emphatically.

"Whatever happened to make you so feel so strongly about using an outhouse?"

"When I was three years old, Hal, my older brother and I were playing cowboys and Indians. I went into the outhouse to hide and I tried to sit on Papa's seat but I fell through the hole. Hal found me and called for my mother, but I almost drowned before she could pull me out. That's why I'd rather fight *'Big Foot'* for the nearest tree than use an outhouse, ever again. I guess that's why I've lived such a *shitty* life ever since!"

"Has your life really been so bad Dani?"

"No, silly; it's just my way of making a joke. And, speaking of bathrooms, I think I'll use ours now and get ready for bed."

The room seemed suddenly lonely without her presence and Digger couldn't bear the silence any longer.

"Dani, what's taking you so long?"

He had piled all the pillows he could find on top of blankets that he had already spread out in front of the fire. Even though he'd been busy, a chill ran down Digger's back and he decided to keep on his long johns. Temporarily, anyway! Anticipating Dani's return, he propped himself on one elbow. Then Dani opened the door, letting in a blaze of light from the bathroom behind her.

"Didn't you know there is electric light in the cabin, too?"

"Don't, Dani!" Digger called out. "Turn out the lights and just stand there. I want to take in every inch of you."

She was wearing a sheer, white peignoir, fully trimmed with feathers and high-heeled slippers that enhanced her long, slender legs.

"Are those real marabou feathers?" Digger was in awe of her.

"I think so, but I just call them boas. I have a kind of a hang-up for fine lingerie."

"God, you amaze me, Dani. How did you get all those feathers up here? You didn't bring them in your backpack, did you?"

"Of course I did. You'll be surprised at all the goodies I've got stuffed in there!"

"You're not only beautiful, but ingenious too. Come and lay by the fire, before you freeze."

The heat from the stove, the endless wine and their own passions ebbed and flowed throughout the night. Their bodies blended well and Dani was in rare shape. Digger gasped as he finally came up for air.

"My God, Dani! We should try to get some sleep now and save some energy for tomorrow, if I even live that long!"

She succumbed to his manly pleas and cuddled down into his arms. He whispered into her ear as they drifted off to sleep.

"Dani, I think I'm falling in love with you."

She snuggled closer, feeling wonderfully safe within the circle of Digger's strong arms.

***

They returned to the main resort the following weekend, both feeling that their time at the cabin hideaway had flown by much too fast. But they also knew that there would be many more months, perhaps even years to come for them both to be together.

Digger went straight to the lodge telephone to get things set up with his boss, ready for their 'State Fair' tour.

During the past week, Dani had given much thought to the problems that still awaited her back in New York. Unfinished business, but she would have to take care of it *'in absentia'*. She felt it would be safe to call her friend, Bill Crawford, for his help one last time. Dani headed for the telephone too.

"Where have you been, Dani? I've been worried sick, not hearing a word from you in all this time. Did you go to the DA, like you planned to?"

"Yes, I did, but it's too long of a story to tell you over the telephone, Bill. I'll tell you all about it someday soon. I'm calling to ask for an attorney's name and phone number. Someone who can oversee the sale of Hearthstone Manor for me…someone I can trust, Bill. Someone who can also oversee the packing up and putting into storage of all my household things. I'll need to sell some stock and to settle some other affairs too, but without my presence there in New York. This *all* has to be kept very hush-hush, Bill."

"It sounds like you don't plan on coming back to the City then, Dani."

"No, Bill, I can't. The Mannellis have already tried to have me killed once. I'm in hiding now and I can't even tell *you* where I am. I daren't let you get involved."

"All right, I'll help you, but you know it hurts me to hear all of this stuff. I told you that you were playing with dynamite, Dani, working for those low-life hoods. OK, here's the number of a guy called Houseman. You'll be safe with him. He's been *my* company's attorney since we were both at Yale together."

Bill paused to give Dani time to write it all down but his next comments took her breath away.

"Dani, why don't you come back to New York? I'll take you to my Connecticut home; no one would ever find you there. I've wanted to ask you so many times, but I'm putty in your hands with anything that concerns your involvements. Each time I came close to asking you to stay with me, that damn black cloud of your connections was there and I'd let you slip through my fingers again."

"I honestly never knew you felt that way, Bill. What are you trying to tell me?"

"Oh, Dani," Bill stammered. "Dammit, I love you, Dani. Please come back. I've missed you so much. I've always loved you, but I wanted you to get your life back in order before I asked you to marry me. I told your mother a long time ago that *I'd* be the one that got you in the end."

"Bill, is this a marriage proposal?"

"Hell, woman, yes! Are you coming back by yourself or do you want me to come fetch you?"

Dani's mind was in turmoil. Digger walked over and listened for a moment before pulling her hair to one side and kissing the back of her neck. He reached over as if to hang up the phone, but Dani frowned and held his hand off.

"I can't come back, not at this time. I just wanted a name and number, that's all."

"Dani, I can't lose you now."

"I don't know where I'm going to be from one day to the next for quite a while, so please don't try to find me."

"But what about us, Dani?"

"I just wish you'd told me about your feelings sooner, Bill. Right now I'm very confused. I need some time to sort my life out."

"Well, I suppose you do, but you're going to drive me to drink, woman. Please keep in touch and don't leave me hanging for too long."

Dani hung up. She frowned at Digger to let him know she didn't appreciate his attempts to hang up the phone while she was still talking.

"What and who was that then?"

Dani decided to tease Digger a little. "It was a very dear friend of mine. And he just asked me to marry him."

"You aren't going to are you?" Concern showed in his voice.

"I don't know, Digger. I'll have to give it some serious thought while I'm travelling on the State Fair circuit with you!"

Seething over Dani's mysterious phone call and her teasing replies to his questioning, Digger drove down into the village to call New York and report to his *real* boss - Tony, *'The Horse'*, Mannelli.

Chapter 21

The telephone line to New York came in loud and clear.

"Tony? It's Digger here."

"Hey, long time, no hear, my man. You made contact with our sweet little 'package', yet?"

"Oh, yeah! And you were right when you said it was beautiful, man. Are you sure we can't we handle this problem without 'burning the wrapper', so to speak?"

"Shit man! Just be sure there's no return address on it, then, if you get my meaning. There's way too much heat back here in the East. How's the temperature out there?"

"Oh, it all seems normal enough, no problems. I'm relaxing and enjoying the trip so far. Things will stay fine, until I'm either pushed into a corner somehow or the right opportunity to deal with 'the package' shows itself."

"So, how are you getting along with her ol' man, the lawman?"

"It's a real kick, Tony. Honest, you wouldn't believe it. Her family actually promotes me! Things couldn't be better on that front."

"Has anything been mentioned about things back here in New York?"

"No, nothing yet. Everyone seems to know the lady is in hiding and doesn't want to leave the mountain, but that's all I've heard."

"OK! Have you made contact with my man in Texas yet, about working the State Fair circuit? Good! You'll be working for my own 'Bonavita Farm' and we'll use my own show horses from there too, since they already work the circuit."

"Thomasina, my trainer, will show you all the ropes and won't hire any other helpers; they'd just get in your way. Now, if you can only talk our 'package' into going on the road with you, we'll have full control over her again and I'll be a happy man."

"Sounds good to me, boss. And after this last week, I think the 'package' will go just about anywhere with me!"

"All right, Digger, but the main thing is to keep her from trying to recoup *any* of her damn money from back here. If you can do that, you can keep the 'package' under wraps for as long as you like."

"I tell you, Tony, this woman's really something. I wish we woulda' met under different circumstances."

"Hell, if only *I* could have gotten into that too..." Big Tony Mannelli sounded almost wistful.

"You mean to say you *didn't*?" Digger was amazed.

"Naw, she was always my kid brother's piece of tail. And I always thought she was a black-widow spider anyway, so I stayed well clear."

"Why in the hell would you call her a black-widow, boss? She seems harmless enough to me."

"Nicky once told me that she has these great long legs and as they made love, she would wind 'em around him and finish up getting on top. Then that long, black hair of hers would fly all around. When he eventually came, the bitch would move on down and *eat* him until he died a slow death."

Digger's brow broke out in beads of sweat as he listened to Tony's words. *'Yeah, I know just what Nicky means!'*

"That's why I'm going to make the most of this assignment, boss."

Digger mopped his brow, hung up the phone and headed back to his jeep, the ski resort and Dani Sutton.

***

On a balmy spring morning, the town of Pomona, California, came alive at first light with the arrival of a mighty convoy. Huge trucks carried farm products, fairground equipment of all kinds and animals for showing and for racing. Giant tents went up in mere moments as merchants and exhibitors prepared colorful and exotic displays to delight fairgoers of all ages.

JR flew down to join his mother for few weeks, during his spring leave from the Academy. It was the first time he had met Digger Rosselli, the exciting new man in his mother's life. The three of them strolled through the fairground, making their way toward the horse barns. Dani sniffed the air and breathed in the mingled, fresh smells of food and animals. She was anticipating what it would be like, working out in the open with all the horses. She found the thought of learning about all the behind-the-scenes activities and getting to know a new, gypsy lifestyle, sensual and exhilarating.

Digger nudged Dani as they passed the stables.

"Look! I can see the van from our 'Bonavita Farms' outfit."

"Where?!" JR looked all around.

"Over there, see? That blue-and-silver *'Mack'* truck next to that other truck with those *'Budweiser'* Clydesdales."

Dani had already stopped dead in her tracks and was staring in awe as six, perfectly matched, Clydesdale horses were carefully unloaded from a luxurious trailer.

"Oh my God! Just look at those beautiful animals!"

She watched their muscles rippling over massive bodies, as the huge horses were led down a wooden ramp. Nostrils flared in anticipation, almost as if the creatures knew that a performance was imminent.

"OK!" Digger was dismissive. "We have ten more days of working next to the Clydes. I'm sure we'll see enough of them."

He led the way over to a small, wiry man who was busy taking bandages off the legs of one of three chestnut mares at the *'Bonavita Farm'* enclosure.

"Hi there, Tommy. Looks like you could use some more helpers. I'd like you to meet Dani Sutton and this big dude here is JR, her son."

"Good to meet y'all."

Tommy stood up, wiped his hands down his jeans and shook hands with Dani and JR. For a small man he sure had a firm grip.

"Be good to have extra help, but have y'all handled horses before?" the little man wanted to know.

"Yeah, some!" Digger cut in before Dani could answer.

"Dani here owned a quarter-horse, back in Washington State and she still has a two-year-old, Standard-bred trotter, out of 'Night Dream', from over on the East coast."

"Strange!" Tommy commented, scratching at his head. "How did ya' get a 'Dream' filly? I heard only the *Mafia* owns that blood line?"

"It's a long story buddy, but we can talk about that later."

Digger steered the conversation in a new direction and Dani took the hint.

"My father's a sheriff around here and he has many horses, for parades and such. I guess I've always had horses around me."

"Well, that's good to hear. The first thing you can do is to get the tack-and-viceroy out of the van. Can you drive a truck, young JR?

"I guess so. I've driven the trucks at military school."

"Okay then, here's the key. After it's been emptied, park it up and lock it. Just look for a big sign that says 'Reserved for Vans and Trailers of Exhibitors'. You can't miss it."

"Tommy!" Dani leaned out of the van. "What's a 'viceroy'? Cigarettes?"

The little man shook his head in despair, muttering, *'Horsewoman, my ass*!'

"It's that 4-wire, wheeled buggy in the back, near the harness and snaffle-bit. Bring those out first, then all the tack trunks."

But for the rest of that day, the new help took Tommy's directions well and they all seemed willing, so he decided to let Dani's *faux-pas* go for now. He would see how they all panned out over the next day or two. That first day was long and hot and the infamous Pomona smog was doing its worst. Dani's eyes burned, her nose was stuffed up, her back ached and she was starving. She craved a long, hot shower and some food.

"Tommy, when can we eat? It's after seven already!"

"Just as soon as you finish cleaning the stalls and get things wetted down."

"You mean I have to shovel horseshit, too?"

The men fell about laughing.

'God, I thought this would be a bit more glamorous, like in the movies,' she muttered.

But as the days rolled by, the routines became easier and any obstacles seemed only minor ones.

It was a far cry from the glamour of New York, but a new phase in Dani's life had well and truly begun.

***

Tommy, dressed in *Bonavita Farm's* blue-and-silver racing silks, looked magnificent astride a racing cart; always placing second or third with *Bonavita Farm's* two, 'Standard' horses. But he took a 'first' at three different fairs with their fine, harness horse; a filly named 'Queen's Knight'.

Smooth, fast and beautiful, 'Queens Knight' was a five-gaited, American saddle-horse. Her mane was long, full and jet black; even though she carried her un-docked tail high, it still almost reached the ground. She went through her qualifying gaits with ease and her high, stylish action set the *'Bonavita Farm'* team well on their way to qualifying for the Santa Barbara National Finals. Dani mused as she groomed the fine, Texan horse after another successful show.

'What a coincidence. She has the same blood line as my own 'Dream of Eden' filly.

As much as Dani liked Digger, she found it difficult living beneath the limitations of his meager income and always having to stay in the cheapest motels. It sometimes seemed that Digger deliberately went out of his way to search out the worst places! Some showers even had scum on their curtains and Dani refused to bathe in them, fearing she might catch some dreadful disease.

On one particular night, it was just too much to take when Digger ordered *one* dinner and *two* plates.

"Honey," Dani spoke tentatively. "For a while now, I've been meaning to talk to you about our money arrangements."

"I don't want to talk about that, Dani." Digger's reply was sharp.

"I told you before we started this trip that I didn't want you touching your own money. We agreed to get along on *my* income or not at all. You *do* remember our agreement, Dani?"

"Well, yes, but it seems such a shame when I have money of my own.

We don't go dancing, or eating out or anything."

"We could be so much more comfortable together if you'd let me share the expenses, at least until you get your back salary from all these fairs we've worked."

"Oh all right then, if it'll make you happier." To Dani's astonishment, Digger gave in without a fight. "You could make me a loan if you like and then I'll pay you back when my boss pays me."

"How much do you need then, Digger?"

"Well, how about $50,000? If we're going to use your money we might as well do it right, eh babe."

Dani was taken aback by the swiftness of Digger's decision and she almost choked on the amount he asked for. But she didn't let her feelings show. She took out her checkbook, knowing full well that *'The Horse'* could still be looking for her. *'But by the time Tony has the check traced, surely we'll have moved on and be in another state.'* Such was Dani Sutton's naive logic.

After receiving the money, Digger became a changed man. He wined and dined Dani and told the whole world that he was in love with her. He even called his parents in Texas and told them that he and Dani were married. She was quite shocked to hear him lie like that, especially to his parents. When she questioned him about it, Digger said that they were just old-fashioned folk; they wouldn't understand him and Dani traveling around together if they weren't married.

And Dani believed him.

***

Moving onward to San Francisco, Digger and Dani checked into the *'Hotel Fairmont'* late at night. She was happy to be back in beautiful surroundings again, but when she looked out of their window the next morning, Dani backed away in alarm.

"Just how high up are we, Digger?"

She could only associate San Francisco with earthquakes and their building seemed to be tipping over already, they were so high up! Laughing at Dani's naïve fears, Digger jumped up into the middle of the bed. He faced the window, stark naked and with his arms outstretched and began singing.

"On a clear day, rise and look around you!"

Dani giggled and hit him with a pillow. He dragged her back onto the bed, pinning her down with his knees and tickling her with a feather pulled from the pillow. Then he asked her the same question, over and over again.

"Do you really love me, Dani? Do you love me?"

"Stop, stop! Yes, I love you, Digger. Now stop tickling me."

"Who do you love, Dani?"

"You, Digger, I love *you*!"

He swept her up into his arms, saying how long he had waited to hear those special words. The two of them were lost in their own special world for the rest of that day.

In the evening they went to see the movie, *'Doctor Zhivago'*. It was one of the most romantic love stories Dani had ever seen. During intermission, they went out to the bar and Digger ordered two chilled martinis. Dani was dreamily thinking about their pillow fight, earlier that day and about the romance of the movie too, when she saw something glinting inside her drink. Using her little finger, she picked out a sparkling, diamond ring from the bottom of her glass and stared at him in amazement.

"Did you put this in here?"

Digger carefully placed the ring on her left-hand, third finger.

"I can't afford a seven-carat diamond ring like the one you said HK bought for you, Dani."

"But I thought he wouldn't mind if we used *his* ring for our wedding which, by the way, will be on your next birthday; June the second!"

"Digger Rosselli, are you asking me to marry you?"

"Yes and you better hurry up with your decision, because the intermission is almost over!"

"Yes, Digger! I *will* marry you!"

He pulled Dani into a long, hard kiss. Then he threw her up in the air with a loud Texas, 'whoopee!'

"Dani Sutton just said 'yes'!" he yelled as they headed back inside the theater. Digger told anyone who'd listen that Dani had agreed to marry him. She was walking on clouds and could hear the applause from the other bar patrons for Digger's performance.

***

JR came over to be best man for his mother's wedding in Portland, Oregon. The wedding party occupied one complete wing of the downtown *'Thunderbird Hotel'* where the manager, a master of his profession, took personal care of all the preparations. The entire Gunther family, along with friends old and new, attended Dani's gala affair.

The bride wore a bone-white, Italian-knit suit for the occasion. Yellow and white daisies were woven into the crown of her long black hair and she carried a matching bouquet. As she walked down the aisle, Dani saw Digger's outline in the candlelight and, for one brief moment, she imagined it was Nicky Mannelli standing there. She knew she would always love Nick but, someday, maybe she could love Digger just as much, but in a different way.

The organist played, *'Love is a Many Splendored Thing'* as Dani gazed into Digger's eyes and they exchanged their vows, 'until death do us part.' Then Dani threw her bouquet of daisies high into the air.

All the young girls were still squealing as Digger and JR hurried the bride outside. A rented limo was waiting to whisk the newlyweds off to the airport, en route to a Hawaiian honeymoon cruise.

As Dani kissed her son goodbye, he whispered into her ear.

"You know, Mom, I'm on summer vacation now with nothing to do. Can I meet you and Digger down in Hawaii, say in a couple of weeks?"

The request caught his mother off guard, which JR had counted on all along.

"Okay! We'll be staying at the *'Colony Surf'*," Dani agreed. "Have your grandfather take care of the arrangements, but give us *three* weeks alone first, okay?"

"Did I hear you right?" Digger cut in. "Did you just tell your son he could come to Hawaii with us?"

"Well, yes! But, honey, in three weeks' time we should be about ready for some company, don't you think? It's not like we haven't already been living together is it and I haven't seen JR much at all during this past year."

Dani gave Digger her best pout. Her new husband looked up at JR's six-foot, five-inch frame, towering above him.

"OK son; see you in about three weeks then!"

JR laughed and extended his hand. "You just take good care of my mom, y'hear."

***

After a pleasant flight to San Francisco, the honeymooners walked up the gangplank and onto the beautiful *'Lurline'*, for Dani's first ever ocean voyage. Coincidentally, she discovered later that the ship was built the same year she was born!

When they got to their stateroom, Digger swept Dani up into his arms and carried her over the threshold. As her feet touched the floor again, he gently kissed his bride of four hours.

"Welcome aboard, my darling."

He bowed to Dani and then turned her towards the interior of the cabin. On a small table, several dozen, red roses surrounded a three-tiered wedding cake and a silver ice-bucket held two bottles of champagne. A lump welled in Dani's throat. Digger was steering Dani toward the bed when their steward tapped on the door.

"Your luggage, sir?"

They both giggled as the steward entered with all their bags and began to help with the unpacking. Digger gave Dani a squeeze.

"I'll go get the layout of the ship while you help the poor guy unpack." And he was gone before Dani could disagree.

After the steward had explained the layout of the cabin and discreetly left her alone, Dani began to notice how strangely warm and woozy she was feeling. She showered and changed, ready for dinner, but the thought of food somehow made her feel even dizzier. Then Digger came through the door singing happily. He kissed her and swung Dani into the air with exuberance.

"What a great time we're going to have, Dani. Some people have already invited us to their stateroom for cocktails before dinner."

He suddenly stopped talking, touched Dani's forehead and then pulled her into the light, over by the porthole.

"Shit, Dani, you're sick, aren't you?"

"I think so, but nothing's happened yet."

"My God, honey; you look green already and the ship is only just leaving the dock," Digger grinned.

Dani looked out of the porthole where she could see the dock being slowly left behind.

"What you need is some fresh air, hon. It *is* very stuffy inside the cabin here."

Digger hurried his wife topside and sat her down before fetching her a warm blanket and a life-vest.

"Just in case you have to lean over the rail," he explained. "I don't want to lose you already."

Even though she wasn't feeling well, Dani could still appreciate the stunning sight of the fogbank rolling in, as their ship passed underneath the Golden Gate Bridge.

"You don't have to stay out here with me, honey, I'll be fine."

"OK then. I'll go have a couple of cocktails and be back soon."

As Dani sat, she noticed that there were many others outside wrapped in blankets too. Even some ship's crew! Suddenly feeling that she might actually be sick, Dani made her way over to the rail, where she got sprayed by high waves. Shocked, she moved away quickly, wondering what the hell deck they were on. Then Digger returned, enthusiastically telling her that the buffet was 'just too magnificent to miss'.

"Maybe if you eat something, you'll feel better."

Dani hesitantly followed her husband into the packed dining room. He introduced her to their personal waiter, Bruce, who would be taking care of the honeymooners during their five day trip. As she glanced over at the buffet tables Dani saw only fresh fish, with dead eyes that stared blankly back at her. Everywhere she looked she saw yet another fish dish. Then she realized why.

"Oh, of course! It's Friday!"

Hurriedly, Dani set down her plate and sprinted out of the crowded dining room. Digger raced to catch up to her, handing her a barf-bag just in the nick of time. Then he led her through the maze of passageways, continually handing her fresh bags, until they reached the privacy of their own stateroom. But in their luxurious, stainless-steel bathroom, poor Dani missed the toilet every time the ship rolled. Digger offered to help, but she was totally humiliated by the mess she was creating and begged him to leave her alone.

"No, Digger; please don't come in here. Leave me alone. I just want to die!"

Dolores J. Guthrie

Chapter 22

The cruise ship's passage continued to be rough until late afternoon on the second day out. Then the wind altered course and they moved into calmer waters. Dani survived her ordeal by eating only apples and dry toast and drinking endless cups of tea, but she looked awful. Digger came and went during her enforced confinement, telling her about all the things she was missing, but the worst part was her husband's pouting; unable to enjoy the fruits of his newly-wedded bliss!

Feeling more stable on the second day, Dani decided she should pull herself together. She found her way to the ships' beauty salon and ordered the 'full-works'; manicure, pedicure, shampoo and set. At last she began to feel almost human again. She chose her white, Grecian-style evening gown with an enormous, white feather boa draped across her shoulders. Finally, she slapped some color into her cheeks.

'I don't look too bad, considering I've been seasick for two whole days!'

She headed out to join her husband in the Grand Salon. On entering the massive room, she stopped and gazed in awe at its handsome decor. A huge spotlight swept over a giant crystal chandelier and rainbows were bouncing all around the ballroom floor. All the bulkheads were covered with white, silk-screened paper, alternated with gilt-edged mirrors and arabesque panels. Even though Dani's eyes passed quickly around the crowded room, she knew that people had already noticed her. She blushingly smiled at Digger, who waved from the bar as she made her grand entrance. As Dani approached him, he extended his hand, bowed and whispered into her ear.

"Gorgeous! You look just gorgeous, Dani."

She took his arm and followed him into the dining room, where he stopped before a table that bore their names on place cards next to small arrangements of flowers. Bruce, their waiter, immediately rushed over.

"I'm so glad that you are feeling better, Mrs. Rosselli. One's first voyage can be miserable, I know, but if it's any comfort to you, many other people were in the same condition as you. Do you think you'll be able to eat tonight?"

"Yes, I'm much better, thank you. And thank you, Bruce, for taking good care of my husband during my illness. He says you taught him to skeet shoot."

"Yes, ma'am. He a fast learner and is already a better shot than I am."

"I didn't know you knew how to use a gun, honey?" Dani queried.

"Well, little darlin', I guess there's a lot you don't know about your new husband yet. I'm like a chameleon, babe. Every time you think you have me figured out, I go and change my colors again."

"I don't know if that's good or bad, Digger. What color are you tonight, then?"

Digger placed his hand on top of Dani's.

"Red! I'm very red."

"And what does 'red' stand for?"

"Hot! I'm red hot tonight, baby!"

They gazed into each other's eyes, thinking of their long overdue wedding night.

"Excuse me," Bruce cut in discreetly as he served them from a silver tureen. "The shark's fin soup is excellent tonight."

Digger fluffed his wife's napkin, laid it across her lap and whispered to her again.

"Later, little darlin'. Later."

***

In such a romantic setting, with all the delicious food and wine and being in love, Dani entered into a new world of fantasy. The two of them had returned to the Grand Salon for an after dinner 'Courvoisier' and espresso, when the orchestra began to play. Digger proved to be an excellent dance partner, making every rhythm change from a samba to a foxtrot. The two of them danced in their own, secretive world and Dani was in complete ecstasy.

"Oh, Digger, I didn't know you could dance so well, either. You truly are a chameleon and influenced by the planet Mercury, I suspect, which would account for your changing moods. Your color now must be mercurial silver.

"Whoa, baby; you are a lot faster than they give you credit for."

As they slowly waltzed around the room, Digger's last comment bounced around inside Dani's head.

'So, who has given Digger the impression that I'm slow then?'

Taking a deep breath, she pushed such niggling thoughts away. She would worry about all that stuff later. *'After all, tomorrow is the first day of the rest of my life'.*

The jovial voice of their MC for the evening interrupted Dani's thoughts.

"Ladies and gentlemen, I would like to introduce a very special passenger, joining us for the first time tonight after having recovered from the dreaded *'mal-de-mer'*. If she will agree to honor us with a song, I would like to introduce to you all, Miss Dani Sutton, from New York City."

Knowing laughter mingled with the crowd's applause. A fanfare sounded and an intense spotlight illuminated their table. Dani was stunned. But, like the professional she was, she quickly recovered her composure and walked over to the waiting MC, took the microphone from him and whispered to the piano player.

"Can you play, *'People'*, from the musical, *'Funny Girl'* and in C minor, please?"

Dani voice flowed with the orchestra and their music as though they'd all been rehearsing together for weeks. Her mood became even more passionate and she was sure that emotional electricity could actually be seen, crackling in the air around her. Her words were for Digger alone and yet Dani knew that everyone felt that she had sung only for them. That natural ability was what made Dani such star material.

'It's a shame I'll never sing again, at least not on the East Coast circuit.'

'The Horse' would make sure of that. Sad thoughts ran through Dani's mind again, even as she took her well-deserved applause. The very memory of Tony Mannelli sent a shiver of fear down her spine. The spotlight followed her all the way back to her table and Digger kissed her cheek as he held out her chair.

"I can't believe that was really you up there. You told me you could sing but, my god, you sound like Streisand!"

"Well now I've finally sung for you, Digger, but next time please tell me first. I don't like to sing without rehearsing. And besides, most musicians don't appreciate folk cutting in on their act, not unless it's in a piano bar. Then they're paid to encourage 'sing-a-longs'."

"Okay, Dani. From now on you tell me if you want to sing and I'll be your manager and set it all up. But I didn't say anything tonight, honest. It was all Bruce's idea."

"Bruce? How did our waiter even know I could sing?"

"Well, while you were sick he was someone to talk to and I like to brag about my beautiful, talented wife you know."

Dani smiled in anticipation as they both swayed through the ship's maze of passageways, toward their own stateroom.

'This will be a night that dreams are made of!'

Dani carried two, crystal champagne glasses, while Digger carried a full bottle of chilled *'Dom Perignon'*.

"Don't shake that bottle too much, Digger, or there won't be enough left to drink."

"Don't you worry your pretty little head about anything, except getting ready for me?" Digger grinned, popping the champagne cork like a professional barman. "See, not a single drop wasted," he congratulated himself.

Dani surveyed their shiny, stainless-steel bathroom again.

'Being in here without being sick certainly makes a pleasant change.'

Dani noticed her dark-circled eyes, reflected in the mirror. She was repulsed by such a reminder of the past couple of days.

"What's taking you so long, honey?"

Turning her thoughts back to the rest of the night, Dani steadied herself and opened the bathroom door, wearing a slinky silk-and-lace gown of creamy brown. She brushed at her long, black hair as she leaned against the open doorway watching Digger. He had created a bed for them on the floor and was sitting cross-legged on it; Indian-fashion and clad only in cowboy boots and his Stetson!

"You look hilarious," grinned Dani, but he ignored her.

"I thought there'd be less movement if we stayed down here on the floor. We don't want you getting sick all over again, do we?"

Digger took Dani's hand and drew her gently down.

"You look just beautiful, honey and *ummm*, you smell so good."

"I always use *'Shalimar'* soap and body lotion when I get ready to make love."

"So that's why you always taste so good, huh?"

Dani laughed and whopped him. She carefully took off Digger's Stetson hat and laid it carefully on the floor. Then she ran both hands through his thick, blond, perfectly-styled hair. Digger was busy slipping the straps from Dani's shoulders and slowly nibbling at her neck and arms. She squirmed out of the gown, to help him along.

"Aren't you at least going to take off your cowboy boots?"

"Nope! If I'm gonna to die tonight, ma'am, I'm gonna die with my boots on!" he declared.

With an abandon she had not yet known with Digger, Dani drew him to her and kissed him, hard and deep. She threw aside any lingering inhibitions. Her eyes wilted closed, her breathing became faster and she almost swooned, gasping at the intensity of their lovemaking. The whole world stopped turning for a long while.

Later, as they lay spent in mutual ecstasy. Dani moaned softly. Her head was still pounding to the beat of her own heart. Digger raised himself up onto one elbow. Carefully, she sat up too and looked around at the disarray in the cabin, but Digger drew her back down again.

"I love the way you taste, woman; you're so clean. You always feel so good…oh, Dani!"

For a brief moment, she felt seasick but put it to the back of her mind as she succumbed once more to Digger's insatiable desires.

***

The next day turned out to be calm and beautiful, so Digger took her on a tour of the ship to show her all that she had missed while being ill. Wherever they went, the ship's photographer was *always* on hand with his camera. Dani was sure the man only saw dollar signs when he looked at the two of them. Their pictures hung on all the bulletin boards and, of course, Digger bought them all by the dozen. He and Dani were in love and he didn't care who knew it.

The whole ship loved them too. They were never without an invitation to someone's stateroom for cocktails or nightcaps. On their last night out, the Captain invited them to dine at his personal table. It was the night of the costume ball. Everyone had spent the whole afternoon making their outfits, using scotch tape, ribbon and crepe-paper in all colors of the rainbow.

Dani wore a pink lace bikini, tucking red crepe-paper around the bottom of it, to make it look like an apple. Then she got some crab apples from the ship's chef and hung them all around her bra, along with a green stem and some paper leaves that she'd made. Shiny red pumps completed her costume and Dani entered the contest as *'Yakima Valley's Forbidden Fruit'*! She won first place.

Digger created his costume to resemble a big yellow banana, with just his bare legs and arms sticking out. He entered as, *'Just a Plain Ol' Fruit'*, which got a lot of laughs but, sadly, no prize.

***

All the passengers were standing on deck when the ship docked in Hawaii. All its whistles and sirens were blowing and the scent of hundreds of gardenias filled the air. Local girls threw flower garlands, or *'leis'*, into the water and young boys dove off of canoes, searching for money that passengers threw into the clear, turquoise water. On the lower decks, a Hawaiian group played traditional music as Dani and Digger bade a sad farewell to all their new found friends.

They walked over to say goodbye to a man in a wheelchair. Dani watched as the wind blew through his full, soft, silvery beard and hair. The man didn't have a single wrinkle on his soft loving face; a face that she had known and loved since her childhood. It was a face that Dani would never forget.

The man spoke to them.

"Ya know, the only place to go, for complete peace of mind here, is to *'Rockefeller's'*, at Mauna Kea, on the big island."

"Well, maybe we'll see you there, sir" Digger bowed and raised his hat to the man. "We plan on doin' some island hopping later."

"Bring your little lady over, Digger, you don't need all this tourist mess over here."

Teary eyed, Dani threw the old man a farewell kiss as he was wheeled down the gangplank.

"I love you, Gabby Hayes."

Digger threw his wife high into the air and then caught her again.

"I never realized you were such a sentimental lady. I love you, Mrs. Rosselli."

Covered with dozens of floral *'leis'*, the pair climbed into their waiting limousine. Dani felt a calmness wash over her; a natural feeling among those who lived in Hawaii, she would soon discover.

'This trip will be a happy diversion from the turmoil I've left behind me.'

Their limo turned into a long driveway that circled around and through one archway of the white, stucco, hotel entrance. The entire frontage was covered in mature vines and tropical flowers. Built back in the late 1940's, the *'Colony Surf'* was *very* expensive and *very* exclusive. Digger and Dani entered the small, intimate lobby, where a proud concierge informed them that *'Michel of France'*, the only restaurant within the hotel, occupied the whole of the ground floor.

"Except for this lobby and the restrooms, of course!"

Laughing, Digger carried Dani over the threshold of their ocean-side penthouse. It had no glass in its windows, only wooden shutters giving Dani the feeling that if she reached out a hand, she could touch forever.

"Damn, this has *got* to be paradise," Digger declared, as he put Dani down and kissed her again.

The much-vaunted *'Michel's'* restaurant was a vision of pure elegance in monochrome, with its black-lacquered grand piano, white, linen-covered tables, crystal gaslight chandeliers and serving carts made of sterling silver. The hotel concierge was well justified in his praise of it. To Dani, no other restaurant would ever seem as romantic. The chandeliers swayed and danced, making their crystals chime, as warm trade winds wafted gently through open windows. Along the beach, the flickering *'Tiki'* lights added to the mystique of the whole atmosphere as the setting sun kissed a shimmering sea with one last flash of fire, before slipping away until morning.

Dani's mornings came to consist of solitary strolls along the beach while Digger continued working at the Hawaii State Fair, along with Thomasina and the horses. In her opinion, they had both worked long enough without wages for that damned Texas firm but she didn't want to argue about it on their honeymoon. Instead, she ignored the situation by withdrawing her own labor. Digger seemed quite happy going his own way, telling Dani that the company would settle up his money when they got back to the mainland.

'I'll believe that when I see it,' Dani thought.

One particular morning, she was sitting in her usual spot at the *'Outrigger'*, a private club next door to the main hotel. In the shade of a palm tree and sipping at a tall iced-tea with fresh pineapple and mint, Dani slipped off her sandals and watched as the tiny pebbles filtered through her toes. She noticed that if she squeezed her toes together tightly, the little puffs of sand and pebbles it created looked just like soft, pussy-willow blossoms. Suddenly, a huge shadow hovered over her. Quickly adjusting her floppy hat, Dani looked up to see a man standing there.

"Hi, there; I'm Walter."

She smiled and reached out a hand.

"Hello! I'm Danielle. Dani for short."

"Do you mind if I sit down and ask you some questions, for my boss over there?"

The man pointed over to a small group of people sitting at an outside table, about fifty feet away.

"I don't think I know you, or your boss, do I?"

"Well, I think you might know *of* him."

Dani looked across the patio to see a gentleman waving to her. She was beginning to feel a little uncomfortable by the whole encounter.

"My husband should be along any minute now."

"Oh, we don't mean to offend you," stammered Walter. "But we have been watching you on the beach every morning and Mr. Ford, my boss, was wondering if by any chance you could sing?"

"And even if I could, why would your Mr. Ford want to know that?"

"Well, if we were allowed to join you, ma'am, Mr. Ford could tell you himself, couldn't he?"

As Dani nodded, hesitantly, Walter stood up and waved the rest of his group over. But Digger walked up and presented himself before Walter had even started the introductions.

"Digger and Dani, may I introduce Betty and Ernie Ford and their son, 'Buck'. And I'm Walter; Ernie's manager."

Dani gave a little squeal as she finally realized who the man in front of her was.

"Tennessee Ernie Ford; that's who you are!"

Digger gave Dani a slight kick under the table to calm her enthusiasm and drew attention back to himself.

"Nice to meet you, sir. I've noticed that name on the room next to our own penthouse. Would that be your suite?"

"Yes, we bought it outright when this place was first built. We come down as often as we can. The reason we asked to meet you, Dani, is because I was told at the restaurant that they thought you were a singer. I am looking for a female lead-singer for my next tour."

Before Dani could answer, Digger cut in again. "You *are* jesting, right."

"No, sir! I'm deadly serious and I'm hoping that the lady can sing as good as she looks."

Digger looked straight at Dani.

"Oh, she can carry a tune alright, but she doesn't really like to sing in front of other people. Do you, honey?"

Dani was totally crushed that Digger would belittle her abilities, without giving her a chance to speak on her own behalf. *'Maybe I would be able to continue my singing career if I could work with someone like Tennessee Ernie Ford.'* If she used another stage name and changed her hair color, maybe even *'The Horse'* would leave her alone.

Betty Ford spoke first, breaking an awkward silence.

"Well, why don't the two of you come over to our place for cocktails anyway, say about eight o'clock tonight?"

Days passed and the group became the best of friends but Dani never spoke of singing, or her future career, to Digger again.

***

Amid a huge commotion, Jacqueline Kennedy had recently arrived at the hotel with a whole entourage, plus a handsome bodyguard and both of her children, Caroline and John-John. Digger had recently signed Dani up for surfboard lessons and the Kennedy children were also signed up in her class. On their very first day out, the instructor suddenly made everyone lie on their stomachs, on their surfboards.

"Everyone, listen to me *very* carefully! Put your hands and feet well up onto your boards! Now don't move at all and *don't* fall off!"

He told them all to paddle, very quietly, to the outer edge of the reef and they all did as instructed, believing it was some kind of training exercise. Dani was quite happily bobbing along until she saw three, large sharks, circling around and eyeballing the group of surfboarders. She began shaking so hard that she feared she would tip over. After what seemed like forever, the sharks turned away and headed back out to sea.

But it was the end of Dani's budding surfing career.

Chapter 23

When it came to their third week in Hawaii, Digger reserved a room in a hotel, just down the street, for JR to stay in. Dani felt guilty when she and Digger went off by themselves, knowing that JR would be left alone, but being alone was the last thing on her son's mind. Digger had tried to promote him among the bikini-clad beauties down on the beach, but JR didn't seem interested. He encouraged Digger and Dani to just 'get on with whatever you want to do'.

He would wave them off each morning, chuckling to himself.

"Bye guys! Have fun!"

Dani would put on a brave smile and leave her son behind but she always wished he was coming with them. One day, as she picked up extra beach towels from the bellhop, the man made a comment to her.

"That son of yours, ma'am, I don't know how he does it. It wears me out watching all his action!"

"What action?" Digger asked, as he handed over a tip for their extra towels.

"Why, he must bring in at least four or five birds a day!"

"What kind of birds?" Dani asked, innocently.

"Oh, you know, 'quail'!" Digger winked at the bellhop.

"Quail?" Dani was mystified.

"Wahines? Broads? Dames?" The bellhop tried desperately to explain. "Gee, I hope I haven't gotten the young guy into trouble?"

Dani was embarrassed at having to be informed what a 'bird' meant, but she tried not to show it.

"I have one more question, then; are these 'birds' all pretty?"

"Gorgeous, ma'am, all of 'em. And they all come out of his room smiling, too."

The bellhop hurriedly excused himself to attend to other guests.

"Well, I'll be damned! And there I was, trying to introduce JR to girls down on the beach!"

"That must be why he's too tired to go out with us at night," Dani giggled. "Do you think I should have a talk to him, Digger?"

"Naw, let the poor kid have some fun. After four years at military school he's just making up for lost time, that's all."

"Digger, do you remember you said you wanted to get your private pilot's license while you were here? Digger nodded. His turn to be mystified.

"Well, if you took JR along, then the two of you could get to know each other better. It'd make better use of JR's time too."

"Boy, I can sure hear that mother hen, a' cluckin'."

"Digger, I've always tried to be a good mother to JR, you know that."

"I know, honey, but you gotta face facts. Your little boy is all grown up now. You gotta cut the umbilical cord, sometime."

"Ouch! You're coming on pretty heavy there, husband." Dani tried to make a joke of it.

"But seriously, as long as JR's in school I'd prefer him to stay closer to us. Besides, he's worked hard all summer, helping you in the horse barns at all those fairs and I haven't seen one single paycheck for either of you!"

"OK! OK! I'll start arranging flying lessons for the two of us. The Hawaii State Fair ends this weekend, anyway, but maybe we could *all* stay a little longer, eh?"

The weather had been perfect recently, so Dani didn't need much persuading. She willingly agreed to extend their stay, happy that her new husband and her son were going to be spending some quality time together.

Dani had a family again, at last.

To amuse herself while the boys got to know each other, Dani took up tennis in the mornings and snorkeling in the afternoons. But she always made sure to stay in the shallows; she didn't want to encounter any more sharks. Spending so much time outdoors had turned Dani as brown as any native. She loved Hawaii; all the friendly, local people and the whole laid-back, island lifestyle.

Digger, on the other hand, didn't really enjoy the sun but he was still keeping busy. Busy spending Dani's money on clothes and jewelry. Busy applying for credit cards and setting up wills and joint bank accounts, always telling Dani that he was looking out for her best interests. Digger had already confessed to Tony Mannelli that he was in love with Dani and that he didn't know how long he could go on playing this game, with her and her family. Digger had never minded stealing from banks, or making the odd 'hit' for the Family, but this current assignment was beginning to gnaw at his gut.

But he was in too deep to turn back.

Every time he looked into those deep, velvet-blue eyes, Digger became more and more confused. But his weekly telephone reports had become less and less important to *'The Horse'* who had far more important things on his plate. He simply told Digger that as long as he kept Dani out of the Mannellis' hair, he could go on playing house with her for as long as he wanted.

***

One particular afternoon, Digger and JR were over at the flight school. Dani was half asleep, on a chaise under her favorite palm tree at the *'Outrigger Club'*, when she became aware of shadows hovering over her. Lazily, she squinted up to see what was blocking the sun. She first gasped in amazement and then squealed with delight.

"Ira! Andre! Where on earth did you come from and how did you find us?"

"We called your folks, Dani. They told us where you were staying and so here we are."

Ira told Andre to go check them both into the hotel, now that they had found Dani. But as soon as his partner left, Ira took Dani's hand and began speaking to her in a serious tone.

"Dani, how could you have married Digger without telling us first?"

"Well, I wanted to invite you both to the wedding, but Digger said you would just feel obliged to drive all the way from Seattle to Portland. And we wouldn't have been able to spend much time with you anyway, as we were due to leave on our honeymoon the very same day."

Ira looked down at her in fatherly frustration.

"Oh, Dani, Dani! When we first introduced the two of you, we didn't think for *one* minute that you'd be fooled by the likes of Digger Rosselli! Not to fall in love with the man and *certainly* not to get married to him!"

"Ira, I'm really surprised to hear you talk like that about your friend. I *am* in love with Digger and we're very happy. It hurts me to hear you talk like this."

"However hurt you might be, Dani, I know things about Digger that you have no idea about. You must leave him, right now. Get away from him before it's too late. *Please*, Dani."

Ira paused and looked around.

"Damn it, Andre's coming back already! Dani, don't tell him or any-one else what I've just told you, but you must heed my warning. Get away from Digger, before they bury you. I'm serious, Dani."

***

That evening they all went out to dinner together and reminisced about all the fun times they had, back on the big, snowy mountain. Digger told them all about their 'seasick' honeymoon and Ira acted as if he had said nothing unusual to Dani earlier. She was completely confused.

When they eventually all retired to their own apartments, Dani sat for a long time in the open window, brushing her hair and looking from star to star. She wondered again if HK was up there, watching over her life. Her hands moved mechanically as her mind searched for answers. *Why had Ira come all this way to warn her about Digger?* The very man she had forced herself to love, hoping that with his love she could be strong enough to forget all about Nicky Mannelli. The man with whom Dani had felt safe, until then.

"Dani, don't you feel well tonight, honey?"

Digger leaned over her shoulder and felt her forehead. A chill of fright passed through Dani, as Ira's warnings rushed back into her thoughts again. She stood up and brushed past Digger, away from the open window, wondering if her new husband really meant her any harm.

'But that's foolish. He could have thrown me out of that window many times already if he'd wanted to.'

Gritting her teeth to stop the parade of troublesome thoughts, Dani climbed into bed and snuggled down into Digger's arms.

"That's right baby; you come over here and give your Daddy some sugar."

***

Next morning, Digger and Ira went off to play tennis. Young JR had taken one of his girlfriends along on his first solo flight and Dani and Andre had gone shopping, to renew their liquor supply and buy groceries. On her return, Dani said a cheerful hello to the desk clerk as she passed through reception on the way to the elevators. She opened their penthouse door to hear the gentle sounds of Hawaiian music coming from within. Digger had spread a sheet on the floor and placed lighted candles all around the room. Naked, he sat on a pile of pillows, eating French bread and drinking wine. Next to him was a huge picnic basket, full of goodies.

"I know it's a little early but I have this humongous appetite, Dani!"

Digger held out his hands toward her. He grinned, opened his legs wide and his beautiful staff bounded up to greet her.

"I can see that you do."

Dani put down the groceries, slipped out of her shoes and knelt down beside him. She took a bite of the bread and a sip of the wine he offered. Her clothes were soon removed by Digger's skillful touch as he gently kissed her. His strong fingers stroked sweet-scented lotion into Dani's beautiful, bronzed skin.

"Relax, Dani, this is our moment. I'm going to take you to outer space," he whispered. "And later this afternoon, we're going to sail with the tide, off into the moonlight."

"But Digger, you don't know how to sail, do you?"

"You'll never know my little darling, will you, unless you come with me? Of course, I could take always take some little beach girl instead!"

"Oh, no you won't!" Dani wrapped her long, tanned legs around his body and pulled him down. Digger stopped talking and savored the moment.

***

The afternoon weather was perfect for sailing but the boatman was a little concerned about the late hour.

"I thought you were picking the boat up earlier, Mr. Rosselli, so please don't go too far out. We insist that all rentals be returned before sunset."

"Don't worry, we'll stay close."

"You *have* both sailed before, haven't you?"

"No," Dani replied," but *I've* had lots of theory lessons, on land."

Digger turned to his wife. "But, I thought you owned your own boat, Dani, when you were back in New York."

"I did, but it was a 'stinkpot'! You know, a diesel-engine, not a sail-boat."

"Well, I can handle it," Digger assured the attendant and gave the boat a strong push away from the dock. He dropped their moorings smoothly and seemed to be well in control.

"When we get a good wind, we zigzag," Dani coached him, "tacking first one way, then the other, with our bow passing through the eye of the wind."

"I know enough about it, thanks Dani! When we tack and the boom comes around, you just keep your head well down."

"OK. Sounds like you know what you're doing, Digger."

Dani relaxed and stretched out to enjoy the trip, drifting off to sleep. The next thing she knew, Digger was talking to her with more than a little concern in his voice.

"I thought we were doing real well, Dani, but to tell the truth I haven't seen the beach for quite a while now and these waves are gettin' a bit heavy."

"I guess so!" Dani raised herself up in order to peek. "It's getting cooler, too, honey. Do you think we should head back in?"

"Get the lifejackets out and put one on, Dani. Best be safe, but first hand me a beer from that cooler."

"Look Digger, over there!"

"What?"

"I saw land there behind us, as we went up over that last swell."

Dani ignored their life jackets and got beers for them both instead. She was feeling romantic again. The ocean view was stunning and the only sound was the slight 'ruffling' of their sails. The sun had begun to set, casting a glowing silhouette of Digger. His golden hair was blowing in the breeze and his bare chest showed his strong muscles as he worked the tiller.

But Dani's moment of reverie was short lived.

Digger yelled at her urgently to find their life jackets, but they weren't where he said they would be. Their boat was making a loud 'splat' every time it hit the water in the heavier waves. Dani looked around, beginning to feel scared. She couldn't see land anymore and it was getting darker. Digger was having trouble holding their mainsail into the wind.

"How far out do you think we are?"

"I don't know, maybe ten miles or so. I've been trying to turn this damn thing around for quite a while and I've lost all sense of direction. I don't mean to alarm you, Dani, but you'd better find those damn lifejackets."

"Digger they aren't under the seats, I already looked."

"Look in all the compartments then, dammit'. They have to be on board somewhere!"

When Dani stood up, she forgot all her sailing lessons. The boat moved sharply and the heavy boom swung around, knocking her overboard. As she surfaced, she was able to grasp the spray rail and hold on tight, but the rising wind had already caught their sails. The boat was moving faster. It dragged at Dani's body, causing her to lose her grip and slip down the side. She managed to grab at the rudder and hung on there for as long as she could, screaming all the while.

"Digger! Drop the sail, Digger!"

'Damn!' Dani realized that he probably couldn't hear her and wouldn't know what to do even if he could. As she hung on for dear life, all she could think about was the arrival of sharks.

"Digg-eer!"

Dani howled as her fingers lost their grip and her whole body went under the raging waves. She fought hard to keep her head above water but the foaming turmoil kept forcing her back below the surface. Whispering voices beckoned her downward. She didn't want to die. She wasn't ready! *'Don't panic. I must keep calm.'* Flashing images of her son and her Mom and Dad made Dani want to live, desperately.

Her mind fought to stay in control, but she felt as if she was falling into the jaws of hell. In despair, she kicked frantically. After a time, she stopped fighting and then the churning water bobbed her upward, choking and coughing. It was as if the hand of God had reached out to lift Dani up.

'I'm still alive!'

She tried to relax into the rocking waves so that her body would stay afloat and her head would remain above water. Through salt-burned eyes, Dani could faintly see white sails as they headed away from her.

"Oh, Digger, you'll never find me now!" Dani screamed, knowing that there was no way her husband could possibly hear her.

She took a deep breath in and rolled over onto her back.

'Why the hell didn't we put on life jackets before we even left the dock?' But Dani knew why; a lifejacket didn't look very sexy, did it? If she could only stay afloat, Dani realized that the incoming tide would eventually draw her closer to shore.

'Surely, they'll be out looking for me at sunrise? JR has his pilot's license now and he'll probably be the first one out there.'

Whenever she started to panic, Dani reached deep into her sub-conscious to keep one thing foremost in her mind; survival. Whenever she relaxed, she imagined that something was touching her and all her muscles would tense up again, keeping her mind alert. After all, it would be so easy just to relax and slip down to the ocean bottom. But there were times when Dani felt it was senseless to carry on.

'No! That won't do!'

She took another deep breath in and counted slowly down from ten as she released the air out through her mouth. All through the night, Dani kept repeating, 'relax, relax, and relax', to keep herself focused and awake. As the morning sun arose, she couldn't believe her good fortune; the tide was indeed bringing her inland. She couldn't tell whether it was boulders on the beach or the shelves of a coral reef that she was being thrown against, but Dani was too tired and weak to lift her arms to defend herself. Then that voice inside her head piped up again. *'Dani, feet first! Get your feet down first.'*

Coughing and sputtering, she turned onto her back once more and worked her feet downward.

'HK is that you? Will you help me, please?'

Dani felt as if the devil was spinning a web around her as, again and again, she was thrust against a protruding ledge. A wave pulled her away again and sucked her down, deeper and deeper to where she became entangled in a clump of seaweed.

Suddenly, some force flung her up again and into the shallows, like a cork popping out of a bottle of champagne.

"Ouch!"

She yelled out as the rough sand scraped against her exhausted body. She wanted to pass out, but knew she must get out of the water. Each time Dani got to her knees, another wave knocked her down and tried to pull her back into that dark, wet womb of Mother Nature. Dani was only dimly aware of the stinging, salt water as it tortured the dozens of tiny cuts all over her shriveled body. She managed to crawl to higher ground before collapsing under the shadow of a big rock. Then, Dani passed out.

***

The sun was beating down on her. Dani's mouth was dry and she could feel something moving all over her body, but she was too tired to care. She dragged herself up onto both elbows, trying to focus through the solar glare. She had a fuzzy vision of three native children, their wide, brown eyes all staring down at her as if she were a prize fish.

One child had a stick and was flicking at small, crawly things that were running all over Dani's body. She was too weak to move. Tears streaked down her sand-encrusted face. Slowly, she became aware of the agonizing pain from the dozens of cuts and bruises she carried. She drifted in and out of consciousness and when she looked up again, the children were gone.

'Dear Lord, am I dead or alive?'

Dani crossed herself in prayer, before closing her eyes one last time.

Dolores J. Guthrie

Part Two

The true colors of Digger Rosselli.

Chameleon

Dolores J. Guthrie

Chapter 24

Digger paced back and forth across the office of the Hawaii Shore Patrol. His golden tan had already faded to an indoor pallor, due to the shock and stress of the past few hours. He shucked off his life jacket and sank heavily into a leather chair that was close to a coffee machine. He leaned over and helped himself to a much needed brew. In the background, he could hear the boat rental agent, telling the whole world and anyone else who would listen that it was not *his* fault, he just rented the boats out and wasn't to blame for any accidents!

The Shore Patrol captain took the man by the arm, walked him to the office door and thanked him for his help, before showing him out. Then he introduced three of the rescue team to Digger. He pulled down a nautical map on the wall as he looked at Digger sympathetically.

"Mr. Rosselli! I know you are not thinking too clearly right now, but please try to follow what I'm saying. The faster we can get moving, the more hope we have of finding your wife alive."

He tapped a wooden pointer against the map and cleared his throat, as if starting a seminar.

"We are here, on Oahu, but Hawaii is made up of 132 islands, reefs and shoals that stretch for 1,523 miles, from the southeast to the northwest. We'll start the search for your wife at first light, so can you tell us your approximate, final location?

Digger shook his head, miserably.

"You mean you didn't you try to take any bearings at all, or at least drop some life preservers into the area so your wife might have something to hang onto? That, at least, would be something we could spot from the air!"

"No! No! No! I didn't do any damn thing right, did I?" Digger began hitting his fists together.

"Mr. Rosselli, you must pull yourself together and study this chart with me." The captain tapped his map again, impatiently, as Digger slumped forward over the desk, holding his head and trying to keep back his emotions.

"Sir, I was confused and lost and I guess everything just happened too fast for me to do anything about it. We should never have taken that damned boat out so far, or stayed out so late, but the sunset was just so incredibly beautiful! And now, my Dani is gone forever."

The captain picked up the nearest telephone and spoke with the air-search crews who were already doing a preliminary sweep of the area.

"For now, go twelve miles out from Diamond Head and circle the leeward side. Then extend your search around Mänana and the Käihikaipu islands and up around Mokulua."

A matronly woman entered the office and quietly sat down across the desk from Digger.

"Mr. Rosselli, while the captain is busy organizing his team I need you to help me to fill out these papers. Are you up to it?" She spoke in a motherly, soothing voice.

"Yes, ma'am, I reckon I'll be OK. What do you need to know?"

"Well, firstly, I need your full name, your address and your phone number here on the islands."

"Digger Rosselli, ma'am. I go by Digger but my real name is Donald; Donald L. Rosselli. My wife and I have been staying at the Colony Surf, Penthouse Suite #1, in Honolulu. Our phone number here is 808-373-1005."

"And your wife's full name?"

"Ah, yes, it was...." Digger paused, realizing that he was referring to Dani in the past tense.

His throat felt as if it were full of gravel and struggling to clear it forced a single tear to trickle down one cheek. Digger swiped a hand hard across his face and looked straight at the lady.

"Her name is Danielle Rosselli, ma'am; *'Dani'* for short."

"And her age?"

"Hell! D'you know, she never told me!" Digger snorted at the admission. "I assume she must be in her early 30's, because I know that she was first married at fourteen and her son is sixteen-years old now. So yeah, my wife must be about thirty-one-years old."

"And how long have you both been here in Hawaii?"

Digger looked blankly around the room at the pandemonium, then shook himself and continued talking to the woman.

"We left San Francisco on the first of June, for a two-month honeymoon. My Dani was an entertainer, from New York, did you know that?"

"Oh, that's interesting."

"Yeah, she was a singer and dancer. She has great legs, you know?"

Digger became caught up in his own thoughts again. He stared at the telephones, thinking that he should call *'The Horse'* soon, to let him know that the 'contract' had been completed. *No one ever suspected that Digger was a hired assassin for the Costa Nostra!* But this was not the time or the place to be calling New York, he decided. He didn't even know for sure that Dani was dead, yet! *'Better to be sure first, eh?'*

Digger struggled to concentrate again.

"May I use the phone please, ma'am? I think I should call Dani's son to tell him what's happened. Maybe he should come down here too?"

"Yes, of course sir, but...."

Before the woman could finish her sentence, JR came bursting through the swinging doors of the Patrol office. Tension immediately crackled through the air between him and Digger.

"I heard on the scanner that there was an air-search-and-rescue going on. Then I heard yours and Mom's names mentioned."

JR was breathless. "I drove here as fast as I could, so will someone please tell me what the hell is going on?"

Digger stood up and laid a hand on young JR's arm. "I'm so sorry, son; it's your Mom."

"What about my Mom?" JR searched everyone's face for answers. "Where the hell *is* she, Digger?"

"She's lost at sea."

Young JR's six-foot five-inch frame moved like lightning and he grabbed Digger by his shirt front, lifting the older man clear off his feet.

"I don't want to hear that crap, Digger." Terror was written all over

JR's face. "How in the hell could you lose my mother at sea?"

"Let go of me, JR! It all happened before I could do anything, I swear. She must have been hit by the boom and knocked overboard."

"But didn't you go look for her?"

"Hell, yes I looked for her. Let go of me, dammit!"

"Was Mom wearing a life jacket?" JR demanded, releasing his choke-hold on Digger.

"Aw hell, JR, I don't know."

"Well, what's this, then?" JR picked up the discarded vest that Digger had worn and tossed it to him.

"Is this yours?"

"Yes, damn it! I put it on after I lost Dani. It was lying on the port deck. She must have been looking for the vests when it happened."

"So were there *two* life-vests lying loose on deck, Digger, or just the one?"

"Christ; I really don't remember, JR. I was struggling to hold our sails into the wind when I realized that Dani had gone. I remember trying to get our bearings but it was getting real choppy and all I know is that I told Dani to go below and look for the life-vests. I'd lost all sight of any lights, or any land, by that time."

"As I tried to turn the boat around, we were struck by a big squall. The wind whipped up and caught the mainsail and the boat shot through the water like a bullet. After things calmed down again, I looked below decks for Dani but she'd just vanished. I searched the whole area, I swear I did JR, but it was getting too dark to see anything. I even took down the sails and floated around like a cork, calling her name, but there was no sound at all from her. All I could think about was that if she got hit in the head, then at least she would have drowned in peace."

Digger lowered his head as he stood up and shuffled over to the window. He threw himself into a swivel chair, turning away from the tortured look on young JR's face. But he was determined to make his point.

"I'm pretty sure there was only one lifejacket on the deck; the one I put on."

JR leaped towards Digger again. He grabbed his arm and pulled him to his feet, then prodded the older man towards the office door.

"So why aren't we out there looking for her right now, then? I know my own mother, Digger. She'll hang in there until we find her, goddammit, so let's get going! We can *both* fly planes and can search for Mom much better up there. She could still be alive, dammit!"

JR pointed up toward the darkening night sky.

"It's not really likely that anyone would find your mother before tomorrow morning," the Shore Patrol captain cut in.

"But it's always possible that she might have drifted ashore someplace, depending on exactly where she went in, naturally and on the movement of the tides. Oahu has some very strong, outgoing tidal currents which oppose the normal offshore waves. That can result in high, steep seas in all the entrance channels, almost certainly roughing your mother up a bit, even if she did manage to get herself ashore."

JR's years of cadet training at the Valley Forge Military Academy finally began to take hold.

"Has anyone notified the Coast Guard yet, sir?"

"Yes, son and they will be starting their own search within the hour. And ships throughout the whole area have already been asked to keep a look out for the lady."

"Come on then, Digger, we're wasting time here. Call 'Gunny' and have him start preparing a couple of planes for us. By the time we get all our clearances in order, it should be light enough to fly."

***

"I guess that was a good idea your mother had, for us to both to take flying lessons, I mean."

Digger talked mainly to pass the time as they waited for a cab to the airfield. "Do you know how our flight instructor, 'Gunny', got that name, JR?"

"Wasn't he in the Marines or somethin'?" JR answered absent-mindedly. He was trying to concentrate on the task in hand; that of finding his mother alive!

"That's right, JR. He was a Gunnery Sergeant in the Marines and the nickname 'Gunny' stayed with him when he retired into civilian life."

Digger's tone grew more serious.

"Do you ever think that your Mom is psychic, JR?"

"I've sometimes thought that," JR agreed, thoughtfully. "She's often been one step ahead of me throughout the years and many of her 'dreams' have come true."

"What kind of dreams?"

"Mostly big, dramatic dreams like hotel fires, accidents, plane crashes and other weird stuff. Like recently, for instance, when she escaped from the 'Mob' back in New York! Mom told me then that she seemed to know all their plans ahead of time and that's what kept her alive! Didn't she ever tell you about any of that stuff?"

"Hell, no!" Digger looked at JR in horror. "But if Dani is so psychic, how come she didn't know she was going to drown yesterday?"

"But, that's just it, Digger. Mom told me before you ever took that boat out that she didn't want to go! She was afraid that you didn't know enough about sailing!"

JR slapped at his forehead in a gesture of disgust.

"Of course! The reason Mom didn't dream about her own death means that she isn't dead yet, Digger! So we have to find her, quickly."

JR yelled at their taxi driver in frustration. "Can't this damn cab go any faster?"

***

After a quick briefing, Gunny led them out onto the airfield.

"I have three planes here, cleared and ready to go, so I'm coming with you. We'll fly along the coast around Diamond Head first and then fan out from there. Digger, you stay on *my* right wing and JR; you hold position off to Digger's right. And keep alert up there, both of you. It could get pretty crowded with all the other aircraft that'll soon be out searching for your wife."

"So what do we do if we spot her?" Digger asked, quietly.

"I'm in constant radio contact with the Coast Guard," Gunny assured them both, "and they're able to move *real* fast, so just call me if you see something, OK? Come on then, let's get airborne."

Digger revved his engine, checking the magnetos. He could feel the adrenalin flowing through his body and allowed himself a smile. *'This will be my lifestyle from now on!'* With all the money he would inherit from Dani, he would have everything he had ever wanted. He thought back to the very first time he'd laid eyes on Dani; to their isolated vacation spent in the mountains and to how beautiful Dani was. *'Of course, she had lots of money too and that made her look even better'!*

Digger recalled standing on top of the mountain with his friend, Ira; waiting for Andre to bring Dani up on the ski lift. He would never forget the first sight of those vivid, violet-blue eyes as her ski-lift came over the brow of the ridge. He suddenly shuddered at a memory that would haunt him forever. *'But why should it?'* As he waited for clearance to take off, Digger tried to reassure himself by thinking aloud.

"But I didn't actually kill Dani, *did* I? I was supposed to, yeah, but this whole thing was a genuine accident."

He grinned, broadly, knowing that he couldn't have planned Dani's death any better if he'd tried. Yet Digger was confused by the strange sadness he felt at the loss of his beautiful, young wife. Such emotion was totally out of character for Digger Rosselli, who was known as a hard-hitting, tough guy with no feelings.

As a child, he used to catch neighborhood cats and laugh as he tortured them. Until the time he threw one down their own kitchen waste disposal and couldn't get it all out. His mother had caught him that time. Digger remembered how she had thrown up and then cried and cried, for hours. *He had always loved to see his mother cry.*

After years of being a good little boy on the outside but cruel on the inside, Digger had developed a heartless need to make people, and animals, love him first before he destroyed them.

To the local mothers, he was known as 'the weird kid on the block'. At only nine years of age, Digger had raped and tortured a seven-year-old boy. Convicted and sent to a mental hospital, he stayed locked away until he was sixteen-years-old. After his release, Digger was rejected by society and even by his own family, rapidly drifting down into the dark under-world of crime. Once there, he quickly learned how to become a 'gentleman killer' and now Digger Rosselli was an acknowledged master in the violent business of 'death-for-hire'!

***

JR, too, was lost in his own thoughts; more determined than ever to find his missing mother. What would he do without having Dani to laugh with, or to talk to and turn to with his troubles? *What a hell of a future that would be!* But what if it *was* JR's destiny to go through life alone? After all, his old man had deserted them both, long before JR was even born. *'Bastard!'*

JR sincerely hoped that he wouldn't turn out anything like his real father and spoke his thoughts aloud. *'Nope! I'll work hard on being more like 'Grandpa Gunther'. He's always been a good provider and a great family man; loved by all his children, nine grandchildren and dozens of friends! That's who I wanna' be like!'*

Flying into the breaking dawn, JR smiled to himself. *'We'll find you, Mom'.* On a pure whim, he banked away from the other two planes and headed east towards Molokai, the next island. He flew low along the beaches; close enough that he could almost touch the sand! JR felt strangely drawn towards one particular, jagged area over by some cliffs.

As he got closer, he saw children playing on the beach, building sandcastles or so he thought at first glance. *'That's no damn sandcastle!'* He made another low sweep over the children, who were now looking up and waving, excitedly. A hot, surge of adrenalin hit the pit of JR's stomach and he wanted to yell out to the whole world. *'I've found her!'*

With a shaky hand he reached for the radio handset but in his excitement, he couldn't remember the proper call sign.

"Breaker-breaker, do you read me?" JR screamed over the airwaves, before he remembered his flying training and pulled himself together.

"JR here; November-Six-Zero-Zero-Seven-Whiskey. I think I've just spotted Mom. I'm about three quarters of a mile southeast of Kalawao, just before some high cliffs. I'm *sure* it's my Mom down there, lying on some rocks at the foot of the cliffs. I reckon the tide must have carried her in. There's a path going inland, away from the beach. Looks like three small children are gathered around her. I'll keep circling for as long as I can but the Coast Guard needs to get a move on!"

"Zero Seven Whisky," Gunny answered, calmly. "I know that area very well, JR. Do not, I repeat, *do not* try to land there. The rocks are much bigger than they look. But don't worry, the Coastguard is already on the way."

Gunny turned his plane toward JR's specified location, with Digger staying close behind. Then JR spotted the Coastguard vessel, heading up the coastline and moving fast so he held his own plane in a tight circle until he was sure they had located the tiny figure that lay motionless on the beach. Then all three planes turned away and headed back to base.

As they approached the airfield, good news was relayed from the rescue boats. Dani was unconscious, but still alive. Alone in his plane, JR grinned broadly and punched the air.

'Dammit, Mom, I knew you could make it!'

Dolores J. Guthrie

Chapter 25

"Easy baby, take it easy now."

A gentle voice penetrated through the fog of Dani's deep sleep. Opening swollen eyes, she saw a haze of dark figures above her. They seemed like shadows from heaven, reaching down out of the morning sunlight.

"Where am I?" Dani tried to rise, but gentle hands pressed her down again.

"Just relax Mrs. Rosselli, don't even try to move."

Then the shadow with the gentle voice began checking Dani's vital signs.

"Her blood pressure is pretty low, from the exposure, but I don't see any broken bones here, just cuts and bruises."

"Keep those kids back," another voice yelled. "Okay, let's get her onto the gurney. On my count of three…two…one!"

The crew carefully carried Dani through the protruding rocks, toward the waiting boat.

"Boat!"

Thoroughly alarmed at the mention of water, Dani fought her way back to consciousness.

"No! No! I don't want to get back in a boat. Please, don't make me go back in the water!" She begged the strangers to leave her alone. "Who *are* you guys, anyway?"

"We are the Coastguard, ma'am and we're taking you to hospital now. Your husband and son are already waiting for you there so don't worry anymore; you're safe and you're going to be fine."

Dani closed her eyes again. She tried to listen to someone talking on the ship-to-shore radio, but everything seemed so far away from her. The effort was too much and the hum of the motors lulled Dani back into a deep, exhausted sleep.

***

Digger walked over to a secluded section of the hospital, leaving JR in the emergency room to wait for Dani's ambulance to arrive. But he was nervous, looking over his shoulder to make sure no one had followed him. He found a pay phone and placed a call to Johnnie Crenziess, in New York. Johnnie still owed him a favor, ever since they had both been involved in the gangland slaying of Arnie, *'The Hawk'*, Ruppilli.

"Hiya, Johnnie boy; 'quick-on-the-trigger' Digger here!"

"Shit man, where the helluv ya been? Me and the boys thought they'd sunk you in the East River. You know, ever since that night a few months back?"

"Nah, I was just lying low and cooling off in the Arizona sun! I heard it got real hot out your way, though?"

"Yeah, the news media had us all killing each other off in some kinda 'Mafia' war! It all died down after a while though."

"Ya still got good connections with *'The Horse'*, in New York, Johnnie?"

"Maybe." Johnnie's voice took on a more serious note. "Why, what's up Digger?"

"I just need some info on a broad named Dani Sutton, that's all. Info like, why she was in New York in the first place and why was *'The Horse'* putting out a 'hit' on a good-looker like her?"

"That's all ya need to know, Digger?"

"That's it for now buddy."

"Shit! Don't even need a pencil for this one," Johnnie snickered. "I met the broad myself, when she was singing in one of Tony's clubs. Man, what a looker and a damn good voice too."

"Okay Johnnie. This is my nickel we're spendin' here so just give me the facts, OK?"

"OK! The way I heard it is that she was engaged and about to marry some multi-millionaire, one of the founders of Xenon."

"You mean the *Gas* Company?"

"No. Some big typewriter, or machine company or somethin'; over in Rochester. Anyhow, the old guy was besotted with her and gave her two or three million bucks-worth of cash and gifts, all in the one year! *'The Horse'* called Dani his 'Cinderella' singer and even though she was his baby brother's girl, Tony Mannelli made it his personal business to get all of her money away from her. He talked the broad into investing a hell of a chunk of her money in some of his corporations. I also heard that Tony transferred some of the gal's stocks *illegally*, through the Bank of North America, where he launders most of his money."

"Well, anyway, Dani's old-geezer boyfriend - I think she called him HK - set the Feds onto Mannelli and not long after that, someone took out the old fool. After his death, the dumb broad went to the DA's office herself and told them how they killed her boyfriend and tied up most of her money!"

"I guess that's why they called *me* in to find her, then."

"But Digger, I heard that the whole thing got a bit too sticky for *'The Horse'* to handle. You see, the million or so that he took from Dani didn't go to the 'Family'; it was a side-deal between him and his brother, Nicky. So if anything happens to this Dani broad now, the Mannellis will be in *way* over their heads, if ya get my drift."

"Yeah, way over their heads and feet first!"

"So, are you still lookin' for this Dani broad then, Digger?"

"Hell no, I'm not *looking* for her. I married the dame!"

"Nah, you're conning me?"

"Would I con you, little buddy?" Digger wound up their conversation. "Gotta go now, though. I'm running out of quarters and I have one more call to make but thanks for the input, Johnnie."

"Hang on, Digger. How can I reach you if we get a good job for you?"

"You can't, Johnnie. I've come to like my new lifestyle so I'm hangin' up my hat for a while. It's nice to have money to spend for a change."

"But, Digger...!"

"I'll call you if I need anything else, OK?"

Digger hung up and walked back to the end of the hall, checking to see if anyone had seen him talking on the phone. But JR was busy talking to a nurse. Digger smiled as he walked back to the phone again.

'That kid never gives up on the skirts, even in a hospital'.

He counted out more quarters and made a call, to *'The Horse'*, back in New York.

"Glad I caught you, Tony. Just thought I should let you know that they found Dani this morning; alive!"

"Ya don't say? I swear that damn broad has nine lives. She could even foul up a wet dream! She managed to elude that hit I had on her, down in Florida, if you remember. I had two of my best men on that job and yet the bitch still managed to outguess us all. She disappeared completely and then turned up in that ski resort in the Washington Mountains, where you found her. Anyhow, I think she's learned her lesson by now."

"As for my kid brother, well let's just say I did him a favor. I've called the hit off now anyhow, so you can do anything ya' want with young Dani Sutton. Just keep her out of New York and well away from me and the kid, OK?"

"To be frank, Tony, this thing in Hawaii really *was* an accident. I didn't arrange it, or nothin'! And after the shock of it all, I've realized that maybe I should keep this Dani broad around for a while. She's great in bed and she's got a load of dough, so killing her would be kind of a waste, if ya know what I mean?"

"Yeah, I hear ya, Digger! My kid brother was only supposed to get close enough to Dani to get control of her money, but the dumb bastard went and fell in love with her, didn't he. That's when all the shit hit the fan! The two of them even wanted to leave the country and be together, so I had to bust a few heads around here, I can tell ya'. By the way, I hear that Bennuchi wants a meeting with you down in Arizona, as soon as you can get away from Hawaii."

"OK, Tony. I guess there's no need to report back to you anymore is there, not unless something unforeseen brews up?"

"Right, no need at all, but don't go screwing yourself to death, eh Digger?"

"Oh, but what a sweet way to go, man!

Digger hung up and hurried back down the hall, realizing he'd been on the phone for far longer than he'd planned. *'Shit! They must have already brought Dani in by now'*. He was just asking a nurse where she was when JR walked up behind him.

"Where ya' been Digger? They brought Mom in already and have been busy working on her for a while."

"I had to go to the 'john' again, sorry. Must be nerves or somethin' JR. Did you talk to Dani, yet?"

"No, she's asleep now. She's got breathing apparatus of some kind over her nose and mouth, probably oxygen and I heard one of the nurses saying something about 'thermal-shock'. You *do* realize, don't you, that Mom was in that cold water for a hell of a long time?"

A doctor came out of the emergency room, looking closely at Digger and JR before glancing down at the chart in his hand. Then he looked back at Digger and extended a hand.

"I am Dr. Brennen, sir and I will be caring for Mrs. Rosselli, unless you prefer to have your own physician present?"

"No sir. We're here vacationing, on our honeymoon actually, so I'm quite happy for you to take care of her. I am Digger, by the way and this is Dani's son, JR. So, how's she doing Doc?"

"Well, we've moved her into the Intensive Care unit now, until she stabilizes. She was in a critical condition when they found her, in and out of consciousness for the whole journey. Plus, she was suffering from hypothermia."

"Is that serious?" JR wanted to know.

"Yes, it is. Exactly how long she was exposed to the cold temperatures will determine if there is any permanent damage to your mother's limbs. She already has some swelling and tenderness in her feet and fingers, but not enough skin discoloration to cause us any alarm at the moment. And, of course, she has swallowed a lot of sea water and has dozens of small cuts and bruises over most of her body."

"But when can we see her?" JR persisted.

"Dani is pretty exhausted right now and she needs to sleep as much as possible. Why don't the two of you go home, get some rest yourselves and come back in the morning. It looks like you could both use some sleep!"

The doctor patted JR on the shoulder.

"Your mother seems a very strong-willed young woman, son. She's responding well to treatment and I'm confident that she will eventually recover completely."

The doctor walked away, leaving Digger and JR to their individual thoughts. As the tired men waited for yet another cab, a thought struck JR.

"How come we keep catching damned taxi-cabs, Digger? Where's that Cadillac that you and Mom rented when you first got here?"

"Hell! I guess it must still be back at the marina! I'd forgotten all about that, JR."

"Take us to the parking lot of the Molokai Boat Marina," Digger ordered, as they climbed into the first cab that came along.

Chapter 26

JR stood in the doorway of his mother's hospital room, watching her as she slept. Dani stirred and her eyes tried to focus on her son's tall frame; his head barely missed the top of the doorframe. It had been a long night, but she was beginning to feel human again. She had been transferred out of Critical Care first thing that day and moved into a regular room, which JR took as being a good sign. Dani's eyes filled with tears of relief and happiness as the fuzziness cleared from her vision and she recognized her only son.

JR knelt down, cradling his mother in his arms.

"Mom, you are going to be just fine. You've already conquered the unconquerable!"

"D'ya reckon? I feel like a complete fool, JR, getting knocked off a boat by its boom. I guess I'll never make a sailor, huh?"

JR rubbed at his forehead, deep in thought. Something was still niggling at him about Digger's explanation of the accident.

"Mom, do you remember whether or not you were wearing a life jacket when you went over the side?"

"Honey, I really don't know." Dani sighed in frustration. "All I remember is drinking a helluva lot of sea water and being very cold, for a very long time. Oh, and I worried about sharks, too! I thought I saw fins circling around me more than once, but then they could have been porpoises, JR, guiding me towards the shore. My guardian angels were with me last night, that's for sure! Sometimes, I think I over-work them, honey" she confessed. "But, where is Digger? Is *he* alright?"

"Sure Mom, he's fine. He'll be here soon. The last I saw of him, he was on the phone. I think he was making arrangements for you both to fly back to Portland, as soon as Dr. Brennen releases you from here. How do you feel?"

"As if I've been run over by a truck!" Dani winced as she shuffled higher up the bed. "I'm so sore, honey. Did I break anything?"

"No! You hit the rocks pretty hard, though, that's why you're all bruised up, but the doc says you'll be out of bed in a few days. Is there anything I can get for you?"

"Yes, how about a big, 'Dairy Queen', chocolate milkshake!"

"That's easy."

"And call your Grandparents too, but don't tell them what happened. Just tell them to make plans to meet us all at Lincoln City, for a week's vacation, when we get back to Portland. I'd rather tell them about this latest episode in person."

Digger arrived soon after JR left.

"Lost in the ocean, they told me. Oh, Dani, I thought you were dead, baby, but look at you now. You've come back to me."

He went over to her with his arms outstretched. A lump came into Dani's throat and tears rolled down her face as she clung to Digger. Yet she stared into space over his strong shoulders, unable to respond to his greeting. Her heart pounded as a flashback of the accident rushed through her mind. *'Do I really know this man?'*

She could picture the sloop as it left her behind and Digger never turning back to search for her. *'He just left me there, in those cold, dark, waters.'* Dani drew a long, deep breath and pulled away from him. Her eyes were blurred and she wasn't really sure of anything, anymore.

Digger panicked at his wife's sudden silence.

"Dani, are you alright? Can you hear me, honey?"

"Yes, I'm fine. But didn't I hear you telling people that you'd circled and circled, looking and calling out for me?"

"That's right honey, I did! But I hadn't seen you go over the side. You could have been gone for a long time before I even started looking."

"Oh! I thought you saw me go overboard. I remember looking for life jackets and thought I heard you say 'duck', but maybe I didn't. My head's still so confused."

Digger kissed Dani's forehead and pushed some stray, black hairs away from her face.

"Well, little darlin', you just stop worrying that pretty head of yours so's you get well faster. The doc says we should be able to take you home in a couple of days."

"Home?"

"No, not back home to Portland yet, just back to our hotel, I mean. The Doc' wants to see you in his office, one more time, before we all fly home."

JR came in carrying three chocolate milkshakes. "How are you feeling now, wonder woman?"

Dani took a Kleenex and dabbed at her eyes.

"My skin hurts to the touch, my head feels swollen and I'm still burping up seawater. But other than that, I feel very lucky to still be here, with my two favorite men."

They all laughed, but Dani still felt a sense of wonder at her own survival.

"I never realized before just how beautiful life really *is*." she whispered. "Do you think it's alright for me to drink this cold drink, though?"

"What the heck," replied JR. "Milk's good for you, isn't it!"

***

After Digger left the hospital, he went straight to *'Macula's'* piano bar, on the first floor at their hotel. He sipped at a Scotch-and-water as his eyes scanned around the large, open room. It overlooked the sandy beach and the ocean where the natives were out doing their *'Tiki'* lighting ceremony, as they did every night at dusk. With eyes closed, Digger lost all track of time as he listened to the peaceful piano music. Several songs had gone by before he noticed a strong smell of scented flowers. Gardenias came to mind. He opened his eyes, turned around on his barstool and almost fell off it!

A gorgeous, slender, olive-skinned, brown-eyed beauty was sitting right next to him. She had long, straight, brown hair and legs that went from the ground all the way up to heaven. She wore a tight, black miniskirt, a red, low-cut sweater that showed off her large, firm breasts and on her dainty feet she wore black, spiked heels. The woman crossed her legs in a way that exposed just enough skin to let Digger know she was not wearing any underwear. Then she leaned toward him and looked deep into his eyes.

"Got a light?"

Digger was lost in the moment, unable to believe what was happening. Only moments before, he had been depressed; thinking of his problems and his sick wife. But not anymore!

"Sure, honey! And do you have a name to go with that pretty face?"

The woman replied in a breathless, husky whisper that set Digger's soul on fire.

"Brenda! My name is Brenda B."

"Hmm! Unusual last name you've got there, ma'am. Would that be 'Miss' or 'Mrs.' B?"

"Miss, if you please. And your name?"

"Digger Rosselli, ma'am, at your service. So, are you a guest here," Digger asked hopefully.

"Yes! And you?"

"Yes, ma'am." Digger couldn't believe his luck.

After a few more drinks and some small talk, Brenda stretched her back muscles and, with a half-yawn, she stood up and smoothed down her skirt. She discreetly pressed her room key into Digger's hand as she moved away from the bar. His eyes were glued to the woman's hips as she sashayed across the floor toward the elevators. *'Wow!' Am I dreaming?'* Then someone tapped him on the shoulder.

"Hi there, 'pops'!"

"JR! Where the hell did you come from?"

"I've been sitting right behind you, having dinner. Some looker isn't she. Is she a friend of Mom's?

Digger didn't respond but turned back to the bar again, slipping Brenda's room key into his jacket pocket and hoping the kid hadn't noticed. He was on edge at JR's sudden interruption. It had changed his mood.

"Aren't you supposed to be back at the Military Academy by next Monday?"

"Yeah! I fly out tomorrow afternoon, at three o' clock. I think Mom is well on her way to recovery now and she has you with her, Digger; right?"

"Oh yeah! She's got me all the way, son!"

***

Two hours later, Digger turned the forbidden key to that find he was still welcome in Brenda B's room.

She had lit candles all around the suite and white wine was already chilling, next to her huge bed. Brenda was sitting on the ledge of the open window and sounds of the ocean rumbled gently behind her silhouette.

"Bring the wine over here, Digger." Brenda spoke in that same low, husky voice he had heard in the bar. "My libido has gotten a little turned off in waiting for you, honey. I hope you're man enough to warm me back up?"

"I'm certainly man enough to try."

"What kept you? Your wife?"

"Wrong! My stepson popped up out of nowhere."

"So, there *is* a wife somewhere then?"

"Let's just say that she's not right here; not right now. We should concentrate on the pleasures that we're obviously both in need of. I feel a strong urge to fly you up to the moon and back, Miss Brenda B; all night long. How does that sound?"

"Let's fly, then!"

Brenda blew him a kiss and disappeared into the bathroom.

Digger slipped out of his own clothes and dragged the bedcovers into a pile on the floor, posing on them to show his best attributes. Digger loved his own body and could see his reflection in a huge, gilded mirror way across the room.

Brenda reappeared wearing a see-through, orange silk gown. As he focused on her magnificent body, Digger's groin began to move of its own accord. He crossed his legs and smiled, pleased that his equipment was still working even though he'd had a bit to drink. He continued watching as Brenda brushed at her brunette locks and dabbed perfume all over her body. Briefly, Digger was reminded of Dani. She was always so clean before sex that it drove him crazy.

His wife was the only woman he'd ever known who douched *before* sex. But his thoughts rapidly came back to the moment. And to Brenda B! The woman was sensual but Digger felt comfortable with her.

Little time was wasted as the pair groped and petted their way toward intimacy. The sex was passionate and the mystique of not knowing the woman at all proved to be a real turn on for Digger. Both of them raced through one orgasm after another. No questions were asked. In fact, no words were spoken at all between them. The heat of the moment was all that mattered. Brenda was definitely Digger's kind of woman. She moved like a cat; one that stalks her mate and then pounces, harshly, until she's completely satisfied.

Planning ahead, Digger was already hoping that this evening could become a routine event in the future. *'Shouldn't be that hard to get Brenda over to Portland. Every woman has her price, after all'.*

He was sure that Brenda had enjoyed the experience every bit as much as he had. But Digger also knew that he would have to figure things out very carefully. Dani must never find out. So far, she knew nothing about Digger's connections with organized crime, neither did she know anything about his once-a-month, unnatural cravings for the affections of virile and very young men! He stretched out on the bed, exhausted and extended one arm until it touched a plant on the bedside table. Suddenly, something stirred in the foliage and Digger jumped up in alarm.

"What the hell is that?"

Brenda laughed. "That's my chameleon. He lives among my plants and he changes colors, depending on where he is, so no-one ever sees him."

Digger realized in that moment how much *he* was like a chameleon, too.

No-one ever really knew *him*; only what he wanted them to know. He pulled Brenda closer and licked her neck from ear to ear.

"So, do you like it all the way, ma'am?"

"Stop talking and come here!"

Brenda grabbed his groin as she bit down hard on his lips and Digger realized that it was going to be a very long night.

***

The hours dragged by and Dani was getting worried. She had tried to call Digger throughout the previous night and all through the morning, but could get no answer. *'Where in the heck can he be?'* JR had already called her from the airport to say his goodbyes. He told her that he loved her and said he would be home for Christmas. But before he hung up, Dani asked if he had seen Digger.

"Not since dinner, back at the hotel last night. I left him in the piano bar at around eleven o' clock. He'll show up soon, Mom, don't worry. You need to get some rest."

"I'll try honey. Have a safe flight and I love you!"

"I love you too, Mom."

Dani started trying to think *good* thoughts instead of worrying all the time. She thought about Digger wanting to settle down in Portland. To her, Seattle would be a much better place to live but for some reason, things were going to be Digger's way, yet again. She realized then that she wasn't very good at saying 'no'! Not to Digger, or to any other loved one for that matter. *'If only I could be more assertive.'*

Dani vowed to try in the future, but her heart was far bigger than her brain. She never wanted to hurt anyone and it always landed her in trouble, every time. Eventually a very tired Digger arrived, just before lunchtime.

Dr. Brennen was already in Dani's room, signing the papers for her discharge. She gave her husband a cold glance. Only after the doctor had left, did she speak.

"You look like hell. So where were you all night, then?"

"I'm sorry, honey."

He tried to kiss her but Dani pushed him away in disgust.

"You stink, Digger! You smell of liquor and stale sex!"

"Honey, I had dinner last night and then I had a few drinks with JR. After he went up to bed, I guess I relaxed and had a few more. After all, I've been through a hell of a nightmare too, you know. I guess I musta passed out when I got to my room. But here I am now darlin' and I'm *almost* sober. Forgive me?"

Digger looked so pathetic that Dani put her arms around him and patted his back like a baby. Digger smiled to himself. The 'Rosselli' charm had worked again.

"Now, let's get you out of here, honey."

When they arrived back at the hotel, a tall, slender, young woman was hailing a cab outside. Although Dani smiled at her, the woman abruptly turned away. *'Strange!'* she thought.

But Digger's thoughts were only of relief. *'My God, that was close.'* After all, if Dani had died in the ocean, Digger would be entitled to at least half of her fortune. But if she were to leave him for adultery, after only a few months of marriage, he would get absolutely nothing!

He realized that he would have to move fast to transfer Dani's money to a place where *he* could have easy access to it. As they waited in silence for the elevator, he turned to Dani.

"Why don't you go on up to the room, babe. I'll stop off and get a bottle of wine to celebrate with, while you make yourself comfortable."

When he returned, Dani was already in the shower. Digger opened the wine and filled two glasses.

"Oh, this shower feels so wonderful, Digger. Why don't you come on in here with me?"

'Time to perform again!' Digger sighed deeply and took a large swig of wine before slipping out of his clothes. He grinned. *'Going to have to plan things much better than this in the future, Digger my man!'*

And he was still smiling as he climbed into the shower behind Dani.

Chapter 27

Dani could feel the spirit of adventure slowly returning to her soul. Soon she would have a new life, far away from the Mannelli brothers and New York City. *'My husband will protect me from now on and everything will be just fine.'*

She wanted to put the ocean incident firmly in her past and decided not to question the version of events Digger had given. It meant that she may never know the *real* truth about that day, but all Dani wanted was to live a normal life. No more 'paper-and-tinsel world' of show business. No more action and excitement. Dani was hopeful that many good things were yet to come in her lifetime, though the terrible memories of New York still brought tears to her eyes. Her mother had given Dani a beautiful, white-marble owl some years earlier. She said it reminded her of her own little 'night owl', Dani, who slept most of the day and was up all night. *'That kind of lifestyle is no way for any respectable young woman to live,'* her mother had said and Dani smiled at the recollection.

Her parents never really approved of Dani's New York lifestyle, but had been willing to let their daughter make her own decisions and live her own life. And Dani loved them for it.

***

Heavy construction on the highway meant that it took longer than expected to get to the airport. And Dani was sure that their taxi driver had taken every side street on the island. She and Digger barely had time to check in their luggage before dashing onboard the aircraft. Dani hated being late for anything but her new husband seemed to have no regard for punctuality. *'If it's important, they'll wait,'* was his personal motto.

'What a honeymoon this has been', Dani sighed. *'It seems an awful thing to say, but I'm glad it's over!'*

She slid over into the window seat so that she could keep her bearings during take-off and landing. Then Dani rested her head on a small white pillow that Digger found in the overhead compartment. Twenty minutes into the flight, her eyes began to close. The sound of the aircraft's powerful engines purred inside her mind and Dani drifted gently away, but her peace of mind didn't last for long.

"Good morning ladies and gentlemen. This is your Captain speaking. The seat belt and no smoking signs have now been turned off, so please feel free to move around the cabin. We should be arriving in Tucson on schedule, so relax and enjoy your flight."

"Digger!" Dani nudged her husband in a panic. "We're on the wrong damn plane! The Captain just said we're going to Tucson, but we're supposed to be going to Portland, Oregon!"

"Calm down, honey. Everything's okay," Digger tried in vain to soothe his frantic wife.

"But we are supposed to be going to Portland," she insisted.

"I thought I already told you, babe, I have a meeting in Tucson tomorrow morning. It's not far out of our way and we'll only be there for a few days."

"What kind of meeting? You don't have a job, Digger, so who the hell are you meeting with?"

"That's just it Dani. I can't live off you forever, you know. My meeting is a for job interview."

"But you never said anything before about getting *any* kind of job, let alone one in Tucson!"

"It's selling some new kind of food blender, like the kind of thing I used to do on the State Fair circuit before I started working with horses."

"Well, you should have discussed it with me first, don't you think?" Dani was getting angrier by the minute.

"I don't want you traveling all over the country again, Digger. I gave up a promising career in show business so that we could spend more time *together*! We were planning to buy our own nightclub in Portland, remember. That's what we talked about, anyhow! So when exactly did you change your mind?"

"Hell, Dani! Enough with the questions! I'm my own man, dammit! I've never been accountable to any woman before and I'm not about to start now."

"Well, it's a little late to tell me all that stuff now." Dani yelled. "Why the hell did you marry me if you wanted to carry on acting like you're still single?" She was beginning to see a different side of her new man.

Digger touched a stewardess on the arm as she passed by.

"Miss, would you please bring me a Vodka Martini, very dry, on the rocks. In fact make it a double, please." Then he turned back to Dani.

"Okay honey! I'm sorry! I admit I should have talked things over with you first, but you've been so sick and I didn't want to worry you."

"But we've always made our plans for the future *together*, Digger. Remember when you and I first met? The A1 Sound Studios were waiting to hear back from me about their offer to replace Barbara Streisand, in their Broadway show. That would have been my first big break, Digger; the one I'd worked so hard for." Dani was determined to press home her point.

"I'd already finished recording all Streisand's songs and was prepared to say 'yes' to their offer, but I gave all of that up to marry *you*! And *you* were the one who chose Portland as the place for us to live, remember Digger; not me!"

"Okay baby! Okay! We can talk about all this later, but I still have to go see about this job in Tucson. The appointment is already made and we're on the plane now, so there's no turning back. You just stay around the hotel and relax, honey. You need plenty of rest anyway, after all you've been through."

"Okay!" Dani pouted. "I'm not happy with you, Digger, but I'm too tired to argue about it all now. We'll talk later."

She turned away and leaned her forehead against the cool glass of the aircraft window, closed her eyes and drifted away deep into thought. *'I don't like the direction that my life with this 'man-of-mystery' is taking.'*

Digger's surprising stubbornness was something she hadn't expected. Dani had hoped that their marriage would give her back some measure of control over her life and get her out of the rat race. But now she wasn't so sure.

'Maybe I should have listened to Ira's warnings'.

Dani couldn't blame everything on her new husband, though. The real reason she had given up the Broadway show contract wasn't because of meeting Digger, although she would never tell him that! The truth was that

Dani had no choice but to give up her budding career *and* her glamorous New York lifestyle. She had escaped from *'The Horse'* and his violent temper, but Dani still prayed daily for her own safety. Her only hope was that if she stayed out of their territory for long enough, the Mannellis would eventually forget all about Dani Sutton and spare her life. As big as New York City is to most people, it had been more like a small town to Dani and she missed it terribly. She had loved the nightlife with all its theaters and restaurants. She had treasured her daytime walks in the green beauty of Central Park. Dani had loved her fabulous home, too and her luxury yacht; all her designer clothes and her fancy cars.

But that was all gone now. Sold off through various attorneys, for half of its true value simply because Dani had been too afraid to go back there. The shadows of her past still haunted the present for Dani.

The humming of the aircraft engines was calming, almost therapeutic. As they drifted in and out of fluffy white clouds, Dani felt as if she could almost reach out and touch the hand of God! Not yet fully recovered from her recent escape from death, Dani dozed for most of the long flight, occasionally repositioning her body to keep from getting muscle cramps. She was so weak and exhausted that the more she slept, the groggier she felt. Then the Captain's voice startled her and she sat bolt upright.

"We are about to begin our descent to Tucson, where the weather is currently ninety-eight degrees. However, we may experience some turbulence on our approach due to high winds in the area. Please remain seated, with your seats in the upright position and your seat belts securely fastened. Make certain that your tray-tables are also secured."

Dani couldn't wait to get her feet back on solid ground. She hated flying. It wasn't so bad flying with JR, or with Digger, in a small plane but the roar of commercial jet engines gave her the jitters. Every time Dani flew in a big plane she swore she'd never do it again, but she kept right on doing it! *'Why does it take so long to land a damn plane?'*

Dani tried to relax but couldn't and Digger acknowledged her fears, patting her leg reassuringly.

"Don't worry honey. We're almost on the ground now. Just try and relax." Then the plane began to sway violently; sideways, up and down and every which way.

"Ladies and Gentlemen, this is your Captain again. We have encountered some very heavy winds so please remain seated and keep your seatbelts securely fastened. Remain calm and our Flight Attendants will give you any further instructions, if needed."

"Oh, my God! I think I'm going to be sick!"

Digger handed Dani a paper bag out of the seat pocket in front of them and she turned away toward the window. *'Just take deep breaths, girl, everything will be fine.'*

Their plane was fast descending toward the runway when a huge gust of crosswind shoved them way off course. Dani stared out of the window in disbelief. All she could see was dirt and huge stones being churned up beneath the plane. The roar of the engines, accelerating back up to full power, caused the plane to shake uncontrollably.

Digger reached over and shoved Dani's head down into her lap. They both grabbed hold of their ankles and held on tight, as instructed, awaiting the imminent impact. Babies and small children began to cry, prompting reassuring comments from white-faced parents. Phrases like, *'don't worry honey, everything will be alright,'* and *'hold Mommy's hand tight now and don't be scared',* resonated around the cabin. Emotional couples faced each other and whispered final farewells. *'I love you.'* and *'I'm sorry if I've ever hurt you,'* would become their epitaphs.

Fear and hysteria slowly turned to total silence as passengers held their breath and awaited the inevitable. The plane lurched upward and began steadily rising again. It swayed and bounced several times, gaining altitude all the time. Then it stabilized. Once the pilot had regained control, they circled around several times before approaching a completely different runway. The passenger cabin stayed as quiet as a tomb until the plane had landed safely. Then the applause was deafening as everyone clapped and cried for joy at the heroic efforts of their Captain.

Eyes closed and silently sobbing, Dani thanked her own guardian angels for once more sparing her life.

'Somebody up there wants me to live!'

***

Later, over dinner at the *'La Paloma'* hotel, she and Digger talked in great depth about their rough flight. Yet, she was surprised to hear him admit to being almost as scared as *she* had been. Dani couldn't wait to go to bed that night, but not for the reasons Digger might have hoped for.

'No sex tonight, then,' he mused, as his wife pleaded exhaustion and shock as her excuses for an early night.

Yet Digger wasn't really too disappointed. All of his greater plans seemed to be working out well, so far. Dani was truly naïve and he had figured her out long ago. He reckoned he could mold his new wife like putty. During the night, his hand wandered, coming to rest on one of Dani's voluptuous breasts. She stirred in her sleep and pushed his wandering hand away.

"Aw, I'm still tired, honey, but we'll have some fun in the morning, okay?"

Digger liked a challenge though. He tweaked one of her nipples and Dani began to breathe more deeply. He moved closer in anticipation. Then came a heavy, rhythmic pounding but it wasn't Digger's heartbeat.

"Shit! There's some fool at the bedroom door."

"Don't answer it." Dani was instantly wide-awake and afraid.

"We don't know anyone here, Digger," she whispered, urgently. The clock on her nightstand showed that it was two in the morning as the loud voice continued to shout from outside the door.

"Open up in there! This is the Tucson police."

Dani choked out a nervous laugh as Digger threw on his jeans. He opened the door cautiously, to admit the hotel's Manager, accompanied by couple of local police officers.

It seemed that Digger had used Dani's 'American Express' card when they checked in at the front desk. But Dani had already reported it missing during their honeymoon, when she thought it was lost at sea. She had yet to realize that Digger was holding *all* of her credit cards *and* her ID! After a few embarrassing moments of explanation, the two were left in peace once more.

"What a night! I'll make it up to you tomorrow Dani, I promise."

***

Next thing Dani knew, she was being shaken awake and Digger was smiling impishly.

"Let's get going, sleeping beauty," he said, kissing her forehead. "Breakfast will be ready in five minutes."

"But I thought you were going to some meeting this morning."

"I am, later. But it's such a beautiful morning that I thought we could have a quick lap or two around the pool and eat breakfast outside."

Digger sat on the edge of the bed and watched as Dani slipped into a pink-lace bikini. He had to admit that, sometimes, she took his breath away. She really was a magnificent woman and he loved the way her long, black hair flowed as she walked across a room. In Digger's humble opinion, she was even more beautiful without makeup. Her blue eyes were like precious stones and her skin was almost pearl-white, like the sky of a gentle dawn. And those large, firm breasts of hers were more than most men could handle!

Digger's eyes followed Dani's hourglass figure as she slipped out through the patio doors. "I'll beat you into the water!" She giggled as she dove into their private pool.

Digger sighed and followed his wife outside.

***

Digger left for his meeting and Dani closed the room door behind him. She leaned back against it, with her eyes closed and moved her hands up to the hollow of her neck. She didn't know why, but she suddenly felt her flesh crawl. Her throat muscles tightened as if she was choking. *'So, where is he really going?'*

Dani was aware that she craved excitement in her life, but didn't like the eerie feelings she was having lately; ever since the boating accident and the whispered, dire warnings from Ira. A shiver washed over her again and Dani walked out onto the patio. She lay down in the sunshine again, trying to get some warmth into her trembling bones.

***

Walking very slowly, Digger approached Joe Bennuchi's front door. *'Wow! This is a bit different from the way things are in New York'.*

There was no iron fence, no gate, no armed guards posted all around the building. Boss-man Joe was long retired and had moved out to Tucson in his later years, with the greatest respect of all the *'Families'*. He was regarded by all as the *'Don of Dons'* and his word was still law.

The large, wooden, southwestern-style front door opened, very quietly except for the creaking of its ancient hinges. He stared at the cute, but very tiny, older woman standing before him.

"Hi, ma'am. I'm Digger."

"Yes, I know." The diminutive servant moved aside and put one finger to her lips in a whisper. "They are waiting for you poolside."

She directed him toward the back patio where Joe was lounging around in the water. He floated on a plastic raft, holding a colorful drink in one hand.

"Hey Digger, fix yourself a drink, son; whatever you want. I'll be out of here soon."

Digger chuckled, quietly. Joe might be the big Mafia boss, but he still looked like a walrus afloat. Across the far side of the pool, his eagle eye spotted a pair of sleek, tanned legs peeking out from under an umbrella. *'But, the old man obviously still has taste'*. Digger strolled over to the poolside bar where a young man had already fixed him an Italian Margarita! The inference was not lost on Digger. *'The old man may be retired but he still knows everything, about everyone!'*

Digger lifted his drink in a toast and Joe nodded an acknowledgement as he labored to get off the rocking, plastic raft.

"Go meet my daughter. I'll be right out."

A young man appeared out of nowhere and wrapped a huge towel around Joe. Then they both vanished inside the pool house. Digger ambled over in the direction of the umbrella and the alluring legs but as he got within ten feet, he stopped dead in his tracks. His whole body jerked in disbelief as the young woman moved the umbrella aside.

"Hello there, Digger!"

His hands were sweating. His heart was racing. *'Oh, my god! Old Joe will kill me for sure. Brenda B is his goddamn daughter!'*

Digger moved over to sit next to Brenda, the illicit beauty from his Hawaiian honeymoon! He didn't even want to look at her, but knew he had to say something before Joe came back out of the pool house. Brenda was enjoying every moment of watching Digger squirm.

"So, how are you, Brenda?" he whispered, struggling to get the words past his bone-dry throat.

"Me? Never better, Digger. How are you?"

He just stared at her and Brenda coolly stared back. The silence between them was deafening. They were so focused on each other that neither of them noticed as Joe sat down beside them.

"I hear that you already met my baby, Digger, when you were holidaying in the Hawaiian Islands?"

With an unlit cigarette hanging from his fat lips, Joe leaned toward Digger and looked him straight in the eyes. "Got a light, son?"

"Yeah! Sure Joe!" Digger fumbled around for his lighter but before he could coordinate his hands, Brenda had flipped her own lighter over to her father and Joe lit his own cigarette. Digger's unease was palpable.

"Strange coincidence wasn't it, Joe; your daughter staying at the Colony Surf hotel, too?"

"No coincidence at all," Joe replied. "I sent her down there to keep tabs on my interests. It's a good thing for you that she wants to keep you on hand as her 'toy boy'."

"Dad!" Brenda jumped up and stalked off in a huff.

"So, let's you and me get down to business shall we, Digger. I need you to fly over to Dallas and do a couple of little 'clean-up' jobs for me; set some of John Rucker's pals at ease. They just can't seem to let go of that guy, HK's, sudden death out there. Somebody keeps digging around, stirring up shit and I'm getting sick of it. Right now a few of our best guys are hiding out in some migrant-worker's farm shack!"

"Well, there's just one slight problem with that request Joe. I'm here in Tucson with my new wife, and…"

"Who cares about that? Take the dame with you!"

"And tell her what, exactly?"

"Hell, Digger! You getting pussy-whipped these days or what? This ain't a 'request', so there's nothing more to discuss, right? Just call me when the jobs are done with."

Joe gripped Digger's hand to reinforce his message as the two of them walked back toward the house.

Brenda was in the main room, plinking out a tune on a baby grand piano. She looked up and winked as Digger passed by the open doorway.

"See you around then, Digger?"

"Er, yeah!"

Digger left Joe Bennuchi's house feeling very depressed.

'So, now what the hell do I do? I've really gotten myself into some deep shit this time!'

Chapter 28

Trying to forge her own identity as a happily married woman, yet still haunted by her recent past, Dani found herself ensnared in a complex relationship. Living with Digger was like being married to three different men all at the same time. She could never figure out what he was *really* up to. Sometimes he was all bottled-up and secretive, yet at other times her husband could be sensual, caring and totally alluring. Dani was beginning to seriously doubt that being married to such a man-of-mystery was worth all the effort. Absent-mindedly, she gazed out of the latest in a long line of hotel windows, fogged up with condensation from the torrential rain pouring down over the city of Dallas.

Dani was thankful that their latest flight, across from Tucson, had been nothing like the trip from Hawaii to Tucson. She was still confused as to why they were in Texas at all but had been told, on more than one occasion, not to ask so many questions. She drew 'tic-tac-toe' on the steamed up window to pass the time. She yawned and she stretched. Dani stared at her watch yet again, which showed her that it was five o' clock in the afternoon. Her husband had now been gone for over eight hours! *'Where the hell is he and what's he been doing?'*

Dani realized that she was asking herself those questions quite a lot, lately. Originally, Digger came from Dallas and so his ex-wife, Debi and their twelve-year old son, Donald Jr., plus Digger's parents, all still lived locally. *'But if he went to visit any of them, why didn't he take me along?'*

Knowing Digger, he was sure to have a convincing explanation when he eventually returned. *'And, knowing me, I'll probably believe him!'* Angrily, Dani swiped a hand across the damp windows, destroying her idle doodling. She picked up her purse and headed downstairs to the bar. Dani was a woman in need of solace.

"A dry Martini, please and you'd better make it a double."

***

Digger took one final puff before flicking his cigarette into a greasy puddle of water on the deserted warehouse floor. That vast, abandoned space reeked of fear, mold and stale liquor. Digger cracked his knuckles and stared down at the pathetic man in front of him, the man tied to his chair.

"It seems you were in the wrong place at the wrong time, my man." Digger taunted him as he ripped the silencing tape from the quivering man's face.

"I don't remember anything, honest." The trembling man wept as he struggled to form words. "You've gotta believe me! I'll leave the country, right now! I'll do anything you want. I only said what I knew the cops wanted to hear. Please don't kill me, man."

Digger shoved the nozzle of his .38 pistol halfway up the man's left nostril and leaned toward him.

"Listen to me, you dumb piece-of-shit and listen good. You have just six hours to get out of the country. No time for family good-byes, do you understand? You simply do not exist anymore. If you surface again, *my* ass will be on the line and then I will find you and kill you. This is a one-time deal; no second chances, pal. Understand me?"

"Anything you say." The man nodded frantically, flinging sweat and drool in all directions. "Just untie me, boss and I'm long gone."

"Get him some new ID papers and escort him to the airport. I don't want anyone tracing this guy's whereabouts, especially not the Feds."

Digger glared down at the wretched man now sniveling at his feet.

"This is your lucky day, pal! I'm still officially on vacation so I'm in a good mood."

Digger wiped the sweat from his own eyes and then left the building. He walked for a while to calm his nerves, before hailing a cab at the next corner.

"Take me to the *'International'* hotel." He looked at his watch and swore under his breath. It was after eleven o' clock at night. *'Shit! Dani will be pissed as all hell!'*

When she wasn't in their hotel room, Digger phoned down to the lounge bar.

"Yeah! Your wife's here and she's feeling no pain, if you know what I mean, sir! She was our entertainer for a while tonight though and, man, what a great voice!"

Dani was sitting at the piano-bar. She looked up blearily and lifted her glass in salute when she saw her husband.

"Hi honey! I knew you would find me, eventually." Her speech was a little slurred and her elbow slipped off the edge of the piano, spilling a little of her drink.

"Oops! I think maybe I've had a few too many." Dani rested the rim of her glass against her bottom lip.

"Come on little darlin, time for bed!" Digger took Dani's glass from her and lifted her up like a rag doll. She tried to regain her composure but in vain, giggling all the way back up to their room.

"Are you gaining weight?" Digger asked, tactlessly as he laid her across the bed. But Dani was out-for-the-count and didn't answer him. *'Great, she's asleep! Maybe if I just continue to keep her high, no questions will get asked'.*

Dani awoke next morning with the mother of all hangovers. She moved slowly around the hotel room, holding a towel filled with ice against her temple. Digger was watching and she noticed his expression.

"Don't say a damn word!" she snapped at him. "I want you to pay serious attention to my condition and realize that you are responsible for all this."

"I wasn't even here and yet it's *my* fault you're in this shape? I'm sick too ya' know!"

"Why are *you* sick?"

"I'm sick from laughing at you," Digger chuckled.

"Oh shut up! This is not one bit funny. You know what I want, really bad, right now?"

"No, what?"

"I'm starving for some spaghetti. Is that good for hangovers?"

"Good lord, woman, it's only ten o' clock in the morning! Most people eat breakfast at this time of day." Digger tossed a toweling robe across to her.

"I already drew a hot bath for you. Go soak in the tub and I'll call down for a Spanish omelet and a large Bloody Mary. I think that would be much better for your hangover than a plate of spaghetti!"

"Thank you! I sure hope it makes me feel better."

"Me too!" Digger declared. "We have a dinner date at four o'clock this afternoon, over at my folk's house. My mom is going to cook us her famous leg of lamb!"

"Ugh! I think I'm going to be sick." Dani ran for the bathroom and leaned over the toilet.

"That'll teach you," Digger yelled after her.

The warm, scented bathwater felt heavenly and breakfast turned out to be just-the-ticket. Dani passed on the *'Bloody Mary'* though, then slept for several more hours.

Digger's family home was set well back from the street. A hedge of beautifully manicured, rose bushes separated the long driveway from a huge, green lawn. On the far side of that lawn, a row of trees led up to the Rosellis' 1920's-era, white-painted, southern style home. A large, covered porch extended all across the front and down one side of the building. A hand-made quilt hung over the railing, blowing gently in the mild Texan breeze. White-wicker rocking chairs and an old fashioned swing gave the porch an inviting, lived-in look.

Digger's mother, Martha, seemed a real grandmother-type, with her grey hair and tiny spectacles. She wore a simple, printed housedress, covered over by a flowery apron. Donald Rosselli Sr., on the other hand, was handsome in a double-breasted suit and tie, giving Dani food for thought. *'I hope Digger looks that great too, when he's in his sixties'.*

Hellos were exchanged, but there were no hugs, kisses or other signs of affection between Digger and his parents. Dani took note of the cool greetings. *'They certainly don't match the impression of welcome that the house gives.'*

"Would you like to see my children?" Martha asked.

Dani was baffled, but didn't want to appear rude.

"Why yes, of course, but I thought Digger was your only child?"

Martha didn't answer as she opened French doors that led into what obviously used to be a music room. Specially-built shelves lined all of the walls and soft, classical music was playing inside the room even though no-one was inside. Dani could not believe her eyes. At least twenty cats, of all colors and sizes were sprawled around on those shelves. Some were on the couch, too and yet more felines occupied the two, well-upholstered easy chairs in the center of the room. Yet everything was spotlessly clean and even the hardwood floors shone with what appeared to be fresh polish!

Dani was speechless. *'My God! What the hell is this all about?'*

Donald Snr. had built the cattery for Martha, she said. Yet it was obvious to Dani that neither Digger, nor his father, shared Martha's obsession with the creatures. Martha directed a sneered remark at Digger.

"Cats are my life. They are so much more loyal than any humans."

Digger glared back at her and Dani understood then, why their reception at the house had been so cool. There had obviously *never* been any love around in that house; only Martha's love for her cats.

She was glad when dinner was over, she was having a hard time socializing with such strange people. After the main meal, cookies, cakes and tea were served in the living room but the conversation still proved anything but sweet. Donald Snr. suddenly spoke.

"Dani, I hope you know how to manage your money, if you have any!" His good looks seemed to undergo a transformation right before Dani's eyes and Digger began to look very troubled.

"Come on, Dad! Don't start that crap again, or…"

"Or what? Does your wife *know* what you do for a living, son?"

Digger jumped up and grabbed Dani by the arm.

"That's it! I knew this was a bad idea. Let's get the hell out of here, Dani!"

Digger shoved her out the front door so fast that she was still in shock as she climbed into the car. Digger started the engine and Dani heard Martha cry out. "You just had to tell her didn't you?"

"Shut up, woman!" Donald Snr pushed his wife aside and stomped back into the house. Martha followed him and the heavy front door slammed shut on the secrets of the Rosellis' picture-perfect, family home.

Their car burned rubber and spewed gravel as Digger sped down the driveway and turned sharply onto the main road. He was silent all the way back to their hotel and for many hours afterward, too.

Dani didn't need to be told that she would never see the inside of her husband's family home, ever again.

***

When she woke up next morning, Digger was looking excitedly out of the window.

"My god, Dani! Come over here and look. Have you ever seen anything like this? There's a real flood down there."

It had been raining ever since they arrived in Dallas but Dani hadn't thought anything of it. What she saw outside then was not what Dallas was supposed to look like, though. Water was already standing about a foot deep all around the hotel.

"Digger, can we get out of this place, right now? I don't like it here and I want to go home. I'm sick of living out of suitcases too and I'm sure my Mom and Dad will be starting to worry about us."

But when Digger called to see if Dallas/Fort-Worth Airport was allowing planes to leave, Dani was bitterly disappointed. "We'll just have to hang out until the weather clears, honey," he told her.

Later that afternoon, Digger remembered one of his old haunts. *'Jack Ruby's'* old restaurant, famous for its connections to the Kennedy assassination, was now a famous bistro and was only two blocks away from their hotel.

"Come on! I'll take you there for dinner."

Dani's shoes were soaked by the time they arrived but, once inside, it was a really cool place. Yet she was shocked at how many people in there knew Digger and surprised, too, at how pleased they all were to see him again.

"This place is my *real* Texas home," he confided and Dani could well believe him after what she had witnessed at his parents' house the day before. By the time they got back to their hotel it had finally quit raining. The floods were subsiding too, so they made plans to leave Dallas the following morning.

***

"Just one more, quick stop," Digger said, as they were on route to the airport and Dani didn't ask any questions, this time. *'I never get a straight answer anyway'.*

The roads were still muddy and rainwater stood fairly deep in places. Dani held her breath, but Digger had driven through many storms in his time and seemed to be handling the car with ease. *'Nothing ever seems to rattle Digger Rosselli!'* she mused. He eventually turned in at the main gate of a cattle ranch but drove past the main house. He drove for a long way, it seemed to Dani, before parking up behind a big barn, in front of a row of migrant worker shacks. Digger motioned, harshly, for Dani to stay in the car.

The one-room shack, marked as number 6, had only one, small window and Dani watched in fear as Digger knocked on its grubby front door. She saw someone briefly pull back an old piece of blanket that was covering the window. Then the door opened and Digger disappeared inside. The door closed swiftly behind him and Dani was left outside, alone, to wait.

✳✳✳

"I hear you have good news for me, Digger?"

The professor beamed and motioned for his visitor to sit down. Digger looked around, but decided against sitting on the dirty bed. He sat at the table instead, pushing aside a plate and some flatware and cleaning a space to lean his arm on.

"That's right, sir." Digger took a large leather pouch out of his jacket pocket and tossed it across the table, toward the professor. After quickly eyeballing its contents, the older man whistled his appreciation.

"Enough?" Digger asked.

"It should get us certainly out of the country for a good while, anyhow. You've done well, Digger my man." The professor sounded well pleased. "Did Joe Bennuchi give you any shit over the amount?"

"Are you kidding? He couldn't afford to quibble. Joe knows you did a good job for him. Did you get the new identities for you and your wife, from his guy, Paulie?"

"Yes and we can't wait to get away from here. This is the third place we've moved to since doing the job for Joe and every time we turn around the Feds are closin' in behind us again. I don't dare think about what they'd do if they caught us."

He patted Digger on the back as the two of them moved toward the door of the cabin.

"I hear you got yourself married, too and into money, Digger?" They both stood looking at the car and at Dani. "Nice looking lady, young man. Good luck to both of you."

The professor waved to Dani as Digger climbed back into the car. She nodded back, wondering what on earth such an intelligent looking man was doing hiding out in this kind of squalor. In spite of herself, curiosity got the better of her.

"Digger, I know I shouldn't ask, but what in the hell are you up to here in Dallas?"

His face was hard and set but Digger didn't respond, so Dani asked again, quietly but firmly.

"Please, honey, answer my question."

"Damn you! Cut it out, Dani! What you don't know can't hurt you!"

The unknown beast had emerged again and the sudden violence in Digger's voice terrified her. *'Just who is this guy I've married?'*

Once more Dani felt herself heading into danger and silence fell between them. Digger's secrets would have to end one day but, for the moment, Dani would wait and see how things panned out.

Chapter 29

The sky all around the plane was a lustrous blue. White clouds, like pillows of cotton wool, huddled off in the distance as their aircraft began its descent. Digger was asleep, or so it seemed but Dani's eyes were scanning the ground below. Their flight path followed the Columbia River, all the way up to Hayden Island where houseboats and marinas lined both banks. As they circled around on their final approach, Dani saw the beautiful city of Portland, Oregon spread out below her.

The surrounding foothills were bejeweled with lavish mansions, evergreen trees and sparkling waterfalls. Mount Hood was off to the right and, even farther out, Dani could see Mount St. Helens. Seeing them reminded her of happier times, skiing on Mount Rainier. It was an awesome sight, majestic and powerful as both mountains were volcanoes and could erupt anytime. Yet those imposing mountains and the mighty Pacific Ocean, with its dozens of busy tourist resorts, were only an hour away from downtown Portland itself.

'Maybe Digger's right and this will be a great place for us to start our new life over, as long as it doesn't rain too much'. Dani had heard plenty about the infamous rains in Oregon!

'Only time will tell', she told herself as she shook her husband's arm.

Digger wasn't really asleep. He had been keeping his eyes closed for most of the flight simply to avoid Dani's persistent questions. His thoughts had been churning, non-stop, worrying about what to do next. His wife was already starting to get on his nerves. They had not had sex since Hawaii, yet Digger knew that if he continued to withdraw from her, Dani's suspicions would only get worse. He had managed to refuse her recent sexual advances by telling her he didn't feel well.

It wasn't really a lie, though; it was hard to feel romantic when you had murder on your mind! Digger's side trips to Tucson and Dallas certainly hadn't helped, putting more strain on their already tense relationship. With Digger refusing sex, Dani was already becoming distant and very defensive towards him. In fact, he couldn't remember the last time the two of them had enjoyed a pleasant conversation. Lately, it always seemed to be, *'why this'*, or *'why that?'* The last thing Digger needed was constant questions from a meddling wife.

The pair stepped off the plane in silence and entered Portland's International Airport. Dani sighed and put on her bravest face.

'Welcome to your new life, kiddo!'

***

The following days and weeks flew by as Dani and Digger looked at house, after house. She knew exactly what she was looking for and the lady wouldn't settle for anything less. Her furniture and personal things had already arrived from New York City; they were being held in storage. Dani owned a twenty-four-foot long, hand carved, French provincial dresser and it needed a dining room with one wall large enough to accommodate it! Dani wanted to find a house as soon as possible and settle down, but it had to be the right one. She wanted Digger to experience her 'domestic'-side and felt sure that he would be more than impressed with all her beautiful furniture and expensive art pieces.

It took three months to find their perfect dwelling; a five-story, twenty-eight-roomed mansion previously occupied by the owner of the 'Oregonian' newspaper group. It was the grandest mansion on Buena Vista Drive and it hugged the hillside overlooking the Columbia River and the whole city of Portland. The two of them jokingly nicknamed it, 'Rosselli's Roost'.

Digger agreed to let Dani organize and decorate the interior of the house, but *he* insisted on taking care of all maintenance and structural issues.

He hired electricians to completely modernize all the wiring. He had the kitchen completely gutted and rebuilt, with the exception of a hotel-style 'dumbwaiter' that went all the way from the basement, all the way up to the fifth floor. Digger was adamant about keeping that. He also hired a domestic couple. Hank would take care of their beautifully laid-out gardens and any general house maintenance, whilst his wife, Lil, would clean and mostly help Dani indoors. Dani told Digger she preferred to do all her own cooking but agreed that she would use the domestic help for larger, dinner parties.

Digger quite liked the idea of his wife planning and cooking all their meals. *'Give her something to do and keep her out of my hair!'*

Yet whilst Dani was busy arranging their new home and planning decor, Digger was zipping around Portland City looking up his former, criminal connections!

Giuseppe Toricello, known as 'Guy', operated a commercial, real-estate company but mainly used it as a front for other, illegal, activities. Within a very short time, Digger had taken the mandatory educational course, obtained his real-estate trading license and started 'working' with Guy. Dani never saw her husband show, let alone sell, a single house much less close any commercial property deals, even though he left the house every morning at eight o' clock sharp and came home whenever he felt like it! He told Dani that his company was working mainly on large, construction projects and that he would get paid as and when the jobs were completed. Digger seemed to suddenly acquire a lot of new buddies too, including an old, Vegas 'pit boss'.

Yet Dani thought it very strange that Digger never brought any of his new friends to visit at their house. It also bothered her that Digger had opened a Post Office box and had all their house mail sent over there. Little did Dani know that her husband was setting up a web of crime and deceit, right under her very nose.

Each day seemed to get longer and longer, as Dani gradually began to run out of things to do around the house. How lovely it would be, she thought, to hear the sounds of music, laughter and happiness filling the rooms of their beautiful home. Instead, the only sound Dani heard was her own sobbing, day in and day out, whilst her husband was out at 'work'.

"Enough is enough, Digger!" she screamed at him one evening. "I'm going out tomorrow morning and look for a nightclub to buy, so that I can start singing again. It's too damn lonely here, being a stay-at-home wife. I need to do something worthwhile with my life, something to make me feel good about myself."

***

Next day Digger came home from work early with the details of two nightclubs that he felt had good potential.

"Get your face on, Dani and we'll go check them out."

First he took her to a place called *'Jake's Crawfish'*; a rustic-style club that had been established for many years. Dani liked the atmosphere inside, but the property was in a very bad neighborhood.

She didn't really feel comfortable about entering and leaving late at night and alone.

The second venue was called *'The 19th Hole'* and it was located downtown on the corner of Broadway and Salmon. The general location was well lit and the club was surrounded by large hotels, so Dani felt much safer about working alone there. During the daytime, the clientele was mostly golfers, stopping in for a cool drink after a long game. In the evenings, it attracted gays and lesbians among its night-time revelers! But it didn't take long for Dani and Digger to close a deal. The old signs were quickly torn down and a building crew moved in to completely renovate the interior. New staff were hired, including a professional piano player and, on opening night, the brand new neon sign above the door lit up as, *'The Carriage Room'*.

The names beneath it stated that Dani and Dale Rogers were its proprietors; Dale being her pianist and musical director. He and Dani made a great team and for the first few weeks customers were lining up to gain admission to Portland's newest nightspot. It was a dream-come-true for Dani. Her life had meaning again. The exhilaration of bright stage lights, the applause of a crowd and being able to wear her glamorous gowns again made her feel buzzing and alive.

For the first time in months she was really happy and threw herself into the project, heart and soul. Digger did his own thing, Dani did hers and that suited her just fine. JR came home from his Military Academy during every holiday and Dani loved spending time with her teenaged son. They took long walks and spent many hours talking together. But at the following Thanksgiving holiday, JR dropped a bombshell on his mother.

"Mom, I've decided not to go back to the Academy for my final year."

"How can you say that, after you've worked so hard to become an officer? Why would you even consider giving up such a great career?

"I've thought about all of that, Mom but I really want to be in the entertainment business, like you."

"For God's sake JR! Are you completely brain dead?"

"Actually, Digger wants me to drop out too and help you, running the Club."

"Doing what? You are only seventeen-years old, son, or did Digger forget that part?"

"Mom, just listen for a minute willya'. Digger said you're going to put in some exotic dancers so I could be your light-and-sound man; working backstage, out of sight."

"Oh he did, did he? And what does Digger think *I'm* going to do in this new cabaret; strip my clothes off too?"

"Sorry, Mom, but I thought you already knew about his plans."

"No; I didn't! So exactly when is this big change supposed to take place?"

"Right away, I think.

***

Dani was deeply hurt and bitterly furious with Digger. When she arrived at the Club that evening, she was even more shocked to see that the piano-bar area was already gone.

"How dare he? Where in the hell *is* Digger?" Dani screamed.

The lounge went deathly quiet as the staff quickly realized that Digger, their supposed boss, was in deep shit. Dani had never told anyone that it was all *her* money; *her* Club and *her* big house. Up to that evening, she had been happy for folk to think that Digger was the wealthy one and not a man living off his rich wife.

Digger materialized from somewhere behind Dani and took hold of her arm, firmly.

"Not here, Dani. Let's go over to the Hilton hotel bar and talk things over. I have both good and bad news."

Digger ordered drinks for them both but Dani could hardly contain her anger.

"Digger, how could you make a decision *this* big without even talking to me about it? I *am* the President of this company of ours, remember?"

"I know! And I know you wanted to be the 'star' in your own place, so I went along with the plan at the start. But it hasn't worked out, Dani and things have changed. I don't know how to break this to you, honey!"

"What do you mean? Where is Dale, my musical director and what the hell has happened to my beautiful piano?"

Digger sighed dramatically, making Dani even more agitated."

"Dale left town already, Dani. He said he couldn't be your partner anymore. To quote him properly, he said 'she's not a good enough singer'. He said he left without saying goodbye because he couldn't bear to hurt you, Dani."

"I don't believe one word of this, Digger. Where the hell did Dale go?" Dani was inconsolable and began to cry.

"Come on! I'll take you home."

They walked to the parking garage but as they approached their car, Digger suddenly stopped.

"On second thoughts, Dani, you go on home by yourself. I've still got things to do back at the Club. I'll catch a ride home later."

With that, Digger walked away leaving Dani wounded and hysterical. She realized then that if the man really loved her, there was no way he could leave her alone in that condition. She sat in her car, with the engine running, for what seemed like hours. It was raining softly outside and the raindrops glistened like tiny diamonds on the windshield. The floodlights in the car park were just a blur as tears streamed down Dani's cheeks. How easy would it be to drive the car away at full speed and smash into something; anything?

"No! No! No!" Dani screamed out loud, pounding her fists against the steering wheel.

"That's just what Digger wants me to do, the bastard! But I'm not going to play into his hands." She took a deep breath, put the car into gear and drove away carefully. She cruised around the city for a while to regain her composure before heading up the hill to home. Dani was alone again, but for some strange reason it felt okay!

Around four o' clock in the morning, Digger slipped into bed beside her. Dani didn't even acknowledge his presence even though she was still awake. She could smell the drink on him but didn't have anything more to say to him. Not then, at least.

***

Dani sat on the patio overlooking her immaculately groomed and terraced gardens. Lil had just brought her some orange juice, a toasted bagel and a full jug of coffee. She breathed in the wonderful aroma and sighed as Lil filled her cup.

"Will Mr. Rosselli be joining you, ma'am?"

"Lil! After all this time, won't you please call us Dani and Digger?"

"Oh ma'am! That just wouldn't feel right somehow."

"Well, whatever you feel comfortable with is fine then. And no, my husband will *not* be joining me for breakfast, Lil. He got home very late last night so I doubt he'll be getting up anytime soon!"

Then Digger strolled out onto the patio, leaned down and kissed his wife on the forehead as if nothing was wrong.

"Good morning ladies! What a wonderful, brisk morning! I'll take my coffee out here too please, Lil."

'Putting on a show for the hired help', Dani thought, irritably.

"I called your father recently, Dani and we're both flying to Yakima later today, to have a talk with him."

"And exactly what do we have to talk to *my* father about?"

"Well, I'm hoping he will move out here and be the day manager of our Club."

"Gee, Digger! You sure like making plans without consulting me," Dani sneered. "But, I don't think that's a very good idea at all. Dad and Mom are very settled in their local community."

"Besides, Papa only has two years left before his retirement from 'un-dersheriff'; he would lose most of his pension if he quit his job now.

"Hell, Dani! Just think about it for a minute will ya'! Your father has been a public servant all of his damn life, but what does he have to show for it? When we finally turn this Club around and give the people what they want to see, your father will be able to retire 'big time'."

"So, exactly what high-flyin' plans do you have for *my* Club, Digger?"

"I've found a great agent who can bring us in exotic dancers, out of Vegas. *You* can still sing, but to pre-recorded backing music instead of the piano and you can do all the MC work, too. If we close down for just *three* weeks, we can still keep the restaurant out front open while you organize rehearsals for the dancers. You can do that Dani, can't you?"

Dani sighed. What he was saying went against all of her instincts, but maybe he was right. *'Perhaps it is time for a change.'*

After all, business hadn't been as good lately as when they first opened. Something definitely needed to change and maybe Digger's big new ideas would work. But Dani hated the thought of disrupting her parents' lives in case things didn't work out. In the end though, she gave in to Digger's grand plans.

She knew that her father would always be there, if he thought Dani really needed him.

'Mom, on the other hand, might need a bit more convincing!'

Chapter 30

Laura Gunther was tormented. She was not about to move away from her home on some whim but if her husband wanted to be so foolish, well he could just go by himself! Laura would live alone if she had to. She hadn't yet made up her mind about Digger Rosselli, but there was something about the man that Dani's mother didn't quite trust. She kept reminding herself that it was Dani's life and if her daughter was happy, well then, 'Mom' should just stay out of it. The problem was that 'Mom' wasn't so sure that her daughter really *was* happy.

Digger had been very convincing over the telephone, telling Harold that he could easily make enough money for he and his wife to live 'very comfortably' for the rest of their lives. Digger even said that the two of them could live on the top floor of Dani's mansion, whilst they were deciding whether moving to Portland was a good idea or not. In Digger's opinion, the Gunthers really had nothing to lose as they could still retain their home in Yakima for the moment, in case they changed their minds.

'Nothing to lose, indeed!' Her husband had worked all his life at the Sheriff's Office and if he were to leave early, then they would surely lose a big chunk of his retirement money. Laura was starting to like her daughter's new husband less and less. But Harold was pretty pumped up about the whole idea and he eventually persuaded his wife to take the risk. They would both move to Portland and try out this new business opportunity.

"Besides," Harold reasoned, "we always dreamed of having some kind of a 'Mom-&-Pop'-restaurant together when I retired, didn't we? And think of how good it will be for us to be closer to Dani."

Laura eventually gave in, but certainly not gracefully.

"Fine! But if I'm not happy, I'm moving straight back here to Yakima! *Alone* if necessary!"

***

Harold discovered that he could actually retire early without too much financial penalty so the gears were quickly put in motion for the start of the Gunthers' new life in Portland. Some of his fellow officers and *all* of their neighborhood friends were shocked at their sudden decision, but other townsfolk cheered them on for being so adventurous at their time of life. Harold finally persuaded Laura into selling their house outright, so everything was packed up and put into storage in case it took while to get rid of.

She was bitterly disappointed when it sold within the first week! *'This idea of Harold's had better work out.'*

***

When they first saw Dani's huge mansion her parents were both in awe, but as time passed Laura became desperately lonely. She couldn't settle down in that massive mansion; it was Dani's house, not hers.

'Foolish, foolish old man! Why ever did I let him talk me into moving here?' Laura read a great deal and she slept more than usual too; anything to pass the time. And Laura cried, every single day.

Yet her husband was in seventh heaven. He loved his new job and the daily challenges it carried. He happily opened up at six every morning to let the cleaning staff in and he stayed there until six or seven, every evening.

Dani's own hours stretched from around eleven in the morning to the wee small hours on most days. She wore many different hats, too, as she and her father worked hard to build up the new business. Dani hired, fired and trained all the staff. She choreographed all the shows *and* she balanced the books. But she and her father were so wrapped up in the Club that they overlooked everything else.

They didn't realize what Digger was getting up to, nor did they notice how depressed Laura was becoming.

Digger was happily doing his own thing, in his own private world. He flew in and out of Nevada several times a week in the Cherokee airplane that Dani had bought him as a wedding gift. Sometimes he took customers and friends out to the *'Flying S Ranch'*, for private party fun and games. At other times he ran weekend trips to Las Vegas, to Marty Rackin's renowned *'International Hotel'*.

Dani really liked Marty. She had only met him once, when Digger had graciously allowed her to accompany him one time, but she took to the older man right away. And now, Digger was an invited guest at Marty's hotel for a long weekend! Dani was really looking forward to a much-needed break. It could have been a beautiful vacation too, if Digger had not been such an ass!

Their five-roomed, penthouse suite was fabulous. It sported red and gold, velvet drapes with matching carpets in every room. A king-sized bed stood right in the center of the huge bedroom, which had mirrors all over its ceiling and walls. Dani anticipated having some real, romantic fun in there with her husband, later that night! She desperately needed a break after putting in countless hours over the past few weeks. But, more importantly, she and Digger needed some quality time together.

But Digger soon diluted Dani's fantasies.

"You're not going to follow me all over the casino this weekend, are you, like the other wives do?"

"Well, I guess not," Dani snapped. "I'd hate to embarrass you by acting like a *wife*!"

Digger ignored her and headed toward the door.

"Marty wants to take us to dinner and a show tonight. He'll be bringing his own 'date' with him so I'll be back around seven this evening, to pick you up."

"What show?"

"I don't know, some big name or other. Marty has made all the arrangements, so just be ready on time and behave yourself."

"Okay!" Dani wanted to add the word, 'honey' to her reply but the emotion just wasn't there.

✳✳✳

During the afternoon, Dani walked around the casino and played on a few of the slot machines but she soon got bored. Every once in a while she would spot Digger across the room and, each time, she consciously removed herself from his view so as not to anger him. She briefly wondered how much of *her* money he was losing. *'Quit being so negative, woman! Maybe he's winning, so go find something else to do'.*

She finally decided to treat herself to some sun by the pool and then spend a few hours at the spa. Dani barely made it to her hair appointment on time and it was six o'clock before she got back to their hotel room. She had already showered at the spa so all she needed to do was touch up her makeup and slip into her evening gown. Just as she was zipping up, Marty knocked on the adjoining door and waltzed in.

"Hi, kiddo! Is Digger here?"

"No, not yet He told me to be ready by seven though, so I'm sure he'll show up soon."

"You look great, Dani! Come on through to our suite and meet my lady friend." Marty looked at his watch. "We're having gin-and-tonics. Do you want one?"

"Sounds great! Thanks Marty!" Dani followed him through to the adjoining room and he made the introductions.

"Dani! Meet Cindy."

Cindy was very young and very pretty but she smiled a friendly enough greeting. Dani noticed a fur coat thrown over a chair and wondered idly why the girl would need a coat like that when it was so hot outside. Marty left the room again to look for Digger, so the girls were left alone and they were soon at a loss for words. It was obvious that they had nothing in common, but Dani tried hard.

"Do you work here in Vegas, Cindy?"

"No! I don't really work at all," the girl replied, mysteriously.

"How do you survive, then?" As soon as the question was asked, Dani realized it was dumb.

"Actually, I survive quite well," Cindy said, coolly. "I'm in investments, you see."

"Oh! That's nice." Dani had no idea what the girl was talking about but thankfully Marty appeared again.

"Digger will have to catch up with us later. We're going to be late for dinner. He knows where we'll be, so let's be off ladies." Marty opened the door for both of them with a flourishing bow.

Digger was waiting for them downstairs and it was obvious that he was not pleased to see Dani. She gave him a sideways look of disgust and wished she had stayed in the hotel room. As there were others present she was forced to be civil, but, deep inside her soul, Dani felt tension building between her and Digger. In truth, it had been building for many weeks, even from *before* the boating incident in Hawaii. The only thing that seemed important to Digger these days was Dani's money and how much of it he could spend. She had no idea how much he had *already* spent, or how much he had lost, or won, on this trip; nor did she really know where her husband *was* for most of the time.

Dani focused all her attention on dinner, which was excellent and on the show that followed, which was spectacular!

Over that long weekend, she and Digger spent quite a lot of time with Marty, who had a new girl by his side on each occasion. Every evening the four ate a fancy dinner together and then watched another new show. On the fourth night, Dani, fortified with champagne, let down her defenses and decided to make a romantic advance to Digger. They had said good-night to Marty and his latest flame, Gloria. But before Dani had finished freshening herself up, Digger had taken off his tie, opened his shirt at the neck, slipped out of his loafers and passed out on the bed.

When Dani came out of the bathroom, in a sheer, pink, flowing neg-ligee, she was not expecting such rejection.

"Wake up! Damn you, Digger; can you hear me? Shit, you're driving me crazy."

With tears streaming down her face, Dani slid into bed and turned away from her husband. His breath reeked of whisky and she knew that he hadn't showered, or brushed his teeth, since early that morning. She pulled the sheets up over her shoulders and cried herself to sleep.

Next day they had a late breakfast in the room, with plenty of black coffee. After a long spell of silence, Dani miserably begged Digger to spend some of his precious time with *her*. So they spent the day poolside, but Digger had his head buried in a newspaper for most of the time. Dani fell asleep and got sunburn! Later that night, when he finally offered to make love to his wife she was hurting too badly. That didn't stop Digger though and that was the moment that Dani realized her husband was a sadist, in addition to all his other faults.

Next day, Digger left their room early to go gambling again. Dani decided to go shopping. *'I might as well spend some of my own money on clothes since Digger is constantly throwing it away on rubbish'.*

She had never even dreamed that her husband possessed such a gam-bling problem. *'Another hidden vice'*, she thought, bitterly.

As Dani came out of a dress shop in the hotel shopping mall, she saw

Digger stepping out of the South Tower elevator. He looked pale and yet sort of red-in-the-face too, all at the same time. She eagerly ran up to him and smiled.

"What were you doing up there, honey?"

"Are you *following* me?" Digger barked the words at her.

"Well, no! I just saw you and …"

"And what? You thought I was up there with some hooker?"

"I don't know *what* to think any more, Digger," she whispered.

"Well, don't think, Dani! Just don't *think*, OK!"

She was left standing alone as he marched over to the Casino and threw himself down at a Baccarat table. He knew she wouldn't follow him there. Instead, Dani went up to their room to pack. The plane would be taking them both back to Portland at nine o' clock the next morning and she was more than ready to leave the whole, miserable weekend behind.

***

"Hello there, darlin'!"

Digger looked up from the gaming table to see Brenda B sliding gracefully into the seat next to his.

"What took *you* so damn long to get here? He demanded to know. "We leave here first thing in the morning!"

"I had to attend to some business for Dad and it took longer than I expected." Brenda replied calmly

"Dammit! I've *needed* you, baby. Where are you staying?"

"Over at the Dunes, in room 448."

"Okay! You head over there now and I'll be right behind you. Dani is still around here somewhere."

Digger realized that he would be in deep shit with his wife in the morning, but what-the-hell; he had been in worse spots before and always managed to smooth his way out. *'Why should this time be any different?'*

***

Dinner was delivered to their room but Dani ate alone. Later, she went downstairs, played a few slot machines and then tried her hand at Black Jack. But her eyes and her mind constantly wandered around the casino, searching for Digger. She finally called it a night and went to bed at around one in the morning, confident that her husband was nowhere within the Casino. Marty told her that he had seen a bunch of guys getting into a cab earlier, to go off gambling at another casino. He said not to worry, but Dani was furious. *'The bastard!'* She closed her eyes and tried in vain to get to sleep but Digger did not come back to their room at all that night.

Next morning, she got up early and called for the bellhop to collect their luggage. Then Dani went down to the casino and made an unsuccessful sweep around the room. Marty told her yet again that she shouldn't worry.

"Digger is a big boy, Dani; he'll find his own way home." But by then she was pretty sure that Marty was just covering for her husband.

So the plane took off without Digger. Dani was far too embarrassed to look at any of the other passengers, much less talk to them. Now she must go home alone and face her folks. But what could she tell them? That this had been one of the longest weekends of her life. That she had married a total ass. That their daughter had made a wrong choice; yet again?

Dani felt thoroughly miserable.

Harold Gunther was standing at the arrival gate when she came through and Dani threw her arms around him.

"Oh, Papa! Thank you for picking me up." She began to cry but stopped when she realized that people were staring.

"Honey, what's wrong? Where's Digger?"

"He didn't show up for the plane, Papa. I think he's drunk somewhere *and* I think he's with someone else. This whole weekend has been a nightmare!"

Harold patted his daughter's back.

"Come on, honey! Let's just go home. I'll get your suitcases. A man like Digger is *not* worth worrying about. If you're really lucky, Dani, somebody will dump him out in the desert and leave him for the birds!"

Dolores J. Guthrie

Chapter 31

Digger turned up at their Club two days later; red-eyed, white faced and feeling ragged. But a genuine apology was the last thing on his mind.

"I guess I made a complete ass of myself, huh? I tried to get on the plane, babe, honest I did, but they said I was too drunk to fly. In fact they kicked me out of the airport altogether, so I went back to the hotel and kept right on drinking. But here I am, alive and well and back to my little 'wifie' again." Digger leaned in for a kiss but Dani turned her head away in disgust.

***

After closing time, Digger was lounging in the back office. His feet were propped up on a spare chair and yet another drink was clutched in one hand. All the lights in the Club were blazing. The janitor was sweeping and the bartenders were busy cleaning and polishing glasses. Dani approached the office after making sure that all was well and was totally unprepared for the conversation that awaited her. Digger slurred his words as he peered at Dani, through bloodshot eyes.

"He's got to go!"

"*Who's* got to go?"

"Your old man, that's who! I already told him to pack up and get out."

"You did what?" Dani couldn't believe what she was hearing.

"Are you deaf? I said your old man has got to go."

"You're drunk Digger. You don't know what you're saying."

"I may be drunk but I know damn well what I'm saying. You're going to have to finally choose between your Pa and me, woman!"

"This is bullshit. My love for you is nothing like the love I have for my father. There is no way that I could ever choose between you. Don't you dare let my Papa leave."

Dani was outraged. Bitterly angry and heartbroken she stormed out of the Club and drove home alone, but the next morning her father confirmed the truth of Digger's decision.

"Digger has ruined our retirement plans for sure, honey, but don't you worry. Your Mom and I will easily find another place to live and I can still find another job. I'm not too old yet!"

"But I can't believe that he could be so cruel, Papa. Last night I thought he was just talking though the booze, you know, but obviously I was wrong. But I still have some say in all this. Digger hasn't heard the last from me yet."

"No honey! Don't waste your breath! There is *no* way that I will ever walk back into that Club, or into this house, ever again. Not as long as that man is around."

"But why is he doing all this, Papa?'

"I don't know *why*, Dani, but I know *what* he's doing and Digger *knows* that I know. And when all of your money is finally under that man's control then *you* will know too, honey. Just remember that money is only money, but if that man ever touches one hair on your head, honey, I'll kill him myself so help me God."

Harold Gunther's knuckles turned white as he punched his fists together.

***

When the household staff heard Dani's news of the problems between her and her husband, they were distraught but stayed loyal to their mistress. Hank and Lil apologized unhappily for not speaking out earlier, but then they recounted lurid stories of Digger's nocturnal activities.

Dani wasn't at all surprised to hear that for several months past her husband had been bringing dancers and other assorted young women back to the house; sneaking them up to the guest wing via the dumbwaiter system. On one occasion Lil had even found a girl in Dani's bedroom, going through her wardrobe. Lil didn't know exactly how long the girl had been there, but had made her leave immediately.

"Damn! I *have* been missing some personal things lately, but I just thought I had misplaced them. You know how scatterbrained I can be."

Dani was gutted to think of some cheap trollop going through, or even wearing, her personal things. "I don't suppose you know any of the girls' names do you, Lil?"

"Some girl called 'Brenda' was one of them but we were never officially introduced to any of them." Hank was apologetic. "I only remember *her* because I overheard Digger call out her name."

"Don't you worry Hank; none of this is your fault, nor Lil's, but I'm going to have to do something about it. Can we agree to keep all this between ourselves until I can arrange to have Mr. Rosselli followed?"

Hank and Lil agreed without hesitation.

"OK, then! We'll see just how powerful Mr. Digger Rosselli *really* is!"

***

Several weeks passed, turning into months. Dani's parents moved away to a new home in Salem, Oregon. Her father got himself a job with the US Marshal's Office, working within their Witness Protection program. He was sent back East for a while, for extra training, so Laura found herself alone again, except for her miniature poodle, *'Gee-Gee'*. But she could cope with that. She was just glad to get away from that nightmare of a mansion *and* Digger Rosselli.

Dani was also alone. Digger popped in and out of *'Rosselli's Roost'* at all sorts of odd hours but rarely came home to sleep. Even when he did, he stayed in the guest wing. He took his meals there too, or ate out elsewhere, but he avoided all contact with Dani.

JR resigned from the Academy to help his mother out. Dani thought he was making a huge mistake, leaving the military for good, but she was too emotionally drained to argue. So JR took over the running of all the lights and music for the Club. In a way Dani was glad he was there, to help her pick up the pieces of her crumbling world. Yet it was unwittingly putting extra strain on her. She felt obliged to remain close by, to keep the glamorous disco dancers well away from her handsome son! She felt that, even at seventeen, JR was still too young for such a life and hated to see him getting more and more involved in the world of show business.

But JR always there for his mother and that gave Dani great comfort. They drove home together each night after work, which was something that Digger had *never* done with her. He always had some other *'business'* to attend to. And JR was always ready to listen whenever Dani needed to talk, or even just vent some of her pent-up anger. Yet she constantly worried about her son, just like any other mother would. They had both made some bad choices in life already and Dani knew that, someday, they would both suffer the consequences.

She often lay awake at nights listening to the nocturnal sounds of the big, empty house. The neighbors had teased Dani about having bought a haunted house and, until lately, she had believed they were joking. Yet the hired help and several of Dani's previous houseguests had already reported hearing strange sounds of tapping and of glass breaking. Other times it was the rattling of venetian blinds for no reason and doors slamming when no one was nearby. On some occasions, cold air would suddenly rush into a room and swirl invisibly around its occupants.

Lights would sometimes come on if a certain drawer was opened. Stuffed animals floated around in the air, as if tossed by invisible hands. Radios and TVs switched themselves on and off at random. And more than once a securely bolted door had opened, all by itself!

Lately, Dani had also begun to experience these 'special effects' but she kept telling herself that any spirits in the house must be friendly, as no one had ever come to any harm there. She also came to believe that there was more than one apparition within her house because, sometimes, several incidents occurred at the same time. She sensed the presence of spirits most strongly when all the room lights would go down, changing from bright to dim in a progressive pattern and often to the beat of any music playing in the background. Dani would smile and talk to such manifestations. It helped her to not be afraid. But as time passed, the disturbances began to get stronger and more violent and Dani began to fear the unknown.

Family members and friends had long ago stopped coming for more than brief, daytime visits. Certainly, no-one ever wanted to stay overnight, except for her own mother. Laura was the only person who had never seen *or* heard anything unusual. *'Mom is much too down-to-earth and practical, I guess!'* Eventually, Dani began keeping a loaded .38 pistol beneath her pillow and locking her bedroom door at night. After Hank and Lil were up and about, she would unlock her door again so the staff wouldn't know how scared their mistress really was!

Dani's life was becoming a living nightmare.

She tossed and turned for the whole of one particular night, mostly worrying about what Digger was planning. Out of sheer frustration, she scanned through the local phone book and made a note of a number that she thought looked reliable. First thing next morning, Dani called a private detective agency!

Ron Woodland, the chief investigator, took her assignment but even after *two* weeks, he still had nothing to report.

"This guy, Digger, is some piece of work, ma'am, but he's definitely hiding something. So far I've had three different men tracking him and the bastard has lost them, every damn time."

Dani tried not to sound too desperate.

"Surely there must be *some* way we can catch him out?"

"Well, ma'am, if you could pin him down to a specific place and time to meet you that would give us the chance to bug his car. Then we could at least track his whereabouts and maybe pick up any action that might occur *inside* the vehicle."

"The trouble with that idea is that Digger hasn't been coming home much at all lately. He rarely shows up at the Club these days either. But I'll do my best to arrange something, Ron and I'll give you a call when I've managed it."

Dani had never felt so guilty in her whole life. In her heart she knew that something had to be done, to save her sanity and to salvage what little money she still had left. But knowing that it was the right thing to do didn't make Dani feel any better. That night she called and asked her mother to come over for a visit; just for a week or so. She felt the need of a familiar shoulder to lean on: someone to help Dani face the ugly scenes that were sure to follow her decision to employ a private investigator.

Harold brought Laura over the very next morning. He left his own Buick behind for the girls to drive around in and took JR's 'Jeep' back to Salem. The house seemed almost happy again with Laura there, but Dani knew that she still had to deal with catching her husband in the act of some wrongdoing. Then, out of the blue, an opportunity arose and Dani urgently called Ron Woodland.

"I'm sorry it's such short notice, but Digger just called and asked if I would meet him for lunch, today. We're meeting at the Hilton Hotel, at noon."

"That's very close to our Club, Ron, so he will most likely park in our own garage. It's *my* car that Digger's driving around in too; it's a white 'Eldorado'."

"Good work, Dani! I'll notify my guys right away and get back to you if we get any results.

***

'Damn the man!' Dani was getting stressed and anxious. Half past twelve and Digger hadn't yet turned up for their lunch date. When he finally did turn up, ten minutes later, he breezed into the restaurant as if nothing was wrong.

"Sorry I'm a bit late but I don't have time to eat, anyway. I just need you to sign these papers, Dani, for my attorneys?"

"What attorneys? And what kind of papers?"

Dani grabbed the sheaf of documents from his outstretched hand and quickly scanned through them. Her eyes grew wider the more she read.

"You are a bigger fool than I thought, Digger Rosselli. Do you honestly expect me to agree to stay out of my own Club and give *you* full authority, just because you say that I'm 'disruptive to management'? To hell with you!"

Dani jumped up and poured her entire drink over Digger's head before storming out of the restaurant. She charged across the street to the Club. There, she made arrangements to change every single lock in the place and at her house too. Then she called her younger brother, Tyler and had him move her fifty-three-foot sailboat farther up the river, out of sight.

Later that afternoon Ron called.

"We've hit pay dirt, Dani! Get yourself over to Beaverton right away, to the 'Hung Lum' Chinese restaurant. We'll meet you outside there in thirty minutes.

***

Dani looked down at the clothes she was wearing and frowned. The Saks, 'Fifth Avenue', white-linen dress and spiked heels she had worn to meet Digger at lunchtime wasn't the best of outfits to go hiding behind bushes in! But there was no time to go home and change. Her adrenalin was pumping as Dani pulled up beside Ron's car.

"Leave your car here, Dani and jump in with us," Ron whispered. Another detective in Ron's car moved over into the back seat and Dani climbed in the front. Ron turned to her "Do you have your gun with you, Dani?"

"Of course I do! I have a proper permit to carry it, too."

"But I can't let you keep it, Dani. Sorry! Hand it over, for now."

Dani reluctantly complied with Ron's request, dropping her gun into his outstretched hand. "But I want it back before I go home tonight, OK?"

They travelled around several side streets until Ron pulled over again, pointing toward a house about two houses down. As they all climbed out of the car, Ron suddenly noticed Dani's glamorous, lunch date outfit.

"Good god, woman! That dress is like a beacon!"

"I'm sorry, Ron, but I didn't have time to go home and change." Dani followed close behind the two men as they all crept up the driveway of a tri-level, white-cladding and brick house. The door to its garage stood wide open and Dani could see her own white, Cadillac 'Eldorado', parked next to a flashy convertible. Ron opened the glove compartment of the sports car and took out its registration documents, shining his flashlight onto the photograph.

The illuminated face belonged to a girl that Dani had first seen on her honeymoon, back in Hawaii. *Brenda Bennuchi* was her name and her home address was shown as Tucson, Arizona!

'So that's why we took a diversion to Tucson, after Hawaii!'

From a room directly over the garage, Dani heard the rhythmic sound of bedsprings shaking up and down. Cat-like moans infiltrated the night air above her head. As she listened to her husband having sex with some-one else, just a few feet above her head, humiliation, anger and hurt consumed Dani's soul. Hot tears rolled down her face and she wanted to scream out loud. Digger had never really loved her, Dani had long ago realized that fact. *'The man's far too selfish to ever love anyone'*. What really angered Dani was the knowledge that he had merely used her, in order to get control of her money.

In a blind, red-blooded rage Dani stormed out of the garage, ran around the front of the house and pressed hard on the doorbell. There was no answer. She pounded on the door with both her fists. Still total silence. Then a bathroom window slid quietly open and a woman's surprised voice called out.

"Who is it?"

"It's Digger's wife, dammit!"

The window slammed shut but still no-one came to answer the door. In her fury, Dani picked up a milk crate that was sitting on the porch steps and began to whack at the front door. The wood was soft and it didn't take long to chip a hole, big enough to get her hand through. She unlocked the door from the inside and flung it wide open. Standing at the top of the stairs was the dark-skinned, dark-haired girl that Dani had seen outside the Colony Surf Hotel, in Hawaii.

"Where's my fuckin' husband?" She screamed at the top of her voice, way beyond all politeness by that time.

"You're trespassing!" The young woman yelled back. "I'm calling the police, right now."

Digger stepped onto the landing, wearing only jeans. No shirt! Not even shoes! His face was so distorted, blotchy and red that Dani almost didn't recognize him. She stepped inside the hallway and flipped on the light just in time to see Digger leaning over the bannister.

"Get out of our home, you fucking bitch!"

"*Your* home? Where in the hell did *you* get the money to buy a home, Digger Rosselli? Do I own *this* damn house, too?"

He came down the stairs so fast that Dani never knew what hit her. Digger smacked her across the side of the head and threw her backward, hard against the wall. Then he planted a powerful fist into her stomach and Dani slid to the floor, helpless. Through blurred eyes, she saw Ron holding a gun on Digger as his assistant handcuffed the raging man to the wrought-iron stair rails. Ron helped Dani to her feet but she shook him off and staggered out of that house of adultery.

"You bastard, Digger Rosselli! I'll see you in court!"

She struggled around to the garage door. *'Well that was stupid of you, Digger, to leave the keys inside my car!'* She reversed her Eldorado out into the driveway and churned up gravel as she left. Ron hollered after her.

"Hell, Dani! They could have shot you when you broke that damn door in."

"But they didn't, did they?" she yelled back, triumphantly.

Dani headed back to the Chinese Restaurant where she and the detectives had rendezvoused earlier. She would have herself a drink to celebrate her victory and wait for Ron there.

Dolores J. Guthrie

Chapter 32

Driving up the rear side of the mountain was a lot steeper and much more winding than taking the usual route, but it was the quickest way to get home. Dani was exhausted and wanted to get back into her own safe, warm bed as soon as possible. It was pouring with rain and the fresh tears streaming down Dani's face made it even harder for her to see where she was going.

"Oh, Mom!" she whimpered. "Why did you have to pick *this* week-end to go visit Papa back in Salem?"

Dani's house loomed dark, cold and forbidding as she sped up the driveway, eager to put the long day behind her. There was almost a threatening aura about it. She parked the car quickly and scurried inside. She would be alone for the night but right then Dani was too preoccupied with anger and hurt to worry about being afraid. She double-bolted the massive, mahogany front doors behind her and started up the marble staircase. She paused, momentarily, looked backward and then heaved a deep sigh.

"Digger, you bastard! You'll never set foot inside *my* home ever again!"

Sudden chills came over her. She felt the presence of someone, or something, all around her and Dani shivered, involuntarily. She tried to think of it as a friendly ghost; one that was trying to comfort and guide her up the long stairway. To keep her mind occupied as she climbed, she concentrated on all the things she needed to do next day. Things like making sure all the locks got changed at the Club.

'They obviously haven't gotten around to changing the house locks yet or I wouldn't have been able to get in tonight, would I?'

It was tough for Dani to keep her mind from thinking the worst. *'What if Digger gets out of jail tonight and decides to pay me a visit?'*

Her husband had already proved himself to be a master of deceit but Dani refused to give in to her irrational fears. *'Everything is bolted down tight, so stop being a silly ass!'* Swiping the back of one hand across her wet cheeks, she continued up the long staircase.

Bong! Bong! Bong!

Her heart skipped several beats until she realized that it was only her antique, grandfather clock, chiming three o'clock. Dani looked down from the first landing and made a quick sweep of the hallway below. All her familiar and precious things were still there. Things like the marble statue of the *'Madonna and Child'*; the hand-carved, French provincial mirror and table and that antique chair that Mr. Fellman, from New York, had given her.

Dani voiced her thoughts aloud.

"Just tell me *why*, Digger? Why did you have to be this way with me? Damn it, I gave you so much and asked for so little in return."

Suddenly, she stopped dead on the second-floor landing. Her bedroom door was closed. *'Lil always leaves it open after she finishes cleaning it!'* Dani moved forward cautiously, because the bedroom light was also on. Creeping silently through her make-up parlor, Dani slowly headed toward her bed. Someone was definitely under the covers! Dani stepped up onto the raised platform around the bed and yanked back the covers. She blew a sigh of relief.

"Where the hell did *you* come from? And how did you get in?"

Dani's younger sister, Brandy, stifled a sleepy yawn. "Hi, Sis! I thought you'd never get home. Lil and Hank let me in before they left for the day."

"Well you scared the hell out of me, you little stinker, but I'm *really* glad you're here."

"Where have *you* been anyhow, Dani? I've called everywhere looking for you."

"Oh, it's a very long story, Sis. It's a complete book of nightmares, in fact. Let me get into something more comfortable and then I'll tell you all about it."

Dani stripped off her clothes, cleaned off her make-up, climbed into her nightie and then flopped down on the green-satin, love seat next to the bed. She picked up the soft, stuffed mouse that was lying there, caressing its little pink ears in an effort to calm herself. After a while, Dani was able to tell her younger sister the whole sordid story. All about the Las Vegas fiasco; about hiring the private detectives and about how they had tracked down Digger's secret love nest just that very evening. When Dani glanced at the clock again, a whole hour had gone by.

"We'd better get some sleep, Brandy. It's going to be a busy day to-morrow."

"What can I do to help?"

"Just give me some moral support, I guess. There's a lot of legal stuff to put in place as soon as possible as I'm sure Digger won't make things easy for me. Goodnight, Sis and thanks for being here. I love you."

"I love you too and I'm glad I came. Something told me that you might need me, somehow. 'Night, Dani."

By the time Dani had settled herself down she could already hear gentle snoring coming from her younger sister. But it took a long while for Dani to relax her own mind. She must have replayed that day's events more than a dozen times inside her head. Yet it seemed only moments before Dani heard the sounds of Hank, busily mowing the lawns below her bed-room windows. She leapt out of bed.

"Wake up Brandy! It's already after eight o' clock in the morning!"

Her sister tried to roll back under the covers again but Dani was having none of it.

"Come on! Get up! I have to file for divorce today before Digger beats me to it. I have to make sure all the locks get changed too."

While Brandy was showering, Dani called the locksmith and ex-plained the urgency of her situation. He was just finishing up a job downtown and agreed to go directly over to the Club when he had finished. After that he would change all the house locks too, leaving *all* the new keys safely with Hank. Dani was quite proud of the way she was coping so far and by the time she and Brandy arrived at the Club, the locksmith was just leaving.

Dani went into the back office to call her attorney. Berry Booth had been the first person in Portland that she had really got to know and trust. He had been hired to deal with the purchase of her nightclub and had come highly recommended. 'Berry Booth will handle any matter safely, big or small', Dani had been assured and she believed she had finally found a lawyer that could be trusted.

"Berry, I need you to start divorce proceedings immediately, for adultery and physical abuse. I should have done this months ago," she added, bitterly.

"If you want it done quickly you'll have to come in this afternoon, Dani. Shall we say at three o'clock? I'll draw up the basic papers right away, but you won't be able to make any implications of adultery because Oregon is a 'No-Fault' divorce state. All we can do is submit papers for the divorce part and file a restraining order against Digger for the 'abuse' part."

"But I have a full detective's report and photographs too!" Dani was horrified at Berry's matter-of-fact manner.

"That man, Digger, has put me through hell!"

"I'm sorry, Dani, but I'm afraid that doesn't matter in Oregon. We have to go by the rules."

"Well what about all my assets, then? You're aware that the house, the business *and* all the money in the bank accounts belong to me?"

"Yes, I know that. But Digger might still be able to get part of your assets, Dani; even as much as fifty percent.

"Fifty-percent be damned!" Dani exploded. "That man hasn't contributed one, red cent to this marriage. All he's ever done is spend *my* money and make me miserable! I'm locking Digger out of *everything*, I possibly can. Do you understand me Berry?" Dani was getting angrier by the minute."

"Go ahead and change all the locks, Dani, but be careful; be *very* careful in how you deal with the man himself. Digger has some very powerful connections here in Portland and word-on-the-street is that he's also associated with the 'Mob' down in Tucson."

"What!" Dani was stunned into silence.

"I'm sorry if that comes as a shock to you, Dani! As his wife, I assumed you knew all about it."

"Shit, Berry! Are you *sure* about all this gangster stuff?"

"I've heard it from very reliable sources, Dani. And if you truly didn't know any of that stuff, there's probably a lot more you don't know as well."

She sighed deeply as she thought back to New York and all that had happened to her there.

"There *was* a guy called *'The Horse'*, back in New York who was involved with the 'Mob'. He used to always call me a dumb broad. He used to call me 'naïve' and 'stupid' too. Maybe I *should* have been more aware of my husband's doings, Berry, but you know what?"

"If the Mob hasn't manage to kill me already, then I'm not going to be afraid of Digger Rosselli. He's just a little pup next to those big dogs!"

"Digger might be a bigger dog than you think, Dani so *please* be very careful and I'll see you later this afternoon."

"Okay! Thanks for the information, Berry."

"Damn! Damn! Damn!" Dani thumped an angry fist on the desk in front of her as she hung up the phone and Brandy came running into the office, alarmed.

"What's up, Sis?"

Dani was shaking with fear and anger as she struggled to hold back her tears.

"I've been set up, yet again! Why can't folk just leave me the hell alone?"

"Settle down honey and tell me all about it?"

"My lawyer, Berry has just informed me that Digger is hand-in-glove with the damn 'Mob'!"

Dani rubbed angrily at her forehead. "When I think back, it all seems pretty obvious *now*. What a damned idiot I was not to see it."

Then JR burst into the office wondering what all the commotion was about and she repeated the whole, sordid story for his benefit, including how Digger had sneaked women into her *own* home behind her back.

"And where have *you* been all week anyhow, JR? I've really needed you these past few days."

"I'm sorry, Mom!" Her son looked a little sheepish. "I thought Grandma was staying with you but I've been busy 'cos I've met the most wonderful girl!"

"Just tell me she's not one of our dancers?" Dani's tone was sarcastic.

"No, Mom!" JR looked a little hurt but his mother didn't notice.

"She's a lovely Catholic girl, her name is Becky and she really wants to meet you."

"This is *really* bad timing, JR, Can't it wait a while, until I'm feeling more cheerful?"

"Aw, Mom! How about we all have dinner together this weekend? You don't have to cook; we can eat out at the Hilton?" JR showed his mother the expression she could never resist and all resistance melted away.

"Oh' alright then! Make reservations for Saturday night, at seven."

"Thanks Mom. I know you'll really like her. Oh, and I have another small confession to make."

"What now?"

"Digger wasn't the only person to use the house 'dumb waiter' system, Becky and I have used it a few times, too!"

He grinned broadly and threw his mother a kiss as he left the office.

"That little shit!" Dani forced a laugh as she headed towards the door herself.

"What's all that stuff about the 'dumb waiter'?" Her sister was curious.

"Later, Brandy! That's a whole new story and it will have to wait awhile. We have a lot of work to do first."

***

That evening's usual, busy dinner-hour at the Club came and went without incident.

No Digger showed up causing trouble and Dani was greatly relieved. She was much too weary to face another confrontation. By eight o' clock, the Club was full and everyone was busy doing their assigned tasks. JR was working the light-and-sound system; her sister, Brandy, was sitting in the audience talking with some young sailor and Dani couldn't believe how smoothly everything was running. At ten o'clock, she went on stage, sang one song and then spoke a few words to introduce the return of the exotic dancers. Then, WHAM!

All the house lights came up to full brilliance and the music stopped dead. Dani looked around to find that her employees had *all* disappeared.

No bartenders! No waitresses! Not an employee in sight!

"Hello? *Hello?* Is there anyone in the sound room?" But Dani got zero response.

"We have a show going on down here, ya' know!" She tried to joke with the audience, but it was so quiet in the room that you could hear a pin drop. Then one of the dancers peeked out through the stage curtains and whispered to her, urgently.

"Digger called earlier and told everyone to walk out at exactly ten o' clock, or they would be fired. There are only us four dancers left that didn't leave."

"But where the hell is JR?" Dani knew her son would never walk out on her.

"He's on the phone right now, waiting to talk to you."

Dani excused herself to her customers and rushed backstage.

"What the hell's going on, JR?"

"What do you mean, Mom?"

"All our staff has just walked out on us on Digger's orders, that's what I mean. And why aren't *you* here, JR?"

"Digger called me over an hour ago and said he had hired a new light man to take my place. He told me to meet him *here*, but he never showed up. I've been waiting for ages so I thought maybe he had gone back there, to the Club."

"No, Digger isn't here and he'd better not come anywhere near *my* Club anytime soon. Just get back here as soon as you can, son."

Dani raced back to calm her restless audience.

"Sorry for the unexpected problems folks, but the show will go on, I promise. Is there anyone out there who could run our lights and music until my son can get here?"

"I'll try!" One young man jumped up and, following Dani's instructions, headed confidently toward the sound room.

"If you could all please be patient for just a little while longer, folks, we'll get this show on the road again! Meanwhile, drinks are on the house, while we re-organize."

That raised a huge cheer and then Brandy stood up.

"OK, I'll be your new cocktail waitress."

The crowd laughed and applauded again. Then the Club's seamstress ran behind the main bar and announced that she could make 'regular' drinks, but nothing fancy!

Dani helped to serve customers too and so the party went on. The cash registers rang louder than ever for the rest of that night.

Next day, employees began calling Dani asking for their jobs back, but she was having none of it.

"Sorry guys, but you made your choice when you walked out last night." Big bonuses were authorized for the four, lone dancers who had stuck by Dani that night and she quickly hired replacements for the staff who had not.

Dani had signed her divorce papers and the restraining order that Berry Booth had taken out against Digger seemed to be working. He was certainly staying well away from all contact with Dani *or* the Club.

Everything was 'business as usual', or so she believed.

Chapter 33

Digger continued to stay away from the Club and from Dani's mansion house but that didn't mean he had changed his ways. Unbeknownst to his wife, he had already taken out a $300,000.00 loan against her home. He had also managed to sneak her seven-carat, marquis-cut diamond ring from the bedroom safe and borrow $15,000.00 against *that*. The ring was set in platinum, with one-carat baguettes on each side of the larger, center stone and it was Dani's pride and joy.

She was in her office at the Club, trying to sort out the growing pile of bills when the phone rang. It was George Brice, manager of 'Security Bank of Oregon'. He had somehow heard that Dani and Digger were in the process of getting divorced. He had no option, he told her, but to call in several loans that Digger had created on *her* behalf. The Bank had already stopped payment on the Club's payroll. They had also frozen any money left in all Dani's accounts and slapped embargos on both her fifty-three-foot cruiser *and* her twenty-eight-roomed mansion! He empathized with Dani, telling her that he was truly sorry she had been caught up in Digger's financial 'anarchy', but his words were no comfort to a woman who was about to lose all she owned.

To add insult to injury, she learned later that same day that her Club's insurance policy had also been cancelled. Digger hadn't paid any premiums for several months past.

***

In the end everything had to be sold off and at a huge loss too, in order to pay off Digger's many debts. Dani tried hard to keep the Club going for as long as she could; after all, it was her only source of income. But as she packed up her personal belongings, Dani wept many bitter tears. Her miserable marriage had cost her dearly. She certainly wouldn't need to hire a large removal truck, unlike when she had moved away from New York and all of *those* bad memories.

Dani's mother had been staying over to provide company and moral support, but the days soon turned into weeks and strain was beginning to show on her daughter. Action was needed, Laura decided.

"Honey, did you remember it's your father's sixtieth birthday this coming Saturday? Why don't you forget all about this divorce mess for a while and come home with me, to Salem? We'll have a big, family, reunion dinner!"

"I have to be in court next Monday, Mom, but maybe I *could* travel over on Friday night. I do need a break from all this chaos."

"Have you been able to salvage much, honey, out of the mess that man left you with?"

Dani shook her head sadly.

"Not much, Mom! Parker Furniture said they would buy all of my furniture back, 'sight-unseen', for thirty-five-thousand dollars and a friend has offered to buy my Steinway, baby Grand piano for another fifteen-thousand dollars."

"My god, Dani! You paid over three-hundred-thousand dollars for all that stuff back in New York. Can't you get any more than that for it?"

"It's *all* considered to be used furniture now, Mom, even though most of it is less than a year old! No-one will give me anything close to what it's actually worth." Dani shook her head.

"Digger has ruined me, Mom and I just can't fight him anymore. I'm tired, I'm weak and I'm miserable!"

JR was helping to pack up things in the kitchen and overheard the conversation. He came in to join them, hugged his Grandmother and then turned to Dani.

"Mom! There's no reason why you can't spend the weekend over in Salem."

"I can manage the Club on my own just for a few days and everything will be fine. You really do need a break you know; you look like death warmed over!"

"Thanks a lot for that, son." Dani knew that JR meant well but his astute observations did nothing for her self-esteem.

"Sorry, Mom, but it *would* be good for you to get away from it all for a while."

"Okay! Okay!" Dani capitulated under the weight of their collective sympathy. "We'll leave this afternoon, Mama! Call Papa and tell him we should get there around six o' clock tonight."

***

Traffic was heavy as Dani and her mother headed toward Salem through a downpour. Huge raindrops splattered against the windshield, making visibility extremely poor. Such terrible conditions added an extra twenty minutes to their journey but once they were turning into the family driveway, Dani breathed an enormous sigh of relief.

"Oh, Mom, It's so good to be *home*!"

Laura busied herself with domestic chores the minute they set foot inside the house. There was a definite chill in the air; the first sign of the changing seasons and Laura turned up the furnace. Dani made hot chocolate for them both, before curling up on the familiar, family couch. Pretty soon she began to feel a warm glow washing over her. Crazily, she felt as if she hadn't a worry in the world. Little by little, Dani's legs curled up into the fetal position and she drifted off to sleep. She stirred slightly when her mother gently covered her with an afghan blanket, but soon glided back into oblivion.

***

On a small table next to the couch, the telephone rang and Laura rushed to pick it up before it disturbed Dani. All the color drained from her face as she listened to what the caller was saying.

"No! Oh, no! Oh, my God!"

Laura was almost hysterical when she hung up the phone. Dani had been jolted wide-awake by her mother's screams.

"What on earth is it, Mom? What's the matter?"

"Oh, Dani, it's your father! He's been involved in a terrible accident! A couple of drunks, road-racing, came up behind him. They ran Harold right off the road and his jeep rolled over and over. They say it was a terrible accident, Dani!"

"But is Papa OK?"

"They're flying him across to Kaiser Hospital, in Portland. Come on, Dani; we have to get over there as soon as possible."

They argued about who should drive but Laura won, much to Dani's dismay. Her mother was a good driver, but also a very careful one and it seemed to take forever to negotiate the Terwilliger curves, to drive across the Broadway Bridge and then to find the right hospital. Except for an occasional exchange of directional information, the trip was completely silent. Their minds were fully focused on a beloved husband and father and they both prayed to find him alive.

Dani and her mother rushed through the Emergency Room doors to find Harold Gunther lying alone on a gurney, covered in blood and mud. He was shaking with shock but had neither blankets, nor pillows. No one was even attending to him. Dani was furious and screamed at the top of her voice.

"What in the hell is going on here?"

Anyone could see that her father needed immediate attention and Dani yelled again.

"For God's sake, somebody *do* something!"

Nurses and orderlies came running from all directions then.

They immediately put Harold into a treatment room and escorted Laura and Dani to the waiting area, assuring them that the Doctor was with Harold now and would do everything possible to save him.

"Check his blood sugar, too; my husband is a diabetic!" Laura shouted at their retreating backs as the doors closed behind the nurses. Then she and Dani wept in each other's arms and Dani prayed harder than she had ever done before. *'Please, God! Please let Papa live. We need him and we love him so much.'*

Three hours later, Harold was taken from surgery and admitted to the Intensive Care Unit. Both legs were fractured and he had extensive internal injuries but the doctors had done all they could. Harold Gunther was in God's hands.

Dani's brothers, Tyler and Harold Jr. had all arrived with their wives during the early evening and Brandy came too, with her baby, Tommy. They were all sitting around Harold's bed when he suddenly opened his eyes. He struggled to speak, but his voice was weak.

"I'll get Digger Rosselli for this when I get out of here!" Then his eyes fluttered closed and he lapsed back into oblivion.

"What was *that* all about?" Harold Jr. queried.

"He must still be mad at Digger for what he did to Dani and to our whole family," Laura spat out the words.

"Or maybe he actually thinks that Digger staged the accident," Dani suggested. "Either way, having angry feelings will give Papa the will to fight back from all of this."

Laura leaned over her husband again. "Just look at this, Dani. They've had him in surgery all that time and yet they still haven't washed all the mud and gravel off him!"

Dani cornered the head nurse at her desk. "What the hell kind of hospital are you running here?"

"I'm sorry, ma'am, but we are *really* short staffed this evening."

Dani thumped on the counter in disgust.

"So what; are there no private nurses we can hire to provide my father with proper, round-the-clock care?"

"I'll see what I can do, ma'am."

***

After several anxious days, Harold Gunther regained full consciousness and life carried on again within the family. Dani moved out of her mother's home and into a hotel, on the advice of her attorney. Brandy and her baby went back to Yakima. Harold Jr. and his wife Lindsay drove back to their home in Klamath Falls. But Tyler, Dani's youngest brother, offered to stay on and help to try and salvage the reputation and revenues of the Club.

JR continued working the music and lights as Dani worked day and night, putting on professional shows and trying to keep the business afloat. It was hard finding and keeping new staff too, because word was already out about the unpredictable financial position of the Club. Naturally, no-one wanted to commit to a job that might not even be there the following week.

Dani's daily life was a nightmare, with no light in sight at the end of her personal, murky tunnel. She was possessed by fears and angry about everything that had happened to her. Angry about the expense of divorcing Digger; angry about the probability of losing her beloved Club and angry about all the worry of her father's recent, near-death experience. She couldn't help wondering if Digger had somehow been involved in his accident. It was odd that the two, young Mexicans who ran her father off the road had been completely unharmed. And that now they were nowhere to be found! *'You will live to regret this'*, Dani promised her 'soon-to-be-ex'-husband as she tore up his photo; one that she had found at the bottom of her purse.

On a sudden whim Dani shoved all her paperwork into a desk drawer. She rang JR and told him not to expect her back for a day or two, but wouldn't tell him where she was going. Then she grabbed her coat and ran out of the Club. She jumped into her 'Eldorado' and set off towards Lincoln City. It was the closest coastal town and only about an hour-and-a-half's drive away. Dani exhaled deeply as she headed down the highway.

"Just one night away from all this, that's all I need to clear this pea-brain of mine! I just need some time to myself and a place to think."

Dani loosened her ribbons and shook out her long, black hair, letting the wind swirl it from side to side. It was the first time she had ever driven her car with the top down and it felt damn good, even on an autumn afternoon. She tuned the radio to a station dedicated to light, popular music and the song, *'Born Free'* surrounded her as Dani raced down the highway. Until she suddenly realized that her speedometer was creeping upward. *'Whoa, better slow this puppy down. I don't need a speeding ticket to add to the rest of my problems!'*

Dani arrived at her destination around mid-afternoon, checking in at the *'Red Lion'* motel with enough time to spare for a walk along the beach before dinner. As she strolled, she picked up a piece of glass that was glistening among the sand, most likely it had once been the bottom of some old bottle. It was milky-blue in color and reminded Dani of an old glass ornament that she owned as a child. Its jagged edges had long been smoothed from years of tumbling around in the sand and salt water on the shoreline. She slipped the tiny gem into her jacket pocket and continued walking along the water's edge, looking for more treasures. Evening fog was creeping in fast, though. As Dani looked back over one shoulder, it was hard to get her bearings in the gathering gloom. A shiver ran through her, almost as if someone was stalking her.

'That's bullshit', she told herself. *'No-one knows where I am'*.

Surely, no-one could still be after her; she didn't have anything left to take! Dani turned back and ran as fast as she could, which was not easy in the deep, soft sand. When at last she saw her hotel's neon sign, blinking through the mist, she breathed a sigh of relief.

At dinner, she stared out of the restaurant windows, depressed at not being able to see the ocean because of all the evening fog. Depressed, too, because she was lonely. And depressed, too, because she'd been so stupid as to lose everything she owned due to the whims of men. After dinner she ordered a *'Grand Marnier'* with her coffee and moved over to sit in the bar, which also overlooked the ocean. The fog lifting again and white-capped surf splashed against the foundations of the hotel. A pale, but still stunning sunset glowed on the horizon yet the sight brought only a stab of pain to Dani's heart. It was the first time she could ever remember watching a sunset alone!

Two men, about her own age, joined Dani at the bar and one of them made an attempt at idle conversation.

"The tide must be in."

"Looks that way," Dani replied, indifferently.

"So what's a beautiful woman like you doing in a place like this?" The second man chimed in with the much overused cliché, hoping to raise a laugh. Dani managed a smile but shrugged her shoulders. She had no need to prove anything to anyone, especially about her womanhood. These two men were so good looking that Dani decided they were probably gay, anyway. Either that or they thought that *she* had money. *'Not anymore, buddies!'*

But the one thing that Digger Rosselli had not yet managed to get away from Dani was her fashionable wardrobe. She still wore the finest clothes and always looked extremely classy. That night she looked an absolute knockout in a red, cashmere sweater with mink collar; red leather pants and matching boots.

'But maybe I shouldn't have worn my Rolex watch!'

The men bought her a couple of drinks and after some more social chatter and a few funny jokes, their conversation turned more serious.

"Hey! We are all adults here, aren't we Dani? So, how would you like to join Jon and me in our suite later, for a special nightcap?"

They smiled at the implication behind his words, but Dani decided that the two men were definitely gay.

"You're putting me on guys, right? A threesome? Thanks, but no thanks! I have a big day ahead of me tomorrow and I need to keep my wits about me. Besides, I doubt if I could keep up with two, young studs like you!"

"Well, it was worth a try!" Jon chided gently as Dani politely took her leave and headed back to her own room. *'No harm, no foul'*, she decided. *'Nothing wrong with a bit of harmless flirting.'*

Dani stripped off her clothes, piled her long hair up into a bun and slid down into her deep, hot, bubble-bath. She closed her eyes and wallowed in its soothing fragrance for a long, long time.

Chapter 34

Early next morning, Dani shifted the 'Eldorado' into gear and headed back toward home. *'Damn!'* She smiled even as she cursed, remembering the night before and half regretting going back to her hotel room alone. Those two guys had been about as good as it got in the looks department but, with her luck, Dani decide she would probably have caught some terrible disease from the pair of them.

'This time you did the right thing, girl!' She reached out a hand, turned on the radio and got lost in her favorite radio station once more. Along the coastal mountain ranges, the customary morning fog was patchy. At times it was so thick that Dani could barely see the car in front of her. Travel was frustratingly slow and it was hard to concentrate on driving. The radio began to fade to a static, fuzzy mush and when the signal disappeared completely Dani switched it off, irritably.

'I wish I smoked. At least that would give me something to do'.

So she started singing instead; partly to while away the time and partly to get her voice warmed up ready for work, later that night. She sang non-stop for over thirty minutes, ignoring the odd looks that came from her fellow motorists. As the fog began to lift again the traffic moved faster, but only briefly. It started raining and, within minutes, movement was reduced to a snail's pace again.

***

Three hours later, Dani finally pulled into the driveway of *'Rosselli's Roost'*. She had stopped there before going to her hotel room because she wanted to check in with Hank and Lil. *'Maybe there have been some new developments'.* JR was busy holding a ladder for Hank, who was cutting down thick ivy that had overgrown its boundaries around Dani's front door.

"I'll be right with you, Mom!" JR shouted over. And by the time Dani had pulled into the garage, JR was unloading her suitcase out of the back seat.

"You can leave that in the car, honey. I won't be staying. I'm going on to the hotel as soon as I've had a quick look around."

"Where have you been, anyhow?" JR quizzed his mother as he followed her up the winding staircase. "You said you were leaving town for a day or two but never said where you were going!"

"It was just a spur of the minute thing, honey. I felt the urge for some R-&-R so I took off for the coast. I just needed some peace and quiet and a bit of time to myself, that's all."

"So, did you have a good time?"

Dani chuckled as she recalled the two guys in the hotel bar but she quickly put on a more serious face.

"Hell, no! There was too much driving involved."

"So you didn't do anything exciting at all, then?"

JR sounded disbelieving as he watched Dani digging around in her coat pockets. She finally found what she was looking for and held it out to show him.

"Well I *did* find this lovely piece of old glass. I bet it has a story of its own to tell."

JR took it and turned it over in his hand. "All I see is a chunk of glass. Where did you get it?" But as he handed it back to her, it caught the light and flashed with brilliant color. "It *is* pretty, though!" he added.

"It was just lyin' there in the sand, sparkling like some big ol' diamond, so I kept it as a souvenir."

JR and Dani entered the master suite and she headed toward her walk-in closet. As she opened the door, Dani yelled for her maid with all the power of her lungs.

"Lil! Lil! All his damn clothes are gone!"

She was absolutely furious. Digger must have gotten into her house somehow. Dani's screams were passionate as Lil came bounding into the bedroom, out of breath.

"I swear, I don't know how this happened, Miss Dani. We never let him in! All the doors have new locks on them and when we came in work this morning, everything was locked up tight as a drum."

JR put an arm around his mother's shoulders. "Locks are only there to keep *innocent* people innocent, Mom. If someone really wants to get in, there is no way to stop them. And if Digger wanted in he would probably have hired professionals to do the job for him, anyway."

"But I would have given him his damn clothes, if only he'd asked me. And why wait 'til I'm away? He's probably too ashamed to face me, I guess."

"I think he's more afraid that you'll kill him, Mom. Digger's not the kind of guy to be ashamed about anything." JR looked all around the bedroom. "Did he take anything else?"

"Not that I can see," Dani conceded. "But Digger did most of his damage before our divorce was even filed, honey!"

Her legs gave way and she sank down onto the bed. Then she brought her son up to date on the list of Digger's misdeeds.

"Digger borrowed money against all my assets, JR *and* he stole some of my diamonds too. It means I have to sell everything I have, just to pay off his debts. I may even lose the Club, too!"

"Fortunately, I took all my personal belongings with me when I moved into the hotel and it's a good thing I did. Otherwise Digger would have ripped me off even more."

Dani began to cry. "The man's an evil demon, JR and I *hate* him! Will it never end?" She buried her face in the bedclothes and sobbed her heart out.

"Calm down, Mom. There must be some way to stop him. Can't you file criminal charges against him now, for breaking and entering or something?"

"Yeah right! Digger can talk his way out of anything, you know that. And with the scummy friends he associates with, he could probably get away with murder, too. It's impossible to pin *anything* on a mobster, JR."

Dani sat up and dabbed at her eyes with the backs of her fingers. "All I can do now is salvage what I can and start over. If I can, that is!"

JR gently guided his mother out of the bedroom. "Come on! Let's get over to the Club and see if he turned up there while you were away."

"JR, I love you, son!"

JR smiled at her. "Me too, Mom! I love you too!"

***

When they entered the Club, Dani was relieved to find everybody busy at their stations. Every seat in the place was occupied and easy laughter was plentiful. Her younger brother, Tyler, walked over and kissed her on the cheek.

"Hiya, Sis! How are you holding up?"

"I've been better, but it's good to see things going so well here. It looks as though you're doing a good job of running things, Tyler. I'm really glad you could stay and help me out." Dani tweaked his cheek.

"Want a full time job?" Then her face turned serious again. "Has Digger been around while I was away?"

"Nope, not a chance!" Tyler was emphatic. "That guy knows better than to show up here. Too many people have it in for him now, after the hell he's put you through. There's no way would Digger show up here, Dani. Not if he values his life!"

"We both know what a jerk he is Tyler, but I don't want any more trouble, please. Promise me that you won't do anything stupid enough to end up in jail for; the bum isn't worth it. Promise me?"

"Relax, Sis; I'm cool!"

Tyler's voice wasn't completely convincing but Dani knew when not to push things. She went downstairs and sat in the darkened office for a while, to collect her thoughts. She could well imagine what Tyler, or her father, might do with regard to Digger and her blood ran cold at the thought. Goose bumps tickled her bare arms and on an impulse she bowed her head in prayer.

'Please God! Let this nightmare end right here and now, with no more traumas to my family. I don't need material things. I don't need my big house or even this Club. Please, dear God, just give me my life back and I'll never ask you for anything again!'

Dani had just finished making the sign of the cross when JR clicked on the light and they both jumped.

"What the hell are you doing, sitting in the dark, Mom?"

"I'm just thinking things over, sweetheart. When this mess is all sorted out, I'm going to get very, very drunk. Wanna join me?"

"Right on! I'll even buy the drinks!" JR grinned and tactfully changed the subject.

"Mom, do you remember a couple of weeks ago, when you agreed to meet my new girlfriend and have dinner?"

"We had to cancel that night, because of Grandpa's accident and then you disappeared off to the coast. I'm beginning to think you don't want to meet her, Mom!"

"Yes, I know honey, but too many things have happened all at once. I'm sorry."

"Well, how about tomorrow night, then? *Please*?"

"Okay! No promises, but I'll try real hard to find the time."

"I'll make the reservations and we'll see you there, then. I love you, Mom!"

As JR left, Tyler appeared and asked Dani if she would mind closing up that night so that he could leave early. She reluctantly agreed, realizing that her brother needed to spend some time with his own family. She moved idly around the Club, chit-chatting with customers and trying to look busy. She was the world's worst waitress and bartender and Dani had not been on stage since the night Digger pulled all her staff away from the Club. She really missed singing with her old friend, Dale Rogers. Dani had always thought they really made great music together. *'What's the real story behind the way Dale left the Club, I wonder?'* That had been another stab in the back from her husband. Digger had tried to destroy everything and everyone that Dani loved.

In an attempt to take her mind off the man, Dani directed her attention to the dancers, hard at work on stage. She had forgotten what a good job she had done on the choreography for the Latin number they were performing. Their costumes looked extremely professional, too. *'Full marks to the seamstress'* Dani thought, proudly. Bright red, green, orange and yellow ruffles on the girls' costumes were accented by contrasting turbans and tiny, ceramic-fruit earrings. She watched, proudly. Her girls were all fine-looking women and *all* their acts were performed in good taste.

Dani tried to run a risqué, but respectable show, allowing the girls to strip down to G-strings and tiny bras but only after beginning their dance routines dressed in glamorous gowns. Her Club did not aim to be the kind of cheap-thrill, strip-joint that enticed weirdoes and creepy menfolk. Dani's patrons were classy, respectable people and usually more couples than singles.

At three o' clock in the morning, Dani finally locked up and headed down to the garage to collect her car. It was a clear night and very quiet at that late hour. Not a soul was in sight and there were only a couple of abandoned cars at the far end of the garage. She hurriedly jumped into her car and locked all the doors. For some reason, her heart was pounding hard. She suddenly realized how foolish it was to close up the Club by herself and walk out alone at that hour. *'I'll never do this again,'* Dani told herself.

She drove out of the garage, heading south, but continued to feel a strange stillness all around her. Absolutely no other moving cars were in sight and Dani's sixth sense began to scream, 'danger'. Suddenly, out of nowhere, a long, black sedan turned the corner and headed straight toward her. The sedan slid sideways to an abrupt stop, in an attempt to block Dani's car. Two men jumped out and ran toward her. Out of desperation, she slammed her foot down hard on the gas pedal and aimed straight for the men. She barely had time to notice their surprised looks, before she clipped one of them. He flew up over the front fender and briefly hung onto Dani's windshield before dropping to the ground, past the driver's door. Frightened and confused, Dani drove home as fast as she could and never looked back.

'Oh God! I hope I didn't kill him!' She decided to stay at her hotel for the rest of the time it took to get divorced from Digger. There wasn't much left inside her big house anyway. Just an air mattress with some linens, a couple of pillows, a change of clothes and an old makeup bag in case she ever wanted to stay overnight.

But, after that experience, it was doubtful that Dani would ever want to visit the big house again; not unless someone else was with her.

Her mini-suite at the hotel was in total darkness, except for a dim nightlight that Dani always left on. She double-locked and bolted the door and quickly did a careful check of the whole place. No one had been there.

She got her .38 revolver out of the dresser drawer and collapsed onto the sofa. She was too afraid to move, let alone call the police. She would talk with her attorney, Berry Booth, first thing next morning. Exhausted, she fell asleep where she lay.

***

Dani awoke with a jerk and a very stiff neck at nine o' clock the next morning, awakened by the sound of the ringing telephone. Hank asked her a few general maintenance questions but then solemnly enquired how much longer he and his wife could expect to be employed. Dani assured him that it would be at least another thirty days before all the legal papers and the foreclosure on the house were completed. She thanked them both for their loyalty and excellent service and, after a moment's hesitation, Dani asked a question of her own.

"Hank, did anything unusual happen over at the house last night?"

"No, ma'am, it was a quiet night. Why?"

She told Hank what had happened the previous night, asking him specifically if there had been anything in the morning papers about 'hit-and-run' accidents. He said no, which eased Dani's mind a little, but later she wondered if she ought to have mentioned anything to him at all. She realized that she didn't know who to trust anymore. *'Christ, I'm getting paranoid.'*

After a long hot shower, Dani fixed herself some breakfast and then called her attorney. She told Berry Booth every small detail she could re-member about the night before.

"I'm sure those thugs didn't report anything, Dani. Even if they were hurt, it would mean jail time for them if they did. You did the right thing by driving away but, *please,* watch your back from now on. I'll try to hurry the legal papers along so that you can get everything settled and move away from here, if that's what you decide to do."

"I'm not going anywhere, Berry; at least not yet. I have a legal permit to carry a gun and that's what I intend to do, starting tonight."

"Oh, Dani! Don't do anything crazy, please. Last night was probably a random attack, meant more to scare you than to harm you. I doubt if you'll ever see those idiots again."

Berry was half-teasing, trying to ease his client's fears. "You need a gun like you need a hole in your head, Dani."

"Thanks for the confidence, Berry, but I *do* know how to use a gun! Papa and I used to go to the local gun club every week and I'm a pretty good shot, too. I do have a head on my shoulders, Berry and it's not completely empty. Trust me!"

Her lawyer apologized and tried to reassure her of his support.

"Seriously Dani; if you need to use your gun, don't hesitate. Better that than getting shot."

Chapter 35

Billy Mo was a happy-go-lucky Chinaman whose famous *'Gold Coin'* restaurant was located on 23rd and Burnside. Billy and his wife, Ida, had managed their establishment for many years and knew every regular customer by name. Folk came from around the world for Billy's famous *'Bib Lettuce-and-dressing'* and *'Crusty Pepper Steak'*. His cousin was also an expert on fine wines and managed the restaurant's first-rate, wine cellar.

The *'Gold Coin'* was Dani's favorite place to dine out. The kind of place where the women clients wore long gowns and furs and their menfolk drove Jaguars and Mercedes-Benz cars. The restaurant prided itself on making *all* customers feel special and Dani felt good handing her black, Russian sable coat over to Ida-Mo for safekeeping.

"Don't you worry now; we will put this in our vault for you, Miss Dani!"

JR stood up as his mother walked into the dining room and she felt proud that her son's military education had taught him such polished manners. *'Too bad he didn't finish at the Academy whilst I had the money to pay for it, though!*

Then Dani's gaze rested on a slightly-built girl, sitting quietly beside JR. Her pale face was framed by long, dark-brown hair. Big, brown, innocent eyes revealed the strain the girl was feeling at meeting JR's glamorous mother. In contrast to the girl's quiet demeanor, JR could hardly contain his excitement as he made official introductions.

"Mom! I'd like you to meet my fiancée, Becky."

It seemed only a few weeks since her son had first mentioned Becky and now the pair of them were engaged! Dani struggled to control her churning emotions and remain polite.

"Wow! When did this all happen, JR?"

"Earlier tonight, Mom. See the ring?"

JR was hopping from one foot to the other with pleasure and Dani's heart went out to her only son. She took the girl's hand gently, to closer inspect the sparkling diamond that rested there.

"It's as lovely as you are, Becky."

Dani smiled reassuringly at the young lovebirds as a waiter brought menus. The girl seemed so quiet and shy. She was young, too and rather plain-looking. *'But at least she's not a dancer!'* As far as Dani was concerned that was definitely a bonus. Yet as the evening and the conversation continued, Dani realized that she was actually quite pleased with her son's choice of wife.

Becky was sweet and innocent. A 'homebody' who did all her own sewing and cooking. She even proudly announced that she planned to make her own wedding dress. Young Becky was most definitely nothing like the girls that JR usually dated! And *that* alone made Dani happy.

***

"Billy, the meal was spectacular, as always and George's wine selection was perfect."

"Thank you, Miss Dani" Billy beamed his gratitude and bowed slightly. "Do you need your fur coat now, or will you be going into the lounge for a nightcap? Tony is playing here tonight, you know!"

Dani looked at JR in surprise.

"I thought this was Tony's night off? Oh, but it would be great to see him." She turned toward Becky. "Tony's my favorite entertainer you see and I haven't seen him for months."

Dani first met Tony soon after arriving in Portland and had taken to him instantly.

The entertainer was a flamboyant, gay man and Dani smiled inwardly at her recollections of him. *'I remember Tony wearing those brightly colored shirts long before they became fashionable!'* The entertainer was extremely outgoing and friendly and lived with his long-time partner, Troy. The pair frequently hosted lavish parties at their fabulous, hillside home and invited guests were carefully selected from among the local entertainers. Dani and Digger had always been at the top of Tony's invitation list.

"I thought you might enjoy seeing Tony again, that's why I suggested coming here tonight." JR smiled at his mother. "Come on, it will do you good to relax a little."

A huge smile wrapped itself around Tony's handsome face the moment Dani entered the lounge. He nodded for her to join him at the piano and, as he adjusted the mike, he introduced her to the audience.

"Ladies and gentlemen, we have a special guest here with us tonight. I'd like you all to meet a very dear friend of mine, Miss Dani Rosselli."

Dani slid in beside Tony on the padded bench and took the microphone from him.

"Apart from being happy to see my good friend Tony, this is also a very special night for me as my son has just announced his engagement!" The audience roared their congratulations. "So I would like to dedicate this love song to my son, JR and his new fiancée, Becky."

Dani then proceeded to bring the house down with her own version of Henry Mancini's wonderfully romantic, *'More'*.

The applause was so great for Dani that Tony nodded for her to sing another one; his personal, Sinatra favorite of *'Fly Me to the Moon'*. The audience still wanted more but Dani took her leave, like the professional she was. *'Always leave 'em wanting more!'* JR escorted his mother back to their table.

"Mom! That was amazing; that's the best I've ever heard you sing!"

"You're biased son, but thanks anyway! It did feel good, though. It's been far too long."

Dani turned toward Becky " So; let's all have a drink to celebrate, shall we? A little cider maybe; what do you think?"

"Cider?" asked Becky, raising her eyebrows. "They don't know that I'm under age here, do they?"

"No honey, but *I* do!" Dani didn't want to get the restaurant owner in trouble by ordering alcoholic drinks for a minor. Nor did she want to embarrass herself. After all, Dani was in business too and clearly understood the ramifications of breaking State licensing laws.

"Cider for the young lady here and I'll have a coke, please." Dani told the waiter. JR ordered himself a draft beer. Then Billy-Mo discreetly walked over and whispered into Dani's ear.

"I thought you should know, ma'am that Digger has just arrived with one of your ex-dancers."

The last person Dani wanted to see was her soon-to-be-ex-husband.

"Where are they, Billy?"

"They just sat down in the dining room, ma'am."

'A true restaurateur', Dani thought, as Billy politely left them again. The man knew everything about everybody.

"Well, I guess this party's over for tonight kids! Mo just told me that Digger is next door, in the dining room!"

Their cars were freshly washed and polished and waiting for them outside the *'Gold Coin's'* front door. *'Just one more reason why Billy's place is so successful',* Dani mused.

"Mom, this has been a wonderful evening. One question, though?"

"What, honey?"

"Well, I've heard rumors that Billy runs hookers out of the restaurant here; is that true?"

"Well if he does, then Billy Mo must be *very* discreet indeed. Digger and I have been coming here for a long time and *I've* never seen or heard any sign of any hookers. Billy has always been extremely pleasant and polite, *but* he's also a very shrewd businessman so, hey; maybe there's another side to the *'Gold Coin'* after all!"

They all laughed at the pun as Dani pointed up at the blinking, golden-yellow, restaurant sign. JR smiled as he closed his mother's car door, then he and Becky waved her off, hand-in-hand.

***

Dani went straight back to the Club. It was supposed to be her night off but everything looked in order as she walked inside.

Linda-Lee Scott was doing her celebrated 'fish-bowl' act. Everyone loved the way the dancer's long, blond hair swayed and flowed as she moved around under the water. Her hair was like corn-silk, swaying in the breeze; golden, clean and pure. Even though he no longer worked there, Dani's father was very proud of his 'find'; he had been the one to hire Linda-Lee while Dani and Digger were away on their ill-fated Vegas trip!

"Have you seen my brother?" Dani asked of one of the waiters.

"Tyler's in the back room, ma'am. Checking the monthly liquor inventory, I believe."

Dani hated doing the first-of-every-month inventory and re-ordering supplies. She wished Tyler had offered to come work for her sooner. *'Maybe he could have kept Digger from robbing my tills blind*!'

She tapped lightly on the storage room door as she entered.

"Thanks for taking care of all this stuff, Tyler. With so much going on I'd completely forgotten about it again. I don't know what I'd do without your help."

"Don't worry, Sis. I'm happy to help out. We were running low on a few things but I think I've got everything under control. I still can't believe that Digger did all this crap to you and our family. Who in the hell does the man think he is?"

Dani heaved a deep sigh.

"I should have thrown him out a long time ago, Tyler. When I finally caught him in bed with that bitch it tore my heart out, but I guess it took the worst kind of shock to wake me up to reality."

Tears welled up in Dani's eyes, unbidden.

"Sis, don't you waste one more tear on that creep. You're a beautiful woman and you'll have no trouble finding another man, a good man this time, when the time is right. Dad always called you his 'beautiful little filly'!"

"I know you're being kind, Tyler but the last thing I need right now is another man in my life."

Dani wiped her eyes on an old bar towel that was lying on top of a dusty box.

"Hey! Don't use that dirty old rag. You don't know where it's been." Tyler handed his sister a clean, pure-linen handkerchief from his pocket and she started to laugh.

"No one uses proper handkerchiefs anymore, Tyler!"

"Well, why the hell not? I'm not about to carry a wad of Kleenex around with me, am I?"

The siblings collapsed into fits of giggles.

"Oh, I feel better for that, Tyler. I needed a good laugh. After you finish up here, come and have a drink with me at the bar. I have some news for you about our young JR!"

"OK, I should only be about another thirty minutes."

"Try not to be too long, 'cos I need to get some sleep tonight. I've got an important court date tomorrow morning."

***

When she arrived back at her hotel, Dani left her car with the valet who informed her that her parents had already arrived and were up in her suite. She was glad of the warning, otherwise she would have been scared out of her wits to find her Mom and Papa sleeping on the spare cot! It was two o' clock in the morning; far too early to wake her parents up so Dani quietly tiptoed past the sleeping couple and closed her bedroom door behind her. But it gave her a warm feeling knowing that her family was there; knowing that she was not alone.

Dani drew a hot bath and lit several perfumed candles, then put on some light classical music, keeping the volume low. She stepped into the inviting bubbles and slid way down, so that only her chin and face were exposed to the fragrant steam rising above the water. She was floating, weightless, on a cloud and her mind drifted off into peaceful thoughts. *'My life is not over; it's just beginning again'.*

The music soothed her soul and Dani lay totally relaxed and almost asleep, until the water turned cold. Then she climbed out and wrapped a large, white, fluffy towel around her glistening body. She climbed into satin sheets and glanced up at her ceiling mirror; the one she had asked the manager to install, just a week after moving into his hotel! She smiled and spoke to her own, lofty reflection.

"Good night, Dani Sutton. Sleep tight!"

***

She awoke to the smell of freshly brewed coffee and knew that her mother, at least, must be up and about. She threw on a robe and went to greet her folks, who were busy eating bagels and cream cheese. She walked directly over to her father, leaned over and kissed him on the forehead.

"Good to see you up and about again, Papa! Are you sure you should be here, though and not resting at home?"

"You're absolutely right, Dani" Her mother quickly answered for him. "I told him he shouldn't come here in his weakened state, but you know your own father! He's just like an old mule when he sets his mind to something!"

"Now don't you go putting me down, Laura. I *need* to be here for our daughter. Nothing, and no one, will keep me from going into that court-room this morning."

"So that's why you're really here, is it?" Dani gently teased her father.

"You're damn right it is! I'm here to see that crook squirm in his shoes! I could still beat him to death with one of these, if you give me half a chance!" Harold raised one of his crutches in the air menacingly.

"Okay, Papa, you can come to the courthouse, but you have to prom-ise me not to cause any trouble. The law will take care of Digger Rosselli."

"Get dressed then, Dani." Laura snapped her fingers. "We'll *all* have to hurry or we'll be late."

Dani swallowed her last sip of coffee and buttered a piece of toast to eat while she was dressing.

***

They all travelled in Dani's car. Since the courthouse was just around the corner from the Club, she parked in the garage and they walked around to the courthouse. As they crossed the foyer, Dani smiled to herself. She loved walking on marble floors; the clicking sound made her feel as if she was tap dancing!

There were quite a few people already inside the courtroom. Digger was there, talking with his attorneys, but when he saw Dani he favored her with her a long, chilling stare. She sat next to her own attorney and tried to avoid looking in Digger's direction. Her parents sat just behind her and it felt good, knowing that she had their support. But she still wondered if all this drama would be too much for her father. He was, after all, still recovering from that appalling car crash.

As she looked around, Dani was appalled to realize that over half the people in the room were attorneys!

Several lawyers represented the Security Bank of Oregon. Another attorney represented Mrs. George; the lady who leased the Club to Dani's business corporation. And even Digger had a couple of his own lawyers to Dani's single one! It was completely mind boggling and Dani shivered in foreboding. *'This should not be happening to me.'* Then the deep, resonant voice of the Court Clerk boomed out and silence descended.

"This court is now in session, the Honorable Judge Kelsey presiding. All rise!"

***

It took a long time for everyone to testify, but the Judge's final decision shocked Dani to the core. She was awarded the house, all of her own belongings, the nightclub, all outstanding bills, her car and her boat. But the Judge then awarded Digger two-hundred dollars a week, for living expenses, to be paid by *her*. Dani was outraged and jumped up out of her seat.

"I will *not* pay that man one single cent," she screamed!

The Judge pounded three times with his gavel.

"Control your client, Mr. Booth, or she will be found in contempt of court."

"Yes, your Honor! *Sit down, please, Dani!*"

"OK, I'll sit down but I will *not* pay Digger one dime," she hissed, angrily.

Then the telephone rang. The bailiff answered it and then passed the handset across to the Judge, who immediately dropped it.

"Everybody out! Evacuate the building immediately; there has been a bomb threat!"

Dani ran to help her father as he struggled with his crutches. He couldn't run down the stairs like everyone else, so the three of them took a chance and went down in the elevator. Everyone waited outside the courthouse for over two, long hours whilst the building was thoroughly searched. No bomb was ever found and, eventually, the whole day's court business was adjourned to a later date. As they walked back toward the Club garage, to collect Dani's car, Laura asked if either of them had noticed Digger squirming around a lot while he was on the witness stand.

"I thought he kept looking at you, Mom but I couldn't turn around to see why."

Her mother smiled. "I kept my hand inside my purse and kept moving it around, as though I had a gun in there. Every time Digger looked at me, I made sure he noticed my gestures."

"*Really*, Mom? I wish I'd thought of that."

Dani was impressed with her mother's inspired notion but Harold Gunther was not amused.

"You girls think you're being real funny, but it's a wonder you both weren't arrested! A courtroom is no place to make threatening gestures, Laura, so don't you ever pull a stunt like that again."

"Behavior like that could hurt Dani's case and our daughter needs all the help she can get."

Harold Gunther, the Sherriff, had spoken and they walked the rest of the way to the garage in silence.

Dani wondered if her ex-husband might have actually arranged for that phony, courthouse bomb scare.

'It would certainly give his lawyers more time to figure out how to get more money out of me!' But she kept her thoughts to herself. Once she had paid off all Digger's debts, Dani would have nothing left to take, anyhow.

Dolores J. Guthrie

Chapter 36

Only two weeks to go before Portland's annual, *'Rose Festival'* and springtime was already in full bloom. The whole city buzzed with preparations for their traditional, massive parade. Dani and Tyler were busy too, preparing her yacht for the annual 'River Run' party. She had even hired topless, dancing girls to dance on deck to welcome home all the US navy ships, into Portland's waterfront. Dani's yacht also sported colorful signs along both sides, advertising her Club. She was going through a terrible divorce, true, but Dani still had to attend to business and the *'Rose Festival'* was a golden opportunity for her. Service men on R&R were everywhere in the City of Portland, which brought the ladies out in full force, too and they *all* needed to drink!

Every year Dani gave generously of her time to help out at various Chamber-of-Commerce events, especially during Festival time. This year she had been invited to accompany one particular ship's Commander to the various social functions. Since she was no longer with Digger, Dani had willingly agreed; it would be a pleasant diversion from her otherwise depressing existence. She had been assigned to one Commander George Pack, but Dani gasped inwardly as the gentleman in question approached her table at the official 'meet-and-greet'. At that time, George Pack was the only black Commander in the entire US Navy!

Dani had always considered herself to be non-prejudiced, but the evening ahead would be a true test of her ideology. Commander Pack was tall and carried himself strikingly upright. He also had unusual blue eyes and his smooth, black skin sported fascinating, dusky freckles. When he spoke, it was in a soft, deep but easygoing voice.

"Good evening, ma'am! You must be Danielle?"

He held out a hand and produced the most stunning smile she had ever seen.

"And you must be Captain, err.....sorry.... *Commander* Pack!"

"Yes, ma'am, but please call me George. May I introduce you to my young colleague, Ensign First-Class, Jerry Carter?"

"Please join us, gentleman" Dani made introductions to her female companion. "This is my friend, Phyllis Maynard."

It was all a bit nervous and tense for a quite a while and Dani kept glancing out of the window at the twinkling lights of a giant Ferris wheel, below. The lights of a 'Human Hammer' fairground ride made sweeping, streaks of color as the giant machine swung up and down. Big ships lined the whole waterfront, showing string-of-pearl lights from stem-to-stern. It was a beautiful sight and Dani felt a tear well up as she remembered other nights; other dates; other men in her life. She began to wonder how to get out of the whole evening without hurting the feelings of that fine officer. The oddly assorted foursome had a few more drinks and shared some small talk, but after about an hour Dani finally excused herself. She walked the ten blocks back to her hotel.

The next evening Ensign Carter, accompanied by two other young sailors, entered Dani's Club and asked for her by name. She invited them to join her at a table, but he politely declined.

"No thank you, ma'am! We are simply here to protest at your behavior last night, toward our Commander."

"I don't know what you mean?" Dani was baffled, but also a little embarrassed by the young man's outspoken comments.

"Tonight is the Queen's Ball, ma'am and you are meant to be accompanying our Commander there to represent *our* ship. But we don't believe you plan to show up tonight, ma'am. We don't believe you want to be seen with Commander Pack because he is black. But if you *don't* show up tonight, ma'am, it will disgrace our entire ship and insult our commanding officer."

"We want you to know that if we sailors had to choose *any* Commander, in the whole of the United States Navy, we would *all* wish to serve under Commander Pack, ma'am. He is an outstanding individual and an honorable leader."

"I'm *so* sorry!" Dani was overwhelmed with remorse and impressed by the young man's obvious sincerity.

"I feel terrible about leaving early last night and I apologize. It's just that I'm going through a tough divorce right now and I really don't think I would be very good company for anyone at the moment."

"Begging your pardon, ma'am, but we feel you're just making excuses."

"Okay! Okay!" The young Ensign's straightforward manner was irresistible and Dani smiled at the solemn young man. "Pick me up here at seven o' clock tonight and I promise to be on my very best behavior!"

"Thank you, ma'am!" They saluted smartly, then turned as one unit and marched out the door.

'That little shit!' Dani smiled again. *'Ensign Carter should be in politics.'*

Tyler was close by and had overheard the whole encounter. He patted Dani's back and whispered teasingly in her ear.

"The black man's gonna get you yet, little sister."

She punched her brother on the arm.

"Get out of here! I'm just doing my civic duty, Tyler Gunther and *you* have a filthy mind."

"Well, while you are going to the Ball, m'lady, I'll keep things rolling smoothly back here."

"Okay! I'll work next weekend then, so you can go out and play, little brother!"

***

Dani was running late, as often happened these days and she had no time for beauty salons. She took a quick shower, dabbed perfume in all the right places and freshened up her makeup. Then she brushed her hair straight back into a knot and attached a hairpiece of flouncing curls. Slipping into a full-length, white, Grecian-style gown and wrapping a white, Marabou stole around her tanned shoulders. Dani admired the effects in her full-length mirror and declared herself ready for the Queen's Ball.

At seven o' clock sharp the three young sailors returned, accompanied by Commander Pack who was decked out in his finest. The man was strikingly handsome in Dress whites, with spotless, white gloves tucked into his gold belt. He stared in awe as Dani walked across the room toward him and gave her his most dazzling smile.

"You are a vision that makes my Navy Seal legs feel like melting rubber, ma'am. Shall we?"

He held out one arm and Dani slipped her hand into the crook of his elbow. She could feel strong muscles working as the Commander pulled her closer to his side. All eyes in the Club were upon them as the fine-looking couple sauntered out into the mild, evening air.

***

The whole evening went by as if she were in a dream. Dani felt like a goddess and danced until her feet were numb. At midnight, just like Cinderella, the sailors escorted her home and George walked her into the Club's lounge. He bowed and lightly kissed her hand.

"We will pick you up at nine o' clock sharp tomorrow, ma'am, ready for the big parade." Commander Pack saluted, turned and marched out the door.

Dani felt every eye in the room watching her; or did she just imagine it, because George was black and she was white?

The weather next day was glorious. Usually it poured down with rain during the *'Rose Parade'*, but not that year! The flowers were beautiful; the themed floats were superb and even the white convertibles, carrying all the dignitaries, had blankets made of red roses spread across their trunks. Dani sat between the ship's Chaplain and Commander Pack. She looked gorgeous, as ever, but still she had found no time for the beauty salon so another well manipulated hairpiece did the job! After the main parade, the guys wanted Dani to carry on partying with them all but she graciously declined.

"Thanks guys, but I really need to get my hair fixed and get rested up before tomorrow's big picnic."

George walked Dani back to the Club and at the door she gave him a friendly peck on the cheek. She handed over one of her hotel's business cards.

"George, I've had the most wonderful time today and I'm really looking forward to the big picnic tomorrow. But why don't you pick me up at my hotel suite, instead of here?"

"It will be my pleasure ma'am. I'll be there at noon, on the dot!"

Dani dashed around the corner and arrived just in time to get her hair fixed before the *'Hilton'* hotel's beauty salon closed. Then she caught a cab back to her own hotel suite, feeling drained and like a limp, rag doll. She planned to go directly to bed but spotted a note peeking out from underneath her door.

Dani snatched it up.

'Your attorney called. You have to be back in court, at nine o' clock sharp, on Monday next. Regards, Lil and Hank'.

Dani kicked her expensive, white-leather shoes across the room in anger and pounded her fists against the walls. "Damn! I'd almost forgotten all about that mess. Will it never end?"

The night was a long one. She tossed and turned for forever, in spite of her tiredness, thinking about her new friend, George Pack. Each time she was with him, Dani felt more and more comfortable about the whole racial thing. In fact the Commander's color was becoming less and less apparent to her with every meeting! The young Ensign had been right in his portrayal of the man. George Pack was indeed a great personality and Dani was starting to feel an attraction to the man that felt very special. She was tired of all the hurt in her recent past. Pain that, until this week, she had not been able to shake. She realized that she hadn't thought of Digger at all recently, not until that note damn had appeared under her door last night!

Spending time with a man of honor and credibility like the Commander had given Dani renewed strength and optimism for her *own* future.

She fell asleep at last and with a smile on her face.

***

The *'Flying-M'* horse ranch is about forty minutes' drive southwest of Portland and was the venue for the *Rose Festival's* grand picnic. It was a huge event but dress was casual, so the men wore shorts and bright, Hawaiian shirts and the ladies wore elegant sundresses. Dani and George were talking with a small group of sailors when another man joined them. Every man stood to attention and saluted as the newcomer approached. Dani assumed that the man was another Commander, but never actually asked his rank. She chattered on in her usual fashion and found him to be extremely friendly and interesting. When he eventually took his leave of the group, the man smiled at Dani and handed her a card.

"Ma'am, it was a pleasure to meet you. If you ever get up to Seattle, please give me a call.

"Thank you! I most certainly will!"

After the man had gone Dani looked down at the card in her fingers and gasped.

"George! Why ever didn't you tell me? That man is the Commander of the *whole* Seventh Fleet!"

"I know that!" George's naturally generous smile grew even wider. "But I was enjoying how comfortable you made him feel, without knowing who he was."

"But why would he want *me* to call him?"

"Because he likes you, Dani! Haven't you looked in the mirror, lately? Those blue eyes of yours are totally bewitching!"

George took her small white hand in his and they set off walking through the vast gardens. His huge hands felt like satin gloves and Dani idly wondered how soft his lips might be! They had just crossed over a small bridge, spanning a winding creek and they were well out of the sight of his men. Dani turned and looked up at George. Suddenly, she was floating. Everything fell into place as the Commander drew her lips toward his own. But then he stopped and whispered her name.

"Oh, Dani!"

He seemed hesitant to kiss her, so Dani put her hands around the back of his head and pulled him gently in. When their lips eventually met she felt that her legs would collapse. There was no sensation of color, it simply felt *really* wonderful and Dani wanted more.

***

The top was down on their convertible and the air was cool as the young Ensign drove them all back toward the city. Dani's skin was stinging a little from a touch of sunburn. *'Too many kisses in the garden this afternoon!'* Neither she nor George had spoken yet but there was no awkwardness between them.

The Commander put an arm around her shoulders, holding Dani closely, but gently.

"Is this better? You looked a little chilled."

"All better!" Dani smiled up at him.

They pulled up in front of her hotel and George got out with her.

"You guys take the car. I'll catch you back at the ship, later!"

Once they were up in her suite, Dani went to change into something more comfortable. She heard George ordering some expensive champagne and two glasses and she peeked around the bathroom door to blow him a kiss. When she returned to the dimly lit bedroom, George had already taken off his shirt and was sitting on the bed. *'What a magnificent specimen of a man!'* She moved closer and George pulled her into his arms, kissing her softly but with great passion.

"Dani! You are a wonderful woman. I have been having visions of what this moment would be like, ever since our first meeting."

The two of them sat on the bed, entwined arms and shared a toast.

"To *us*, Dani! When I sail away tomorrow, I will always remember the feelings we have shared these past few days."

"George, I will always remember you too!"

Crystal champagne glasses clinked, echoing in the darkness. Then Dani stood and untied her powder-pink peignoir. It dropped to the floor, revealing a pink, satin nightgown beneath. George dragged back the bed-covers and called her name again.

"Oh, Dani, baby! Come to me!"

She stepped out of the nightgown and collapsed into his arms. In the dimmed room, Dani's pale skin glowed bright against George's honey-brown, satin complexion.

The man's hugeness gave Dani pleasure, as well as a little pain. Yet the strength of their body movements was both passionate and sensual. Commander George Pack was electrifying.

They finally collapsed into each other's arms, utterly satisfied. It had truly been a night of truth for Dani. She had bedded a man of color and loved every second of it.

She glanced at the clock on her nightstand. Five-o'-clock in the morning! George was already asleep and Dani snuggled down beside him, cradled within strong, loving arms. She closed her eyes, reflecting on the brief time that she and George Pack had spent together.

'This short-lived, but incredible love affair is not something I will ever forget!'

And Dani even dared to believe that neither would the Commander!

Chapter 37

Dani lay in bed, watching the rain drizzle down outside her bedroom window.

'Maybe if I hang my head outside, I could be drawn inside a raindrop!' Dani always did have a fanciful imagination. She tried her best to be positive about the day ahead, even though her stomach was churning. Her hands were cold, damp and sticky from restless sleep and she wiped them, absentmindedly, on the sheets. She could hardly bear to drag herself out of bed, but her adjourned court hearing was due to begin again in two hours.

'At least the sun is trying to come out', was Dani's best effort at being cheerful.

In spite of trying to put off the inevitable, she arrived at the court-house a full thirty minutes early. As Dani approached the entrance steps, her nose detected the moist, fresh scent of recently cut grass. She reached down and plucked a large, dandelion seed-head that had escaped the wrath of the county's gardener and his lawnmower. Dani was still stalling for time before she faced the Judge again. She held the delicate wildflower in front of her face, almost reverently, recognizing that even weeds can be beautiful. Then she blew gently, scattering its dozens of tiny seedlings into the breeze.

'If only my own problems could be swept away so easily'.

But, no matter what happened in court later that day, Dani vowed to stay calm. Like the dandelions in the grass, she too would survive. She bowed her head and closed her eyes in prayer.

'I wish, I wish, that my nightmare will finally be over today. This is now and tomorrow is tomorrow but, no matter what happens, my life will go on.

"Dani! It's time for court. Come on, let's go."

A man's deep voice called Dani's attention back to reality. She jumped in alarm and her eyes shot open. Berry Booth, her attorney, held out a hand and they climbed the courthouse steps together.

"Are your parents not here today?"

"No, I made them go back to Salem. Dad wasn't feeling too good. He's still getting over his accident, if you remember. But they know you'll take good care of me."

Dani presumed that her lawyer had his clients' best interests at heart, anyway. Berry Booth was a tall man, with sandy colored hair. His cheeks always had a touch of ruddiness in them, not from drink but from his many weekends spent skiing. He seemed to be a happily married man, with five handsome children and Dani sincerely hoped that he wouldn't turn out to be anything like her previous attorneys, back in New York City. The court-room was filled to capacity as Berry nudged her ribs, reminding her to stand.

"All rise! This Court is now in session. The honorable Judge Murphy presiding!"

Her eyes scanned the courtroom again as everyone sat down. She couldn't see Digger anywhere, although his attorneys were already seated at a table to Dani's right. Feeling on the verge of throwing up, she sucked in a deep breath and held it for as long as she could, trying to push the sensation of nausea down. Berry noticed Dani's pale face and patted her hand, gently.

"Hang in there, Dani! Things won't be so bad."

She tried to smile but felt a chill run through her body as her mind flashed back to the bomb scare at her previous court hearing. In spite of all her best intentions, Dani's mind drifted in and out of awareness during the morning's lengthy and complicated proceedings. Lawyers, for both parties, batted legal arguments around like balls at a tennis match.

Berry Booth restated Dani's position; that she was the President of the *'Gigo'* corporation; that she owned all of its stock and that the company had over eight-hundred-thousand dollars in its bank account. Her home, which was worth nearly half-a-million dollars, had been free and clear of debt until Digger Rosselli borrowed money against it without Dani's knowledge. Her husband had subsequently opened five different bank ac-counts, all in his own name and had fraudulently moved most of Dani's money into those accounts. Digger had also purchased several other prop-erties in his own name, including a large interest in some dubious, land-development project.

Then Digger's attorneys filed their countermotions, ultimately trying to force Dani to turn her house over to *their* client so that he could pay off his loans to the bank. Dani returned to full consciousness with a jolt. Something in her subconscious mind acknowledged the implications of Digger's lawyers' remarks and she shot to her feet.

"No! That's *my* money. Digger Rosselli will not end up with *my* home by using my *own* money!" Dani was totally distraught.

"Motion dismissed!"

The Judge turned to Dani. "But one more outburst like that and I will have you jailed for contempt of court, young lady!"

"I'm sorry, your Honor; it won't happen again!"

But Digger's next motion tore at Dani's heart and she almost fainted. His lawyers were now claiming that she, Danielle Sutton, was emotionally unstable. They moved that her entire company, *'Gigo'* corporation, should be sold off and that all stocks pertaining to the Club should be turned over to Rob Kendall & Co: Accountants. All moneys were to be placed into 'escrow' and held there until *all* debts of said nightclub were satisfied. The sum of one-hundred-and-fifty-thousand dollars would then be paid to the seller, Danielle Sutton.

Dani turned to her lawyer in panic.

"I agree to sell the Club to this Rob Kendall person, but we can't allow *his* accountants to handle all my money, too! Do something, Berry, before it's too late."

But it was already too late.

"Motion granted. Court is adjourned!"

The Judge appeared to hang his head in shame but the damage was done. His gavel came down hard and Dani sat down on her bench with a thud. Everyone stood up, except her, as the Judge swept out of the courtroom.

"That damn Judge *knows* what they're doing to me, Berry, yet he won't stop it."

"Come on, Dani! I'll walk you back to your hotel."

She was dog-tired and deeply depressed as the two of them walked away from the courthouse. Absent-mindedly, she voiced her innermost thoughts. *'Bitter is the death of love!'*

"What did you say, Dani?"

Berry was busy checking his watch. Five-thirty in the afternoon meant that it was too late to meet his wife at her parents', for dinner. Maybe he should offer Dani a commiseratory drink instead. He excused himself and made a quick phone call, then repeated his question to Dani.

"I said, *'Bitter is the death of love',* Berry. It's just something I read in a magazine but it seems appropriate for the way I feel right now. I'm feeling *very* bitter, Berry. It feels like my heart has died and I don't think I'll ever be able to love, or trust, another man again."

"You will, Dani, you will."

Berry Booth's well-practiced lawyer platitudes kicked in. "Time heals all wounds my dear, so why don't we start by having a drink to-gether?"

Dani exhaled deeply as they entered the lobby of her hotel. She felt exhausted.

"I'm sorry, Berry but I'm not going to say 'thank you for a nice day'. When this thing is all over, I'll probably not receive even one, single cent. I doubt if I'll even have enough money to pay your legal fees, you do real-ize that don't you.

Berry's gaze deepened as he took Dani's arm and escorted her inside the bar. "I think we both deserve a drink right now, or maybe even two!"

***

Dani sipped at her martini, stirring the olive around her glass with one finger. Berry was drinking a tall scotch and water.

"So that's what attorneys drink when they want to forget about their bad day in court?"

Dani had a twinkle in her eye.

"No! I just like scotch. Dani, do you recall when we first started working together? It was on your lawsuit against the United States of America.

"I sure do. When was that? Three years ago?"

"Almost *four* years ago now and that particular lawsuit may go on for years yet, you know."

"But *why*, Berry? If I owed the US Government over a hundred-thousand-dollars in back taxes, like they owe me in rebate for when HK overpaid my taxes; hell, they would throw my 'you-know-what' in jail, quick as a flash!"

"That's right, Dani, they would! But the government is entitled to do that; keep your money and build interest on it for as long as they can get away with. Legally, it's up to the courts to push the issue."

"In the meantime, since you haven't yet paid me for any of my earlier work, I would like to put this current case on a contingency basis."

"What do you mean?"

"Well; my partners would prefer me to drop you altogether, Dani, because you are tying up too much of our company's time and money. And after today, all of your free cash is being held in escrow so you won't be able to touch it! I've been thinking of how we can best work things out so that all parties are satisfied."

Dani didn't have the heart for a squalid argument over legal fees.

"Anything you say, Berry, but I really can't afford to lose this present lawsuit. There'll be at least half-a-million dollars coming to me once they pay off Digger's debts, even with the interest they'll charge me."

The three large Scotches that Berry had already consumed were starting to kick in.

"I know this case is important to you, Dani but my job is important to me, too! I just thought we could work out some way for me to keep on representing you, that's all. I have been attracted to you for a long time, Dani. In fact, I think you are the most sensual woman I've ever known."

Dani was utterly stunned at what she was hearing.

"Good god almighty, Berry! Yet another man tries to take advantage of me; *you* of all people! I trusted you, but a lot of good that's done me, huh?"

"Now, Dani! I haven't had any worries about payment until now, but....! Oh, what the hell! Why can't we deal with this in the privacy of your room, Dani? This plan of mine will benefit both of us, but let's go *now*. I can't stay out all night like single guys can you know."

"No, I guess you can't."

Dani's tone was sarcastic as she picked up her purse and headed toward the lounge door. She walked toward the elevators, then stopped and turned. Sure enough Barry Booth was right behind her; glass in hand and tongue hanging out.

'Oh, why the hell not?

Dani had been used by others so often during her short life that she suddenly decided it was time to do some 'using' of her own. But she was well aware that tonight wouldn't be anything like the night when she took Commander Pack back to her room. *That* night had been exciting. Hot, steamy and full of passion and emotion. *This* evening would be completely different.

And it was. The rendezvous was cold and completely unromantic. No scented candles flickered and no soft music played. Berry's thin lips felt like sandpaper upon her own soft, tender mouth. His hands were rough too; toughened by the cold mountain weather during his frequent weekends outdoors. The sex act itself was quick, almost animal-like and not in the least bit enjoyable for a woman like Dani. There was no foreplay and no kisses, no soft caresses afterward. The man simply finished what he came to do, dressed himself and left; all within one hour!

Dani was sitting up in bed as he prepared to leave. She managed to keep a straight face but it was a pretty funny sight, watching Berry Booth, respected attorney-at-Law, struggling to put on his shoes while repeatedly checking his watch.

'And I thought I could trust this man!'

"Got to run, Dani, but you were fabulous. We'll do this again soon I promise."

Berry gathered up his phone and briefcase, blew her a quick kiss and the hotel room door closed behind him. Dani couldn't help herself.

'Fabulous, my foot! I don't think he even know what fabulous means.'

She spoke her thoughts aloud to the empty room. Then she almost sprinted to the bathroom. Dani couldn't wait to draw a hot, bubble-bath, light a few scented candles and turn on some relaxing, classical music. Gratefully, she sank down beneath the gently popping bubbles and breathed a sigh of relief.

'I wonder how much that little session knocked off my legal bill, then.'

Dolores J. Guthrie

Chapter 38

When the phone rang at ten o' clock next morning, Dani was coming out of a very deep sleep. She was so drowsy that the handset fell onto the floor as picked it up. When she eventually got it to her ear, she heard Berry Booth's concerned voice at the other end.

"Dani? Dani? Are you there? Are you all right?"

'Dammit, what does he want now?'

But she kept her voice sweet.

"Hello, Berry. I'm fine. I just dropped the telephone on the floor, that's all. Sorry about that."

"Oh, OK!" The attorney paused to clear his throat. He sounded quite nervous.

"Well, firstly I wanted to, err… thank you for yesterday evening, Dani but I also have some other news for you. Not good news either, I'm sorry to say. The Judge has already granted the foreclosure order to your bank. That's because of the three-hundred-thousand dollar loan that Digger took out against your house, remember? Anyway, you have only sixty days in which to vacate the property, Dani."

She was wide awake at that point and sitting on the edge of her bed.

"How can they take away my half-million-dollar home, just because of a three-hundred-thousand dollar loan? I've already sold most of my stuff to pay off Digger's debts and now they want my *house*, too? Damn it, Berry, I don't believe this garbage?"

She was lost for words at the injustice of it all, so Berry tried to fill the gap with a few words of reassurance.

"I'm trying to help you, Dani, *really* I am."

"I suppose you are, but it doesn't feel like it." Another awkward silence floated on the airwaves between them. Dani was bitterly disappointed but then her naturally practical nature shifted into gear again.

"Oh, what the hell! Most of my furniture has already been sold off so what good is an empty mansion to me? My personal belongings are all here with me at the hotel, so I might as well stay put for the next sixty days."

"But if you do *that*, my dear, you will have to pay your own hotel bill."

"My God!" Dani exploded in bitter anger. "Can things get any worse? You know I don't have that kind of money, Berry."

"Well, you *do* still have your Eldorado, don't you?"

"Big deal, so I have a car! How the hell can I *ever* get back on my feet if everyone keeps screwing me over?"

This was not the start to the day that Dani had anticipated.

"I really have no choice then, do I Berry. I'll have to move back into my empty house until the sixty days are up. Fortunately the electricity and phone lines are still hooked up, so my stove, refrigerator and telephones will still work. And I think I still have one leather chair over there, next to the pool table."

Dani was simply doing her thinking aloud, trying hard to stay positive in spite of such bad news.

"I can ask JR and some of his friends to help me move the rest of my stuff back over to the house. So much for my meager savings, though. They'll have keep me alive for quite some time, won't they?"

"You'll be fine, Dani. And I promise to get some money released to you just as soon as I possibly can. Just hang tight for now, OK?"

"I don't feel able to trust *anyone* anymore, Berry and can you blame me?"

Her lawyer agreed with her, but then dropped another bombshell!

"I've heard through the grapevine that Digger got beaten up recently, Dani. So badly, in fact, that he ended up in hospital for a while. *Please*, tell me you had nothing to do with that?"

"Of course I didn't!" Dani was horrified at her attorney's lack of faith. "Even after all that man has done to me, I could never wish him any real harm. Yes, of course it crosses your mind when you hate someone as much as I hate Digger, but I would never go through with such a stupid idea, Berry."

"OK, I believe you Dani, but you understand that I had to ask? Digger got out of the hospital yesterday anyhow, but he might well think you were behind his attack so *please* be very careful. That man is ruthless when he's riled up and you know that from first-hand experience!

"Hell, Berry; I would hope Digger knows me well enough to realize I could *never* be a part of something like that!"

Dani hung up the phone wishing she had never answered it in the first place. Then the ramifications of their conversation hit home and her mind spaced out. She tried to picture Digger's face but her awareness seemed to have erased it from memory. Dani imagined her ex-husband, lying crumpled and hurt and tears streamed down her face, unbidden. She couldn't help it; it was in her nature to be compassionate but Dani was also angry at the inevitability of the attack on Digger.

'He was probably left for dead by the same thugs he runs around with'.

She stood up too quickly and, for a brief moment, couldn't remember where on earth she was. Sunlight streamed into the room, filtering through sheer, white curtains. One window was open and a gentle, but cool, breeze danced around Dani's face and shoulders.

She rubbed at her slender arms and gazed down in amazement at the blue, flowery, flannel nightgown she was wearing. It didn't look at all familiar. *'When and where did I buy this and is it even mine?'*

The brisk air caused her to shiver but it also brought Dani back to reality. She rolled her tongue around the inside her mouth. *'Cotton mouth!'* She hadn't brushed her teeth yet! Eventually, Dani recollected her lawyer's phone call and all that they had talked about. She sat down again and applied her mind to the problem of getting all her personal possessions back over to *'Rosselli's Roost'*. She considered asking Hank and Lil to help her, instead of bothering JR.

'But that won't work, will it? How can I pay them for their time?'

In the end she decided to load everything into her trusty Eldorado and do the job herself, even if it meant making several trips. That way she could stop at a jeweler's store on the first trip and, hopefully, sell one of her diamond rings. Dani needed money to live on, at least until her lawyer could get some of her assets released.

'And, thankfully, Digger didn't steal all of my good jewels!'

Poking around in her jewelry box yielded a three-carat, yellow, diamond ring; one of the first gifts Dani had ever received from HK. She paused before slipping it onto her ring finger, one last time. She thanked HK with all her heart and soul. With head bowed and eyes closed, Dani wiped away a tear and silently gave thanks to her late fiancé's memory.

'I miss you, darlin'. If you were still here, I wouldn't be going through any of this mess, would I?'

Dani wished she could afford to travel to Pennsylvania to place flowers at his monument. HK had been the *real* true love of Dani's life. They would be soul mates forever and she firmly believed that they would be re-united someday, in the spirit world.

***

Dani stepped out of the jewelers store with a ten-thousand-dollar cashier's check, tucked away safely in her purse. HK was still helping her, even from the grave.

Her car was stuffed full as she made her final trip up the driveway of her once-beautiful mansion. She checked all around the outside before pulling the 'Eldorado' into the garage. Was it just her vivid imagination or did she see movement in one of the fifth-floor windows? She shook her head and silently rebuked herself.

'Dammit' Dani, stop being so paranoid'. But she closed the garage door securely before getting out of her car. She entered the house through the utility room, rather than going outside and in through the front door!

The house had been empty for some time now and it felt cold and unloved. Dani's footsteps on the tiled floor sounded loud. She missed Hank and Lil, who always used to greet her whenever she came home. Now there was no Hank; no Lil; no family; no husband; nothing! The only sounds Dani could hear were the echoing creaks of a lonely, empty house. There was no laughter, no love, no smell of dinner cooking nor any heady waft of fresh coffee brewing. Only the echoes of emptiness.

Dani was not looking forward to the next few hours but time went by faster than she expected. She unpacked, then double-checked that all the doors and windows were securely locked. She turned off all the lights, except for one small lamp in the kitchen in case she needed to come downstairs during the night.

On her way upstairs, it dawned on Dani that there wasn't much for her to come downstairs for anyway, not until she made a trip to the food market, tomorrow. The few things she had picked up on her way over there would barely keep hungry mice alive, if there were any!

'Oh well, I don't suppose leaving one light on in the kitchen will run up my electric bill too much!'

As she continued up the stairs, Dani made a mental note to watch her pennies more carefully. Her financial future was going to be unsettled for quite some time to come. She lit the fireplace in her bedroom to make the room feel cozier, then made up the fold-a-way bed that Hank had already brought over for her. He had also brought all of Dani's towels, bedding and other linens, as well as a portable television and a small chair! *'What a sweetheart!'*

Dani sighed, locked the bedroom door and ran herself a hot bath. She sank down into fragrant bubbles, courtesy of the hotel she had recently been staying in. Dani had packed every complimentary bottle she could find from her bathroom there! The only items she lacked were some scented candles and a glass of wine, but she could shop properly the next day! Today there had been no time and Dani had the aching bones to prove it. She leaned her head back on the rim of the tub and instantly dozed off.

The sound of breaking glass, downstairs, brought Dani up and out of her bath in seconds. Her heart was pounding but she was fully alert. She dried herself quickly and threw on a robe. Too afraid to leave the bedroom, she got her gun from under the pillow. She moved her chair to where it gave her a good view of the bedroom door. Then Dani sat, watched and waited. She heard footsteps moving, up and down the stairs, for well over an hour. Occasionally the bedroom doorknob slowly turned but no-one seriously tried to open it. Dani snatched the phone that lay on the floor next to the bed, but it wasn't working. Either someone had deliberately cut the line or had taken the kitchen extension off its hook. Dani listened intently. It sounded more like a phone off its hook than a severed line. Her heart was beating loudly as she screamed into the handset.

"Whoever you are, get the hell out of my house. I have a loaded gun here and I'm not afraid to use it!"

She fell back onto the bed, exhausted. Dani still gripped the gun in her right hand but had dropped the phone. Sobbing and crying, she pleaded with her invisible intruder.

"Please! *Please*! Just leave me alone!"

She pounded one fist against the bed until she could barely lift that arm, but fear and panic eventually wore her down and Dani cried herself to sleep.

***

At noon next day, she awoke to pounding on her bedroom door and the sound of her son's worried voice.

"Mom? Mom? Are you in there? Are you alright?"

Dani was exhausted and, at first, she wondered if the events of last night had all been some terrible nightmare. Then she felt the gun in her hand. She slipped it back under her pillow again before opening the bedroom door.

"JR, honey! I'm so glad to see you!"

Dani's eyes were so swollen, red and puffy from crying that she deliberately kept her face turned away from him.

"I went over to the hotel to help you move your stuff, Mom, but they said you'd already checked out. I've been trying to call all morning too, but the operator said your phone was off the hook so I decided to come over here in person. I saw your car in the garage, so I knew you were here."

JR suddenly realized that his mother wouldn't look at him. He gently put his hands on Dani's shoulders and turned her face toward him. It was obvious that she had been crying for hours, but he also saw fright and confusion in his mother's eyes.

"What's going on, Mom?"

Dani tried to speak but nothing would come out. She began shaking all over instead. JR cradled her in his arms and walked her over to the bed. They sat, side by side, until she had calmed down.

"There were all kinds of noises, all night long. I'm so scared, son. I feel like I'm losing my mind. I sat in that chair all night holding my gun, until I eventually cried myself to sleep. It was terrible!"

Dani started to tell him more but JR cut in. "It was probably just one of the house's friendly ghosts, Mom, welcoming you home!"

JR chuckled as he tried to ease his mother's fears but his face clearly showed his own, real concerns.

"It was no ghost, JR, friendly or otherwise. I heard glass breaking downstairs, I heard footsteps moving up and down the stairs for hours and then the kitchen phone was deliberately taken off the hook.

Dani took a deep breath and looked him in the eyes.

"There was definitely somebody else in this house last night!"

Dolores J. Guthrie

Chapter 39

JR left when all seemed normal again. They had checked the house together, every nook and cranny, so Dani felt brave enough to creep downstairs to prepare herself a suppertime tray. Yet when she reached her own landing again, she suddenly stopped. The fear came flooding back. It flowed over and around Dani like an invisible, shadowy fog as she once more heard the thumping of her own heart. She stood perfectly still with one hand on the door to her bedroom, certain that anyone close by would be able to hear her heart, too. She tried to mentally talk herself back into sanity.

'Come on, woman! If this is the same person, or thing, that was here last night; well, it didn't hurt you then so it won't hurt you now, will it?' Stay calm and don't do anything stupid.'

Dani had to force herself to enter her own bedroom. Still holding the tray, she took a deep breath and peeked inside first. She pushed the door open wide, in case someone should be lurking behind it. The terrace doors were wide open and a slight breeze wafted the sheer curtains.

'Those doors were definitely closed and locked when JR and I searched the house earlier!' Dani tiptoed inside and quietly placed the tray on her dresser. Slowly, she crept toward the bed to retrieve her gun from beneath the pillows. She was shaking so badly that she couldn't get the safety catch off. *'Don't panic, dammit; you'll only make things worse!'*

She knew that JR wouldn't return for several hours yet; he had gone over to his fiancée's house. Dani reached for the phone to call 911 but the line was dead, yet again! She hung up and hurried over to lock the terrace doors once more. But fear took charge and she froze. Her mind wandered off at tangents, intuitively aware that something dreadful was about to happen but having no idea what it might be.

Was Digger simply trying to drive Dani crazy, or did he really mean to kill her? She prayed that he was only trying to scare her, but couldn't understand *why*. Dani made a wry face as she recalled one of her granny's old sayings; *'revenge has a sweet foretaste but a bitter aftertaste'*. Could mere revenge be what such unrelenting harassment from Digger was all about?

Dani had once truly loved the man. She had given him a life of luxury that he could only have dreamed of before he met her. Digger had everything a man could want yet it had never seemed enough for him. All Dani did was to catch him in bed with another woman, but did Digger honestly expect her to live her whole lifetime with such cheating ways? *'Why is it so important to Digger to completely ruin my life?'*

It was all about money, Dani knew that in her heart, but she still couldn't understand how a person could become so evil and twisted over mere money. Her late fiancé, HK, had been a billionaire, yet he was the most generous man Dani had ever known. Digger had youthful good looks, wit and charm but had turned out to be a real low-life. The kind of selfish scrounger who stops at nothing to get whatever he wants.

Dani always tried to see the best in people. She couldn't help it; it was in her nature *and* in her upbringing. Even at that moment, afraid for her very existence, she tried hard to think of something good to say about her ex-husband. But the only thing that kept coming to mind was how badly Digger had deceived her from the very beginning. Dani's money was the only thing the man had really wanted. And now that he had taken most of it, he was about to move on to some other unsuspecting victim. Yet even knowing all that, Dani's trusting nature still refused to consider that she might be at risk of death, at the hands of the man she had once given her heart to.

She tried to breathe shallowly in order to listen. She had heard movement again above her, as if someone was walking around up there.

'Hopefully, it's just one of my home-grown ghosts.'

Dani's mind was a wreck. She badly needed to relax. She spied the jug of hot cocoa and peppermint 'Schnapps' sitting on the food tray she brought upstairs with her. It would be cold now but that didn't stop Dani from drinking the entire pitcher! The relaxing effects kicked in almost instantly. As alcohol-mellowed sensations warmed her soul, Dani heard another noise. This time it came from the sitting room, right next to her bedroom. She sobered up fast!

'I can't take much more of this.'

Dani suddenly saw things clearly. In her mind's eye, she could see Digger breaking into her suite through the terrace doors. He would have been disturbed when Dani came back upstairs. But he could have climbed up the ivy outside, gained entry again on the fifth-floor and then ridden the 'dumbwaiter' back down again. Very few people knew about her mansion's dumbwaiter system but Digger was *one* of the few!

'I just know it's him!'

With gun in hand, Dani hurried over to the terrace doors. She stepped outside, closing the doors quietly behind her. With one hand braced on the stucco wall of the house, she peered over the wrought iron railings. There was nowhere to go from that terrace, except down!

Dani gently moved a ceramic pot containing a large, evergreen bush and crouched down to hide behind it. She remembered to take off the safety catch this time before cradling her gun against her chest, holding it tightly in both hands. It was aimed directly at the French doors like a bomb waiting to go off. Dani's eyes were wide open and her teeth were clenched in terror.

She was well hidden but after a while her legs started to cramp up. She would have to move again soon, in order to relieve the pain. Very carefully, Dani moved the planter just enough to allow her to peek inside, through the open slats of the louvered-terrace doors.

At first she couldn't see anything, then she caught a brief glimpse of someone taking a drag from a cigarette. She jerked her head back and her heart began to pound again. A tight lump of fear filled her throat, but Dani forced herself to stay calm and concentrate. If she were to shoot and kill some total stranger how would she ever live with the guilt? Even if it were self-defense, how could Dani *prove* it? The way the courts had been shaft-ing her over money lately, what was to keep them from simply hanging her outright? Then there was no more time for thought as a well-remem-bered, silky-smooth voice, sent chills of terror down Dani's spine.

"Honey? Is that you?"

The French doors opened and Digger stepped out onto the terrace.

"Dani, my love; why on earth are you hiding from *me*?"

Digger switched on a flashlight and its beam swept all around the terrace, coming to rest on Dani's face. He shifted the light downward just far enough to realize that she was holding a gun. Dani said nothing, but pressed against the stucco wall to balance herself. Slowly, she rose into a standing position whilst keeping the gun aimed at the center of Digger's chest. As he spoke again, she began to shake so badly that the weapon nearly slipped out of her hands.

"Hey little darlin, it's *me*! Digger? I'm not going to hurt you, babe; I'm a lover, not a killer. See, I don't even have a gun; just this little ol' knife here."

The blade flashed in the torchlight and Dani screamed.

"Get out of here Digger! Just turn around and leave my home right now or I swear I'll shoot!"

"Now why would you want to kill me, Dani'?"

"Ha! Why *wouldn't* I, after all you've done to me? Get out of my house, right now, Digger or I'll shoot!"

"Give me the damn gun, bitch!"

The tone of Digger's voice turned violent in an instant and he lunged forward, slashing wildly at Dani. The knife blade gouged her forearm, from wrist to elbow. As he pulled away from her, Dani's gun exploded and he fell backward onto the terrace, blocking the doorway.

Dani stepped out from behind the planter and made to climb over him, but Digger reached up and grabbed at her arm. He gripped it firmly, turning the gun downward and dragging himself up off the floor at the same time. Leaning all his weight on Dani whilst shoving her backwards, he pinned her up against the wrought-iron railing. Digger's eyes frantically searched around for the knife but he couldn't locate it in the dark. He tried once more to yank the gun from Dani's inexperienced hands, but she was fighting for her life. Letting go was not an option.

In the intense struggle that followed, the gun went off again. The two of them fell over the railing together, landing on the third-floor balcony, twenty feet below. Dani felt bones breaking as she landed flat on her back, with Digger on top of her. She could hardly breathe for the excruciating pain and the extra weight of her ex-husband. Warm blood was oozing all over her neck and chest, but Dani had no idea whose blood it was. In a blind panic she tried to push Digger off, but the unconscious man was far too heavy for her to move.

Dani's desperate screams went unheard, her voice subdued by her agonizing pain. Then everything went black in her world.

***

At the sound of the very first gunshot, Dani's neighbors had already called 911. She was faintly aware of the harsh sound of sirens all around her, but had no memory at all of getting down from that third-floor floor terrace and into the ambulance, parked in her driveway.

Dani briefly regained consciousness, but felt as though she were taking part in some disaster movie. Police officers and their patrol cars were everywhere and medics were about to load Dani into the back of the ambulance. She was firmly strapped to a backboard, with supporting braces on her neck, arms and legs. As the medics tilted her gurney up to get it into the ambulance, Dani saw a second gurney off to one side. It held a shapeless lump inside a blood-stained body bag. All that remained of Digger Rosselli.

Some of Dani's neighbors were whispering in a huddle. Others were giving statements to the police. And there were other folk simply drawn in off the street, gawking at the spectacle. As the medics closed the ambulance doors, Dani looked back at her beautiful home. She would later swear that someone looked out from one of her fifth-floor windows. Then darkness enveloped her once more.

***

With disbelief in their minds and hearts at everything that had befallen their beloved daughter, Laura and Harold Gunther drove up from Salem. They waited for JR in the lobby of St. Vincent's Hospital. When he arrived, Laura placed loving arms around her worried grandson and told him all she knew, which wasn't very much.

"Honey, it seems that Digger was actually trying to kill your mother. Dani either killed him in self-defense, or her gun went off accidentally, during the struggle. But we won't know for sure until the police have finished their investigations."

"The bastard!" JR eyes were full of more questions but they would have to wait. His first concern was for his injured mother. "But what are Mom's injuries?"

This time it was his grandfather who answered.

"We're waiting for the doctor to come out and talk with us again, son."

"Your Mom is still in surgery, but he *did* say that he thought she would be fine. He was a little concerned about her spine, because she fell hard, son, but mostly they're worried about her mental condition."

"Why? What did that sonofabitch do to her?"

"No one knows exactly what happened, JR, but he attacked Dani in her own bedroom! They both somehow fell over the terrace railing and landed on the balcony below. Your Mom landed flat on her back, with Digger on top of her. She was drifting in and out of consciousness before they took her into surgery, so she wasn't able to tell us much of anything at all."

"Shit! I should have been there with her. "JR was gutted that he hadn't been there to defend his mother.

"She asked me to stay overnight but I had already arranged to go over to my fiancée's house. I know Mom was pretty scared, because a lot of weird things had been happening in that house lately, but we checked the whole house together before I left! *Damn!* Why didn't I just stay with her for *one* lousy night? This would never have happened if I had taken Mom more seriously. I thought she was only imagining things; you know, because of all the stress she's been under lately"

"*I* can't believe you left her alone either, JR."

Laura Gunther was not normally an angry person, but she was beside herself with worry over her eldest daughter. "Nothing is more important than your own mother, JR. I know she's been through a lot lately, but Dani isn't crazy. At least not yet!"

Laura began to cry as her grandson begged her forgiveness.

"I'm really sorry, Grandma."

Tall, handsome JR looked down at his tiny grandmother. "But who could have thought that Digger would really try to *kill* Mom?"

"Not your fault son. *I* should have killed the asshole myself, a long time ago!"

Harold Gunther was pacing back and forth, slamming one fist into the palm of the other hand. "Now look what that crazy bastard has done to my little girl: she may never be the same again."

Silent tears ran down the rugged lawman's cheeks and JR moved over to give his grandfather a hug.

"She'll be fine, Grandpa. You know how strong-willed Mom is. You should have seen the mess she was in when they pulled her out of the ocean, back in Hawaii. If it was ever Mom's time to go it would have been back then, believe me."

Laura moved over to join them both and they all linked arms. The three of them bowed their heads and Laura instinctively began to pray.

"Our Father; we come before you today to ask for your blessings on the precious life of our daughter and JR's mother, Dani Sutton. She has suffered terrible injuries after an unprovoked attack and needs your strength to see her safely through this ordeal, Lord. Amen."

They finished their prayers and were drying their tears as the senior doctor came into the lobby. He held out a hand to each of them in turn.

"I'm so glad to see that you made it here safely. As you probably remember, Dani and I grew up in the same neighborhood so I know your daughter very well. Even as a child, she always lived on the edge and seemed invincible to the rest of us kids. Nothing and no-one could get the best of Dani, it seemed, but this time she has been one *very* lucky lady indeed."

"But what *are* her injuries, Doctor?" Laura wanted the full details.

"Dani has extensive bruising to her spine but, amazingly, no fractures there!"

"She *does* have a fractured right fibula though, with a below-the-knee walking cast already put in place. She also has a cast on her right wrist, to fix some small breaks there."

"My poor baby!" Laura moaned. "But the police said something about her being stabbed as well?"

"Yes! She has a long, slash wound on her right forearm but we've cleaned it up and sutured it well. It should only leave a faint scar. We've also put her on antibiotics, to help prevent infection. All in all, Dani's medical injuries are quite minor considering the terrible fall she took."

"So when can we see her?" Laura, like any mother, was anxious to see the damage for herself.

"You can probably see her in a couple of hours, after she leaves the recovery room, but I must insist on only a very brief visit today. I want to keep Dani in the ICU for at least a day or two, so that she can be monitored for any other injuries that could show up later. She's very heavily sedated at the moment, as you can imagine, so we won't know what her mental state is, or how much Dani remembers, until she wakes up fully; probably in a few days' time. The police will need to get a statement from her, too, just as soon as she is able to talk."

"Are you saying that our Dani might have some brain damage?" Harold Gunther had remained quiet since his earlier outburst.

"No, but she does have a slight swelling of her brain. The scan didn't show any actual bleeding but this is something we always watch out for during the first forty-eight hours after *any* fall. Dani landed on a very hard, tiled floor and hit the back of her head pretty hard. We have a top Neurosurgeon already lined up, just as a precaution, but we don't expect to be using his services anytime soon. Believe me; we have a very experienced trauma team here and Dani will be monitored very closely. Your daughter's in very good hands, folks."

"Thank you, very much, Dr." Laura's voice sounded weak, even to her own ears.

"After you see Dani tonight, I want you all to go home and get some rest. You all need to take care of yourselves because Dani will need to draw on *your* strength in the days and weeks to come. The staff will call you immediately if there are any real concerns about her condition."

Dr. Mackey shook their hands again, before leaving them waiting for Dani to return from surgery. Laura grabbed hold of Harold's hand and looked her husband in the eye.

"We won't have to stay in that horrible house of Dani's when we leave here will we, dear?"

"Not on your life." Harold patted his wife's arm reassuringly.

"It will have been sealed off as a crime scene by now anyway, so we'll get ourselves a room at the Hilton. It's closer to this hospital, too. JR, are you coming with us?"

"No! I'll stay over at my girlfriend's house, but I'll meet you folks back here in the morning."

***

Dani's family met up next morning and it was obvious that no-one had really slept. They were all worried about Dani but mostly about her mental state. It was extremely fragile and they knew it. But they silently celebrated the fact that Digger was finally out of their lives forever. The man had caused so many problems for Dani *and* for all her friends and relatives.

Her parents and her son kept a continual vigil at Dani's bedside over the next few days; praying hard and waiting for her to wake up. For the first thirty-six-hours she squirmed around a lot, moaning and groaning. Dani's eyes opened properly on the second day but she simply stared vacantly, up at the ceiling.

She showed no signs at all of recognizing her family, either by sight or by their voices. Instead, she had a terrified expression in her eyes and every so often a single tear would roll down her pale face to drip onto the pillow.

Laura Gunther bent to kiss her daughter, trying hard to hold back tears of her own. She was determined to stay positive for Dani's sake.

"Dani, honey? Can you hear me? You are safe now and in the hospital. And we are all here with you, too; me, Papa and JR. We love you very much and we want you to get well, my darling, so don't you worry about a thing. Just rest, now."

Laura rejoined her husband in the waiting room, where he was already talking with Dr. Mackey again. Harold squeezed his wife's hand as she sat beside him and then turned his attention back to the doctor.

"What has happened to our baby? Will Dani *ever* recognize any of us again?"

"We believe that Dani's reaction is due to the prolonged strain that Digger Rosselli put her under. Not just this final attack on her life, but the mental and emotional abuse that he subjected Dani to over a very long period of time."

"Is it treatable, though?" Harold Gunther's voice cracked, in spite of his best efforts.

"I have discussed her case with our neurosurgeon and *he* feels that Dani would benefit from some shock therapy treatment."

"Shock therapy!

Laura put her hands over her mouth in horror. "Surely that kind of thing is cruel and inhumane?"

"Please, Laura, hear me out." Dr. Mackey had been expecting such a reaction from Dani's immediate family.

"Shock treatments have proved extremely effective in producing short-term amnesia, which is exactly what Dani needs in order to forget the horrifying memories of Digger Rosselli. And these modern treatments are not like the ones of twenty years ago, you know. The patient is sedated first and has absolutely no memory of the procedure afterward." Dr. Mackey's tone became more serious.

"Our psychiatric team feels that a series of three to five treatments would probably bring Dani out of her severe depression and give her the best opportunity of living a full life again. In my opinion too, it's certainly worth a try."

"When would they start?" Harold wanted to know.

"Assuming that you, as Dani's family, all agree with this option, Dr. Babson has made arrangements for her to be transferred to the State Psychiatric Hospital, in Salem, sometime next week. Her physical condition should be stable enough by then to allow her to be moved."

"She will then be evaluated extensively before any treatments commence to confirm that she meets all the criteria and is an appropriate candidate for such drastic therapy. Please, believe me, I wouldn't support this option if I didn't truly feel it was the best thing for Dani, in the long-term."

***

Dani remained awake, but non-responsive, for the rest of that second day. She gazed straight ahead, face expressionless. After a bath she was helped into a wheelchair for the first time. Her right leg, in its cast, was supported in front of her and her right arm, also in a cast, rested on a pillow in her lap. She responded to her name with a slight nod, but showed no interest in what was happening around her. People came in and out of her room and they all looked familiar, but Dani didn't know who they were. If someone spoke directly to her, she kept her eyes locked, facing forward. *'They know my name so I must know them, mustn't I?'*

From time to time she opened her mouth, as if to speak, but no sound came out. Up until then, Dani had been on medication so sleeping hadn't been a problem, but she didn't sleep at all that night. She stared up at assorted, damp stain patches on her ceiling, trying to remember.

'What happened to me? Where the hell am I and why am I here? Who are all these people that keep hovering around my bed? Am I dead, already?'

Dani spent a full week in St. Vincent's Hospital. Her broken bones were healing well and the Occupational Therapy team had taught her how to walk with crutches and how to dress and undress without help. Having casts on her right arm *and* leg made the process more difficult, but Dani quickly mastered the technique. Yet during the whole of that week, she had not uttered one single word, nor recognized *any* of her family.

On the eighth day, Dani and her wheelchair were loaded into an unmarked white van by a nurse and a driver. Dani felt good. She was out in the fresh air and there was so much to see. She had no idea where she was going but seemed not to care. When the van pulled up outside the huge, dirty, brick building that was the *'Oregon State Mental Hospital'*, Dani had no idea that she was entering an asylum. The nurse who had accompanied Dani handed over her medical records to the receptionist and then left.

"Hello Dani! This will be your home for a while, until you get completely well again."

The new receptionist sounded friendly enough, but that did not change the fact that Dani was now alone, frightened and among strangers. Her eyes grew large as she tried to concentrate on what was happening around her. A lot of people were milling about aimlessly in a large room off to Dani's left.

Some were drooling uncontrollably. Some were crying. One man was even tied to his chair by a belt-like device. He was naked and his clothes were scattered on the floor, all around him. The overpowering smell of urine was appalling! This wasn't like any hospital that Dani had ever been in before!

'Oh, my god! Where am I?'

She started to cry, though she didn't know exactly why. An older, black male orderly took charge of Dani's wheelchair and he gently guided her down a long, narrow hallway. They entered a bare room. It had no furniture, except for twin beds with super-flat mattresses and there was only one blanket on each bed. There was no private bathroom, either. There were no pictures on the walls and no curtains at the window. Dani gasped when she saw tiny, mesh wires embedded in the window glass. Then she saw that the window glass in the door had the same wires. *'Where in the hell am I?'*

As he was leaving her, the black orderly spoke quietly.

"Don't you worry now, honey; you'se goin' t'be just fine. You'se here to get yo'self well again and we'se here to help you."

Dani struggled out of the chair and sat on the bed. She looked down at an ugly hospital gown, lying on the bed beside her and then at her two casts. She was hungry but couldn't remember whether she had already eaten that day or not. When she tried to call for help, no sound came out of her mouth. She couldn't seem put any coherent thoughts together, either. Dani lay down on the bed and curled up into the fetal position. A single tear rolled across the bridge of her nose and plopped onto the sparse bed-covers. Then another tear fell. And another. As each hot, salty tear fell Dani counted them until, at last, she fell asleep.

***

After that the days and nights all seemed to run together for Dani. She had absolutely no conception of time.

There was no meaning to anything for her, either. She was in a whole new world and didn't like it one bit. At least three different doctors examined her daily and asked countless questions, but Dani still said nothing. She only nodded or shook her head in reply. Therapists and even the regular nurses constantly tried to get her to talk, but without success.

Dani had tests every single day, for what seemed like forever. Blood tests; heart tests; brain tests, you name it! She had Occupational Therapy working with her, too, trying to improve her walking skills. Dani showed her reluctance to use her crutches by throwing them on the floor, each time they were handed to her. The therapist finally gave up and watched Dani hobble around on her own until she felt that her stubborn patient was safe enough, doing it her own way.

Nurses gave out several pills every day, which Dani tried to pocket in her cheeks to spit out later, but that didn't work. The nursing staff were 'hip' to *all* the patients' tricks and watched her swallow each and every pill! Dani became so bored with the whole process that she took to sitting in a corner by herself and watching the *real* 'crazy' people all around her.

One lady had already pulled out most of her own hair. Another patient, a man, walked around hunched over all the time. He was constantly picking up dirt and lint off the floor and eating it! Another man rocked silently in his chair for hours on end. And there was also the naked man who was always secured to his chair. The staff re-dressed him constantly but to no avail. He would immediately pull all his clothes off again. Staff and patients alike did their best to stay clear of him as much as possible, because the man had a mean attitude, grabbing out at anyone who walked by.

The terrible urine smell that Dani noticed when she first arrived had either gone or she had become used to it, because it didn't seem to bother her anymore.

But watching all these strange people, for hours on end, made her increasingly uneasy until she couldn't stand it any longer. On the evening of the sixth day, Dani screamed her first words, at the top of her lungs!

"*Somebody,* help me! How did I wind up in this goddamned loony bin? I need a cigarette, too. I need a damned cigarette. And where the *hell* is my family?"

Dani was enraged and began hobbling around the massive room on her walking cast. With her one good arm, she started throwing other patients' dinner trays onto the floor and knocking over all the empty chairs she could reach. Within seconds, aides came running from all directions and physically subdued Dani. It all happened so fast that she didn't have time to count them all.

"Well, *that* got a response didn't it?" She overheard one of the staff members chuckling and whispering to the others. "At least she's talking now and that's usually a good sign!"

Four male staff struggled to carry Dani to a small room without any windows. It had padded mats on the floor, ceiling and walls. They put a straitjacket on Dani's upper torso so that she couldn't take a swing at them. Then they secured leather restraints around her ankles too, to stop her from kicking out. It took a while to fasten one around her plaster cast but the staff managed to do it without hurting her. There were so many hands on Dani, all applying gentle pressure so that she could hardly move at all. But she could still scream and spit and Dani did plenty of that! At least before the medications they injected her with took hold.

Just before dozing off, Dani smiled and whispered to the nurses.

"All I asked for was a cigarette and I don't even smoke!"

Dani awoke as aides were removing all her restraints three hours later. The friendly, black man was back on duty and he helped Dani to her feet.

"Sorry ma'am! We really *are* here to help you, you know. But now that we know you can talk again your stay here will be much shorter, especially if you cooperate with us."

His strong arms helped Dani back to her room where she clambered into bed, utterly worn-out. She slept right through the night, for the first time since leaving the other hospital.

***

The next morning heralded a big day for Dani. Now that she was talking again, her doctors decided to take advantage of their window of opportunity. They scheduled a family conference to obtain permission for future treatments and included Dani in their discussions. They wanted to explain things to her, obviously, but they also wanted to try to determine the depth of Dani's returning comprehension. Her parents and JR arrived early, as they had done every day since the shooting incident.

It was a pleasant surprise when Dani called all of them by name, even though she spoke in a strange monotone. It brought tears of joy to Laura's eyes but Dani was still not her old-self, not by any means. Doctors explained the pros and cons of using 'electroshock' therapy. They said that Dani's lucidity would come and go for quite a while as a result of the treatments and they also said that the family shouldn't expect too much right away.

"Even though Dani spoke yesterday and again today, her speech and behavior patterns will be quite sporadic during what will be a long, healing process. The purpose of using electroshocks is to give Dani amnesia of the more recent events. A sort of 'resting' of her brain, so to speak."

"Then we can then use regressive hypnotherapy and other analysis techniques to uncover the real roots of Dani's problems. Only then will she be able to go forward and become healthy again. As we tap into her subconscious, we will see a wide range of behaviors from her. These will depend, to some extent, on her family history but mostly on her own ability to handle the stress of slowly remembering extremely traumatic, past events."

The head doctor was gentle, yet firm as he continued his deliverance of Dani's prognosis.

"We must *all* be very patient during the coming weeks. Recovery from mental stress is always a very slow process. It can take a patient many weeks, if not months to make real progress. And, more often than not, progress involves taking five steps backward to accomplish *one* single, step forward! But I am confident that Dani will be fine when this is all over."

The neurologist smiled and winked at Dani.

"From all that I've observed, Dani here seems to be a very strong-minded, young woman!"

Dani said nothing at all during the whole consultation but her medical team was certain she had understood at least a part of what they were saying. They had been studying her facial expressions and body language throughout the entire meeting.

Her son was also quiet. JR sat with his head bowed, occasionally nodding to show his agreement with whatever was being discussed. Dani's parents, however, said plenty; mostly about their understandable safety concerns. After ninety minutes, the family had *all* agreed to proceed as planned, knowing that there were no guarantees but feeling hopeful because of all that the doctors had told them.

Circumstances didn't really leave them very much choice; not if they wanted Dani to lead a full and happy life, ever again.

They signed the consent papers without hesitation, but with heavy hearts at the enormous gamble they were taking with Dani's health. The first treatment was to be given that same afternoon.

Dani understood that the doctors and her family were trying to help, even though she was still confused about these 'treatments' they kept talking about. She, too, wanted nothing more than to be back to her old self again. So when the nurse delivered the pre-op medication, Dani accepted it without a murmur!

Next day, she remembered nothing at all of the procedure, nor did Dani have any memory of the treatment room, or of any equipment that had been used. Her muscles were stiff and sore and she felt extremely tired, so Dani simply lay down and drifted in and out of sleep for several hours.

Chapter 40

Three months later, Harold and Laura Gunther returned to Dr. Babson's office for an update on their daughter's progress.

"Good to see you both again!"

The doctor strode out from behind his massive, mahogany desk and held out a strong hand to greet them. The Gunthers were obviously disappointed at their daughter's apparent lack of progress. He could see the hurt in their eyes but Dr. Babson did his best to make them feel comfortable. He moved across to a side table which contained a wide variety of drinks and snacks, offering them their choice.

"Two black coffees please, but nothing to eat. We've just had lunch, but thanks for the offer."

There were two armchairs in front of Dr. Babson's desk and Harold motioned for his wife to sit down. There followed a short period of nervous, small talk between them all, which allowed their coffees to cool down a little before Dr. Babson began to speak more seriously.

"I have asked you here today because I need to get a better insight into your daughter's past life experiences. As we've already discussed, the electroshock treatments have been very successful, so far, in blocking Dani's short-term memory. But her progress now seems to have come to a standstill. Some quite large pieces seem to be missing from her 'life-puzzle'. That is most unusual and not at all what we expected, so we must adjust our treatment plan."

"We now need to concentrate on regaining Dani's long-term memory, because she needs to work through those issues that her subconscious mind has blocked out."

The doctor took off his glasses and polished them carefully, giving Harold and Laura a few moments to absorb his explanations.

"You see, in humans, the subconscious mind is able to block out the memory of certain catastrophic events, in an attempt to protect the individual from too much stress. This can often be a good thing but in Dani's case it most definitely is *not*. Before we can begin to tackle her recollections of Digger's death, we must tap into Dani's past so that she can begin to put any *older* traumatic events into proper perspective. In the beginning, we believed that Dani's was a clear-cut case of 'sudden-onset amnesia', caused by a single, traumatic event. But I'm afraid her case is much more complicated than that."

Dr. Babson paused again before delivering his radical proposals for Dani's future treatment.

"We now believe that Dani is suffering from a condition called, 'PTSD'. That means 'Post-Traumatic-Stress-Disorder' and the syndrome is especially common among military personnel, as a result of the dreadful events they may have witnessed during the heat of battle."

"We would like your permission to use a new technique, known as 'regressive hypnosis' on your daughter. I want to take Dani back to the very earliest years of her life and then slowly bring her forward to the present, identifying any traumatic issues she may have experienced along the way. Only when Dani can talk openly about past events can she even begin to process Diggers violent death and express her feelings concerning it. I honestly believe that with this new treatment program and plenty of time, your daughter will make a *full* recovery."

"So what can we do to help?" Harold and Laura spoke in unison.

"I need you to tell me *everything* you can remember about Dani's early life, starting from the moment she was born, or even *before* that if you think it might be significant."

"Oh, Harold, you should tell the doctor all about that stuff. You can explain it much better than I ever could."

Laura Gunther lowered her head as if somehow ashamed and her instinctive gesture was not lost on Dr. Babson. He made a few brief notes and committed the incident to memory as Harold Gunther cleared his throat, squeezed his wife's hand and began his recollections.

"Well, Doctor, it seems to me that our Dani has always lived kind of a stormy life! It started on the very day she was born, with the worst storms in the history of Oklahoma City. That day was June 2, 1932, when all electric power in the city was shut down by storms."

"I was just nineteen years old at the time. Laura here was even younger; only seventeen she was and pregnant with Dani, our second child. Neither of us will ever forget that dreadful day. I was driving around fallen trees and 'hot' wires from all the downed power lines. There were overturned cars too and all kinds of debris from the tornados and torrential rains that were destroying Oklahoma City."

"Laura was lying down in the back of our 1931 Plymouth as I glanced in my rearview mirror. She was being very brave, yet she seemed frail as she tried to hold back her labor pains. All I could do was to keep reassuring her. *'Yes, we would get to the hospital in time and yes, everything would be just fine!'* But about ten minutes later, she started screaming."

"I must confess to feeling a bit angry, because Laura hadn't told me she was in labor until she was in real serious pain. I was scared to death that our new baby would be a breech birth, like our firstborn, Harold Jr. Young Harold was nineteen-months old by that time. Sweat was pouring off me as I negotiated all the obstacles on the road, but I knew I had to stay calm for Laura's sake."

"In an attempt to put her sobs out of my mind, I forced myself to think about all kinds of other things. I even thought about where I used to live as a kid and about the irony of it all. You see, I grew up on our old, family dairy farm, five miles south of Oklahoma City."

"We owned eighty acres of prime grazing property land until we lost it all during the great depression of 1929. Nowadays, we rent a house from the *very* same bank that foreclosed on our family farm."

"I remember thinking about Franklin D. Roosevelt, too; he was our President at the time. He promised to repeal prohibition, eliminate all the soup lines and reduce unemployment. His predecessor, Herbert Hoover, had also promised us poor folk *'a chicken in every pot and prosperity for all'*. Them promises had all sounded splendid but instead, everyone in this country lost not only their pot, but also the place to put it!"

"You should have seen him then, doctor." Laura suddenly spoke up with a dreamy look in her eyes. "My Harold was six-foot, two-inches and weighed one-hundred-and-eighty pounds. He had jet black hair with long sideburns and beautiful, olive skin that showed off his deep-brown eyes. Everyone in town knew him, you see. He was known as 'the Gunther boy'; always dashing around town in his 1929 Bentley! He reminded us girls of a young Rudolph Valentino; always with a smile on his face, love in his heart and the world at his feet. Oklahoma City was built by and named after, Harold's great-grandfather, you know. I couldn't believe that *I* was the girl who had won his heart. I was only fifteen years old, then!"

"OK, dear, thank you!" Harold Gunther was more than a little embarrassed. He actually began to blush but the doctor merely smiled.

"I need to finish Dani's story, dear. I'm sure Dr. Babson doesn't have all day."

Harold patted his wife's hand to lessen the rebuke before carrying on with his recollections.

"Anyway, right then lightning struck the road a few feet ahead of us, forcing me back to reality."

"It tore up the street like a whip ripping at bare flesh and the force of it rocked our car violently. Laura was flung to the floor as I had to slam on the brakes. I pulled over and helped her get back onto the seat but we were both in tears by that time. Her waters had broken during the fall, which meant that her labor was already in its final stages. I placed a pillow under her back but I could smell the hot, sweet, smell of blood and I knew that my wife was not doing well."

"She was afraid that the baby would be stillborn and it was obvious that panic was setting in with her. I saw that large, jagged, hole in the road ahead and knew I had no choice but to turn around and head for a different hospital. I prayed like never before, begging God to keep them both alive and safe until I could get us over there. I made promises from the bottom of my heart and I even threw in one about moving us all out west, far away from that Oklahoma dust bowl and all its bad memories!"

"You see, earlier in that year of 1932 several members of our family had already pulled up roots and moved away from Oklahoma, to 'God's country' as they called it. They meant the State of Washington, sir, but our plans to join them out there were scuppered by the expectation of our second child. I had heard from my Uncle Herbie that food was plentiful out there in Grandview, Washington State. Good fruit and produce were all going to waste, he said, because no-one had any money to buy them!"

"I turned the car around, but Laura had become as quiet as a church mouse. I thought she may have already bled to death, but I kept on going anyhow. The storm raged on, slamming sagebrush, dirt and all kinds of debris against our car. Fine sand totally covered the windscreen, making driving a nightmare."

"The tornado was getting closer too, roaring louder and louder like a thundering locomotive until it completely enveloped our car. Then, in a split second, it was dead calm again!"

"It seemed as if long minutes of silence passed us by, but it was really only seconds before the wind tore at us again; rocking the car, lifting it up and slamming it down again against the dirt road. I managed to hang onto the steering wheel but I could see my poor wife's limp body being bounced around in the back seat. The wind was so strong it even picked up a cow and slammed it against our car. The poor animal's front hoof came right through the windshield! The impact threw me against the windshield too, leaving me stunned and bleeding."

"But then I heard Laura crying. Only weak sobs at first but they were music to my ears. It meant she was still alive! The driver's door wouldn't budge, because our car was lying on its left side in a drainage ditch. So I waited for the tornado to pass, then I climbed out through the rear door. Then I carefully pulled Laura out the same way."

"I laid her on the ground, making her as comfortable as I could. Then I pulled large pieces of glass out of her foot, but the blood flowed freely. I bandaged the wound as best I could, using strips torn from my shirt. I checked Laura for other injuries, as her pulse was very weak and irregular, but I was overjoyed when I felt movement inside her swollen belly. I prayed again for the safety of my wife *and* our child."

"No-one was around to help us. I could see a farmhouse on fire in the distance but those poor folk had enough problems of their own. My chest felt as if the steering wheel was stuck inside it, but after one look at Laura, I knew I would lose them both if I didn't get help soon. Then the moon appeared through a gap in the storm clouds and the sky stayed clear long enough for me to get my bearings."

"The tornado had moved off into the distance by then and as I slowly turned around, full circle, I saw the sign of another hospital, about a half-mile away. I thanked God, over and over again, as I scooped up my wife into my arms. By then she was limp and unconscious again but I carried her all the way there."

"Debris in the hospital parking lot was evidence that it had only narrowly escaped those evil winds from the sky."

"Emergency staff met us at the door and took Laura from my aching arms and began working on her immediately. It was obvious, by all the blood and the size of her belly that my wife was well into her labor. I'd forgotten all about my own injuries until a nurse dragged me into the ER, where she stitched and bandaged my wounds."

"But before they were finished with me, a nurse came rushing in to ask if I knew Laura's blood type. Seems she had lost a lot of blood and needed a C-section immediately if they were going to save our baby. Luckily I did remember; it was O positive. I sat on a stool, watching the nurses and doctors working and I cried and prayed non-stop. I felt dizzy and sick, but before I had the time to pass out, someone shouted that our 'miracle' baby was here. One nurse swung our screaming little Dani by the ankles whilst another cut and tied-off the cord. And that's how she was born!"

"My heart sank again when someone yelled that Laura had quit breathing. The doctor grabbed a syringe of somethin' or other and rammed it directly into my wife's heart and I got to her bedside just in time to see her jerk, gasp and then take a massive breath. I just stood there blurry eyed, speechless and numb and then passed out! I think they were glad that I did though, so they could focus on my wife and child and not have to worry about me. I remember someone giving me a pillow and throwing a blanket over me but they left me on the floor where I lay!"

Harold chuckled as he recalled that.

"I remember sleeping really well that night but woke up feeling as if I'd been run over by a herd of cattle! And when I heard the sounds of chirping birds the next morning, I was amazed at how such tiny creatures could have survived such terrible tornados."

"My first visit to the Maternity Ward was a bit of a shock. Laura was as white as a sheet and had all kinds of tubes and needles going into her hands and arms. It was hard to believe that, three years earlier, she was the top, female gymnast at her High School. My Laura has always been strong, but she weighed only ninety eight pounds at that time and stood all of five-feet-two-inches tall!"

"She and our baby were in hospital for ten days, giving us plenty of time to choose a name for our miracle daughter. We eventually decided to name her after two beautiful and famous movie stars, in the hope that she would grow up to rival, or even exceed, their beauty and charm. That's why our little girl was christened Danielle Jean Gunther."

"On November 1 that same year the rest of the Gunther family, twelve of us in all, began our journey north to Grandview, Washington State, to join the rest of our clan. We even took along my seventy-year-old grandfather!"

"Harold Jr. was 2 years old by then and little Danielle was just five-months old. The four of us traveled in our ancient, patched-together Plymouth which was packed full with us and our worldly goods. We even towed a homemade trailer, loaded with the rest of our prized possessions. I had just thirty-four dollars to my name by that time, so my father paid our expenses for the trip."

"The stars served as our candles and God was our guide. It took us three, long weeks to get to Washington State but it was well worth the trip, doctor. We camped by streams at night, so we always had fresh water to drink, cook and bathe with. Most of the time we were dreadfully cold, though and about half way through our journey we began to wonder why we hadn't waited until spring! But we had no money left, you see, so we had no choice but to travel when we did. How little Danielle survived that long trip, I will never know. Old Grandpa Gunther said, *'That baby o' your'n will go far in life, Harold. She has the constitution of a government mule!'*

"As a small child, our Dani was pretty much a loner. She rarely played with the other children, she preferred to be around adults and of course her big brother, Hal. Our Dani worshipped Hal. Looking back, I suppose we were a bit too over-protective of our little girl, because of almost losing her."

"When she was about five, Dani started having nightmares and those lasted for almost four years. But we never knew *why*. Maybe with this new treatment you want to try, doctor, we might find out. Anyway, during her childhood we pretty much gave Dani everything she wanted and tried to keep her out of harm's way. We didn't want her to get sick, you see, nor to be afraid of anything so we kept her away from other kids until she went to school. Now I can see that perhaps we were wrong in many ways but we did the best we could at the time."

"The older Dani got, the needier she became. She seemed very inse-cure and craved lots of love and attention; much more so than other kids seemed to do. She used to cry a lot, saying that kids her own age didn't like her. Physically, Dani developed much faster than other girls did and was barely into puberty when she first started getting the attention of older boys. Of course, we tried to stop her having any contact with those older guys but we didn't have much success. I guess that's why our Dani rebelled and took off with an older boy. They got married when she was still chewing bubble-gum!"

"I guess Dani kept most of her growing up experiences to herself, so as not to worry her mother and me. So I can't help you with any problems she might have been going through during those early years, doctor."

"Our daughter is definitely a survivor, though. She has an iron will but still needs to be taken care of, in spite of my ol' Grandpa's prediction. I guess that's why our Dani has had more than her fair share of men, all of them losers."

"I think she thought that if they slept with her, it meant that they loved her. Now can you see how our Dani is so dependent on others, especially men?"

Harold Gunther was an excellent storyteller and hoped he had remembered enough to be helpful. But as her father, he hoped he hadn't said too much!

"Very interesting, Mr. Gunther. That was very interesting indeed!" Dr. Babson sounded genuinely intrigued. "Young Dani certainly had a unique beginning in life, there's no doubt about it. And yes, Harold; the information will be very helpful to me. I thank you both for sharing it with me."

Dr. Babson escorted them to the door. He had been given far more information than he could have hoped for, but he also realized that he and his team had a lot of work ahead of them.

"What will happen next then, with our Dani?" It was Harold who asked.

"I plan to start her on the regression-therapy next Monday. I'll take her back as far as she is willing to go and then, each session thereafter, I will bring her forward in time. It's a very slow process, I'm afraid, so we will have to wait and see how she progresses. Each patient goes at their own pace."

"Can we be present, doctor?" Laura asked, hesitantly.

"You may wait in the waiting room if you'd like to be close to her but, because of confidentiality issues, you may not *legally* be present during Dani's sessions. If you stop at the desk on your way out, my nurse will give you a copy of our schedule."

"Thank you doctor, very much." Harold spoke sincerely. "We just want to support our daughter in any way that we can."

Dolores J. Guthrie

Chapter 41

"Dani, can you hear me?"

Dr. Babson spoke in calm, even tones and leaned closer to his patient as she relaxed in the chair. Dani nodded her agreement so he continued to address her in the same steady, rhythmic voice.

"Do you remember me, Dani? I am Dr. Babson, one of your medical team."

He squeezed her hand. Dani's eyes were wide open, but she simply stared up at the ceiling with a blank expression on her face. She squirmed a little as if trying to get comfortable in the plush, fabric recliner beneath her. Dr. Babson gave her a pillow for her neck and she quietly thanked him.

Ever since completing her electroshock-treatment program Dani had been very quiet. She spoke every day, but usually only when she was spoken to. Occasionally she would say 'please' and 'thank you' for some service rendered. Dani was always very polite, but she never got involved in a real conversation. But her angry, raging episodes had subsided and so that was progress of a kind.

Today was to be Dani's first experience with hypnosis and Dr. Babson was cautiously optimistic.

After speaking with her parents, he had requested all of Dani's medical and psychiatric records from the previous ten years; the legal requirement for keeping such records. After evaluating an absolute mountain of paperwork, Dr. Babson was of the opinion that Danielle Sutton was a much stronger personality than her father portrayed. Yes, Dani had suffered trials and tribulations, all involving men, but in most instances she had managed to hold her head high and continue putting one foot ahead of the other. Dr. Babson felt that his patient was more naïve and lacking in education than anything else.

She was definitely not the smartest woman in the world, but Dani was kind and generous in her soul. Even though she tended to need a man in her life at all times, she had also demonstrated the ability to make some good decisions on her own.

Quite surprisingly, she had shown herself to be an effective business-woman, too; at least until she allowed men to step in and destroy her, both emotionally and financially. Dr. Babson's long-term goal for Dani would be to rebuild her self-esteem to where she was confident enough to live alone, comfortably and to manage her own life. He continued to speak in a quiet, measured tone of voice.

"Dani, I am going to help you to get your life back under control. Would you like that?"

"Oh, yes," she whimpered softly, "but will it hurt?"

"No, Dani," the doctor smiled, "there will be no physical pain, but recalling memories that you have kept buried for a very long time may prove uncomfortable for a little while. Just believe that I am here to help you and put your trust in me, Dani. It's important that you feel able to trust me for this new treatment to work properly, so can you do that, Dani?"

"Uh, huh!" Dani answered, a little shyly.

'He's a very nice man and very handsome too. That starched, white jacket and silver hair make him look very professional, not like those other men in white jackets that used to hold me down. Yes, I feel comfortable in this room, I feel comfortable in this chair and I feel comfortable with this man.'

Her rambling thoughts were interrupted by the doctor's soothing voice.

"Very well then; let's begin, Dani."

The doctor turned the room lights down and settled himself into a sofa chair about three feet away from his patient. He flipped the switch on a tape recorder on a side table, then crossed his knees to make a place to rest his note pad.

"Close your eyes now, Dani. I want you to take a deep breath in and then slowly let it out. Let go of all your tensions, Dani and forget about everything else except the sound of my voice. Let go of all your tensions and fears, now."

The doctor's naturally deep voice was soft and gentle, a soothing monotone to Dani's ears. He allowed himself a smile as she began to visibly relax.

"Starting with your feet, Dani, I want you to tighten all of the muscles in your toes. Now tighten those in the balls of your feet and your heels and then allow *all* of those muscles to relax until they begin to feel very, very heavy. Just relax, Dani. Now I want you to do the same with the muscles in your calves, in your knees and in your thighs. Tighten them all as hard as you can and then relax them until they begin to feel very heavy. Good! That's very good. Now take another deep breath in, Dani and as you slowly release all the air in your lungs I want you to concentrate on your feet and legs. Let go of any tension or stress in them and completely relax. Allow your legs and feet to feel very heavy and then completely r-e-l-a-x, Dani."

Dr. Babson continued speaking in the same monotone voice, slowly and softly.

"Keeping your eyes closed, Dani, I now want you to tense your abdomen, your pelvis and your buttock muscles. Hold them tightly for a moment and then release every single muscle until they feel completely relaxed."

"Let go of all the tension in your body, Dani and simply relax."

"Concentrate on the sound of my voice and on becoming completely relaxed. Now tense all the muscles in your chest and back as hard as you can and then let them go, until they also feel heavy. Take in another deep breath, Dani and as you slowly breathe out you will blow away all the tension and stress from your body."

"Let go of all your tension Dani, right now. Relax all of your muscles until they feel so heavy you can no longer move. But you don't want to move, Dani, you only want to relax."

Dr. Babson paused to give her time to follow his repeated instructions.

"Now I want you to squeeze your hands into fists, Dani. Focus on every single finger and every little joint. Then release your hands and tighten all the muscles of your arms, as if you were preparing to 'box' an opponent. Now, relax your arms again until they feel heavy beside you, so heavy that you are unable to move them."

He paused again.

"Now I want you to rotate your neck from side to side, Dani. Tense your neck muscles and all of your jaw and face muscles. Tense even your lips, your eyelids and even your forehead and then relax all of these muscles, very slowly."

"Now take in a really deep breath once more, Dani, and as you slowly exhale you will blow away any remaining tension, stress and anxiety from within your body and mind. Let go of all of your stress and all of your fears. Your body is so relaxed now, Dani, that you couldn't move a muscle even if you wanted to. Now, clear your mind until you can think of nothing at all, Dani…nothing…nothing."

Dr. Babson's voice had become more insistent, but he maintained the same steady, rhythmic, monotone as before.

Dani's body was so totally at ease that she felt as if it were melting into the recliner that held her.

She no longer felt an empty, frightening numbness inside her brain. Her fears and emotional pains were gone, shooed away like a flock of starlings disappearing into the evening sky.

'What a wonderful feeling. Is this really me?' Dani marveled at how good she felt as she drifted off into a totally, unconscious state.

Dr. Babson was satisfied that his patient was completely under hypnosis. Her body was totally limp and flaccid and her eyes moved rapidly under closed eyelids; the 'rapid-eye-movement' phase that indicates a natural, 'dream' state.

"You can hear only *my* voice now, Dani and you will do everything that I instruct you to do. Breathe very slowly and easily, now. You are feeling really good, Dani but I want you to go down into an even deeper sleep. I want you to go back to a place in time where you are happy and laughing. Go back there now, Dani. Go back now."

Dr. Babson had taken complete control of Dani's mind and together they began the long journey back into her past. A smile came over her face and she began to giggle like a little girl.

"Dani, what are you doing right now?"

"I'm laughing at myself," Dani replied in a 'sing-song' voice.

"And why are you laughing at yourself?"

"I'm playing 'jacks' with my friend, Eileen. I moved my hand to catch the ball and fell over onto the sidewalk. I broke my front tooth off." Dani continued to chuckle.

"Why is that so funny, Dani?"

"Because Eileen says I look funny, I suppose. She's laughing at me and that makes me laugh too."

"How old is Eileen?"

"She's the same age as my big brother, Hal. They will both be thirteen next August."

"So you must be about eleven or twelve years old then, Dani?"

"Yes, I'm eleven."

"OK, so, let's move forward a bit. You are thirteen years old now, Dani. You're a teenager."

"Oh that's wonderful. I must be a woman."

"Why is that so wonderful, Dani?"

"You don't really want to know." Dani spoke, coyly. She even snickered a little.

"But I *do* want to know, Dani. I want to know everything about you" Dr. Babson continued to probe, gently but firmly.

"Well, I'm having my first period this week, you see. Isn't that wonderful! That means I'm a woman now."

"That's great, Dani." Dr Babson made copious notes, even though he was recording the session.

Dani sighed. "I think I'm in love."

"What makes you think that, Dani? You are very young to be in love at thirteen. Don't you think perhaps it's only puppy love?"

"Oh no, I'm sure it's *real* love. I feel so good you see, whenever I see Johnny or even think of him. And he loves me too."

"How do you know that Johnny loves you, Dani?"

"Because he's always trying to touch me in my private places, *you* know?"

Dani screwed her face into a shy smile and pulled at her clothes.

"Is this your first experience with sex, Dani?"

Dani pouted and her face transformed into a frown.

"I don't like sex. It hurts when we do that. Johnny said he was going to give me my first experience in sex so that I could become an adult. But it was really painful the first time and I was scared. I cried and told Johnny 'no' but he still did it anyway. I got used to it after a while, though. Now it only hurts a little bit each time we do it, but I'm still afraid."

"Why are you afraid, Dani?"

"Because my brother and Eileen are on the other side of the haystack and they will know what we're doing."

"So why do you let Johnny have sex with you then, Dani?"

"Curiosity, I guess. And I'm afraid he won't love me if I don't let him do it."

"How old is Johnny?'

"He's sixteen and he's my brother's best friend - next to Eileen, of course."

"So why do you think Johnny likes *you*, Dani, instead of going around with girls of his own age? He's close buddies with your brother, isn't he, so Johnny must know how old you are?"

"Oh yes! He knows how old I am but I look much older, you see and I have a *really* good figure. Johnny says I have bigger and better boobs than any girl he knows. He says he's liked me since I was only ten! Back then he used to try and kiss me and if I was off guard, he would grab my boobs. I used to push him away back then, though, because my boobs were tender and they hurt when he squeezed them. Johnny got really mad when I wouldn't 'play' and then he would say I was nothing but a goddamned kid."

"Johnny was a star athlete at our school and it made me feel real good to be around somebody like him. He could have any girl in our school if he wanted and said that he had already laid most of them."

Dani suddenly started to cry, rubbing at her eyes in a childish gesture.

"Dani, why are you crying?"

"Johnny says that if I won't let him touch me and all that stuff, then I'm just wasting his time, so he just left! He says I'm to give him a call when I want to act like a real woman. He didn't bother with me any more after that day. It hurt my feelings a lot and I missed him so much. He even quit coming over to our house to see my brother. Hal goes over to Johnny's house instead, now."

"Do you start seeing Johnny again, Dani?"

"Yes, a few months later. I sneaked in to see a football game and watched Johnny make the most awesome play ever. He had been hurt during an earlier session and was sitting on the bench, but then the coach put him back in as 'running back'. I was so afraid for him. I didn't want him to get hurt anymore, but in one wonderful play Johnny caught a pass and ran the whole length of the field to score the winning touchdown. He was grinning from ear to ear as he came off the field and tossed me the game-ball as he passed the bleachers where I was hiding. Johnny is my hero and I was so excited that he had acknowledged me again."

"What did that day mean to you, Dani?"

"It meant that Johnny's rage was over and that maybe he would love me again."

"And was that what happened Dani?"

"Oh, yes. It was just like old times when Johnny came over to our house later that night, to have dinner with us all."

"I was surprised to see him there and ran up to the bathroom to freshen up, so that I would look older to him. It had only been months, but it seemed like years, since Johnny had been to our house. When I walked back into the kitchen, Johnny said, 'you look great, kid!'

"I hated it when Johnny called me kid so I told him that I was all grown up by then. He grinned a big grin and said I had a great 'rack' and that he couldn't wait to touch them again, just like he used to. All evening he kept saying, 'wow' and we were both hoping that my Mom couldn't read our minds."

Dani sounded really excited."

"So what happened next?"

Dr. Babson had to ask the question, even though he already knew the answer.

"Well, everything happened, didn't it?" Dani giggled. "We got back together, didn't we? And we're *still* together, too, unlike a lot of couples at our school. Johnny's in High School now, but I'm still in the seventh grade. Most of the kids in *my* class don't even date yet!"

"Dani, you're thirteen years old right now, so do you ever think about things that might worry you?"

"Do you mean, like, worrying about stuff after it happens?"

Her face took on a puzzled frown as she tried to fathom what the doctor meant. But Dr. Babson remained silent. It was important that Dani figured things out for herself. Then her face suddenly brightened and she became very enthusiastic.

"Oh, I see what you mean. Stuff like, what if Johnny hadn't tossed me the game ball that day. And, what if Johnny hadn't hurt me with his 'you're just a kid' remarks and those 'when you grow up' comments? And what if my Dad hadn't given us tickets to go to the wrestling tournament that night?"

Dani stayed deep in thought for a moment, but then continued.

"And, what if Harold, Eileen and Johnny and me would have gone straight home after the wrestling tournament, instead of going to 'play' in the haystacks?"

Dani sighed.

"What do you learn, though, from all those *'what ifs'*, doctor? Can you really help me to turn back the clock?"

"Yes Dani, that's exactly what I'm going to do. I'm going to help you to remember the important facts from your *past* life, so that you can learn how to deal with the things that have affected you badly. Then you will be able to go forward with your *future* life and be healthy and happy. You are going to rest now, Dani and you won't remember anything about our discussions today. I'm going to count backwards now, from ten down to one and when I snap my fingers together, you will wake up feeling completely rested and refreshed."

"Ten – nine – eight – seven – six – five – four – three – two – and one. Wake up now, Dani."

Dr. Babson snapped his finger and thumb together loudly and Dani instantly opened her eyes. He shook her hand and said they had done some good work together that day. He also told her that they would continue to meet every Monday, Wednesday and Friday over the coming weeks. Dani was feeling totally relaxed and calm. She even smiled at the orderly who came to take her back to her room.

"That will be fine with me doctor. I feel really good right now."

Harold and Laura Gunther had been waiting outside all this time. And they were overjoyed to see a smile on their daughter's face as she held out her arms for a hug. It was the first time Dani had *really* smiled in many, long months.

Dolores J. Guthrie

Chapter 42

Dr. Babson started their next session exactly where he had left off. He needed to learn *much* more about Dani's troubled youth.

"Dani, it is still 1945 and you are still thirteen years old. So tell me what's on your mind today."

"It's very hot today. Everyone is really emotional and crying a lot."

"Who is crying, Dani?"

"*Everyone* is."

"What date is it, Dani?"

"It's August 6th, 1945. Mom and Dad came home from work early today and President Truman just announced on the radio that a plane called the 'Enola Gay' successfully completed its mission. The plane was a B-29 bomber and it was commanded by Colonel Paul W. Tibbetts. It dropped something called an 'atomic bomb' on a place called Hiroshima, in Japan. The bomb was nicknamed *'Little Boy'* and it was dropped at eight-fifteen in the morning, after waiting three days for bad weather to clear. Everyone is saying that World War Two is almost over! They are all crying tears of joy and some of sadness too, I guess, but isn't it wonderful news?"

"Yes, Dani, it is wonderful news. You remember the details of that day very well."

"My folks talked about that day for months afterward, it was such a big deal."

"Yes it was a very big deal, Dani, as you say. OK, let's move on to 1946. Where are you now?"

"Oh! I'm fourteen-years-old today and it's also my last day of school."

"All of my girlfriends are here, too and we are waiting for Johnny to pick me up. We are all very excited because Johnny and I are driving to Idaho today, to get married!"

Then Dani's expression suddenly changed and she began to cry.

"Oh no! Oh my!"

"Dani, what is happening? Why are you crying?" Dr. Babson probed gently for every small snippet of information.

"Oh, no! It's not Johnny in the car! It's Johnny's father and *my* father too. Oh, I'm so embarrassed. My friends are all watching this scene and I *hate* myself. Oh, why is this happening to me?"

"Calm down Dani, everything is alright. You are quite safe here with me."

But she covered her face with both hands and sobbed uncontrollably.

"No! No! Leave me alone. *Please*, go away and leave me alone."

"What is happening now, Dani?"

"My father is dragging me across to the car and yelling at me to get inside. As soon as he slams the door shut, Johnny's dad drives away, really fast. Johnny's father has a big black car, too and he's a detective, just like my father. Oh, where are they taking me?"

"Keep talking Dani!" The doctor was furiously scribbling notes.

"They've taken me to Johnny's house and now we're all sitting in their living room. Johnny's folks and mine are trying to convince me to give up my baby. No! No! I won't do it. I love Johnny and I want to have our child. Please, Mom; won't you help me?"

"How does the day end for you, Dani? What is decided between the adults?"

"After talking and talking and talking for hours, they finally decide to allow Johnny to marry me. They say they will help us to get settled with our baby, when it comes. Oh, I feel so relieved to hear that, but I'm so tired now."

Dani sighed and her whole body shuddered with relief. She appeared to doze off. After giving her a few minutes to recover, Dr. Babson pushed on in his search for answers.

"Where are you now, Dani?"

"I'm at my wedding to Johnny and everything is beautiful. I'm dressed in a powder-blue suit, with a white, wedding hat and a pair of white, high-heeled shoes."

She chuckled at the images inside her head.

"This is my very first pair of high heels and I can hardly walk in them.

I feel so silly, trying to be all grown up. I wonder what everyone is *really* thinking about me. They probably think I'm stupid and I guess I am, huh?"

"How is Johnny behaving, Dani, now that you are married? Is he there for you? Is he being supportive?"

"Heck no! He's just a dumb kid, like me. Johnny was very quiet all during our wedding and he's been angry all the time ever since. He blames me for getting pregnant, you see and says everything that goes wrong is *my* fault. He tells me I used to look so sexy that he couldn't keep his hands off me before I got pregnant, but now he says the only thing he ever wanted me for was sex!"

"Johnny says he hates kids and that he hopes I miscarry. He's told me lots of times that he'll do whatever it takes to make me lose our baby!"

Dani began crying again but Dr. Babson persisted. This was important information.

"Tell me why you are crying now, Dani? What did Johnny do to you and your baby, Dani?"

"Johnny is being horrible to me. Right now, he's holding my finger into an open light socket and screaming about how ugly I look, now that I'm big with our child."

Dani's heart-rending sobs filled the room.

"Tell me what else Johnny has done to you, Dani."

"He once chased me with a gun, shooting it into the air and laughing as I ran away. He was shouting awful things to me, too; things like, *'You look fat and sloppy, running away like a pig. The gun is full of blanks anyway, you stupid bitch.'* When that didn't work, he tried to push me down the stairs but, thank God, I was able to grab hold of the railing. I only broke my wrist."

"Where are you both living, Dani?"

"We live in his parents' basement and to make things worse, Johnny hates his step-mother, Dori. She is a devout Jehovah's Witness and won't allow us to celebrate Christmas, or *any* holidays. Johnny is *so* angry at me, all the time. He yells and throws things and he already broke some of his mother's family heirlooms. I hate Johnny now. I *hate* him. But I love him, too. Oh, why is that, doctor?"

Dani wrung her hands and shook her head in her distress.

"I never thought I could ever say this but, as much as I love Johnny, I'm also afraid of him and I want him out of my life!"

"Settle down, Dani. I'm here beside you and you're quite safe. You're doing just fine. Let's move ahead again, just one more week. Where are you now?"

Dani's voice lowered and she became very solemn.

"Johnny left the house today. I'm all alone now and it's so hard to be pregnant and alone."

"I miss my family so much and I wish I could go back home. I hope Johnny *never* comes back. I wish he was dead! Oh, I miss my family so much. They are so wonderful to me."

"Does Johnny ever come back, Dani?"

"Yes! He came back about two weeks later. But I think the only reason was so that he could torture me some more."

"And how did Johnny do that, Dani?"

"He said I could go 'jack-rabbit' hunting, with him and some of the guys. My brother, Hal will be there too and I'm so excited. Maybe things are getting better. But when we get out to the desert, the guys all take off running to flush out rabbits. But Johnny runs back to the car and yells for me to get out and follow him. He says if I stay in the car, I might get shot."

"So what do you do, Dani?"

"I was afraid, so I did as Johnny said, but I couldn't keep up with him. Then I realized that he was just playing with my head. The faster I ran, the faster Johnny ran, to stay ahead of me. He kept turning round and yelling at me; *'hurry up bitch or you'll get shot'*. I was half-running and half-stumbling over hot sand and gravel. The sage brush scratched at my legs until blood ran down in streaks. Then I got shooting pains in my lower back."

Dani started to cry again, but struggled on.

"I couldn't go any further so I fell down and screamed for someone to help me. That's when my brother, Hal, ran back and he cradled me in his arms, cussing at Johnny. *'Are you crazy, man? What the hell are you trying to do, kill Dani and the baby?'*"

"Then we all got back into the car and headed for home."

"But Hal and Johnny kept on arguing and yelling at each other, until Johnny stopped the car and kicked him out. My brother had to *walk* the ten miles back home, along those awful desert roads."

"When we got back home, Johnny screamed at me some more. He said I should get out of his car and out of his life. He told me I had ruined his relationship with Hal. Johnny said he lost his best friend, all because of me. Then he tore off down the street before I'd closed the car door properly and it knocked me to the ground."

"Are you OK, Dani?"

"Yes! I got up and walked back to the house, but it was a real struggle. My back was really hurting and a sharp pain was stabbing into my right side. I figured I'd feel better once I took a hot bath and relaxed. It took me a while, but I eventually fell asleep, until Johnny came home and staggered into our bed. I pretended to be asleep, though."

"What happens next, Dani?"

"Nothing, thank God. That night was like all the other nights since we got married. Johnny just lay there with his eyes open, not saying a word. He never touches me in a *nice* way anymore. He says my pregnant body is disgusting to him and just yells at me *all* the time."

"When did Johnny hurt you again?"

"I think it was the next night. I got up to go to the bathroom but I tripped over Johnny's shoes and fell down. He jumped out of bed, screaming at me again, *'Get up, you fat pig'.* He started kicking me in my back. I curled up to protect my baby as he kept on kicking me and eventually I blacked out. When I woke up, I was in an ambulance. I was terrified that Johnny would come back and kill me but the medics told me that he was in a police car, on his way to jail!"

Dani was panting and moaning, holding her stomach with both hands and writhing around in her chair.

"Let's move on a little farther. Where are you now, Dani?"

Dr. Babson wanted his patient to travel away from the bad memories for a while. Gradually, her breathing slowed and she visibly relaxed.

"I'm still in the hospital, but I'm feeling much better. I have been here for four weeks already. I can't move my legs. When Johnny kicked me in the back, it bruised my spinal cord and that's why I can't move my legs. The doctor also tells me my baby has shifted too far and is pressing on my kidneys. He says the paralysis will be temporary, but I really don't care as long as my baby is OK."

"Let's move ahead a little more then, Dani? What happened to Johnny?"

"After he got out of jail, he ran away and joined the paratroopers, but he wasn't in the Army for long. He didn't tell them that he was married *or* that his wife was pregnant! When the authorities found out that Johnny lied on his paperwork he was given a dishonorable discharge."

To the doctor's surprise, Dani began to smile.

"But I don't care. I'm back at home now and my parents are taking *real* good care of me. During these long, lonely months of being only fif-teen-years-old and pregnant, I've lost all my girlfriends, except for Eileen Mackie. I quit school, you see and rarely go out of the house any more, but Eileen comes over almost every day after school. While I'm waiting for my baby to be born, Eileen helps me to walk every day around the house, since the feeling and movement came back into my legs."

"Are you still married to Johnny?"

"Yes! My parents want me to have the marriage annulled but we agreed to wait until after the baby is born, so that it will have a proper name."

Dani went very quiet again.

"What is it, Dani? What's happening to you now?"

"It's January 25th, 1948 and I have a beautiful, curly red-haired, baby boy! I've named him 'JR'. The 'J' is after Johnny and the 'R' is for the russet color of his hair. It was all so quick, too! He was born on a cold marble slab in the prep room, before the doctor even got there. I still can't believe I had a natural birth after all I'd been through. The nurses tease me, because you are supposed to be at least sixteen-years-old to be allowed on the baby ward!"

"And how do you feel now that your baby is here?"

"I feel sad during visiting hours. I share a ward with five other mothers, but they are all older women with husbands. *My* baby's father has never even seen his beautiful son. I can't believe how much I've screwed up my life. Not just for myself, but for my family too. I've hurt everyone around me, especially my parents. I have really shamed them. And my own life will never amount to anything now, will it? I didn't even finish school, which was stupid. I will *never* get a decent job now and I'll probably never meet a decent man, either. Who will want *me*, with a child? Oh, I'm way too young to be a mother. I have no idea what I'm doing and I'm *so* afraid!"

Dani sobbed uncontrollably for a few minutes and then became silent for a long time. Suddenly, she started waving her arms around and laughing hysterically.

"What's happening now, Dani?"

"I'm watching Johnny screw up his life, too!"

"How is he doing that?"

"After he got kicked out of the Army, he married some girl named Lucy. Sounds like a cow's name to me. *Ha, ha!*"

"Anyway, Johnny went on a deer-hunting trip but took a girlfriend along, instead of his wife. Then he came down with some weird disease called, 'Bulbar Polio'! The girlfriend had to call in the flying paramedics to rush Johnny to hospital. He lived, with no serious after-effects from the disease, but his wife left him after that. Serves him right! I heard later that his wife had been Johnny's girlfriend whilst he was married to me! Nice guy, that Johnny, huh?"

Dr. Babson smiled but said nothing. He simply continued talking in his comforting voice.

"Dani, you have done very well today! I'm going to count backwards, from ten down to one. When I clap my hands together, you will immediately be wide awake. You won't remember anything about our discussions today. You will simply feel as if you have been resting peacefully. 10 - 9 - 8 – 7 - 6 - 5 - 4 - 3 - 2 - 1."

Dr. Babson clapped his hands together loudly. "Wake up now, Dani!"

She stretched, lazily and sat up, looking all around the room in bewilderment. She stared hard at the doctor, so he introduced himself again. "I'm Dr. Babson. Do you know *your* name, my dear?"

"Yes! I'm Danielle Sutton. But why am I here?"

"You've had some health problems recently and have been with us for quite some time. I have been using something called 'regression therapy', to try to help you understand any traumas you have experienced in the past."

"What does that mean, doctor? Am I crazy?"

"No, not at all, Dani. After a few more sessions you should be able to return home and continue with your life."

Dani looked deep into Dr. Babson's eyes.

"Home? Do I still have a home?

Chapter 43

Normal hospital routine was to rouse all the patients at seven-o'-clock in the morning. Aides would bathe and dress those who needed assistance, before shepherding everyone into the dining room for breakfast. After that, they were all herded into the enormous, impersonal day room. As Dani became more and more aware of her surroundings, she was both amazed and horrified by all that was happening around her. In the beginning, the odd behavior of her fellow inmates had been a source of entertainment, even amusement for Dani. But as her own treatment developed and she became more aware of reality, Dani felt only pain and sorrow at the way some patients behaved and at the circumstances which might have brought them there. Apart from breakfast, lunch and dinner, Dani and her fellow patients spent every day within the confines of that vast recreation room, until bedtime came at nine-o'-clock each night.

Dani had become more and more independent in her daily living. She would bathe and dress herself before staff members escorted her to join all the others. She was also allowed her own choice of where to spend her days. She could go to the 'big room' with the other patients or she could stay in her own room and amuse herself there. Most of the time she chose to join the others, but she would sometimes watch television, work on a jig-saw puzzle or even play Ping-Pong with a member of staff. Such were the surroundings in which Dani spent her days. But lately some aides had told her that she really didn't belong in hospital anymore, a thought which made Dani very happy.

***

It was a beautiful day outside. Sun was shining through the windows, above where Dani was stretched out on a mat on the floor. She usually sat up and leaned her back against the wall, but today she was lying down flat so that the pool of sunlight that was spreading over the floor like a warm, bloodstain could warm her entire body.

That particular area of the day room had become Dani's own, 'special spot'. Over time every patient found their own special place within the dayroom, except for those poor souls with weird routines and obsessive rituals. They would perform anywhere they could find a space!

The warmth of the sun made Dani drowsy but just as she was dozing off, a nurse gently shook her arm.

"Dani, it's time to see Dr. Babson again. Wake up honey."

She had long since come to associate Dr. Babson's room with a place of safety. The atmosphere was always peaceful and calming, but today Dani felt strangely sleepy, too.

'Maybe it's just from too much laying in the sun, or maybe they gave me some special medicine during the noon-time med rounds.'

But she felt so comfortable, safe and relaxed that she decided it didn't really matter.

Dr. Babson smiled as she entered. His face showed empathy as he observed her demeanor. Dani's condition had greatly improved during their sessions, but she still had a long way to go. The nurse helped her to get comfortable in the familiar, brown-leather recliner. The lights were lowered and the customary, spinning disk was put on the table in front of her, to help speed up Dani's descent into the necessary, trance-like state.

'I wish I could remember what I tell this man when I'm asleep. Oh well, the quicker we do this, the faster I'll get out of this hell-hole, won't I?'

Dani crossed her hands over her chest, drew in a deep breath and looked straight ahead at the spinning disk. It was really quite peaceful watching the twirling, colored lights and her mind flashed to an image of herself, dancing on stage. Stage lights and sequins flashed briefly before her eyes.

Dani snuffed the thought out as if it were a candle. She looked straight ahead again, but her face showed an uncertain expression.

'Could I have ever been a dancer?'

"Dani? Are you completely comfortable?"

"Yes, thank you!"

"And do you know where you are, right now?

"Yes! I'm here with you for another treatment session. I can't really remember what happened to me but I know I've been very upset, for a very long time."

Dr. Babson nodded, happy with her response.

"That's right my dear. You have been in our hospital for quite some time now. There have been many traumatic events in your past life and the purpose of our sessions is to help you to recall them, but in a safe environment. Once you learn to deal with the past, Dani, you will be able to move on with your life."

She was silent for a while and then cleared her throat.

"So have I recovered fully yet, do you think?"

"Not quite yet, Dani but you are getting very close." Dr. Babson reassured her with his words and with the sound of his voice.

"You are feeling very relaxed already, Dani but now I am going to count down, from ten to one, in order to take you down into bottomless relaxation. 10 – 9 – 8 – 7…."

It didn't take long. As with all therapy patients, the more times they are hypnotized, the faster relaxation kicks in. Dani felt like an astronaut; floating above herself, totally weightless and relaxed.

"Dani, can you hear me?"

"Yes, I can hear you, doctor."

"I want you to go back to the year of 1948, Dani. Are you alright with that?"

"Oh yes! I'm staying with friends in a small place called Milton Freewater, in Oregon. I'm taking care of Bob and Verla's baby while they go out to work and, of course, I have my own baby too. I get free room-and-board and Verla also gives me five dollars a week for spending money!"

She smiled and began humming, quietly.

"What's happening now, Dani?"

"Bob arrived home today with a man friend and he's staying over for dinner. The friend's name is Freddy Walker. He's a very quiet man, a bit on the small side and not really very good looking, but he does have a kind face. I think he likes me, too. He says I'm pretty. Freddy seems a bit lonely and unsure of himself. He told me that he once wanted to be a Catholic priest. He was studying hard for that but decided that he wasn't smart enough, or strong enough, for the calling. So he and his brother, Larson, set up a taxi company together."

"Do you start dating this man, Freddy?"

"Yes, but after I meet his brother there's a problem. I couldn't believe how handsome Larson was! I wish Freddy wasn't in business with his brother. I could never be in love with Freddy, you see, because I am attracted to his brother. That creates problems, because I don't want to hurt Freddy. He is very good to my baby son, but Freddy is fifteen years older than I am. His brother is more *my* age."

"And how old is that now, Dani?"

"I'm sixteen. Freddie takes me out on drives in his taxi sometimes and sometimes we play cards with Verla in the evenings."

"Are you having sex with Freddy?"

"Oh, no! That's why I care for him so much. He has never even touched me, or tried to kiss me."

"OK, Dani; move a little farther forward in time and tell me what is happening now."

"Freddy is teaching me all about the Catholic Church and telling me about the kind of life he could provide for me and my baby."

"You are smiling now, Dani. Why are you smiling?"

"Freddy has asked me to marry him but he says I will have to go to something called 'catechism' first."

Dani suddenly began flailing her arms around and shouting.

"No! No! I *won't* go home with you. Freddy loves me. I'm all grown up now and I can make my own decisions. Stop it! I won't go home with you."

"What's happening, Dani? Who wants to take you away?"

"My parents are here. They are telling Freddy that I've been hurt too much already and that if he really cares for me he should come to visit me at their home, in Yakima. My folks are very upset with me."

"And do you go with them, Dani. Does Freddy come to see you in Yakima?"

"Oh yes, he came lots of times! We got married too, after a lot of problems with our local parish priest. *He* believed that it was *my* fault that

Freddy left the priesthood, but it wasn't. The priest never forgave me, though. Anyway, Mom and Dad gave us a big reception in the *'Knights-of-Columbus'* hall! That was a wonderful day, at least until we went to bed."

She stayed silent for a long time and Dr. Babson had to prompt Dani to move on.

"Why wasn't your honeymoon night good?"

A mortified expression crossed Dani's face and she hung her head. Dr. Babson had to strain to hear her subdued reply.

"We hadn't *ever* had sex before you see and that first night was a terrible disappointment. I guess I had expected more from an older man, but I am so ashamed of myself. I don't even want to think about it."

But the doctor wasn't about to let the subject drop. "Is that because Freddy hurt you in some way?"

"Oh no! Freddy is a very holy man." Dani wrung her hands in despair and embarrassment as she tried to explain.

"My aunt had given me a beautiful, sheer-black, nightgown to wear on my wedding night. I wanted to look good for my new husband, you see. But when I came out of the bathroom wearing it, Freddy shouted at me for not being properly covered up! He said that I should wear something more decent. I felt so cheap and dirty. Freddy made me wear his old pajama tops to bed after that."

"Did the two of you make love that first night?"

"I guess so." Dani shuddered at the memory. "I was so embarrassed that I just lay there, afraid to move. I think maybe it was Freddy's first time ever, too. It only lasted about five minutes but that was long enough for me to get pregnant! Freddy says that men's desires should be aroused only to create children and he means it! Every night we kneel beside the bed and say the rosary together. Then Freddy asks God to cleanse everyone's mind and soul, especially mine!"

Big, hot tears rolled down Dani's cheeks.

"Why are you crying, Dani?"

"My new life is horrible! The women of our church are always med-dling into my life. They are always asking me if I say my prayers and such, but I don't think that's any of their business."

"They even believe that Freddy and I were *forced* to get married and they tell me I'm a sinner. They are all crazy."

Dani wiped her face on her sleeves before resuming her desperate story. "Every Thursday night I have to cook dinner for Father Beard, but that man makes me really nervous."

She began wringing her hands again and shaking her head, fiercely. "I wash our clothes and hang them outside. I churn our own butter; I pick and can all our own fruit and vegetables; I clean the house *daily* and I bake our own bread. I even kill and pluck our own damn chickens! But I *hate* this lifestyle! I was not raised to be a slave."

Dr. Babson was gentle with his patient but was also determined to get her to recall every word of her wretched, life-story.

"What happens next, Dani?"

"All that hard work took a massive toll on my body, but being so young and having a second child on the way, was even more damaging. When I was six months pregnant, I became paralyzed again and was bed-ridden until our baby was born. My beautiful, baby girl was born a full month early, by C-section, but she did really well."

"I'm having a rough time with my own recovery, though. The doctor tells us that I should never get pregnant again; it could kill me. I was even given a diaphragm to use for birth control, but Freddy refused to let me use it. He says it would be sacrilegious. He was *very* upset with the doctor for even giving it to me and told him that 'God will always guide our way'."

Dani took several deep breaths but remained silent.

"Talk to me, Dani. What happens next?"

"I have no choice but to carry on, do I? Freddy and I never, *ever* have sex for enjoyment. We only have sex to procreate and he believes it is his duty to fill the world with children!"

"Three months after Shannon was born, I became pregnant *again*. I was so terrified; I believed I would die!"

Dani began to howl as she recalled the anguish of those dark days. "Freddy was *so* wrong about everything. God certainly didn't take care of me, did he?"

"Calm down my dear, you are quite safe now, so there's no need to cry." As always, the doctor's voice was gentle, smooth and comforting. "Why do you think you are going to die, Dani?"

"Because my insides are all messed up with scar tissue, from all the beatings I've had and from all my pregnancies. I'm *too* young! This new baby is already lying on my kidneys and the doctor says they will rupture and shut down as the baby grows."

She began to wail again.

"But that didn't happen, did it, Dani? You didn't die; you are here now, with me and you are fine so let's move ahead a little farther in time."

"No, that didn't happen, thank God, but I was bedridden and in great pain for weeks. Father Beard visited daily and was preparing me for death until my Mom and Papa took me away to Yakima Memorial Hospital, to see the specialists there. They did an emergency 'C-section' next day, to abort my baby. That's how close I came to dying. They also tied my tubes so that I can *never* get pregnant again."

"You were a very lucky girl, indeed." The doctor was appalled by what he was hearing but he made no other comment. "Tell me what happened *after* that day."

"Oh, it was terrible! I woke up and my Mom was there, which was good, but Father Beard was there too. He had come to give me absolution, he said. He told us both that my life was only spared to allow me to care for the two babies I already have!"

"Because my recent baby died, Father Beard says I've committed murder in the eyes of the church and he's going to personally see to it that I'm excommunicated! I will never be able to go back to Freddy's hometown, or his church."

"Did you ever go back, Dani?"

"No! And I didn't only lose one child back then, I lost two; my newborn boy *and* my baby girl, too. After I got out of hospital, Freddy drove over to Yakima and took my little girl away from me. I'd never seen him so angry. I thought he would kill me."

Dani was sobbing again.

"Why didn't Freddy want to stick by you and take care of you, Dani?"

"He said I was no use to him anymore, because I could no longer have babies. According to Freddy and Father Beard I had *murdered* his newborn son and wasn't fit to be a mother, nor his wife."

"Did you ever fight for custody of your daughter, after you got well again?"

"Oh yes! An attorney told me that I would certainly, at the very least, get visitation rights, just as soon as I got back on my feet. He said I would have to prove to the family court that I was a good mother and that I could afford to give *both* my children a good home and all that. But that never happened, did it?"

"Freddy had the weight of the Catholic Church behind him and plenty of income from his taxi business. He fought for full custody of my little girl and got it!"

Dani felt such a failure. She didn't like remembering all this past stuff, yet in the back of her mind she recalled the doctor saying that it was *good* to remember. Then her thought vanished, like smoke in the breeze, as Dr. Babson spoke again.

"Dani, you are going to wake up soon, but this time you will remember *everything* that we have talked about this afternoon and in all of our previous sessions. Even though you may feel sad about some of the things you remember, you will be very happy that the pain is all in the past now. It cannot hurt you anymore and you will learn from those past mistakes."

"You will also feel wonderfully calm and relaxed when you wake up. 10-9-8-7-6-5-4-3-2-1. Wake up now, Dani!"

Chapter 44

"Hello Mr. and Mrs. Gunther, nice to see you again." The receptionist smiled a welcome. "Please follow me. Dr. Babson is waiting for you."

The doctor was business-like, as always, yet kind and reassuring. He let them get comfortable before outlining his plans for the final phase of Dani's treatment.

"Thank you both for coming today. Dani has made tremendous progress during the hypnotherapy treatment, so today I plan to bring her forward to the very date of Digger's shooting."

"Does she remember *everything* now, doctor?" Laura asked, timidly.

"The new treatment has worked very well, I'm pleased to say. Dani now remembers a great deal from her youth and is much more aware of the present, but we're not quite at the end of the road yet. Your daughter experienced *many* life-changing involvements within a very short period of time, you know. But today I plan to take the lid off the box of secrets that has been blocking Dani's access to her most significant memories. Today will be very important for your daughter's future."

Dr. Babson looked at Harold and Laura Gunther intently.

"Now, you must both bear in mind what I said before with regard to patient confidentiality. The *only* reason I am able to allow you to remain in the room during our session today, is because we are moving Dani forward into dealing with events that you, her parents, are already aware of. But you must not speak at all during this meeting; not to Dani and not to each other, no matter what she says or how upsetting her words may be for you both to hear."

"Not *one* word must be spoken by either of you, until the session has ended and I have returned Dani to complete wakefulness. Is that quite clear?"

Laura Gunther looked terrified but Harold squeezed his wife's hand and spoke for them both.

"We understand Dr. Babson. Not a word from either of us, we promise!"

"Then let's begin, shall we? Nurse, would you please bring our patient in?"

Dani walked unaided into the familiar surroundings of the therapy room. She was surprised, but very happy, to see her parents there and greeted them with enthusiasm. Then she climbed into the comfortable, reclining chair as easily as a child would climb onto a favorite fairground ride. Over the long months, that chair had become Dani's sanctuary. A place where she could feel safe and secure, whilst Dr. Babson and his team worked on salvaging her mental health.

The doctor pulled the shades down and prepared for their session as usual, the only difference being that Dani's parents were in the room.

'I hope I don't freak them out with anything I say!'

But it was only a fleeting worry and Dani quickly forgot about it. She wriggled her bottom to get more comfortable and reached down to pull the lever that would raise her legs higher.

"Very good, Dani. You know the routine well by now don't you?" Dr. Babson smiled at her parents and Laura visibly relaxed.

"You are showing so much improvement, Dani, that I want to see if we can dig a little deeper today, OK?"

"Sure!" Dani lay back and gazed at the colored disk, already spinning in front of her. The doctor's voice rapidly faded farther and farther away as she listened to the usual countdown.

"Are you feeling relaxed now, Dani?"

"Very relaxed, thank you."

"That's good, because I want you to dig even deeper into your memories today. There are no more secrets now. You will be able to talk about anything I ask you to Dani. Right now, I want you to remember back to the days immediately after you lost your baby boy. Go back to the point where you were recovering from the complications of his aborted delivery. What are you doing now, Dani?"

"Just milling around at my parents' home."

"Doing what?"

"Absolutely nothing! My folks think I should look for a job and try to start a new life for myself and my son, JR."

"And do you plan to do that, Dani?"

"Yes, I already found myself a job; earning eighteen-dollars a week by selling candy and popcorn at our local theater. And now I've moved into an old boarding house, with my Aunt Wanda. She is two years older than me and I really love her. I work afternoons at the theater and Wanda works nights, singing at the *'Elks Club'*. I go to work at noon and get home at about seven-thirty in the evening. Then Wanda goes to work at eight o' clock in the evening and gets home at about one o' clock in the morning. It works out well for both of us. We take care of little JR between us, so I don't have to pay money for a babysitter. And every week, my Papa brings over a big bag of groceries. He always leaves a little note in the bag that says, *'I love you, from Santa'*."

Dani smiled contentedly at the recollection. But her father swiped at an unmanly tear; covering his face with the hand that his wife was not gripping tightly.

"Things are going well for you right now then, Dani?"

"Yes! This is a good time in my life."

"Let's move ahead a year or so. Where are you now, Dani?"

"I'm still living at the boarding house. Most of the girls that live here are either going out with, or are already married to, soldiers from the nearby Yakima Firing Center. I've recently been introduced to one of the servicemen; a guy called Peter Sutton, from New York. He's tall and lanky, a sort of 'Gregory Peck' look-a-like but he's handsome, too. He's twenty-two-years old and he's kind of poor, like me, so we play a lot of cards and we eat popcorn and drink lemonade. Sometimes we go to a movie, because I can get free tickets. I hate it when Peter goes into a tavern for beer with his buddies, though. I have to wait in the car, you see, because I'm not old enough to drink yet. I'm old enough to have a baby but still too young to go into a tavern with my friends!"

"Let's move forward to 1952 now, Dani. Tell me what's happening in your life now."

"Peter has just been discharged from the Army and we are all on our way to Cincinnati, New York. He has family back there, you see."

Dani became suddenly animated, like an excited child. "I just saw my first 'television' program today, as we travelled across the country. It was wonderful."

She smiled, happily and then carried on with her recollections. "Little JR, is four years old now. He has always been such a good little boy. He loves collecting bugs and things but I've promised him a dog after we all get settled. JR has never had a *real* pet before."

"Do you get married to Peter, Dani?"

"Oh, yes! It was a very quiet affair though. Mom and Papa refused to come. I guess they're ashamed that I'm being married for the *third* time, at only eighteen years old."

Laura put a hand to her mouth but a glance from the doctor kept her silent. Harold Gunther stared fixedly at a spot on the floor and shook his head, slowly.

"Wanda and some of our friends from the boarding house gave us a very small reception, after the wedding ceremony at City Hall. And our wedding night was a real hoot!"

Dani laughed out loud. "Peter and I had to sleep on the bathroom floor, because Wanda and little JR were sleeping in the only bed we owned!"

"It must have been a big bathroom, Dani." Dr. Babson chuckled with her.

"Actually it wasn't that big, but we had a lot of fun that night. Peter couldn't keep his feet covered up so he put his combat boots on to keep his feet warm. We didn't get much sleep; we laughed most of the night!" Dani giggled again as she remembered.

"Move forward in time a little more now, Dani. Are you still in New York with Peter?"

"Yes, we are still in Cincinnati. Peter's mother and father are from old, Pennsylvania-Dutch stock. They live in a very old, very big, white farmhouse, with green shutters. It has five bedrooms; a bathroom; a dining room and the big, family living room has a sun porch. The huge, kitchen at the back also has a porch. Several milk churns are stored there, all covered over with cheesecloth to separate the cream off for making butter.

They have buckets full of eggs on the porch, too and a special light that they shine through each egg to check for bad spots. They only eat and sell those eggs with no spots, you see. There's a big, red, barn too for all the machinery. Peter's folks have a very different lifestyle from the way *my* folks live. But they have taken my son, JR and me into their home and way of life as if we were their own flesh and blood. I love them both very much."

"Peter has a lot of good friends, from the old days and they are now friends to me, too."

"Because of his good schooling Peter got himself a good job in the optical trade, so the three of us are now settled over in Baldwinsville, a suburb of Syracuse, New York. We have a beautiful, waterfront property on the Seneca River and because of Peter's good job, I can afford to stay home and make it a warm and beautiful place for us all. Little JR, with his red hair and freckles, lives a regular *'Huckleberry Finn'* lifestyle out here!"

Dani's face glowed and her body melted into total relaxation as she remembered those happy, family days.

"During the summers, JR often camps out with his friends on one of the many small islands in the middle of the river. We have a fifteen-foot ski boat and we take trips up and down the river, too. Sometimes we visit one of the local lakes and sometimes we just have picnics onboard and enjoy the scenery. Young JR uses our boat mostly. It didn't take him long to become a really skilled, water-skier."

"We have wiener roasts, too and patio games like 'horseshoes' or 'croquette'. We even have hay-rides in a horse drawn wagon, with lots of singing! JR is very musically inclined and can play several different instruments. He once played *'Flight of the Bumble Bee'* all the way through on our old, upright grand piano, when he was only seven-years old! He also learned the clarinet in school and started playing the guitar when he was a teenager."

The pride that Dani felt for her son was tangible. Her love for him filled the therapy room, bringing tears to even Dr. Babson's eyes. Yet Dani was oblivious to the emotions that she was stirring up among those seated around her and she chattered on, happily.

"In winter, we had snow and sub-zero weather from 'Thanksgiving' right up until springtime! The big pond behind our house was perfect for ice-skating parties and JR and his friends sometimes played ice-hockey, too. I didn't like that though, it's such a very rough sport"

"Dani, let's move forward again, to the year of 1963. Is that OK with you?"

"Oh, yes!" Dani clapped her hands together, excitedly.

"Isn't it wonderful? I was just crowned, *'Miss Cleopatra of New York,'* and now I'm living at the 'Barbizon Hotel', in New York City!"

"Why are you living there, Dani?"

"Because I'm working full time now, as a bathing suit model for 'Pandora Sportswear'."

"So what happened to Peter and young JR then?"

Her face crumpled, like damp tissue paper.

"I *do* feel bad about Peter. We were very happy together for almost twelve years, but I had *always* dreamed of being in the entertainment business. Several opportunities came up for me to be a model, a singer and even a dancer whilst we were together but Peter would never agree to let me do it professionally. I was only ever allowed to do those things as a hobby."

"But after I won the *'Miss Cleopatra'* thing I had no choice, you see. I have to live and work in New York in order to fulfill my obligations. At first I drove home once a month to see Peter and little JR, but it wasn't the same. I was too much concerned with myself, I guess. I so desperately wanted to be a *'star'*, to be somebody famous. I enrolled young JR into the 'Valley Forge Military Academy' and later I filed for divorce from Peter, in Mexico."

"But how did you afford private schooling for JR?"

Dani squirmed in the chair, hung her head and giggled, coyly.

"Well my new boyfriend, actually he's my lover, is the Vice President of Xenon Corporation!"

"HK is his name and he's a millionaire, you see. He's much older than me but we are *very* much in love and are to be married soon."

Dani suddenly gasped and sat bolt upright in the chair. Hot tears flowed down her face.

"Oh! No! No! HK is dead. And *they* killed him. The 'Family' I mean; the *'mafia'* family. They had my fiancé killed. HK is gone forever and I must move away from New York because I know too much No, *please*; I don't want to talk about this anymore!"

"Dani, just remember that you're quite safe here, with me. Nothing can hurt you in this room, so let's move ahead again. Say, a couple of years?"

Dr. Babson knew they were getting very close. Closer to the death of Digger Rosselli and to the moment of Dani's mental meltdown. He trod very carefully as he moved his patient slowly forward in time.

"Yes, doctor. I'm OK now! I'm driving up to my empty, mansion home, in Portland, Oregon. It's dark and my car headlights are full on. JR should have come home with me, from the Club, but he had a date with his fiancée. I've told him all about the strange noises I keep hearing in this house. I'm sure he thinks I'm imagining things but I don't think I am. I've had so many problems lately, with the divorce and everything."

"I *really* think someone is after me, though. Maybe I should turn around and go back to Salem, to stay with Mom and Dad? No! It's too late. It's too late to turn back now. Besides, I'm really tired. But I'm so scared. Oh, no! No!"

Dani grabbed the arms of her chair and hung on with bone-white knuckles." Help me! Someone, *please* help me!"

Both parents jumped out of their chairs and Laura made as if to reach out to her suffering daughter, but Dr. Babson held her back firmly. Dani could still hear the doctor's voice, although it sounded very far away.

"Dani! This is Dr. Babson and I am right here with you. You are perfectly safe, Dani, you must believe that. Can you hear me talking to you, Dani?"

"Yes, I can hear you, doctor." Dani's voice was calmer but her face was still filled with fear.

"You need to relax again, Dani and feel completely at ease. Nothing is going to hurt you, I promise you that. But you must tell me *exactly* what happened that night at *'Rosselli's Roost'*, on Buena Vista Drive. Don't be afraid, Dani. When this is all over everything will be fine, but I need for you to tell me, right now, everything that happened that night; just the way it happened."

Dani looked dreadfully stressed. Her cheeks were pale and the pulsing veins in her temples showed that her heart was beating fast. Her tears ran in rivers but she made no attempt to wipe them away.

"Tell me what you see, Dani?"

"I see… I see… cowboy boots. It's very dark but I see his cowboy boots. He's coming out of my bedroom now, out through the French doors and onto the terrace."

"Who is 'he' and what is he doing, Dani?"

"It's Digger and he is looking for me! I'm hiding behind a big plant in the corner of my terrace. Digger has a light in his hand now. Oh, my God! He sees me! Oh! Oh! He's stabbed me. It hurts and it's hot! I can't believe how much it burns. Oh, god; the pain is so bad and I'm bleeding."

"Keep talking to me, Dani. Tell me what is happening?"

"He's trying to get my gun away from me. I'm struggling but he is too strong for me and now Digger has the gun. He is trying to push me over the balcony. Oh, the gun just went off. Oh, God help me! I daren't let go. Somebody, *anybody*, help me *please*."

Then she let loose a blood-curdling, deep-throated yell of pure terror.

"Dani, listen to the sound of my voice. I'm still here with you and *nothing* can hurt you. Does Digger still have hold of the gun?"

"Yes! Yes! But we're both falling."

"It's all over now, Dani. You are alive and you are here with me. You are healthy and you are safe. It's time to wake up now, Dani. When you do wake up, you will remember *everything* that we have talked about today and yet you will feel great. You don't have to hide secrets anymore, Dani. You have nothing to fear from your memories, ever again. I'm going to count backwards now, from ten down to one, and then you will awaken feeling refreshed, relaxed and comfortable."

"10-9-8-7-6-5-4-3-2-1! Wake up now, Dani!"

She sat up, blinked and looked across the room at her waiting parents.

"Mom? Dad? Is that you? Oh, god, I think I have been to hell and back but I love you both, so much. Can I *please* come home now?"

She leapt out of the chair and ran into her parents' waiting arms. The three of them clung to each other like drowning rats on a chunk of floating timber!

Dr. Babson wiped his own eyes and beamed at the sight before him. Then he sank back into his chair and breathed a deep sigh of relief.

"Thank God; Dani's back!

www.ingramcontent.com/pod-product-compliance
Lightning Source LLC
Chambersburg PA
CBHW051433260626
47162CB00001B/78